METALTOWN

TOR BOOKS BY KRISTEN SIMMONS

Article 5
Breaking Point
Three
The Glass Arrow

METALTOWN

KRISTEN SIMMONS

TOR TEEN

A TOM DOHERTY ASSOCIATES BOOK

NEW YORK

METALTOWN

Copyright © 2016 by Kristen Simmons

A Tor Teen Book
Published by Tom Doherty Associates
175 Fifth Avenue
New York, NY 10010

www.tor-forge.com

Tor® is a registered trademark of Macmillan Publishing Group, LLC.

The Library of Congress Cataloging-in-Publication Data is available upon request.

ISBN 978-0-7653-3662-0 (hardcover)
ISBN 978-1-4668-2879-7 (e-book)

Our books may be purchased in bulk for promotional, educational, or business use. Please contact your local bookseller or the Macmillan Corporate and Premium Sales Department at 1-800-221-7945, extension 5442, or by e-mail at MacmillanSpecialMarkets@macmillan.com.

First Edition: September 2016

Printed in the United States of America

10 9 8 7 6 5 4 3 2 1

For Ren
I will always stand beside you, no matter what

1

COLIN

"Go halves with me—you want pigeon or rat?"

Ty swiped at her nose with the back of her hand, making the threadbare, fingerless glove bunch around her wrist. The cold had drawn bright blotches to the exposed skin between her hat and tattered scarf, and as the line to Hayak's corner cart shortened and pulled them beneath the yellow glow of the streetlight, Colin could make out the hooked scar on her chin, and a fading brown bruise on her jaw.

"What's the difference?" They all looked the same to Colin: charred fists of meat. He stamped his feet and shrugged deeper into his wool coat. It was too big—big enough to fit another sweater inside if he'd had one, which he didn't. The bitter predawn wind clawed right up his stomach and back, freezeburning his skin.

Ty's thick, straight brows lifted, but refused to arch. "One flies, Prep School. Surprised you didn't know that." She snorted, revealing a crooked front tooth.

Colin frowned. He hadn't been to school since he was thirteen, more than four years ago. That life was in the past.

"Rat," he said, because it was her less favorite of the two. "And I call the nose."

"Course you do." She spat on the ground, then rubbed it into the cracked sidewalk with the heel of her boot. "You talk. Hayak likes you better."

"That's 'cause I'm likable, Ty." He grinned now, and she rolled her eyes.

Another customer served, and they moved to the front of the line.

Hayak, a greasy man three times their age with a shock of white hair and a peppered beard, looked up from his rotisserie and grimaced.

"No," he said. "No, not you two. Not today. Hayak cannot feed you today. You go away."

Colin flashed his best smile and pulled off his hat in an attempt to look less shifty. "Come on, Hayak. You said we could pay at the end of the week—"

"*No.*" He shook his finger at them sternly. "No, *you* say you pay at the end of the week. Hayak say you can pay now."

Colin looked over his shoulder and winced at the grumbling line behind him. Stepping off to the side, he cuffed the man's burly shoulder. "You know I'm good for it, Hayak. You know I wouldn't lie."

He hid a smirk as Ty eased up beside the cart behind him and stashed a handful of fry scraps up her coat sleeve. If he could just turn Hayak a little more, she could reach the black spit and the hunk of charred meat pierced on the end.

The man directly behind her was crowding up in line, making a quick circle with his hand for Ty to pass him some. She raised a silent fist, like she might punch him, and he fell back a step.

"Hayak, you're right, I should have given you money last week. Only I didn't get paid, okay? So it wasn't my fault." That much was true. Hampton Industries was fat on green. So fat, it didn't get off its lazy ass to pay its workers half the time.

As Hayak shouted back, his face turned progressively redder and his eyes began to bulge. It was just a matter of time before he went for the tongs to beat Colin upside the head. Colin pulled his hat back down over his ears, taking the lecture with a feigned look of shame. Shifting left drew the cart man's gaze further away from Ty. She was just about to make a grab for the prize when motion behind her caught Colin's eye.

A man approached, wearing clean trousers and a coat swollen with enough stuffing to make Colin shiver at his own lack of protection from the cold. He had that yellowed, sunless skin, pockmarked at the tops of his cheekbones, and long hair, greased nice, and pulled into a tail at the back of his skull.

Jed Schultz. The People's Man. The voice of the Brotherhood— the people who represented the workers' rights at the steel mill where Colin's ma was employed. He was flanked by a man twice his size but half as bright. A hammer, hired to watch Jed's back so the greenback bosses couldn't stick a knife in it. Colin thought his name was Imon, and had heard he'd come from somewhere in the mountains, north of the Tri-City. A place so cold your breath turned to ice before it left your mouth.

Colin coughed once, and Ty abandoned her mission without so much as a glance up.

"Morning, Hayak," said Jed. He walked straight to the front of the line. Those who'd been waiting didn't mind—Jed did right by the poor folks, so Jed got whatever he wanted in Metaltown.

"Mr. Schultz, good morning. Yes," Hayak recovered, keeping Colin in his sight.

"How's the bird?" Jed asked.

"Good, good. I give you my best one. Here." Hayak stepped back behind the center of his cart, and rotated the rotisserie once over the flames to warm the round carcass Colin had been eyeing. His stomach grumbled. Saliva filled his mouth. He'd eaten yesterday, but it felt like longer.

He swallowed as Hayak wrapped the bird in paper and handed it to the People's Man. Jed nodded, just slightly, cuing Imon to step forward and withdraw a wallet from the breast pocket of his coat. There was a stack of bills in the fold, and as he unfurled one after another, Colin's eyes grew wide as dinner plates. Jed was flush as a greenback. There was a bite of jealousy, then a swell of admiration. He wondered what it would be like, just once, to walk up to Hayak's cart and buy whatever he wanted.

"Your money's no good here, Mr. Schultz," said Hayak, a huge smile plastered across his face. Colin couldn't help gagging, to which Hayak responded with a glare.

"Good man," said Jed. Imon put his money away. Jed turned to Colin. "You like pigeon, Mr. Walter?"

Colin's eyes went wide. He wiped his hands off on the front of his coat, aware of ten pairs of eyes that swung his way. They were surprised, Colin knew, that Jed knew his name. He was surprised himself.

"Yes, sir." Colin's mouth gaped like a fish when Jed handed him the steaming, charred meat. White bubbles of fat had already begun to congeal against the puckered skin in the cold; a good sign the bird was thick, not hollow. "Whoa. Thank you, Mr. Schultz."

"How's Cherish, Colin?" His eyes were dark and piercing. Powerful, Colin thought. He wondered if he was capable of such a commanding stare himself. Jed and Imon had stepped in front of Ty, and she was slowly backing into the line opposite them, head down, hat pulled over her ears. Colin gave her a puzzled look—it wasn't like Ty to back away from anyone, famous or not.

"She's okay. The money you sent helped, thank you, sir. The doc said she needs clean water for drinking. That's what we bought." Colin had stiffened at the mention of family but tried to play it cool. Jed didn't need to be bothered with all the details.

"Good boy," said Jed, nodding with interest. Colin relaxed. "So Colin, Hayden was supposed to meet me this morning. He say anything to you about it?" Jed reached for another hunk of meat—rat or pigeon, Colin couldn't tell—and returned Hayak's smile.

Colin tensed again. His brother had grown unpredictable these last few years. Hayden was three years older than Colin, but had never adjusted to Metaltown the way Colin had. Ma said it was because he'd gotten his heart broken when they'd pulled him out of school. She didn't know the half of it.

Colin's fingers were beginning to thaw beneath the crinkling paper holding the bird. Dawn was coming, turning the darkness to the chronic steely haze that burned off the chem plant across the bridge in thick, white plumes. The air had a sweet, heady odor that would only grow stronger as the day plowed on.

"He's been sick," said Colin. "He did say he was going to meet you, but I guess he fell behind. He was up puking all night." Which was probably true, wherever he was. Colin hadn't seen him in two days. Ty's chin lifted in surprise before digging back into her scarf.

Jed scowled. "Not the flu, I hope."

"No sir, just ate something rotten." He was going to punch Hayden square in the face when he surfaced.

"Well, that's okay then," said Jed. "Since he's indisposed, maybe you can do me a favor." Jed leaned against the cart, tearing a hunk out of the meat in his grip with his chew-stained teeth.

Colin took Jed's lead, and bit straight into the wing. It was tough and gamey, but warm. He felt Ty's glare from behind Jed.

"Yeah. Sure, okay," said Colin.

"A friend of mine lost his girl to the corn flu a few weeks past. He's been missing work, and I'd hate to see them lose their place over it."

Colin nodded. Jed did this kind of stuff a lot. Just two weeks prior, Colin's ma hadn't made her quota at the mill and the foreman had refused to pay her. Their cupboards were already bare, and just before the heat was shut off, Hayden came home with a wad of cash, courtesy of the People's Man. It had been enough to keep their lights on, and put food in their bellies for days.

Jed stepped away from the cart, and the people in line tentatively resumed their shuffle.

"They live in Bakerstown, by the Cat's Tale, you know where that is?"

"Sure," said Colin, taking another bite. He used to live in Bakerstown before he'd left school.

Imon removed the wallet again, this time taking out a stash of green bills half an inch thick. Colin had to remind himself to keep chewing. Just one of those bills could fill six jugs with clean drinking water. Another could pay the power at his apartment through the next month. One more could mean food, *real* food—bread and beans and salted pork—for dinner, not just broth like they had every night.

"Can you take this down to him this morning? One-fourteen Fifth Street."

Colin waffled, glancing at Ty. She was shaking her head no, but when Jed followed his gaze she immediately fixed her eyes on a hole in her shirtsleeve.

He faced Colin again. "I can count on you, right Colin?"

"Yeah. Of course, Mr. Schultz. It's just that I've got work in an hour, and the Cat's Tale is way up Fifth Street. I mean, I'll do it, it's just . . . You know how the foreman gets if you're late." Colin couldn't afford to push his luck with Minnick. The man had fired two workers just last week for getting sick on the job—something that happened a lot on account of the hazardous materials they dealt with. But he didn't want to get on Jed's bad side either, not after how good Jed had been to his family.

Jed smiled. "I'll talk to your foreman. You're in Small Parts labor, right?"

"Yes, sir," said Colin.

"Good. Go ahead and take your pal." He stuck a thumb behind him in Ty's direction.

"Okay."

The concern that had come into Jed's face while he'd been talking about the family dissipated. He slung a hand around the back of Colin's neck and gave a companionable squeeze. "You're a good kid, aren't you? Remind me of me when I was your age. Man of the house."

Colin grinned, and felt his ears grow warm under his hat. Technically, Hayden was the man of the house, but Hayden wasn't here, was he? Colin wasn't so irritated that his brother had blown off Jed anymore. In fact, Hayden could go right ahead and stay gone as long as he liked.

Imon handed him the stack of money, and Colin, fighting the urge to count it, folded it into the front pocket of his trousers.

"Say hello to Cherish for me." Jed turned back the way he'd come, disappearing into the gray smog.

Colin felt ten feet tall. Breakfast, a personal hello from the biggest man in Metaltown, *and* the morning off work? It couldn't get much better than that.

"Wipe that grin off your ugly face." Ty snatched the remainder of the bird from his loose grasp. He pulled his hat back, smoothed one gloved hand over his buzzed head, and winked at her.

"Ugly," Ty repeated. Then they turned the opposite way, toward Bakerstown and the rising sun.

TY

Ty bit down on something that crunched, and pulled a white shard of pigeon bone from her cheek. It was thin as a needle, and she used it to pick at the food stuck in the gaps between her teeth. She may not have liked where the feast had come from, but she wasn't about to turn it down. Pride didn't fill your belly like a roasted pigeon.

"Smells good out here," Colin said from beside her. She glanced over, but he wasn't smiling like he had been for the last mile—he was biting his pinky nail. She felt her own brows draw together in response.

The air did smell cleaner; anywhere outside the grasp of the factory district did. But though the sun didn't have to cut through a filter of smog, it wasn't like the place was perfect. The poor ran thick here, crowding the street beside them, begging at each red brick shop front for food and work.

Funny how they didn't come to Metaltown to beg for work.

"Don't lie. You know you love the smell of nitro in the morning," she said, glad to see his hand lower from his mouth and his grin return.

The crumbling sidewalk they walked down ran beside an iron fence that twisted and spiraled like the ivy that clung to it. It would have been posh had the park within not grown over like a jungle.

It was even stocked with wild animals: dopers and sellers and the kind of people who knew how to get anything you wanted—for the right price. At least half of them were in the earliest stages of the corn flu.

She felt the switchblade lodged into her boot, and another knife in her waistband. Always ready, just in case.

"How much did Jed's man give you?" she asked, changing the subject. She would have suggested pocketing a few bills for themselves, but she knew better. Nothing was free in Metaltown. She'd bet a week's pay that Imon's muscle work wasn't limited to greenback thugs.

"I don't know, but it's burning a hole through my leg." Colin was thinking of lifting it too, she knew he was. They were two like minds. Had been since she'd taken him under her wing four years ago, fresh out of prep school.

She glanced his way, noticing the changes in him. Metaltown had made him hard. His sky blue eyes had turned to steel, and his dark, shaggy hair had been shorn close to the skull to cut the heat inside the plant. Hands used to writing facts and figures had grown strong and calloused, and he had muscles, too, beneath those baggy clothes.

She'd been eleven and he'd been thirteen when they'd met, but their ages might as well have been reversed. He'd known nothing about work, and for some unknown reason she'd taken pity on him and called a *safety*. According to street rules that made her responsible until he could stand on his own two feet. Now he was a leech. She couldn't shake him if she tried.

"Let's count it," she said, feeling a different, greedy kind of hunger take over. Even if they couldn't lift it, she could feel the paper in her hands and imagine what it'd be like to buy whatever she wanted.

"Yeah right," he said, and his shoulders pulled forward again. "We passed the beltway. We're on McNulty's turf now. One sniff of green and they'll be on us like flies on rot."

"Let 'em come then," she said, tapping the handle of the knife she kept in her waistband. "I'm not scared of any Bakerstown pansies."

His barked-out laugh had her cheeks suddenly warm. "Just like you were going to take Jed and his man, right?"

She fought the urge to sock him between the eyes. "I could take 'em."

"Course you could've," he said. "Imon only outweighs you by a hundred and fifty pounds."

She tossed the bird carcass into the trash-filled gutter. "I'll take you in a second."

"Such a tease." He shoved her off the sidewalk.

She pushed him back, maybe a little too hard, irritated that all the layers of clothes she wore suddenly made her too hot. He bounced off the iron fence, laughing.

The clang of a doorbell from one of the shops across the street drew their attention to a couple exiting a deli. They were flush, that much was obvious. Smart clothes—a black peacoat and slick leather shoes on the man, a swanky black dress on the woman—and clean, brown skin. The woman's small brimmed hat with its fishnet veil had Ty wondering what purpose such ridiculous clothes could possibly serve.

The couple waited for the doorman to clear a path through the beggars, then headed down the sidewalk around the corner, making no attempt to hide the shiny handheld defusers they each wore on their waistbands. The crowd cleared around them; one shock from those things and a person would be out for hours.

"Must be hard being so damn rich," said Ty. "Wading through all this muck. It's disgusting really."

She hiccuped a laugh, pleased with herself, but Colin didn't find her funny. His eyes were round as he watched them go. What was wrong with him? He was standing taller. And smoothing down the front of his shirt. He'd been acting strange all morning, ever since they'd run into Jed and Imon.

She shifted her weight from one side to the other. They shouldn't have left Metaltown. Jed was trouble—she refused to trust a rich man she'd never seen work. He probably wasn't even going to keep his word and tell the foreman. Then they'd be sacked and she'd be no better than these bums here, begging for a job.

Colin had begun walking again.

"If I was flush," he said, "I'd buy a separate sidewalk so me and my greenback friends didn't have to get our shoes dirty."

Ty's shoulders loosened, and she fell into step beside him.

"If I was flush, I wouldn't walk at all. I'd make scraps like you pull me around in a cart."

He smirked. "If I was flush, I wouldn't even need a cart. I'd make scraps like *you* go get me everything I need."

"Anything for you, Great One," she said. But her laughter failed when he lapsed into silence. Most of the time the quiet didn't bother her. She preferred it actually; there was nothing more annoying to her than mindless chatter. But here, so close to a home she knew he still missed, she felt a strange pressure to keep him talking.

"Where is Hayden, anyway?" she asked, thinking back to the whole reason they were on this venture. "And why's he working for slick Jed Schultz?"

Colin scowled. "He's not slick. He's all right."

Ty took this answer to mean that he didn't know where his brother had landed. He was all doe-eyed again, thinking about Jed, and she didn't like that one bit.

A couple stiffs in black uniforms walked by, and Ty pulled Colin down off the sidewalk so they could pass. Bakerstown police were as crooked as they came. Word was their chief was owned by big boss Hampton himself, who could use them as his own private army if the mood struck. They wouldn't take kindly to a couple Metal-head kids with pockets full of cash.

"Here's Fifth," she said when they reached a corner. A bike messenger swept by them, nearly clipping Ty's arm. She swore and gave him the finger.

Old rusty cars were parked on the curb, relics from a time when gas wasn't just for the rich, before the war between the feds. Most people used them now for shelter, though half of them had been dismantled for parts. A parking garage entrance came up on their left, and though their pace didn't quicken, both of them kept their eyes sharp. A lot of shadows in there. A lot of places for someone to hide.

Two guys were sitting on the concrete exit ramp and jumped up as Colin and Ty approached. They were both shorter than Colin, and well fed, dressed in hand-me-down wool slacks—nice ones, but not new—and shirts tucked into their waistbands. Their belts were painted green, flaking around the buckles. Muscle, hired by McNulty. Ty thought they looked soft and out of practice.

Colin sighed beside her, which made her lips quirk into a small grin. But when a girl about their age sauntered out of the shadows with her shirt tied in a tight knot behind her lower back, the scowl returned to Ty's face.

"Well hello," said Colin, eyes traveling from her darkly painted eyes and thick brown curls down her curvy form. She smirked and pushed her chest out, hand resting on one cocked hip. Ty made a noise of disgust.

"Let's see," said the first guy, a dark-skinned boy with dreadlocks. "Holes in their boots, eyes dumb as a dead pig, and the stink of acid. Must be Metalheads." His friend laughed into his fist.

Colin smirked, then wiped his grin away with the back of his hand. "Was that an insult, Ty? I . . . just . . . can't . . . seem . . . to . . . catch . . . on." He scratched his head.

"I *think* so." She shrugged. The other two looked at each other and laughed, but the lines around the first boy's eyes had gone tight.

"Damn," he said. "That's a girl. Thought for sure she was a man."

"That's 'cause she's twice the man you are," Colin shot back. His hand on Ty's arm stopped her from smacking those smirks right off their fat faces, even as her skin prickled with resentment. He'd meant it as a compliment, but it didn't feel that way.

The girl giggled, maybe at them, maybe just to flirt with Colin. Girls were always losing their heads around him. He sent her a smile blocked immediately by the second boy, whose hair was curled so tightly against his skull it looked like it might break.

"Why'd you cross the lines, Metalhead? You know better."

"Jed Schultz sent us to see a friend of his," Colin told them, easy as he might've said *nice weather today* or *say, you all have matching belts, how 'bout that.*

Ty's jaw locked. Why was he pulling the Schultz card? They could have handled this on their own. It took a second for her to figure out he probably didn't want them finding out about the money in his pocket.

Jed Schultz had immunity in Bakerstown, which meant *they* had immunity in Bakerstown. She wasn't used to that kind of protection. She wasn't sure she liked it. A reputation like that came with a cost.

McNulty's boys sighed and took a step back.

"Yeah, all right," said the boy with dreads, the disappointment thick in his voice. "Why didn't you say so? McNulty and Schultz go way back."

"I'll bet they do," said Colin.

Jed was the white knight of the gray city, the middleman between the people and their wealthy employers at Hampton Industries. McNulty was the king of the underworld—a big Northerner who made his money from the wealth of Bakerstown through girls and gambling and dope. Word was, McNulty used to run Metaltown before Jed came along, but after Jed won the workers over, he booted McNulty across the beltway. There was a truce in place: as long as their interests didn't clash, their people didn't clash. But that didn't mean they liked each other.

"Shouldn't you Bakerstown pricks be in school?" Ty asked. "I think I hear your teacher calling."

"*School?*" Dreads' patronizing tone made her hands curl into fists. "Surprised you know what that is, she-man. Are they teaching factory workers to read now?" His friends laughed.

She laughed with them, despite the bite of annoyance. She could read. Kind of.

"We graduated early," said the boy with the curly hair. "McNulty handpicked us to run his crew."

"Least he got it right with one of you." Colin leaned around them to grin at the girl.

She twirled her hair around one finger.

Ty's eyes narrowed. "Look, interesting as this is, some of us actually got things to do."

A long, hard stare passed between her and Dreads, kicking up her pulse. He was the first to back down, bringing a smirk to her face. When he turned away, Curly Hair balked, but followed. McNulty's clan let them pass without further trouble, though Ty could hear them arguing with the girl all the way down the block.

"Still think he's slick?" said Colin when they were out of earshot. "Jed's even got Bakerstown showing some respect."

Ty grunted. If McNulty was letting Jed do business in Bakerstown it could only mean one of two things—that McNulty didn't see Jed as a threat, or that Jed was even worse than his Bakerstown rival. Either way, she would have rather they'd fought—better than hiding behind some slick's back.

The intersection opened to reveal two twin stacks of apartments up ahead, cut down the center by the remainder of Fifth Street. The place was worn by the weather, and by the hodgepodge add-ons that folks had done over the years. Tattered sheets and clothing hung to dry outside the windows, some of which were covered by cardboard or trash bags. Half the place was marked by graffiti—most of it green for McNulty's clan. Somewhere in the distance, a baby was crying.

It was good, somehow, to see that even Bakerstown—the middle ground between the empty pockets of Metaltown and the high society of the River District—was just as sorry as where they'd come from. She hoped Colin saw that too. Then he might stop thinking things were so much better across the beltway.

"We're here." Colin stopped before a bar with dark windows and a set of stairs that went down into the entrance. The sign protruding from the door front said "Cat's Tale" in pale gold letters. Harsh words and harsher laughter filtered outside.

Beside the stairs was another set of steps, these leading up to an enclosed concrete landing. They climbed around the paper trash and a stray tabby that hissed at Ty, and stopped before the first door: 114 Fifth Street.

Colin took a deep breath, reminding Ty to breathe too. She registered the nerves in her belly then—they'd been brewing since she set foot out of her own territory this morning. They needed to get this over quickly and get back where they belonged.

Colin knocked twice and they waited. *Stupid,* Ty thought, for them to come now, in the middle of the day. But Jed had said this man hadn't been to work in a while, so maybe he was home.

They didn't wait long. From the inside came the sound of locks releasing, one at a time. Three clicks, and then the door pulled inward. A skinny boy about their age with yellow hair and dark rings around his swollen eyes answered the door. He was wearing a thermal shirt and pants that were too short, and his apartment stunk of boiled cabbage.

Ty heard Colin's quick intake of breath and braced defensively, but he didn't make a move. A second later the stranger's eyes rounded with recognition.

"Colin?" the boy said. "What are you doing here?"

3

LENA

Lena set down her electronic reader and stared out the study window at the stone steps that led from the great room downstairs to the gardens, and then to the dock. The river was bright blue, as it always was after a recent color treatment. An illusion, of course; the water was filthy. The street people from the surrounding districts bathed and laundered in it—and, disgustingly enough, fished in it as well—leaving it even more sludgelike than the sticky black oil water of the Whitewater Sea.

"Is there a problem, Miss Hampton?" asked her tutor, an angular, birdlike woman with a hooked nose. Her dark hair had become speckled with gray over the last year, and she wore it in a short cap around her skull.

"I'm tired of this, Darcy," said Lena. She rubbed her eyes, the satin fingers of her gloves making the perfect blue water disappear behind her fine lids. "If I have to read one more word of this nonsense I'll be forced to throw you in the river."

Darcy flattened any expression she might have had, and adjusted her simple black dress.

"Now Miss Hampton, there's no need to be hostile."

"Not according to the Advocates," she argued, pleased to have elicited a sigh from her tightly strung tutor. "Hostility seems to be working quite well for them."

Just last week she'd read that the Advocates—Eastern Federation radicals, desperate for food—had taken out a supply train headed toward the southern border. The contents, not rations but Hampton Industries weapons, had all been stolen, a large painted *A* marking the side of the empty boxcar. For a group who claimed they wanted peace, they seemed to have no problem killing Northern Federation soldiers to get it.

She glared down at her reader again. Poetry was useless, especially poetry in a foreign tongue. If the purpose was to make her worldly, she'd rather learn about the war, and what news there was from the front lines. She certainly wasn't getting any information about it from her father and brother, who rarely included her in business discussions.

"The Advocates are misguided," said Darcy, looking out the window now as well. "Hunger makes people dangerous."

Hungry or not, they were ignorant if they thought there was enough food and clean water for everyone to share. Resources were thin. Just last week the Hamptons' cook had run out of bread for her morning toast. A flour shortage, he claimed. The effects of the crisis were felt even in the River District.

"Well, crates of military-grade weapons make people dangerous too," said Lena. "Maybe they should try eating *them* if they're so hungry."

Sometimes her father liked to say that it wasn't a war about resources, but a war about entitlement. People fighting for what they thought they deserved, rather than what they actually needed. Even the North, who claimed defeating the Eastern Federation's military would enable them to offer aid to the poor starving citizens there, really just wanted their enemy's land. She wasn't naïve. More than once she'd heard her whispers during her father's parties at the house of what Hampton Industries could do if they expanded their factories into the Eastern territories.

"You've been doing some extra reading, I see." Darcy's thin brows pulled inward. There was a fine line between geography and politics, and her father's orders were that Lena only study the first.

"I read that their leader—Akeelah something—wants a seat on the Assembly," Lena pressed. The article about the supply train attack had mentioned as much. Apparently he'd lived on the streets, and worked in the cornfields. There were no pictures of him. Perhaps he was hiding, just like his Advocates.

She could hardly imagine a laborer from the East serving on a board entirely composed of Northern citizens. Her father had served his elected, six-year term alongside military commanders, police chiefs, and other businessmen and women when she was a child. Every other month they'd met to discuss Northern Federation issues, to govern the *North*. Including anyone from the Eastern Federation, much less the leader of a rebel group, would have been like inviting a traitor over for dinner.

"Perhaps he just wants their voice heard," said Darcy.

"Then perhaps he should tell his people to stop stealing our weapons and ambushing Northern troops."

"Sometimes people feel opposition is the only way to get attention." A vein appeared on Darcy's forehead. She appeared as if she might say more, but her mouth snapped shut at the creaking of footsteps in the foyer. They both turned toward the front of the house, but the noise had stopped. It was probably a maid, dusting the hallway paintings.

"Let's return to task," Darcy said quickly. "Did you encounter a problem with the poem?"

"I just want to know—"

"The poem," she said firmly, ending their previous talk.

"Yes," said Lena. She leaned forward in her desk chair; the bolts of fabric tightened around her waist and made it difficult to breathe. "The problem is it's pointless to learn the ancient languages when they serve absolutely no practical purpose in the real world."

"And what would you know of the real world, my dear?"

Lena stood sharply at the sound of her father's voice from the study door. Josef Hampton was statuesque as always, his face clean-shaven, smooth as bronze, his black hair neatly combed. The gray suit he wore had been pressed to crisp lines. Its gray vest was open at the front, an indication that he'd just finished his morning meeting. She hadn't expected him home so soon; he normally kept to his office, a separate cottage on their estate, until the evening.

Lena smoothed down her hair, tucking a flyaway into the tight knot at the back of her neck. She cleared her throat, noting the way Darcy's hands had folded in front of her hips and her head had fallen forward in respect for her employer.

"Good morning, Father," said Lena, unsure yet if his cool smile meant he was pleased to see her. She hoped he hadn't overheard too much.

"Good morning, Lena. Please, continue," he said. "You were just telling the tutor about the faults in your curriculum."

Lena's neck warmed. She lifted a gloved hand and waved off the comment. "I was just trying to lighten the mood." She laughed. She couldn't hear Darcy breathing. Lena hoped she didn't plan on passing out.

"I only meant," continued Lena, "that I wish I could study something more useful. The old languages get their best use as party tricks these days. Everything now is in the common tongue."

Josef's face did not change. "And what if I told you an education in the arts is one of the few things that separate us from the working class?"

Lena turned back toward the window, wondering how it was possible that her father, the most brilliant man in the Northern Fed, could be so impractical. "Then I would say that Hampton Industries rests on the backs of the workers, not the back of the arts. And that there are a great many other things that separate us beside that. Circumstance, for instance."

"Circumstance?" chided her father. "Is that what children are calling money these days?"

She wouldn't know. She rarely socialized with others outside of committee parties, and her father didn't approve of her mingling with the families of their subordinates. The Hamptons remained untouchable, leading the Northern Federation's Tri-City area—the River District, Bakerstown, and the factory district—in revenue. But they hadn't always been so fortunate. Her great-grandfather had worked his way up from poor means, living in a space smaller than her bathroom while he built the foundation of their empire. She often imagined him alone, tinkering with various forms of ammunition in his tiny shop while the people who would one day make him rich squabbled outside on the streets.

Because of his diligence, her family had a legacy, one that thrived on a bloody violence they would never see up close. Their various factories manufactured military supplies—bombs, guns, all grades of weapons and ammunition. A necessary business, according to her father. The survival of the Federation depended on it.

"Miss Hampton," piped Darcy. "Perhaps we should study outside today? It's quite lovely."

Lena chewed the inside of her cheek, unable to turn around and face her father for fear of the disappointment in his eyes. She didn't know why her mouth ran away with her sometimes.

But Josef had begun to laugh, a deep, honest sound of amusement. Lena faced him then, consciously holding back a smile.

"Such a sweet girl," he said, dark eyes gleaming. "Darcy, perhaps you should be teaching Lena a trade of some kind. Welding perhaps. Or sewing. There are always open positions in the kitchen."

Lena acknowledged the chill in the room and forced her chin to stay level.

"I meant no disrespect, Father."

He smiled at her, and approached slowly, stopping a few feet away.

"I know," he said. "It's in your nature to question. I sometimes wonder, if you had a mother . . ." He trailed off, eyes focusing on the river outside.

Lena felt herself drawn forward, wanting to hear more. He rarely spoke of her mother apart from when he was acknowledging Lena's faults. She felt an emptiness creep into her chest, a feeling of loss. But that was ridiculous, of course. The only mother she'd ever known had been her nanny, and even if as a child Lena had wished for more, the woman was no more bound to the Hamptons than the rest of the staff.

"What was she like?" Lena found herself asking.

"She was beautiful. Like you." If he'd meant it to be a compliment, she couldn't help feeling disappointed, like there was little else to her.

"I was thinking I could work," Lena said. "Perhaps not in the kitchen, but somewhere else. Surely there's something I can do for the factory? Otto can barely keep up the books for his division—"

"Your brother is still learning," responded Josef. "He's only been manager for a year. He'll figure out what needs to be done."

"He'll run it into the ground," Lena said under her breath. She'd heard her brother just last week telling the foreman to do whatever he wanted, just as long as the division's output increased. If she had to guess, she'd say he hadn't spent more than an hour in his factory in the past month. If her father knew Otto was drinking his days away at the Boat House, she doubted he'd have such confidence in his tone.

"But since you're so eager, there is something you can do," said Josef, either not hearing Lena or ignoring her. "We'll have guests this afternoon. Clients, the kind with deep pockets. I'm sure you recognize the importance of fostering such relationships."

"Yes, Father," said Lena, sparking with hope.

"Clever girl," he said. "You'll sing for us, I hope. Let them see the Hamptons' softer side."

Lena's shoulders fell. He didn't want her to sit in on the meeting, to be a part of negotiations. Of course he didn't. Otto was called in for wining and dining, and she, just a year his junior, would be the entertainment.

Her father faced her, waiting for her gaze to rise and meet his. When it did, he nodded once, and left the room.

* * *

Lena climbed the stairs to the third story, the heels of her shoes clicking with each contact against the cherrywood floor. In the hallway mirror she caught a glimpse of herself and paused, blowing out a controlled breath she hoped would dispel the flush that had climbed her neck and blossomed on her high cheeks.

Automatically, one hand went to smooth her black hair, though it hardly needed a touch-up. It was neat and flawless, as were her olive skin and the arches in her brows. Not alluring, not like the women who attended her father's parties with their wealthy patrons, but polished. So like her father.

She sighed in frustration, removing one glove to fix her makeup. Leaning toward the mirror she could see her amber eyes clearly, and wondered as she had a thousand times if her mother's eyes had been this strange lion's color. Her father's and Otto's eyes were dark, nearly as dark as the black hair they all shared. Perhaps that was why he favored his son so much more than his daughter. Because he was a nearly perfect replica of the powerful, untouchable Josef Hampton. Quickly, she replaced the glove and continued past Otto's bedroom to her own.

Her quarters were large, composed of a sitting area, walk-in closet, bathroom, and sleeping room. Antique furniture had been sparsely arranged by her family's interior designer. Lena moved immediately to the window, before which hung a white decorative cage, half her height and shaped like the palaces across the sea. Inside was a bird, a brilliant yellow canary that trilled a happy greeting and hopped sideways along the wooden dowel.

"Good," Lena said. "Why don't you go downstairs and sing for Father and his colleagues if you love it so much."

She poked one finger through the cage, frowning when the songbird only tilted his head from side to side, but drew no closer. When he warbled again, Lena's lips turned up into a small smile. He was extraordinary; she'd thought so since her father had brought him home three years earlier from a business trip. They'd set up the cage together, one of the few tasks not left to the servants, and he'd told her she must take care of him herself in order to learn the value of responsibility. Sometimes she wished her father would come upstairs to see what a good job she'd done, but he rarely came to this level unless to look for Otto.

"Pretty thing," Lena murmured, longing to feel the soft downy feathers but only feeling the inside of her glove. Outside, the breeze rattled the gray limbs of the oak tree against her windowpane.

"How exciting," said Darcy, stepping into the room in one jerky movement. "What will you sing, I wonder?" Her tone didn't reflect her words; she was always on edge after a visit from Lena's father.

Lena rose, already defeated, and walked to the table beside the tall bureau where she kept her clothes. "I don't think it really matters, do you?"

In the center of the room, Darcy had already begun riffling through the sheet music on its intricate wire stand. "Something that shows your range, I think. Not that piece you performed at the last recital. Something classic. Your father will like that."

Darcy wasn't listening to her. She had a way of picking through a conversation and only extracting the things she wanted to hear. It was that way with all of Lena's servants.

All but one.

Ignoring Darcy, Lena went to her sleeping room and closed the curtain separating the chamber. Her bed was neatly made, the plush gold comforter hanging nearly to the floor, a menagerie of decorative pillows scattered around the head. She kneeled beside the mattress, and shoved one hand beneath it until she came upon what she was seeking: a doll no larger than her fist, handmade from rope that had once belonged to a mop.

Smiling wistfully, Lena laid down the doll's dress and removed her glove once again to feel the knotted rope that made up the head. Then, taking care, she placed it back in its hiding place, where the servants could never take it out with the garbage.

COLIN

"Colin, you know this kid?" Ty sized up the tenant before them, eyes scanning over his lanky arms and tired face as if he might try to get tough.

Colin knew better. Gabe Wokowski was a runner, not a fighter—had been since they were kids. But that didn't mean Colin knew what to say. His mouth opened then closed like a fish's. He wiped a line of sweat off his brow. The apartment was hot as a damn furnace.

Gabe's family had lived down E Street. Not on Fifth. It pissed Colin off that they lived here. Bakerstown held enough memories of what he'd had to leave behind without him running into old ghosts.

"What are you doing out here?" Gabe asked, glancing at Ty with a confused expression. "I thought you moved."

"I did," said Colin finally. "Sorry. Took me a minute to remember how I know you."

He didn't know why he said it; four years was a long time, but the guy didn't look *that* different. Not like Colin did. Standing in the doorway of the Wokowskis' home, he became acutely aware of the holes in the elbows of his coat and the scar slicing through his eyebrow—a badge he'd earned in a fight a few years back that served as a warning to others that he wasn't afraid to take a hit. But as Gabe glanced over it, the look on his face was more pity than fear, and Colin didn't know what to make of that.

"School." The boy frowned. "Gabe Wokowski."

"Right. I remember now."

"We had class together every year." He turned to Ty. "Assigned seating charts. They always put you in order by your last name."

"Yeah, they do that in the factories, too," said Ty with her usual bite. Colin wished she'd stop glaring at him.

"You work in the factories?" Gabe asked her. "In Metaltown?"

"Is this kid for real?" Ty jabbed a thumb his direction. Gabe's face turned red.

Colin cleared his throat. "Listen, Gabe, we need to talk to your dad." They were here for business, not to catch up. Maybe flush schoolboys didn't have to work, but Colin had responsibilities.

Gabe withdrew into the house and let them in. It was a small apartment for Bakerstown; dingier than the Wokowskis' old place on E Street. They could hardly take a step before bumping into a blue patchwork couch, which they had to shuffle by sideways in order to get into the kitchen. The walls were decked out in old-lady needlework pictures—flowers and such—and several pairs of shoes had been kicked off randomly across the floor. Colin remembered when he'd had more than one pair of shoes. He remembered when he'd had a bicycle, too, like the one hanging from a hook against the back wall. He and Gabe used to race home from school.

Ty crinkled up her nose at the cabbage boiling in the pot over their single-burner stove. It was hotter in here; the oven was cranked high and had been left open to heat the room. Dishes, coated with crud, were stacked up on the counters. A fly buzzed against the window frame.

"There's stew," said Gabe, picking through the mess in the sink. "It's mostly cabbage, though."

"Smells like it," said Ty. "Not as good as pigeon, huh, Colin?" He winced when she elbowed him in the ribs.

"So you live in Metaltown?" asked Gabe, testing the word again. "I thought your family did all right."

"Who said we don't?" asked Colin.

"Oh, right. I only meant . . . I thought you were moving uptown, that's all. I thought that's what you said." Gabe scratched his head.

"Looks like you heard wrong," said Ty when Colin didn't respond.

Colin loosened the scarf around his neck but didn't take it off. His eyes flicked down to a worn book on the kitchen table, and stumbled over the title. *Flight of the Fox,* it was called. Probably a kiddie book with a name like that. Maybe Gabe had a screw loose or something.

It had been a long time since Colin had read anything but factory manuals.

"Well, I'll just go get my dad then," said Gabe after another moment. He wound his way around the chairs and down a narrow hallway.

"You going soft in the head?" whispered Ty. "If it's bad blood, let's just drop the green and be done with it."

Colin didn't know what was wrong with him. It wasn't bad blood. In fact, he and Gabe had hung out together as kids. So it didn't make sense why this apartment, which was twice the size of his place over the beltway, seemed to be shrinking, or why he didn't care what Gabe had been up to for the last four years, or why he wished Ty had stayed in Metaltown.

"Colin." A man in a loose-fitting shirt and slacks approached from the back of the apartment. He was fair-skinned, like his son, with light hair that had lost some of its luster over time. He smiled warmly, but his eyes were tired.

Only then did Colin remember that Jed Schultz had sent them here because Mr. Wokowski had lost his daughter to the corn flu. He pictured her now—red hair, mouthy, always trying to tag along. She'd been a few years younger than him. Kali or Kaylee or something.

"Hi, Mr. W.," said Colin. "I . . . I heard about your daughter. We came to pay our respects."

Mr. Wokowski's face fell. "Thank you." He nodded slowly. "And how is your family? Your mother? And her friend, I heard . . ." His voice broke.

"They're real good, thanks." Colin glanced down at the book again.

"What about you? Gabe says you're working in the factory district."

Colin pulled at his scarf, wishing they'd crack a window to let in some air. The room was as hot as the factory floor. "Just for a little while," he said. "Then I'm going to the coast—place called Rosie's Bay. My brother was out there for a while working a fishing boat. One of those rigs that go way past the oil slicks to the clean water and net sharks and tuna and stuff. Real stuff, not the synthetic kind. I'll be doing the same."

He pictured the route he would take from the train map Hayden had brought home not long after his return. The Northern Federation was mountainous, marked by swells and potholes where the people and the smog had gathered and stuck throughout the ages. Winding through valleys, the train would climb the Yalans, higher and higher until you could look down and see the southern border of the Eastern Federation—where most of the fighting took place. His brother had told him the North's military guarded the supply trains heading toward the ocean. Once he got to the water, it was just a matter of walking the coastline until he reached his destination.

"That sounds wonderful," said Mr. Wokowski.

"It is," said Colin. He saw Rosie's Bay clearly in his mind, just as Hayden had described it: green cliffs cutting down into the frothy waters of the Whitewater Sea, a small fishing village right on the sand. Lots of space and as much food as you could catch.

Mr. Wokowski nodded. "It's a good day when friends come

calling." Behind him, Gabe shifted, and moved something across the stained carpet with his bare foot.

"You have some good friends, I guess," said Colin, feeling more at ease talking to Gabe's dad. "Like Jed Schultz."

Mr. Wokowski's face shot up. His eyes had narrowed. "Why do you say that?"

Ty, who could always read a room, sucked in a breath.

Colin reached in his pocket. His fingers, calloused and cracked from the cold and the factory, closed over the smooth bills, and he felt a pang of regret. With this kind of money he could set up his folks and get the hell out of Metaltown. He could be on the northern coast within the month.

But Jed Schultz had been good to his mother when few others had. He wasn't about to stick a knife in the man's back.

"Gabe, go to your room," said Mr. Wokowski suddenly.

"Dad, I—"

"*Go.*"

Colin scowled, seeing his old friend bow like the child he'd once been and withdraw into the shadows.

Mr. Wokowski stepped forward. "Please thank Mr. Schultz. Tell him we could not be more appreciative. Tell him that, will you? Tell him we're fine without his money, and I will return tomorrow to work." His voice had gone all wobbly and thin.

"He didn't want you to lose your house," explained Colin. "He wasn't mad or anything. He was just trying to help out."

"Of course," said the man, eyes so round you could see the whites circling the brown irises. "His gesture will never be forgotten. I was planning on returning tomorrow anyway. And my wife's pay has covered the rent this month. We are all right."

"But . . ."

"Come on," said Ty. "Let's get out of here."

"Jed told me to give you this money," insisted Colin. "Turning it down is crazy."

"Colin," said Ty. She grabbed his arm. He shook her off, staring at the old man, who seemed to wither before him. Colin didn't like that, either. He didn't want Mr. W. to be afraid of him; the man was acting like a child.

"Here," Colin said, slapping the money down on the arm of the couch, where it spilled across the floor.

"No!" Mr. Wokowski dove to the ground, scooping it up like melting snowflakes. Still on his knees, he shoved it at Ty, who took it with a look of bewilderment on her face. She stuffed the bills into her coat pocket.

Colin couldn't believe it. When someone offered you something so generous, you didn't turn it down. You said thank you, and used it to keep a roof over your head.

"Fine," he said. "I guess you were right, Ty. Bakerstown *is* full of pricks and pansies."

Mr. Wokowski's jaw locked, but he didn't say another word. As Colin left, he saw Gabe in the hallway, braced with a tire iron over one shoulder but looking more like a kid than ever.

TY

They moved fast out of Bakerstown, like their own shadows were chasing them. Fast enough to make Ty's shins burn, but not fast enough to leave Colin's dreams and demons back where they belonged: in the past.

She watched him, ready, but for what she didn't know. His shoulders were bunched, his fists balled, his eyes shifting side to side, looking for a fight. She felt strangely powerless, and had the urge to hit something just to know she still had control over herself.

It wasn't until they'd crossed the empty beltway marking the barrier to Metaltown that Colin finally exploded.

"Stupid, hardheaded bastard!" He kicked the ground and sent rocks spraying into the concrete partition separating the empty lanes. "How could someone turn down that much green? That was two months' rent!"

"At least," said Ty.

"At *least*," repeated Colin. "I get he's sad about his daughter, I get that, but come on. That's no excuse to be stupid."

Ty kept walking, hands in her pockets on the cash. It felt dirty. Just like slick Jed Schultz.

"What's with you?" she asked. "Why do you care so damn much?"

"I don't."

"Right," she said. "You must think I'm pretty dense, Prep School."

"Stop calling me that!" He turned on her, stare burning, and she glared right back at him.

"Then stop acting like it!" Ty's voice echoed off the empty streets. "You're not one of them anymore. You don't belong there anymore. You think you're all big and bad because stupid Jed Schultz knows your name? Well, you're not. You may have been high and mighty once, but you're scum just like me and the rest of Metaltown now and don't you forget it."

She was breathing hard, watching his face change from fury to shock, then back to fury.

"How," he said through his teeth, "could I ever forget it?"

Something pinched inside of her. She hadn't meant to spout off like that. She didn't know how he got under her skin the way he did sometimes.

"That guy's dumb as a rock," she said finally. "Forget him. Forget this whole place."

He started walking again, and she walked a few feet back, feeling the anger still clouding the air around him. Hating herself for adding to it.

Push him back home, she thought. *He'll be all right. Just get him back home.*

"Jed won't be bent at you for bringing the money back," she said.

"I don't care if he is," said Colin, but his tone told Ty differently. It was important that he play nice with Jed. If he didn't show he was grateful, Jed wouldn't give Colin's family a bump. And if they didn't get the money, Colin was going to lose Cherish, just like Gabe Wokowski had lost his sister.

She hated Jed Schultz. They wouldn't have even had to come to this stupid place, and Colin wouldn't be in such a bad spot now, if it weren't for him.

"Let's just steal it," she said. "Go to that place you always talk about. Go fishing."

The sky was growing overcast. A change that had nothing to do with the weather, but with the chem factory across the river.

"Rosie's Bay," he said after a while.

"Yeah," she said. They'd never go there, of course; they'd never get out of Metaltown. But it was nice to think about sometimes.

*   *   *

Jed's office was at the back of Market Alley, where the vendors set up their wares in handcarts and canvas tents, or sometimes right on the ground. Most anything you wanted could be found there: clothing, ripped off from Bakerstown or the River District; discarded food that hadn't met control standards at the testing plant; and piles of junk to swap—teapots and cracked dishes and scrap metal.

It was late in the afternoon by the time Colin and Ty picked their way down the main drag. Colin had taken the money back from Ty a few blocks back and stuffed it in the hidden breast pocket inside his coat. Market Alley was full of pickpockets, and someone could stand to make a fortune if Ty and Colin weren't careful.

They came to a water cart, and Ty gave up her last two coins to buy them both a drink from the metal cup. As soon as she was finished, she wished she could hand over one of those bills in Colin's pockets, but knew that wasn't an option.

She found herself hungry again passing by a fire pit, edged with bricks. A little woman with short black hair and close-set eyes shoved a skewer of yellow bulbs in Ty's face.

"Roaches," she said. "Crispy. Try a wing."

Ty felt a sudden clenching in her gut. Anything fried was dipped in cornmeal batter, and anything on the street hadn't passed food inspection standards. Roadkill was one thing, synthetic corn another. And even if she had occasionally taken her chances, she wasn't about to do so in front of Colin, not with Cherish in the shape she was in.

At Ty's dismissing wave, the vendor's eager smiled flipped upside down. Colin chuckled as she flung curses at their backs, and Ty felt a knot loosen inside of her at the sound. There was something strangely comforting about Metalheads: what you saw was what you got.

At least that was the way with most Metalheads.

Ty cringed as the warped wooden door at the back of the alley came into view. Two clasped hands, the mark of the Brotherhood, were carved into a sign hanging from a peg just below a peephole. As they approached, the door pushed outward and Imon wedged his enormous body through the opening.

"What am I supposed to say?" Colin said under his breath.

Imon stepped aside, allowing them entry. It was creepy the way he never talked. Ty found herself wondering if he had a tongue—if he was one of the poor, unlucky saps who'd burned their mouths out in food testing.

"Tell him the guy wasn't home," said Ty, suddenly worried that Jed really would be mad they'd botched the delivery, and what that would mean for the both of them.

Colin nodded, and they stepped through the dark entry into a tight corridor. Imon squeezed past them, sending a jolt through Ty as he brushed by her. She didn't like tight quarters like this. She preferred an open area, enough room to move, to defend herself if necessary.

Colin walked just behind Imon, making an immediate left into a small office, thick with the bittersweet stench of cinnamon cigarettes. Fancy stuff, Ty thought. Not your typical hand-rolled tobacco.

Jed was sorting through some papers atop his desk while he stood behind it, a heavy scarf hanging loosely around his neck despite the warmth of the room. He'd changed since this morning. He was wearing a clean suit, beige with fancy black stitches, but his hair was just as greasy as ever.

"There he is," said Jed as they entered. He didn't even glance at Ty, and she was glad for it.

"Hi, Mr. Schultz," said Colin. He sniffled, and wiped his nose with the back of his hand, then reached into his pocket and withdrew the money, carefully folded, just like when it had been received this morning.

Jed's smile melted, and in its place flashed a look so cold, it made Ty's spine tingle.

"Bad luck, eh?" With his words came an expression of understanding. Colin released a breath he'd been holding, but Ty was still on edge.

"Sorry," said Colin. "We went to the place you said, but no one was home." He placed the money on the desk before Jed, and took a step back, bumping into Ty.

"If you ever need anything else, I'm good to help," he added.

Jed picked up the bills slowly, flattening them in his hand and counting them, one by one. The tension thickened the air between them. Colin's face darkened.

"I didn't take any of it. Sir," he added.

"I know that, son," said Jed, continuing to count. "You're a good man, like I said."

They waited. Ty glanced back toward the door, but Imon was still blocking it. Her toes stretched to the ends of her boots.

"I used to work in Small Parts, like you, back in the day. Did you know that?" asked Jed, still counting. Ty rocked forward and back on the balls of her feet. "I was about your age when some slots opened up at the Stamping Mill. It was a pretty ugly place then. Wasn't unusual to go weeks without pay, or have the foreman knock you around for looking at him wrong. McNulty let it all slide. He used to run this town back then." At the name of his old rival, a wistful look spread over his face. "I know it's not perfect now, but it's better. You know why it's better?"

"Because of the Brotherhood," answered Colin.

The corner of Jed's mouth lifted, but he didn't look up from his task. "That's right. Because of the Brotherhood. I started the Brotherhood because the people needed protection from the men upstairs and the gangsters that controlled them. Because they needed some-one they could trust to take a hit when they couldn't, or help them meet the rent when they were short. That's what the Brotherhood does, it helps people. For a small fee, of course."

Ty knew what the Brotherhood did for the Stamping Mill. The employees handed over twenty percent of their pay to Jed Schultz, and that tax went to help the needy. Small Parts didn't have a Brother-hood. Small Parts was made up of small people—kids—and no one cared if a kid got a check, or if a kid worked long hours, because kids were hardy, and had their folks to fall back on.

Well, not *all* kids.

When Jed got to the bottom of the pile, he pulled two bills out and handed them back to Colin.

"For your troubles," he said, smiling. "You could use some new trousers, looks like. A sweater, too. It's cold outside."

Ty swallowed. She willed Colin not to take it—owing money to the wrong sort was worse than being poor—but what choice did he have? Like Colin had said earlier, when you got a generous gift, you took it, and you survived.

"Thank you," said Colin. He reached for the bills, but Jed didn't let go when Colin went to pull back. Ty's jaw tightened. *Sick joke,* she thought. So they were in trouble after all.

"Colin, you don't have to lie to me," said Jed softly, leaning forward over his desk.

"Sir . . ."

"They didn't want the help, no problem," said Jed. "I didn't intend to make anyone feel awkward, least of all you."

He released the green into Colin's hand.

"I . . . okay," said Colin. "I just couldn't believe he didn't want it, I guess."

Jed laughed then, and Colin joined in, weakly.

"Isn't that the truth?" said Jed. "Some folks just don't know what it means to struggle. Not like you and me, huh, kid?"

Colin nodded. "Sorry, Mr. Schultz. Won't happen again."

"All right," said Jed. "Get out of here. The foreman at Small Parts is expecting you back in an hour. Why don't you get some new things before then?"

With the conversation closed, they left the office, but the cinnamon smoke had given Ty a headache, and left a nasty taste in the back of her throat.

* * *

Colin bought new wool trousers that only had a couple fixable rips in the back pocket. He bartered fiercely with a vendor over a pair of boots, but when it was all done, he ended up with a fleece blanket, thrown in for half-off with a thick-knit sweater.

"Wanted this anyway," smirked Colin, folding the blanket under one arm as they exited Market Alley. "You sure you don't want anything? I still got some change."

"No," said Ty quickly. She had a bad feeling about spending Jed's money. A feeling like he might want it back someday.

"Suit yourself," said Colin.

Just past the alley on Factory Row was Whore's Corner, where half a dozen girls were flaunting their goods. They were all fishnet and cleavage, even as the cold patched up their skin, and Ty swung into the street to give them a wide berth. She'd work doubles every day for the rest of her life, long as it meant she could keep her clothes on.

As they passed, a blonde in red leather whistled at Colin, and he winked back at her.

"Two for one, baby," called another. She opened her waistcoat and flashed them. "I work for small parts too." She cackled.

"I still got some change," Colin repeated, tripping over his own feet.

Ty pushed him on past the daunting stone archway that marked the entrance to Division I—the Stamping Mill, owned by Hampton Industries, just like the rest of Metaltown. Even outside you could hear the loud crunch and squeal of metal through the tall barred windows behind the gate.

Another block and they came to Small Parts, a fat, deep building just as gray and drab as the rest of Factory Row. There were no windows here, no chance for break-ins, or break-outs as the case may be. That was because Small Parts worked in explosives.

Not all the unstable stuff—that was done at the chem plant just across the river. But in the back of the factory, in a corner they called the "hot room," was enough white phosphorus to blow the cap off half a city block. So Small Parts was kept locked down, with a deadbolt across the door and a signed contract that sent thieves straight to lockup in the district prison.

Ty didn't have to read well to know the sign said "HAMPTON INDUSTRIES—DIVISION II." They passed the front double doors—there more for show than anything else—and rounded the alley to the employee entrance on the west side. Ty had never been late before, and the nerves were already dancing in her stomach when Colin banged three times on the metal grate.

Jed Schultz better have kept his word and talked to the foreman.

Colin stepped back as the familiar sound of a chain pulled off the inside handle. A moment later the door flung open to reveal a short, ill-tempered man with a glistening bald spot right on the top of his head. Minnick, his thick, red brows furrowed, glanced down the alley as if to make sure they weren't followed, then picked at a sore on his grisly jaw.

"I bet you two think you're pretty hot stuff, don't you?" he growled. "Sending the Brotherhood to my door."

"I thought it was Hampton's door," said Colin. Ty shot him a quick glare.

"Oh, very nice, very nice. Schultz got you on the payroll, does he? Guess you won't be needing your job here anymore then, will you, smart-ass?"

"Colin," warned Ty. They were two of the most productive

workers on staff, but that didn't mean Minnick wouldn't fire them. The foreman was a pain, but not someone you wanted to push.

"Mr. Schultz said he talked to you, Minnick. That you should expect us back this afternoon."

"Oh, my apologies!" bellowed Minnick. "Yes, my liege! I have indeed been expecting you! May I show you to your regular station?" He grabbed Colin's collar and jerked him down. Ty's hands fisted in her pants pockets, fighting the urge to strike out in defense.

"Brotherhood has no jurisdiction over Small Parts, you little brown-nosed rat. Brotherhood protects the Stamping Mill and the chem plant. The grown-ups. You know who protects Small Parts? Me. And I'm about to take real good care of you." White-flecked beads of spit sprayed from his mouth onto Colin's cheeks. One ruddy fist wound back, daring them to do something. Anything.

Colin didn't even flinch.

"We can work something out," said Ty. "Overtime. Janitorial. I know you got something for us." She hated giving in to slime like Minnick, but where else were they going to go for work? They weren't old enough to catch a shift at the chem plant, and she'd rather die in food testing than start working a corner like the whores outside Market Alley.

Colin breathed in slowly through his nostrils, then stuck a hand in his pocket and retracted a handful of coins that he held out for the angry foreman.

"Oh my, oh my," said Minnick. "Now we're talking. Something shiny for your good friend Minnick."

"That's right," mumbled Colin.

"What else you got? Let's see that scrap of blanket there. What else? New duds?"

"Given to me by Mr. Schultz," said Colin, and even if Minnick talked a hard game, Ty knew he wouldn't try to steal something Jed had given Colin. He liked to rough up the kids, but when another adult dressed him down he practically pissed himself.

Minnick spat a brown wad of chew out the corner of his mouth while he considered this.

"Get your asses inside," he finally said. "Cross me again and you're done here."

Ty exhaled.

They followed him in, placing their personals and weapons in the employee lockers while Minnick bolted the door. Colin, still grumbling over the lost green, stripped down to a thermal, frayed around the neck and thin enough to show patches of his skin. Ty glanced away quickly. Fool should have bought one of those when he had the chance.

She took off her coat and hat, but kept on all three sweaters she wore. She'd grown used to the heat of Small Parts. It wasn't comfortable, but it was a lot better to be hot than to remind a room full of guys that she wasn't exactly built the same as the rest of them.

They picked a high locker, like always, where anyone trying to lift anything would have to make an obvious show of it. No one tried much anyway. Stealing got you fired as fast as fighting, and besides, they all came in and out at the same time of day for the most part anyway.

Past the metal detectors, from out on the floor, came the familiar grind of gears and the consistent hum of the supply belt. The heat hit Ty like a furnace, and with it, the sharp tang of sweat. She moved to the rail, looking down over the factory floor at the hundred young workers who stood at their line stations as they had since dawn. Cutting tube casing or fuses, attaching wiring to batteries, springing the waterproof coils. Placing their finished products on the belt that snaked across the floor. This was what Ty had done every day for half her life. Ever since she'd been kicked out of the orphanage and sent to find work.

It was better than begging. That's what she always told herself, anyway.

"Uh-uh," said Minnick from behind them. "I think we're going to go with that idea you had earlier. Janitorial, right? I don't believe anyone's cleaned my toilet since last summer. We'll start there, then move to the floor latrines, how's that sound, little rats?"

Ty sighed.

Better than begging.

LENA

The businessmen came in the late afternoon and gathered in the parlor room on the bottom floor of the Hamptons' home to smoke cigars and drink. Otto, a younger, less serious version of Josef, had graced them all with his presence, wearing a pressed black suit to match Lena's floor-length gown. Their attire was one step more formal than the rest of their guests'. There was never any doubt whose children they were.

Lena was positioned in the center of the room, fully exposed on all sides. Eight men, including the two from her own family, surrounded her, and half a dozen of the house staff were serving liquor and hors d'oeuvres. Otto was near the bar speaking to a man she'd never seen before. Middle class, from the look of his suit, and with a tail of hair that hung down to his sweat-rimmed collar. Her mouth tightened with disapproval as her brother withdrew his wallet and passed the other man a series of bills. She wondered why Otto owed him, and imagined it had something to do with a gambling debt at the Boat House. This would not be the first time she'd seen him pay out for losses.

Her father approached through the sweet-smelling haze, accompanied by a man with thinning gray hair. He wore strange boots—unfinished leather with a wide heel—and pants creased right down the center of his legs. A thin bolo tie was fastened by a silver clip just below his collar. She couldn't place where he might be from; no one around here dressed that way.

"My daughter Lena is a master of songs," boasted her father, and despite her irritation at being dragged to this party as a centerpiece, she found herself blushing.

"Lovely dress," the man said with a lopsided smile. The hand not holding a tumbler reached for her waist, and before she could sidestep, it slid along her stomach.

Lena fought the urge to jerk back, and remained composed despite the swelling anxiety. Her father had raised his glass to summon the staff for another drink. When he looked back his flat gaze met hers, dipping to the man's hand for only a moment. He said nothing about it.

Gracefully, Lena slid away.

"May I sing for you?" she asked, a calm tone masking her revulsion.

"Yes, please," said the man. "But only if you answer one question."

Lena froze. Her father's stare had hardened, his intentions clear. *Do not let me down.* Normally he would have redirected the conversation away from her. The fact that he was letting this man say whatever he liked made her realize the significance of their pending deal.

"Why should I do business with your father?"

Lena balked for only a moment before composing herself. She didn't know what this man did, much less how his company could serve to support Hampton Industries. How could she answer correctly without the proper background?

"Well, Lena?" Her father smiled, though the lines of his throat twitched. Perspiration beaded on her hairline.

"Anyone who goes into business with Hampton Industries is making an excellent decision," she said slowly, gauging her father's response through her long black lashes. She tried to remember everything she'd ever heard her father say to a client. In his silence, she continued. "The company evolved during the war, and though we have no hand in agriculture or food production, our profit margins increased twelvefold during the famine. Why? Because we make weapons, sir. Mass produced, of the highest quality. And as long as humans roam this world they will find something worth killing each other over."

Lena held her breath, bracing for her father's disappointment.

The man's mouth had held a straight line, but when she finished he placed his cigar between his thin lips and clapped generously, spilling liquor from his glass onto the floor. A maid hurried to clean it up before he could slip.

"Quite a showing, Josef. Ice cold." The man began to ogle Lena's body in a way that made her want to slap him. She hated that her father still had said nothing. Had her words earned none of his pride?

Finally he smirked. "What can I say? She's a Hampton." The man in the boots chuckled appreciatively.

She recognized the cue, and smiled pleasantly, though she felt ill.

"Sing something, dear," said her father. As if she were one of his factory machines he could command with the press of a button.

But she was a machine. She was a Hampton. Emotionless and hard as steel.

Lena closed her eyes, summoning calm, drowning out the smoke and the boisterous male voices. Gradually, her pulse slowed. She took a steadying breath, and sang.

It was a ballad. She'd chosen one in the old language despite her earlier argument. She knew immediately from the silence filling the room that she'd made the right decision. This was what they wanted to hear, a song about a working man who'd become rich on love, only to see his beloved killed by a storm. A song about things as foreign to them as the lands across the sea. A song about a love that didn't exist.

She ended on a soft, haunting high note, and the room erupted into cheers. But when she opened her eyes, she found her father was no longer standing beside her. He had disappeared.

Lena gave a small curtsey, and quickly excused herself before the man in the boots could follow. By the time she stepped through the double doors onto the patio a sharp pain had lodged inside her chest. She hated these parties, hated being put on display. Hated the drinks and the smoke and the men's careless hands.

Her father hadn't even stayed to hear her sing.

Lena's eyes drifted over the river, to the district beyond Bakerstown, smoldering in the distance. Metaltown, the staff called it—the third section of the Northern capital, Tri-City, where Hampton Industries was located. A gray haze hung over the place, like a perpetual storm cloud, blocking out everything beneath.

"Brava." Lena stiffened at the sound of her brother's voice.

Otto left the patio door swinging open and stalked toward her. She read his face; a lifetime of training had taught her to be ready when the lines beneath his dark eyes tightened, and when he threw his arm over her shoulders and squeezed, she went rigid as a flagpole.

"I'm so glad you liked it," she said flatly.

"Did I say I liked it?" He rubbed his jaw with his free hand. "Oh well, it doesn't matter what I think. The rube did, and that's all that matters. What did you say to make him so interested? He needs a bib for all that drool."

"Shouldn't you be down at the club?" Lena asked. "I hear they send out a search party if you roam too far away from the bar."

He whistled through his teeth. "Don't be nasty."

His arm lowered, hand gripping her waist as he jerked her closer. He pinched her hard on the ribs, grabbing the skin and twisting it, until she knew it would be black and blue and perfectly hidden beneath her clothes. Aware of voices near the door, she sucked in a harsh breath and held it while her eyes watered. She had to bite the inside of her cheek to keep from crying.

"I'm sure you'll be happy to hear that whatever you said got Father all out of sorts," Otto said, finally releasing his hold. "He wants you to come to the factory with me tomorrow. Thinks it might be time you learned the family business."

"He does?" Lena asked, still gritting her teeth.

"You know him. He's probably trying to teach a lesson of some sort. The importance of failure or something."

Someone called him from inside, and he raised his hand, waving companionably. As he strode away, the pain in Lena's side receded, and she turned a curious gaze back toward Metaltown.

COLIN

At the end of the day Colin smelled like bleach and piss. If there was one thing he hated more than scrubbing toilets, it was scrubbing toilets while Minnick the perv watched, and knowing there wasn't a damn thing he could do about it if he wanted to keep his job.

Didn't stop him from visualizing forty different ways he could kill the bastard.

At least he and Ty were released on time with the others. Everyone knew that if Minnick didn't bring a fix to work, he got twitchy near closing time, and today the foreman wasn't about to stay late.

They lined up like usual, and walked one by one through the metal detector into the locker room. Colin was itching to get back out on the street. Maybe they'd only stayed half a day, but it had felt like three times that long with Minnick drooling at his back. After this morning, patience wasn't on his agenda.

"Johns look real shiny." Zeke, a boy near Colin's age with a shaved head and deep brown skin, elbowed in beside him. "I could see my reflection in the bowl."

"I aim to please," answered Colin.

"So did I," said Zeke.

"Why were you out, anyway?" Colin turned to see Matchstick, a kid Ty had known from St. Mary's who'd earned his name because he liked to lift the defective pieces from the scrap bin and rig mini explosives. He was only fourteen but as tall as Colin.

"We thought you'd been sacked," said Martin Balzac, scratching his yellow, spiky hair. He lisped a little on account of several missing teeth.

"Heard you were doing work for Jed Schultz," said Zeke. "He ever needs more guys, you tell him I'm good, okay?"

"How'd you hear that?" Colin asked, straightening up a little taller.

"Noneck saw you guys at Hayak's cart. Said Jed bought you something to eat."

"He did," said Colin. "Bought me some new duds, too."

"You'll tell him I'm good to work?" asked Zeke again.

"New duds," said Martin, laughing. "So that's why Minnick keeps giving you the eye." He batted his white-blond lashes Colin's way.

Colin shoved him into the lockers as they headed toward the door.

*　*　*

They snagged what they could from the corner vendors and met on the beltway, the stretch of road over the train yards that separated Metaltown from Bakerstown. It was deserted, just as it had been when Colin and Ty had walked back from Gabe's house that morning. Folks stuck to their side of the tracks, especially at night. Even the cops, who housed themselves in McNulty's territory. That's why Colin and the others liked it. No Minnick breathing down their throats. No one telling them what they had to do.

Most were from Small Parts, though some of the younger workers from the uniform division or the chem plant came there to set fights, to make trades or make out, or smoke the herbs they stole from Market Alley. Zeke was still pressing Colin about the morning, and how he might get on with Jed. He had a sister to look after, currently over with a group of older girls getting her hair braided. Colin watched them, a scowl on his face. The more he talked about

Jed, the more he thought about Gabe Wokowski, and Bakerstown, and how different things had been before Cherish had gotten sick.

"Hi, Colin." A girl waved to him from the pack of females, curly hair tied back with a rag. She smiled sheepishly, and when he returned her wave she ducked back into the huddle and giggled.

"Hi, Maggie," said Zeke, far too late. He made a show of waving, though the water girl from Small Parts didn't return the gesture. "What do you think they're talking about, anyway?"

"Probably you."

Zeke looked hopeful. "You think?"

"No." He tensed his gut a second before Zeke punched him.

Other days Colin would have braved the group, flirted with Maggie, maybe even convinced her to go somewhere private, but he didn't feel up to socializing. He should have been home, anyway. It was Hayden's night to take care of Cherish, but that didn't mean anything. Colin had been hoping to find him here, but he was probably down at Lacey's or one of the other bars gambling.

A lone figure sat on the cracked sidewalk, staring out into the divide between the two towns and the still train cars below. Colin tossed the blanket he'd bought in Market Alley on the ground and took his place beside her, fitting his legs through the railings and letting his feet dangle, as she did. This was often their spot, and always Ty's. They didn't talk about all the places they might go like they had when they were younger, but they thought about them all the same.

"I need to go get a bunk," Ty said after a while. She slept at the Board and Care, where beds were doled out on a first-come, first-serve basis.

"I need to go home," he said. Neither of them moved. An icy wind swept over the beltway, and he hunched deeper into his coat. The sun was setting; here on the edge of Metaltown you could actually see the sun—or at least a round white ball—through the haze.

"Your home or Maggie's?" Ty launched a pebble onto a train car below.

He didn't know why he was surprised Ty had seen Maggie wave at him. Ty saw everything.

"She's a pinhead, you know," Ty added.

Colin smirked. Maggie did have a pretty narrow face. But so did Ty. For a moment he looked at her, wondering if she might be pretty if she cleaned up a bit, or smiled every so often. Then he felt weird, like he was staring at his ma, and shook the thought from his mind.

"What do you care?"

"I don't," Ty retorted. "I don't care what you do. Do whatever you want." She crossed her arms over her chest and shivered against the cold.

Colin suspected the black mood had followed her from the morning. He passed her the blanket, and she jerked it around her shoulders.

They were quiet for a while, watching the crane trucks below load freight into the rusted metal cars. Then Ty said, "You ever have one of those toy trains when you were a kid? The wood ones with the metal tracks."

An image formed in his mind of the small rectangular blocks on tiny wheels. He'd painted it red, but only because the store had been out of yellow.

"Sure. Didn't everybody?" He regretted saying it when she gave an exasperated sigh.

"No, Prep School. Not everybody." She tightened the blanket around her shoulders. "I had a dream about one last night."

He didn't know why she was frowning.

"That's sweet," he said. "I'll get you one for your birthday. You can set it up on the line and play with it during your break."

He braced for a shove, but instead she just snorted.

A hiss behind them caught their attention, but before either could untangle their legs from the railing, there was an earsplitting crack from over by the concrete dividers. A flash of light, and a spray of dirt, and then silence.

"MATCHSTICK!" Martin, smeared with grime, emerged from the cloud of dust and charged after the rail-thin boy, who darted through the crowd. A cheer rose from those around, always game for a little demolition.

"Lifting from Small Parts again," said Ty, but her lips quirked up. From the opposite side of the street, Matchstick hollered for someone to save him.

Colin laughed, and then Ty laughed, the ugliness of the day having burst like Matchstick's explosion. He laughed so hard the tears burned his eyes and his stomach cramped, and it was only when he saw that Ty wasn't laughing anymore that he realized he'd slapped his hand on her leg.

He followed her gaze down, and then withdrew, feeling a little awkward. Not that he should have. Ty was family.

He stood.

A kid rammed into him from behind. He was smaller than most, pushing through the others like he owned the whole beltway. His dark hair was crunchy with sweat, and his shirt was dusted with the white powder all the workers used to keep their hands dry. That meant he worked at Small Parts, though Colin had never seen him before. As he went to shove past, he tripped over his own feet.

Colin reached down automatically to grab his arm and almost laughed. The kid's shoes were huge—men's shoes. Clown's shoes more like it. And white leather, like part of a chem factory uniform.

Exactly like part of a chem factory uniform. The kid was a thief—you had to be eighteen to apply there, and he couldn't have been more than ten. Plus, it was just plain stupid to steal uniforms—the workers all wrote their names on them so they wouldn't mix them up.

It rubbed Colin the wrong way. Not that he hadn't taken things he'd needed before, but the way the kid was tromping around, showing off, irritated him. It was plain disrespectful.

He kept a hold of the boy's arm, mind set on telling him to watch himself. But when he leaned down, he recognized the inscription on the instep, scratched in black marker.

H. Walter.

Hayden Walter.

In an instant, he'd wrapped the boy's collar in his fist and shoved him against the railing. Small, narrowed eyes burned up at him with fury, though not as hot as Colin's. Ty jumped up in surprise.

"What are you doing?" She'd immediately gone for their hands to break them up.

"Where'd you get those shoes, kid?" Colin rammed him against the railing again. The metal clanked, drawing the attention of those packed closest.

"*Colin,*" Ty hissed.

"Get your hands off me!" the boy squeaked. No one dared defend the kid. No one pushed Colin when he was angry.

"Fight!" someone called. The word caught like wildfire, and after a brief, frustrated moment, Colin released the boy. He wasn't looking for attention, he wanted answers.

"The shoes," Colin said, jaw locked.

"There could be ten H. Walters working there," Ty said after a moment. But Colin recognized the handwriting, and he remembered the night Hayden had marked them, just after he'd started at the plant.

The kid tried to run, but Colin snagged the back of his shirt and dragged him back into place.

"Where did you get those shoes?" Colin asked again. "Last chance to tell me before I make you tell me, kid, and trust me, I don't care if you're six or sixty, I will."

Ty swore under her breath. She was going to intervene. There were rules about picking on someone half your size, rules she'd taught him once upon a time. Even Metalheads had a code.

Fine, so Colin wouldn't kill him.

"Try it, you big stupid . . . giant," the kid managed, practically walking on his tiptoes as Colin hoisted him up.

The crowd of bodies grew denser as Ty attempted to drag them away from the railing, toward the center of the bridge. In order to get a better grip, Colin abandoned the shirt for the kid's arm, bending it at an awkward angle behind his back. He was careful not to break it. Good God. It didn't hurt nearly as bad as the kid was carrying on.

"Ow!" the kid whined, falling dramatically in a heap against a concrete barrier. Several workers Colin knew had stopped what they were doing and were watching with interest.

He stepped forward.

Ty slapped a hand on his chest, a stubborn look on her face. "Don't make me stop you."

He glared at her.

"I lifted 'em fair, okay?" the kid belted. "From some junkie sleeping off his bender underneath the bridge."

"When?" Colin bent down and ripped one shoe off, then the other, tying the laces together.

"Hey! I got those fair, I told you!" said the kid.

"You stole them. How's that fair?" But he knew as well as anyone, what you didn't claim was ripe for the picking.

"Last night." The boy pouted. "I got 'em last night. You happy?"

Ty kneeled beside him. "There's free shoes at the Charity House."

"Wood shoes maybe," he spat. "Shoes that don't fit, maybe. Shoes that got holes in 'em, maybe."

Ty crossed her arms over her chest. He was mouthy, that much was for sure.

One good smack across the jaw, that was what the kid needed. God knew Colin had gotten his fair share of them after moving across the beltway. But the flash of fear in the boy's eyes stayed his hand. Ty was right. What did picking on a kid prove? That he was Minnick, that's what.

A final hard look, and Colin stood. He had to find Hayden. Make sure he was alive. He hadn't been home in three days now. A shudder passed through him as he considered just how cold the previous night had been.

He shrugged into his coat and tucked the blanket under one arm. The switchblade in the front of his belt beneath his shirt moved, reminding him of its presence. Turning toward the river, he paused when he felt Ty's hesitation. She was staring at the shoes hanging over his shoulder.

"Go get your bunk," he said, letting her off the hook. He could have used her help, but winter nights in Metaltown were too cold to sleep outside; maybe Hayden knew firsthand, but Ty didn't have to. He was on his own.

"Get out of here," she said, the strange, sad look on her face sticking with him as he jogged away.

* * *

He searched for hours. Hayden wasn't under the bridge where the kid had said. Even the normal bums had scattered, leaving the tagged concrete pylons and asphalt to the rats. Part of him was grateful for it; his brother could have frozen so near the murky river water.

After clearing the area, Colin pulled up his collar, hid the blanket inside his coat, and began his normal drill—a systematic check of all the places he'd found Hayden before. He ducked into shady clubs and talked to bouncers, a few who knew his brother by name. He asked a couple working girls if they'd seen someone tall, like him, but a couple years older and with longer hair. Not a sign.

Dusk had long since faded to black, and with the night came a familiar tingling at the base of Colin's neck. He palmed the blade from his waistband and cursed himself for telling Ty to get her bunk. He could have used an extra pair of eyes, if for no other reason than to watch his back.

Resigned to kicking Hayden's ass all the way to Bakerstown when he found him, Colin returned to the bridge and climbed the concrete steps to the pedestrian path. Half the suspension wires had busted since the famine, but that was back when cars traveled this route. Now it was all foot traffic, and only chem plant employees who came this way. Though he doubted they did so this late at night.

He kept his eyes sharp across the bridge, ignoring a man near the edge who was yelling at no one, and a trio that eyed him suspiciously as they passed around a glowing dope pipe. The air smelled sweeter over here—sweet enough to make the bile rise up Colin's throat. Still, the river rushed twenty feet below him, and for a moment the water, lapping against the man-made levies, brought a small sense of calm. He wondered if the ocean spoke this language, or if it made a different sound when it hit the sand.

In the dark it was impossible to see the hulking stone asylum, or the sign that hung from the edge of the bridge, but he knew it was there. Hampton Industries, Division III. Chemical Plant. Half a dozen biohazard signs had been erected on the path, but most of them were rusted or tagged with graffiti. At thirteen he'd thought this was the creepiest place he'd ever seen. His opinion hadn't changed much in the last four years. He gripped the knife harder, wishing he had some source of light.

If Hayden wasn't dead, Colin was going to kill him.

The gates were close. He could hear the clink of metal on metal as a breeze came through. And then the slide of a chain against it, like fingernails scratching up his spine.

"Hayden," he called. And damn it all if he didn't sound like a Bakerstown pansy. He swore and stood a little taller.

Something stirred near the base of the gate. Everything inside of Colin told him to run. Every muscle flexed against his skin. Who knew the type that came out here this late. The type who killed people and pawned their effects, that's who. The type who'd gone crazy from the food testing plant. Who lured orphans down to the river and maimed the girls that worked the Metaltown corners.

The thing moved again—a shuffle of cloth and a scrape against the dirty pavement. Colin almost guessed it was a rat until a distinctly human moan whispered over the breeze.

"Who's there?" Colin's voice cracked. Now part of him was glad Ty was across the river; she would have ridden him for weeks about it.

Another moan.

"I'm looking for Hayden Walter," Colin said, taking a risk and stepping closer. He was only a few feet away now. The knife was braced before him, but the stranger wouldn't have been able to see it unless he had cat's eyes.

"Hayden," the man repeated. In a voice Colin knew as well as his own.

"Damn you." Colin tucked his knife away and knelt down beside the pile of rags on the cement. A sliver of skylight, just for a moment, revealed the soiled white canvas of his brother's uniform. A deep breath, and Colin's head spun. Hayden smelled worse than he did. Sticky sweet, like the air. Like the plant.

"*Nitro?*" Colin asked in disgust. He swore again. Nitroglycerine. The stuff was worse than dope. Workers in Hayden's team breathed the heavy, colorless oil all day while they packed it into bomb shells. Anyone outside would have gotten a headache from the fumes, even had a heart attack if they'd gotten too much, but those on the inside developed a tolerance. Which turned the hours after work into a slow grind of withdrawal.

Good thing you could huff the fumes to fight off the tics and aches. Took the edge right off those clenching muscles. Of course, after a while, your body couldn't survive without it, but who cared about that?

Obviously not Hayden.

"Get up," said Colin. "We're leaving. Get your sorry ass up."

Hayden groaned when Colin squatted beside him and felt around for his arm. He stood up fast enough to tweak his brother's shoulder, and relished in the little grunt of pain. He wished Hayden was sober enough to fight, because Colin would have worked him up and down the walls.

"Whatcha doin'," Hayden slurred.

"God, you reek."

"Colin?"

"Walk, asshole."

They took a few steps toward the bridge, and Hayden stumbled, taking both of them to the ground. Colin pushed him off, feeling a sudden, uncontrollable swelling inside his chest. He couldn't look at his brother. He shouldn't have come out here. This was unbelievably stupid. If Hayden wanted to die he should just get on with it and leave the rest of the family alone.

The air stunk, and he stunk, and Hayden was high on nitro. *Nitro.* Why was it that Colin felt like an idiot, when Hayden was the one stoned out of his mind?

"Little brother?" Hayden said slowly. In the darkness, Colin could see his brother's glassy eyes blink once. His chest clenched again, harder than before. So hard he could barely breathe.

After a while he stood and helped Hayden back up. "Come on," he said. He moved slowly this time, so that Hayden could take each step.

"Don't tell them," Hayden said.

Colin sighed. "I won't."

TY

Watching Colin walk away, Ty felt the cold shudder through her. A reminder that she was about to face another night alone.

She wasn't scared—she refused to be scared. And she didn't need anybody looking out for her. But having Colin around did make it a little easier to breathe. Sometimes, being around him was the only time she ever really relaxed.

And sometimes, she couldn't relax around him at all.

"Looks like that makes two of us got stiffed." The boy with dark, sweat-crusted hair shoved off the wall to a stand. She'd forgotten about him.

"What?" Ty frowned.

"He stole my shoes, and you got ditched."

"He didn't ditch me. I told him to go." She didn't know why she was defending herself to a boy half her age. "Anyway, you're the one who stole the shoes first."

"Yeah, whatever."

The alley outside the employee entrance had cleared; most of the workers scattered as soon as they realized there wouldn't be a fight. Just a few remained now, people she knew but wasn't friendly with, and this boy.

The gray haze was lowering, turning purple with the sunset. The boy glanced upward warily. He wasn't looking forward to the night any more than she was.

"You hungry?" she asked. As he turned to face her, it hit her how small he was—a bony body draped in tattered, oversized clothes. The chill blisters on his cheeks were easier to see when he wasn't mouthing off, and the curls at the ends of his hair made him seem almost babyish. He stepped gingerly down the alley, holey socks providing limited protection from the cold, dirty ground.

"Why? You sharing?" He tracked the movements of her hands down by her pockets like a stray dog, and she wondered when he'd last eaten. Her stomach was already grumbling; it had been since they'd gotten back to Small Parts.

"Come on." She led him down the alley, watching the way his eyes darted to every shadow, how he hesitated before every corner. "What's your name, kid?"

"Augustine," he said. "But the guys call me Chip."

"Augustine," repeated Ty. "You're from St. Mary's then." She knew the orphanage well enough. She'd been brought there when she was little after a woman had found her wandering the streets. For five years she'd schooled under the iron fists of the nuns, only to be turned out when she was eight with a half-assed prayer and an order to find work before she starved. If she had to guess, it hadn't been long since Chip had been given the same farewell.

"There were three Augustines when I was there," she continued when the boy didn't answer. "The nuns like that name, I guess."

"I said to call me Chip." He glared up at her. The corner of her mouth turned up. "Where we going, anyway?"

"You'll see."

She led him the back way, down a dingy cart path, past a pawn shop to a dimly lit bar. *Jack Sly's*. The windows were covered with plywood and tagged with graffiti, but hard, growling music seeped out from beneath the door.

"In there?" Chip asked.

"Not unless you're paying." She led him around the back side of the building and dragged him down behind a stack of cardboard boxes.

"What are we doing here?" he whined. She shushed him.

They waited with bated breath as the minutes passed. Ty's legs began to cramp, and her stomach became more demanding. Unable to hold still, Chip started tearing the boxes into chunks, and shoving the pieces up his shirt. Kid was smart, Ty thought. Cardboard was a good barrier against the cold.

The back door opened, and a hefty man in a white undershirt, stained around the pits, hoisted a bag of trash toward the green metal trash bin. The garbage was already overflowing as it was, and after attempting a few times to push it down to make more room, he simply tossed the bag on top. Then he wiped his hands, hocked up a mouthful of phlegm on the wall, and disappeared back into the bar.

"Dinnertime," whispered Ty, eyeing the trash bin. It said a lot that Chip's eyes were round and eager, and he didn't get snobby.

They tiptoed across the way, grabbed the bag, and pulled it behind the Dumpster. One rip of the plastic and a blast of fumes hit them—rotten vegetables, probably, but deeper inside was a mix-meat sub, half-eaten, and a few pieces of fry bread.

"You gotta get here before midnight, okay?" Ty told him. "That's when they throw rat poison on it." When the kid didn't look up, she snapped a finger in front of his face. "I showed you my stash, now when you find one, you show me, got it? Those are the rules."

"What rules?"

"Street rules," she said. He nodded.

Fat on their feast, they cut through an abandoned building filled with squatters, and made their way to the Board and Care. Ty found she didn't mind Chip's company. He hadn't said much, and she liked that. Still, she couldn't help wishing Colin was there. She wondered if he'd found Hayden, and if he had, what kind of shape he'd been in.

Stupid junkies. Colin should just cut ties and be done with it. He couldn't see that Hayden wouldn't have gone looking for him. Sometimes you chose your family—like she'd chosen him all those years ago.

The light of day was just barely hanging on by the time they reached the Tribelt Interchange, or Beggar's Square as the people in Metaltown called it. There, three roads converged into a narrow roundabout encircling a small, dry fountain. Any day of the week that fountain was lined with pigeons and bums, and tonight was no exception.

On one corner was St. Mary's orphanage. On another, the Board and Care. And on the third, Charity House.

"Go get some shoes," Ty told Chip, lifting her chin toward the flimsy wooden building. So many additions had been tacked on to Charity House over the years that it hardly looked like a house at all, but more like a big, cancerous mass.

The boy shifted back and forth.

"What's the problem?" asked Ty.

"Nothing. I don't need shoes," he said. She barked out a laugh, but swallowed it down when his obstinate little face scowled up at her.

"Come on," she prompted, leading the way. Across the street, outside St. Mary's, the orphans were cleaning up the broth bowls they'd given out to the first hundred lucky people in line.

"No." Chip dug his heels in. "I know what's in there. I'm not catching it."

Ty tilted her head, then huffed. "You can't catch corn flu from another person."

You can't catch corn flu from another person. Someone had told her that when she was little. She couldn't remember who. Probably someone from St. Mary's.

"Oh, yes you can," he argued.

"Oh, no you can't," she retorted. "I promise. My friend's mom got it from food, and he sees her all the time, and he's not sick."

"Your friend who stole my shoes? That friend?"

"That friend."

"Like I'm gonna believe anything *he* says."

Ty sighed. "Fine. Suit yourself. I'm going to get a bunk, and unless you're planning on sleeping outside, you better get in there, too."

Chip lifted his chin defiantly, glancing back at the Charity House. "Swear on your mother's life I won't catch it."

She barely remembered her mother, but supposed it wouldn't hurt swearing on someone who was already dead. "Sure, Chip. I swear."

Ty pulled Chip through the swinging doors, not giving him a chance to waste time thinking. The sight that greeted them always made her insides turn to jelly, but she wasn't about to show it. Not while the kid was watching.

The low-ceilinged room was packed with cots, drawn so close together the workers had to inch sideways to get between them. The bodies on the beds were in different states of decay—the worst were gray and ashy, so thin they might blow away, with lips tinged red by the blood that spewed from their lungs. Others still had a normal color to them, but were marked by the unmistakable red blotches on their cheeks and skin. And the best off, the newly diagnosed, they worked the place, having come here before they couldn't walk in hopes of gaining a bed when the sickest kicked the bucket.

Thick, hacking coughs ricocheted off the walls. Chip, eyes wide with fear, covered his mouth and nose with his dirty hands. Ty made a note to ask for mittens, too, if they had some to spare.

"They're just people," she told him quietly. "Like you and me."

"Not like me," he said, voice muffled through his sleeve.

A frail man hobbled by, his cheeks cherry red, his eyes bloodshot. A handkerchief, stained with blood, was held tight in his fist. Ty stopped him, careful not to knock him over.

"Can we get in the donation room?" she asked.

He nodded and pointed toward the back. They'd have to walk through the clinic to get there, and he was too busy, and too weak, to lead them.

"How'd they all get so sick if they didn't catch it?" Chip asked. She flinched when he grabbed the tail of her coat, but didn't make him back off.

"It started with the famine," she said, picking her way through the cots. Her stomach began to pitch—the smell made her want to vomit. She focused on the back door. "Too many people, not enough for everyone to eat. People were starving, so they started fighting for food." *And for the land to grow it on, and the sea to fish it from, and the rights to transport and pack it.* The nuns had given this lesson more than once in her youth. "Then the fighting turned into a war, and even more people went hungry. Then these scientists started making synthetic corn, you've heard of that?"

"I'm not stupid, you know," he said from behind her.

She rolled her eyes. "They thought it would end the fighting because people would have enough to eat. They made a ton of it in factories all over the world, but it wasn't tested, and it made people sick."

They reached the donation room, and Ty commanded herself to stay calm as they passed through the threshold. There were stacks of clothes here, piled from floor to ceiling. Shoes, too. Nothing was organized. It was as if the workers had just thrown it all inside and slammed the door.

Which was exactly what they'd done. Soon as someone at Charity House died, they stripped them, recycled their clothes, and burned their bodies in the incinerators out back. She could smell it working even here. The charred, sour smoke dried out her nostrils.

"I never knew all this was here." Chip dove into a pile as if he were being timed. Ty didn't tell him where the clothes had come from.

Chip sat on the floor, trying on mismatched shoes. She sorted them for him, hoping he would hurry up. He may have been more comfortable, but she was about ready to pop. They needed to get back outside fast.

"So why do they keep making the poison corn?" he asked.

She cleared her throat. "They don't. But too many people had already eaten it, and it was already put in all sorts of food. That's why you've still got to be careful." She threw a pair of gloves down for him to try. "And that's why the Federations are all still fighting. Because testing food is so expensive, half the world's starving to death."

"Why doesn't somebody just make some medicine?" He laced up a pair of scuffed boots, prodding the toe with his thumb. The look on his face said they were a good enough fit.

"You don't think they're trying?" The Medical Division tested their cures on the inmates at the local jail. Sometimes the inmates were released when they were no longer considered a danger to society. Most of them were so sick they didn't last long.

A worker opened the door and tossed another armful in. Before the door closed, they caught sight of an emaciated, naked male corpse being pushed outside on a gurney.

Chip jolted up, face pale. "Can we go?"

"Yeah," Ty said.

* * *

Later, Ty lay in the bunk she'd chosen, the one closest to the door and flush against the wall. She kept her knives out at night, one in her hand, the other close to her chest, attuned to the snores and heavy breathing of the fifty others that occupied this wing. Chip was upstairs with the juniors, probably curled up around his shoes snoring like a baby. He was a brat, but he was tough, and she liked that about him. She hadn't been all that different at his age.

Alone, her mind drifted to Colin, and whether or not he'd found his brother. She hoped so, more for Colin's sake than Hayden's. He was a worrier, always trying to keep track of too many moving parts. His family. Work. Cherish. She thought of the look on his face when they'd left Bakerstown and blew out a heavy breath. There was nothing to be done about that, but maybe she could talk to Hayden. Convince him to clean up his act. Colin had called him out more than once, but if Hayden heard it from someone else he might listen. Normally she'd say it wasn't her business, but it was different with Colin. The things that hurt him, they hurt her, too.

She made up her mind to do it the next time she saw him, and immediately felt something loosen in her chest. Imagining Colin's grin, she smiled, and then quickly wiped the look off her face, feeling like an idiot.

* * *

A heavy hand fumbled over her chest and she bit back a scream. Like a shot she was up, scanning the darkness to see who'd had the stones to touch her. One of her knives was knocked to the floor with a clatter. When she dove for it, something hit her hard against the side of the head. Bright white stars burst in the darkness. A slimy hand clutched around her mouth. She bit down hard, drawing a muffled scream from her attacker.

She was thrown down on the thin mattress and it squeaked and groaned beneath her weight. Her mind was reeling. *Fight, fight, fight.* She kicked, opening her mouth to bite again, but a putrid sock gagged her as it was shoved inside. Her arms were pinned overhead, locked in place by a strong grasp.

She began to panic. Not this time. Not again.

Hands on her shins, her thighs. More than one pair. Two. Three. Pulling at her waistband, trying to get past her belt. She squeezed her knees together as the tears burned her eyes.

Fight.

People were getting up—she could hear them shifting on their nearby cots. But no one came to help. Two bodies laid across her to pin her down.

"Hold her," one spat. She could smell the corn whiskey on his breath. Fury broke loose inside of her, burning down her limbs. She bucked back, knocking one of them against the wall. Again she was hit. Her eyes felt like they would pop out of her skull. Her mouth opened wide in a silent scream. But she didn't stop. She *would not stop.*

The clothes she wore twisted around her, but this was why she wore so much. They might get through one layer, but then they'd find a second, and a third. Finally, somehow, she twisted, and with a thud, landed on her back on the floor.

She spat out the gag, and a second later was out the door, running through the entryway, past the snoring patrons in the other rooms. Running. Running, and no one was ever going to catch her.

LENA

Lena sat at the table in her bedroom, surrounded by neat stacks of paper, staring at her wall monitor with tired, blinking eyes.

"Miss Hampton, it's time for bed." Darcy was perched beside her, on a stool Lena often used during her singing lessons. The fatigue was heavy in her tone.

How late was it? Midnight? No, Lena realized, several hours past.

"I had no idea how ill prepared I would be," Lena said, straightening her back. She was still wearing the slim-cut evening gown that she'd performed in, but it was now wrinkled and losing its shape. Her satin-gloved fingertips pressed against her temples.

"You'll do fine," assured Darcy. "No one will expect you to know any of this." She motioned to the electronic files on the screen displaying countless facts and figures that defined the rise of Hampton Industries, and the history of Lena's family.

"*I* expect myself to know it," said Lena. "And if people are going to do business with me, I'll expect them to know that I know it."

Darcy turned to face the dark window, her expression hidden by shadows. "Very well, then. What exactly have you learned?"

Lena looked at her a moment, the sudden wave of relief washing away some of the tension between her shoulder blades. Sometimes she forgot she wasn't alone in this massive house, that Darcy was here beside her.

"The company was started by my great-grandfather before the war," Lena began. "It was just a small arms shop then, with a firing range attached to the back of the building." Shooting had once been a recreational activity, an activity for stress relief, or hunting practice, as the game still ran thick in the mountains surrounding the Tri-City area. But the droughts changed everything. Season after season passed with little or no rain, and the farmland in the center of the country dried up, forcing a mass migration into the already packed cities.

"The famine brought a surge of business as people began to quarrel," Lena continued. "Hampton Ammunition, as it was then called, was able to expand. Neighbors wanted guns for protection from each other, and increased violence led to increased sales. The statistics from that time show that one out of every three people in the Tri-City had a weapon. Orders were being shipped from the northern border to the small farming communities south of the Yalan Mountains."

"South?" said Darcy, a wry smile quirking her mouth. "But everything south of the Yalans belongs to the Eastern Federation."

Lena changed wall screens to a map of the Silah Peninsula, finger trailing down the eastern coast to a series of bays on the southern tip. Darcy was testing her, but she was glad for it. "It was before the Federations were formed," she told her tutor.

From their history lessons, she knew that the fishing industry had survived only a little while after the start of the famine. Overfishing and pollution from the congested coastal cities had turned people back inland to farm the last viable crop: corn. Scientists developed chemicals to increase the harvests and prolong the growing seasons, not knowing that they were actually creating the first strains of the deadly corn flu, a disease that would kill hundreds of thousands. People were starving, too desperate to think of the consequences. They fought over control of the fields and how to distribute the rations, forming alliances. Those in the East used their Hampton Industries weapons to defend the southern crops, defeating the Northern troops that retreated behind the protection of the Yalan Mountains. There, the Northern Federation became self-sufficient, withdrawing trade agreements with the East, who ended up with nothing but dry fishing ports and deadly fields of corn.

Her grandfather, Kolten Hampton, had taken over the company as soon as he turned eighteen, only a year older than she was now. He'd died when she was three—a hunting accident in the Yalans—and her memories were only what her father had told her of him, mostly that he was stern and hard-working. She'd found a picture of Kolten on the stone steps in front of Division I, surrounded by smiling workers and cutting a fat red ribbon with a comically large pair of scissors. Though he looked like he could have been Otto's twin, Kolten's drive was far greater.

"My grandfather made the company what it is today," Lena said. "He branched out from the small munitions orders and purchased similar businesses, putting them all under the Hampton name." After the Northern Federation was established, the companies in other nearby cities were closed, and moved to a more manageable, central location in the capital, later known as the factory district. "The various focuses were organized into divisions—everything from handheld weaponry to military-grade arsenals, including explosives—and now, thanks to my father, Hampton Industries is the exclusive provider for the Northern Federation's military."

And Otto was next in line to take control.

She slumped in her chair, as much as the dress would allow. The men in her family had worked too hard to have a spoiled playboy lose it all.

"That's very good." Darcy rose to stretch her back. When she leaned closer to the desk, her gaze landed on a small scrap of paper bearing an address. She squinted at it, but before she could ask, Lena tucked it beneath the stack of papers. Perhaps too tired to care, her tutor turned away and walked the length of the room.

It *was* a good start, but there was still so much Lena didn't understand. She looked back down at the statements, brows drawing together.

"I didn't even know that we owned a medical division," she said. "I mean, *the* Medical Division. It oversees the hospital, the medical school in the River District, the clinics in practically every town, even *research facilities*. Basically everything that involves a pill or a bandage in this entire Federation belongs to Hampton Industries, and I can't even find any contract outlining the transfer of ownership."

"Oh?" asked Darcy.

"The branch's income is noted on every quarterly report for the last decade. It constitutes *half* of our earnings."

"Once upon a time it was a lot more than half," Darcy said.

Lena glanced up, surprised that Darcy knew this. "It was?"

"Once upon a time saving lives was more important than ending them." Her tutor rubbed her eyes and shook her head. "I mean, there wasn't so much need for the weapons divisions because we weren't at war. I'm sure the contract is in there somewhere," she finished quickly.

Lena returned to the screen, sliding through the documents with the sweep of her finger. Darcy was probably right; healthcare would take priority in times of peace. But this was wartime, and it was still earning a substantial chunk.

"I bet Otto lost the documents," she muttered. "I'm sure the previous owners will be ecstatic to hear that we've been profiting off a company we don't even hold the title to."

"The owners died," said Darcy, and Lena again met her gaze with curiosity. Her tutor sighed, looking away. "You were talking about the Medical Division, correct?"

Lena nodded.

"Yes, I believe the family that owned it all died of the corn flu. Ironic, isn't it? The people dedicated to finding the cure succumb to the illness." She blinked away a rare jaded expression. "Their heir disappeared. It was all the gossip at the time."

"What if this heir still lives?" Lena asked, thinking of the earnings on the quarterly income statements she'd seen. How much would Hampton Industries owe them? The losses would be devastating.

"If such a person existed, they would have claimed their family's fortune by now, don't you think?"

Yes, Lena supposed so.

"Besides, your father had people looking into it, and when they didn't find a lead, the company was absorbed. I believe the people across the river call it the *food testing* division now. Something like that." Darcy stood, putting the stool back against the wall. "Better to leave the past in the past. You have more pressing things with which to concern yourself. Now, if you're not going to go to bed, Miss Hampton, I'll have to say goodnight."

"That's fine, Darcy," said Lena absently. Her thoughts were still on the hit the company would take if they ever lost the Medical Division—the hit the entire Federation would take. Beyond the economic implications, it absorbed a huge amount of responsibility. Research facilities within that division had created the quality standards that deemed foods safe, hazardous, or consumed at one's own risk. They were researching a cure to the most devastating epidemic the world had ever known: the corn flu.

It was not the sort of business one wanted to misplace the title paperwork to.

Her concentration was broken by footsteps on the stairs, and her father's voice from the landing below. "Is this humorous to you? You don't cancel important business meetings just so you can go gallivanting with pretty young women."

The footsteps stopped. Both Darcy and Lena froze, listening as her brother answered.

"She was *very* pretty."

He spoke too slowly. Drunk, Lena realized. Drunk and in trouble. It was not the first time, nor would it be the last.

The click of hard-soled shoes on wooden floors, and then a slam that made both Lena and her tutor jump. Near the door, her framed pictures rattled, and in his cage, her bird fluttered his yellow wings and jumped from one dowel to the next.

The next words were low, and too muffled to make out. A few moments later, she heard the quiet click of Otto's bedroom door, and her father's steps descending down the stairs.

"Well," said Darcy. "I suppose it's time for me to go to bed."

Lena nodded. Whatever her father had done, her brother deserved, but that didn't stop her stomach from twisting.

Locking the door behind Darcy, she turned off the wall screen and walked to her dresser. There, she removed her satin gloves and placed them neatly beside her hairbrush. With effort, she unzipped her dress, and slowly peeled out of it, wincing at the purple welt Otto had left on the right side of her rib cage. She touched it gingerly, biting down against the responding ache, and looking again to the door where a nearby picture frame still hung crooked from her father and brother's argument on the stairs. The house was quiet now; Otto was probably already passed out.

The dress went in the hamper, and she hesitated, as she always did, before opening the tall mahogany bureau. She had to check to make sure the lock was still broken, that the metal bar would not emerge with the twist of a key. Only when she was satisfied at its defectiveness—the only imperfection she allowed in her life—did she open the double doors.

"Now, Mr. Bird, what shall I wear tomorrow, hm?"

* * *

An hour after dawn, Lena paced in the foyer, a storm cloud brewing over her head. She'd learned from the house staff that Otto had left only minutes earlier to breakfast with a Ms. Dwyer, the young daughter of one of the Hamptons' investors. It was hardly a shock—

expecting Otto to follow through on anything was like expecting a rabid dog not to bite—but it still surprised her after their father had chastised him for gallivanting only last night.

It was possible she'd misunderstood their fight, that the bang against the wall hadn't been a manifestation of Josef's anger. For hours she'd lain in her bed, staring at the ceiling, listening for any sign that Otto might be creeping across the hall to make her suffer for his own transgressions—he only ever pinched her or said nasty things when her father had first done something of the like to him. But the house had remained still. She hadn't even heard him sneak out.

Unwilling to let him ruin her plans, she asked Aja, their driver, to transport her to Otto's division in Metaltown so that she could await his arrival.

With Aja in the driver's seat, Lena slid across the padded bench in the back of the electric carriage. She disliked car travel—the passenger compartment was much too small and the bumps gave her motion sickness, but the factory was several miles upriver, and it was too cold to have Aja pull her in a handcart.

"Are you ready, Miss Hampton?" came his low, polite voice from the front. He was a big man, with skin the color of red mud and hair as black and thick as hers. He barely fit in his singular driver's seat, and was forced to drive with the window open to have someplace to stash his elbow. For this, he wore a long, heavy trench coat, and a thick wool scarf.

"Yes, Aja, thank you," Lena answered. The engine wound to life, and they pulled out of her family's circular cobblestone driveway. Away from the main house with its three sprawling stories and landscaped grounds. Past the coach house, where the help lived, and the driving range where her father took his associates to golf.

By the time they hit the main street, Lena's heels were tapping hard enough to dent the floorboards.

She didn't know why she was nervous. She was a Hampton, and no one crossed a Hampton. But her father had taught her at a young age that a hungry dog will bite the hand that feeds him, and these people, though grateful for their employ, were unpredictable. Lena didn't do unpredictable well.

What she did do well was organize, and that was what she intended to do, starting today. First with Otto's division, to show her father her capabilities, and then with the rest of Hampton Industries. She'd be the first woman to run the company. A legacy, like the line of men before her.

She'd dressed professionally, in fitted black pants that disappeared into knee-high boots, and a cream-colored button-up blouse topped by a short, rib-hugging coat the color of cherries. Her black hair was tucked in a bun at the nape of her neck, and she'd worn leather gloves, to show the workers that she wasn't afraid to get her hands dirty.

In her breast pocket was a scrap of paper, and on it, an address she'd looked up from the payroll department. It was from an old file—a domestic worker who had taken care of her as a child. Lena hadn't seen the woman since she'd left the Hamptons all those years ago, but she thought of her often. For more than a year, she'd held on to this address, convincing herself that it was probably no longer good. But now that she was heading across the beltway, there was no reason not to check it out. Once the work was done, anyway.

She was just going to shadow her brother for a little while. Nothing was going to go wrong. But in case something did, she'd tucked a defuser—an electroshock weapon meant to incapacitate an attacker without fatal damage—into the back of her waistband. She'd been trained to use one when she was five, and felt more than competent to defend herself should the need arise.

They passed through Bakerstown, where most of the Hamptons' extra staff who didn't stay on the grounds lived. It was a rundown place, but there were pockets of good shopping, including the markets where the cookstaff bought their groceries. Only a few electric cars, like hers, were on the street. Mostly people traveled by bike cart, or handcart, or walked among the homeless.

She shivered at the thought, glad for the firm feel of her defuser against her lower back.

A few miles farther and the way cleared of all traffic, car and pedestrian alike. The sky, which had been glowing with a hint of morning light, grew heavy with a sweet, suffocating kind of fog as they continued on a desolate beltway. Below were the train yards, and the chug and high-pitched whine of steel penetrated the car's thin windows. They'd been driving less than an hour, but she had the distinct impression they'd traveled a world away.

She saw the gray buildings first. She'd heard talk of how drab this area—Metaltown—could be, but her father didn't think it was fitting for a lady, so she'd yet to see it with her own eyes. As they drew closer to the factories, her excitement began to crystallize into a cold, hard ball in the bottom of her stomach. People—the kind she didn't want to find herself alone with—were all around, a sea of dirty clothes and dirty faces. They were all staring at the car like a cat tracks a mouse. She placed a hand on her weapon unconsciously, and leaned forward.

"Otto said he would meet us here?"

"Yes, Miss Hampton. Within the hour."

Which meant at least two, in Otto-speak.

She removed the address from her pocket and passed it up between the seats.

"Aja, can you bring me here? I'd like to check on someone. It will only take a few minutes."

"Miss Hampton." Aja's tone was wary. "Your father wouldn't be pleased with any unexpected stops. This isn't the kind of area where . . ."

"It's fine, Aja. I'll have you with me."

He hesitated. "Very well, Miss Hampton."

They turned down a side street and passed by what looked to be a flea market. Most of the carts and tents were still covered for the night, but there were a few people up and about, picking through the leftovers.

Aja slowed the car, and looked out the opposite window.

"We should be close, Miss Hampton. I believe the address you're looking for is just down that way. Who are we visiting?"

"Just an old friend . . ."

A woman with a red shawl around her shoulders caught Lena's eye from across the street. Her long, dark hair was braided down her back, and she'd tucked her pants into worn boots that blossomed around her ankles. Even though her clothes were baggy, Lena could tell that she was slim.

Familiarity had her hands pressing against the window, had her straining her eyes for a better look. As if the woman could sense she was being watched, she turned to the side, giving Lena a glimpse of her profile.

Everything within her snapped into place. Every muscle, every nerve, every piece of her once-broken heart. Joy lifted her mouth to a grin.

She was here.

"Stop!" Lena screeched. Aja slammed on the brakes, but he was too late, the woman had already left the flea market and disappeared around the corner.

Lena jerked the handle of the door open and spilled out onto the street.

"Miss Hampton!" she heard Aja yell, but the choice was upon her. Follow the woman, or wait for protection. Her feet made up her mind; she was already jogging toward the corner.

"Aja, come *on*. Hurry up!" she called over her shoulder.

There were a few women—prostitutes—sitting on crates against the stone wall, and Lena felt their confused stares pull toward her. More people were emerging from the nearby streets, dressed in their work clothes, moving with a sense of purpose.

"Look at Miss High Class," one of the girls yelled.

Lena's throat grew tight as her happiness plummeted. Her eyes strained in all directions, but the place was becoming more and more crowded. Where was Aja? There was plenty of room to park the car; he should have reached her by now. Instead, she found herself alone in a sea of sneering faces, all staring at her clothes. She looked at the doors of the buildings around her, but none of them were marked.

"Sorry," she said as someone bumped into her. "Oh, I'm sorry, I didn't see you," she said to a tall man, but he had already passed and did not look back.

She scanned the area, searching desperately for that familiar face. For that red shawl. The force of her impulsivity caught up to her, slamming around her rib cage. She'd never done anything so uncalculated and reckless.

"What do we have here?" a man asked, fixing his hat as he moved toward her. She felt for the defuser in her waistband, and gripping the handle, turned her head down and skirted to the side. Again, she wished for Aja to appear. She ducked into a narrow alley, glancing back out onto the street with a shudder of panic. He should have caught up with her by now.

She'd made a mistake. The woman wasn't here. The address was wrong—there weren't even numbered apartments in this area, and she wasn't about to go knocking door-to-door like a crazy person. Defeat sagged her shoulders. Her old nanny could have gone anywhere in the Northern Federation after her father had laid her off. She had no reason to come to this place.

Feeling intolerably stupid, Lena forced one solid breath and peeked out into the street at the heavy flow of people. Part of her considered stepping into the rush, but it was hard to see exactly where she'd left the car or to know where she should go to find Aja. If she was being honest, the crowd frightened her a little, and staying put seemed like the best course of action.

"Damn it all to hell," she said to herself. And then in a burst, recited every curse she'd ever heard Otto say.

"I always thought pretty girls weren't allowed to say dirty words."

She spun around to find a boy leaning against the alley wall with his arms crossed. He was dressed warmly, like the others she'd seen, in an oversized wool coat and heavy slacks. A gray knit cap was pulled back, revealing his eyes—piercing blue, like the river water just after it had been dyed. He had stubble on his jaw and chin, and a cockeyed smile that made all sorts of warning bells sound the alarm in her brain.

He must have come out of one of the dented metal doors that lined these rain-stained walls, or climbed down the fire escape from a window above them when she wasn't looking. Surprised, her mouth gaped, but she shut it quickly.

"Excuse me?" she asked.

"You don't have to excuse yourself," he said. "I've heard a lot worse."

"I . . . no," Lena said, shocked by his forwardness. "I'm sorry. I'll say what I like."

"So why are you apologizing?" He moved toward her with long, confident strides, slowing when she took several quick steps back and nearly tripped over a broken chair someone had discarded.

"Stop right there. Please," she added, pulse flying. If she backed up any more, he'd push her right into the crowd, and she'd be swallowed up.

He stopped, grinned. "Since you asked so nicely."

Irritation heated her blood. She was not about to be undermined by a cocky boy from the factory district. She set her feet, set her jaw, and stood up as tall as she could. Even in her boots she didn't quite reach his shoulders. "If you're trying to intimidate me, it won't work." She tugged at her gloves. "What's your name, anyway?"

His head tilted to the side, and as he gazed slowly down her body, a flush rose in her cheeks. Whoever had taught this boy manners had failed. Miserably.

"Tell me your name, and I'll tell you mine," he said.

She gawked, but quickly pulled herself together. A Hampton remained composed, even under the most trying of circumstances.

"Lena," she said, cursing the waver in her voice. "It's Lena."

He held out his hand, calloused fingertips extending through the holes in his woven gloves. "I'm Colin."

10

COLIN

She was pretty enough, he'd give her that much. Pretty, and definitely in the wrong place.

Her smooth, honey-colored skin and soft, clean hair stuck out just as much as those high-society clothes. Girls in Metaltown dressed for the cold outside and the heat inside the factories—layered up so bulky you could hardly tell their shape. Their faces were pale from long hours of work, and they certainly didn't wear makeup. Not unless they were working a corner. She'd been the last thing he'd expected to find when he'd come up from the basement apartment, and he'd been caught so off guard that he'd glanced back inside just to make sure he'd dumped Hayden in the right place.

Once he'd figured out he wasn't crazy, he settled in for the show, entertained by her nervous pacing and the curvy shape of her thighs. She was little, but full in all the right places, and something about the way she spoke made him think of the way kids balance on a curb, teetering faster and faster right until the moment they fall off.

"So," he said, "how's your stay so far in Metaltown? Has the staff been helpful?" Obviously she was lost, but for some reason he didn't want to point that out. She was probably from over the beltway.

Bakerstown, maybe, though if that were true, he had no idea what she was doing here.

One gloved hand rose to smooth her perfect hair. "I'm fairly certain no one would come here for vacation."

He smiled at her condescending tone. "I don't know. Metaltown is full of secret hot spots, you know. If you wanted a tour—"

"I'm here for work." Her eyes darted to the flow of people outside the alley, then quickly back to him.

The muscles in his chest clenched, just for a moment. A Bakerstown kid, clearly out of her element, looking for a job. Something about that story rang familiar.

"What a coincidence, so am I." Colin took another step forward.

She backed into the wall, her face drawn with worry. "You should know I have a weapon."

"Three guesses where you stashed it."

Her cheeks turned bright red, the same color as her snug little jacket. One hand shot behind her back.

"Easy," he said, realizing he'd scared her. "I surrender." He raised his hands over his head to prove it.

She was shivering, trying to hide her chattering teeth, but the breath was clouding in front of her face. Not the smartest move, dressing so thin, but he'd made mistakes when he'd come here too. If not for Ty setting him straight, he wouldn't have lasted a week.

He wondered if she had anyone setting her straight. Not from the sounds of it. Definitely not from the looks of it.

"Here." He took off his scarf and offered it to her, more than a little regretful when the cold air gripped his throat.

"Oh. I couldn't."

"Don't want to freeze to death. Besides, you can give it back next time you see me."

She didn't laugh. That was promising.

Her prissy little nose crinkled up, but she took it, and folded it around her neck. He liked the way it clashed with her outfit. Soon enough, Metaltown would work its way into her clothes, and her pretty skin, and that scarf would blend right in.

It was kind of a shame, when he thought about it.

"I'm a little lost," she admitted after a moment.

"You don't say."

Her eyes narrowed, and now she took a step toward him. "You don't need to make fun of me," she said. "I haven't done anything to deserve it. I've got things to do, and I don't have time to play games."

"Is that what we're doing?" he asked, amused at her scolding. "Playing a game?"

Her lips parted slightly, and his gaze lowered there and stuck. Then he looked up, hoping she hadn't noticed, and jammed his hands into his pockets.

"Miss Hampton!"

A big man in a suit barreled into the alley, a line of sweat dripping from his black hair down his jaw. As his gaze moved from Lena to Colin, he bared his teeth.

"Finally," Lena muttered.

Colin staggered back quickly.

"*Hampton?*" he managed.

"Miss Hampton, the car is waiting across the street."

Lena nodded, eyes flicking between the two of them.

"Hampton?" Colin said again. Then he began to laugh. "You've got to be kidding me."

So much for both of them having the same sad Bakerstown story.

"Is this boy harassing you?" The man glared at Colin.

"I suppose that depends on your definition of harassment," said Lena, clearly more comfortable in the other man's presence. Colin choked a little, and she waved a hand. "We barely spoke, Aja."

Barely spoke? It became immediately clear that she didn't want to be seen associating with him, and he nearly laughed at the irony of it.

She looked at him a second longer, as though expecting him to say something more, but what was he going to say to a Hampton? What was a Hampton even doing out here? They had middlemen like Minnick to run their factories. There was no reason for them to cross the beltway.

"Well . . . good-bye," she finally said, shoving her hand out so quickly he flinched. Tentatively, he shook it. Again. And when he squeezed her fingers, just a little, she jerked away.

"Good-bye," she said again.

"Bye." He tipped his head forward, and she huffed, like he'd done it to annoy her.

With her servant clearing the way, she marched back into the crowded street, leaving Colin, bewildered, in the alley.

*　*　*

On his way to work, Colin stopped at the smoke shack outside the employee entrance of the Stamping Mill. The night crew was just about to get off, and there was still a half-hour before he had to report for his shift at Small Parts. As he waited outside the door, the chill hit him. The girl had taken his scarf, he realized, a little annoyed now that he knew she probably had thirty of them at home. He could still see how she'd turned up her nose at the offer.

He could still see all of her, perfectly.

I suppose that depends on your definition of harassment, she'd said. Cold. Why he'd expected different was beyond him.

But something about her *was* different. The way she'd acknowledged him at all, instead of blowing him off. The way she'd shaken his hand when they said good-bye. He didn't know how she was related to the big boss, but it didn't matter. She wasn't just flush, she was powerful, and that meant hands off. Not that he was ever going to see her, anyway.

The door opened, and a rush of people exited the building. A few he knew greeted him with tired smiles and slaps on the back.

"Ida, your boy's here," a man named Fritz called, one hand clasped on Colin's shoulder. Sweat had etched lines through the powder smears on his forehead and cheeks. "One more day down, eh, Colin?"

"Till what?" Colin asked.

"Till I die," Fritz answered with a wink. "And I can get out of this rat hole."

"Fritz, stop pestering my baby."

Colin's ma was tall for a woman, built thick and strong. Her face was much like his, with a broad jaw and tired, blue eyes. The sleeves of her stained shirt were rolled up to her elbows. Colin leaned in automatically for her to plant a kiss on his cheek.

"You look tired. Everything all right at home?" She cracked her neck, rolled her shoulders.

"Yeah," he said. "Everything's fine. She slept through the night." He didn't really know if that was true, of course—he'd only been home for a few minutes after he'd dumped Hayden at their friend Shima's to sober up. But when he'd come in, he'd heard Cherish's heavy breathing from the bedroom, and she hadn't roused when he'd rinsed her blood-soaked rags.

"Did Hayden check in?" With a heavy sigh, she pulled a hand-rolled cigarette from her pocket and stuck it between her teeth. It took her four strikes to light the match. He hated that his brother made her worry.

"He did," Colin said. "He left early for work, though."

"He look okay?"

"Looked fine to me." Which he had. When he wasn't doubled up with the fever chills on Shima's floor.

Ida took a handkerchief out of her pocket. A few crumbled crackers were inside, and she handed them over to Colin.

"I'm okay." He'd eaten at Shima's, and besides, he knew this was all his ma would have until the end of her shift.

"All right." Ida pulled his collar tighter around his neck, her lips thinning to hold the cigarette in place. "Anything big I should know about?"

I talked to a Hampton this morning. "Nope," said Colin.

"Anything new at the factory?"

Minnick made me scrub the johns because I ran an errand for Jed. "Where's your coat?"

"Inside."

"Another full?"

She nodded. Colin felt bad for her; she'd been working more double shifts over the past few months. She paid her dues to the Brotherhood like everyone else, but her salary was barely enough to keep the lights on, and the money Jed Schultz sent was never enough.

If Hayden could get himself together, they'd do better. If Hayden could get himself clean, he could be the one helping out, and Colin, like Fritz, could get out of this rat hole.

Bastard was set on ruining everything.

Colin chewed a sharp edge off his pinky nail.

A buzzer went off inside the factory. Ida crushed the end of her cigarette against the wall, and tucked it back in her pocket. Then she hugged him, and Colin could feel how skinny she was getting.

Damn Hayden, and damn his stupid nitro.

"Love you," he said.

"I love you, Colin. Be good today. Do the right thing."

"Don't I always?" He smirked.

"Yes," she answered, her brows still furrowed. "You always do."

* * *

Ty was already inside by the time he reached Small Parts. He recognized her things in the locker, and placed his beside them. Minnick didn't even glance up as Colin passed through the metal detector; either he was in need of a fix or they had an inspection today. He was pastier than normal, and his collar was already soaked with a ring of sweat.

The warehouse was warm, but the machinery had just started up and it would only be a matter of time before the room was blazing. The place was already alive with the crank and hum of grinding metal. He wasn't surprised by Matchstick's black eye, or by Martin's self-satisfied smirk. Zeke only yawned when Colin passed.

He ducked under the moving belt, and made his way toward the center of the floor where he and Ty were stationed. She was in the usual place wearing her usual padding. How she could stand the heat, he'd never know. Her eyes were down, her bare fingers twisting together two narrow metal rods.

"You're late," she said irritably. "I've already done a dozen pieces so far. You'd better hurry and catch up."

Beside her on the hip-high table were the fuses that Colin would connect to the waterproof copper wiring and transport down the line. Another few stops and that detonator would be packed into a plastic sheath, and screwed onto the nose of a bomb. By the time they reached the hot room—a curtained area in the back—the workers would pack them with white phosphorus and nitroglycerine, sent over from the chem plant. Those jobs were the worst: first the burns on the hands, then the red eyes, then the sores around the nose and inside the mouth. Most workers there lasted six months before they started getting really sick. Once they started missing work, they got sacked.

They didn't have protective gear like they did across the bridge at the chem plant. There was no reason to; they were just rats, like Minnick always said.

Colin made certain he was so good at building detonators that Minnick would never have reason to transfer him down the line.

"How'd you get in here so early?" he asked Ty.

"Minnick crashed in his office last night." She wiped a line of sweat off her cheek with the back of her hand, and it came back streaked with blood.

Colin's muscles went tight. He removed the handkerchief from his pocket, and walked to the water barrel to dampen it. When he came back, he passed it over to her without a word. She hesitated a moment before pressing the rag into the side of her head. When she looked up, Colin could see that her lip was split open again, and that half of her short, messy hair was matted with dry blood.

He took his place beside her and picked up one of the pieces, exhaling slowly as he fitted it to the wire. His palms were already beginning to sweat, though, so he put it down and dipped his hands in one of the powder bowls near their station. When they were dry, he grabbed some needle-nose pliers and went to work.

"Where we headed tonight?" he asked. She knew what he meant.

"I took care of it," she said. "You find your brother?"

"Where," he said carefully. "The Board and Care?"

"I said I took care of it."

Colin pierced his thumb with the sharp copper wire and swore. He didn't look at her. "You hurt, Ty?"

"I'm fine, all right? Just drop it."

He shook his head. He knew Ty, and he knew when she'd taken care of business. She came back haughty and good-tempered, and talked more than usual. But when she was like this, when she wouldn't tell him what had happened, he knew she'd lost.

If he hadn't been with Hayden, he could have had her back.

"I found him," said Colin. "He's burning it off at Shima's."

Shima made her rent money watching people's kids while they worked. He'd met her just after he'd moved here—she'd made Ty and him rice after she'd found them begging in Market Alley. She'd been there for him ever since, cleaning him up after a fight, nursing Hayden through a bender. She was a lockbox of secrets, and he thought she was as good as gold.

Ty nodded, glad for the change of subject.

They worked in silence as the time passed, finding a rhythm twisting wires, inspecting pieces, throwing defective parts into the incinerator carts. They stretched their necks and backs, and dried their hands with white powder, but did not sit down. Minnick would have had their asses if they had.

The hours were marked by Maggie, the water girl, coming through with her jar and cup. She liked to linger. Normally Colin didn't mind, but today he found himself wishing she would just move on.

"Don't you have a job to do?" Ty finally barked. Maggie glared at her, and continued down the line.

"On the floor!" Martin yelled from the battery section.

"On the floor!" Colin automatically passed on to Plastics. The workers focused on their jobs, heads down, backs straight. The foreman was coming through.

Minnick appeared at the top of the stairs, flanked by two individuals: a slender man in a dark suit that Colin recognized immediately as the boss of Small Parts, and . . . Lena.

Colin dropped the part on the table, and the coil snapped off the metal bar.

"What the hell are you doing?" Ty said between her teeth. "Quick! Throw it in the pile before you have to count it as an error."

He spun around and tossed it into the defectives cart just as Minnick walked through.

"And as you can see, we do the detonator piecework here," the foreman was saying, an unnatural, almost scary smile plastered on his face.

Lena was still back with Martin, watching how he put together the batteries. Colin thought the poor guy was probably pissing himself being that close to a girl like her.

Ty followed his gaze and grumbled, "If I was flush, I'd buy some damn clothes that fit."

Colin thought Lena's clothes fit her just fine.

"Lena, for God's sake, will you please focus?" Otto Hampton said. "I don't want to be here all day." Colin's shoulders tightened involuntarily.

Lena's head cranked back, a tight look in her eyes that her brother disregarded with a wave of his hand.

"Good work," she said to Martin.

She wasn't wearing Colin's scarf anymore, and he was more disappointed at that than he would have guessed. She'd probably burned it the second she'd left the alley. He kept watching her, ignoring Ty's hiss that he keep his eyes on his work. He willed her to see him, to recognize him, to say anything.

It was killing him that she didn't see him.

"What's down that way?" she asked, pointing to where the chemicals were packed into the metal canisters.

"Oh, nothing you need to be concerned with," said Minnick quickly. "Just more wires and coils."

The foreman didn't want her to see the kids with the red eyes. With the burns on their fingers. Didn't want her to smell their puke in the trash can. Colin wondered what she would think when she saw that—if it would bother her, if she'd care, or if she'd just ignore it like her brother.

Then her gaze turned and caught his. Her eyes went wide with surprise. She gasped. He smiled.

And she lowered her eyes and walked by.

"What are you doing?" Ty snapped. "You want to get us fired? That was the boss and his sister, you idiot!"

Colin scowled. She'd acted like they hadn't spoken. She hadn't even acknowledged that he existed. He didn't know what he'd expected. She was a Hampton; so high above him she probably had to squint to see him at all. The anger sparked inside of him again. This whole town was pathetic. Ty getting jumped, his ma working doubles, his brother on nitro. He needed to find a way to make some green, and then he'd be gone, on a fishing boat, netting tuna and stuffing his face with food. Never before had he wanted so much to get out of Metaltown.

He was still pissed when he saw Lena and her brother climb the stairs and disappear out the main doors. Seething by the time the runner came in carrying a message from one of the other factories and knocked on Minnick's door. But when Minnick came out, his face back to its normal ugly expression, Colin's anger turned to curiosity.

"On the floor!" he called, warning the others.

Minnick stomped down the steps and made his way to the sorting area, where the youngest kids worked. He grabbed one off his stool—the mouthy boy who had lifted Hayden's shoes—and dragged him toward the stairs.

And then Ty, who would have cut off her own foot to keep this job, left her post and began to follow them.

11

TY

"Whoa, Ty," she heard Colin call behind her. "*Ty!*"

He grabbed for her arm, but she was already jogging toward the stairs, following Minnick and the boy up to his office.

"Let go!" Chip was yelling, wriggling in the foreman's grasp. "I got work to do, okay?"

Minnick boxed him hard against the ear, bringing a bright angry mark to the side of his face. "Stamping Mill needs someone to go over and help with something," he said. "You do whatever they need, then get your scrawny ass back here and finish up."

"I won't finish if you make me go," he threatened.

"Then we'll stay as late as we need to until you do." Minnick's mouth twitched, and he licked his peeling lips.

Ty's stomach twisted. She didn't know what she was doing. Her head was pounding—had been since last night. Combined with the heat and the noise it felt like her brain was about to explode.

Pure foolery, that was the only explanation for abandoning her station, for why she was standing right behind them. She didn't know this kid, not really. They'd only spent a few hours together. She hadn't called a safety on him—he wasn't hers to protect. But for some reason she was remembering all kinds of things she didn't want to remember. All the times she'd taken a beating. All the times no one had had her back.

She watched her hand lift, saw her fingers knot in the shoulder of Chip's shirt.

"What the hell is going on here?" Minnick slammed her back into the banister at the top of the stairs. Her breath caught. She tilted back, and nearly would have fallen over the ledge if not for her grip on Chip's shoulder.

"Kid has work to do," she said, blinking back the vertigo. "If he doesn't sort my materials, I can't do my job."

Minnick scoffed. "Well, look at this, Small Parts pride is alive and well!" He raised a fist toward the sky. "Why don't you go with him? Is that what you want?"

"Ty, come on," said Colin, behind her on the stairs.

"Oh, I see. It's a mutiny. Abandon ship!" Minnick went to shove Ty again, but Colin stepped between them.

"Don't push me, boy." Spit flew from Minnick's mouth. He jerked Chip toward his side, but the boy arched away. Ty's lips curled back in rage.

"We need this kid or else we'll *all* be here for the rest of the night," said Colin, and Ty felt a surge of affection for him. He didn't like Chip, but he trusted Ty.

Minnick considered this. "He's that good, huh?"

"He's a solid worker," Ty growled.

"And you," he said, looking up at Colin. "We all know you're good, don't we?"

Ty swallowed thickly. "Colin's always over goal." Her friend was ramping up for a fight, she could feel it. She didn't want him to get fired—she didn't want anyone to get fired. She just wanted to make sure Chip was all right, that's all, and he wouldn't be with Minnick.

"Then I think the choice is clear. You two rats," Minnick pointed to Colin and Chip, "if you're not at your posts in thirty seconds, you won't ever be back at them again. And as for our hero . . ." He side-stepped when Colin moved closer to Ty. "You can go see what the

Stamping Mill wants. And I swear if they fall behind while you're gone, all three of you can kiss this fine establishment good-bye."

* * *

The Stamping Mill was only a block up Factory Row from Small Parts. She entered the gray stone building from the employee entrance, where she and Colin met his ma sometimes. Ty had never been inside before, but always thought the screaming grind of the metal inside and the tall, barred windows made the place look like something out of a nightmare.

Inside wasn't much better.

The noise hit her first, like she'd walked straight into a wall of screeching gears and crunching steel plates. It stole her breath, and intensified the throbbing in her head. The main factory floor was so congested with machines and bodies it was hard to see what was really happening, but the ceiling was three stories high, and some of the metal monsters went straight to the top.

She followed the runner around the edge of the floor, searching for Colin's ma, but it was impossible to tell who was who when they wore those face masks and goggles. Small Parts didn't make them wear gear like that. Probably better—they'd just fog up in the heat.

"What the hell is this?" Ty looked up to see a burly man with an orange beard and a handkerchief tied around his forehead. He was wearing navy coveralls, same as the other workers, but had a clipboard in one hand.

"I said a kid—a little one. What's so confusing about that?" The runner, a jaundiced boy with stringy black hair, shrugged.

"I'm small enough," said Ty, fearing they'd send her back to retrieve Chip.

"You're tall as me," he said. "And hefty."

"I'm small enough," she repeated. Taking a deep breath, she pulled off her sweater, and another underneath, until she was just wearing a long-sleeved thermal. The bottom had ridden up over her knife handle, revealing two puckered, circular scars on her stomach, and when he narrowed his gaze there, she shoved her shirt back down. She felt practically naked.

"Christ almighty you stink," he said. "And if I can smell you over sulfuric acid, that's saying something."

"So don't stand so close," she said, avoiding his eyes.

He blew out a long breath. "All right, all right. You're scrawnier than you look." He cut straight through the middle of the room, and Ty followed, feeling too crowded with all the noise and people. Her heart was pounding by the time they reached the problem—a squat steel machine, still smoking, with red lights blinking near the handlebars.

"It's a steel press. The sheets go in there." He pointed to the right side of the belt, which was currently frozen. "They get treated there with the acid." He showed her a spray bar that was meant to move down the pieces. "Then they get flattened when you pull this lever. Clear?"

"Yeah," said Ty. "Yes, sir."

"Something's jammed in the compression chamber. Need you to shimmy up there and get it out."

It looked easy enough, Ty thought. She'd have to climb the belt, move through the chamber, and jerk whatever it was free. If she did a good job, maybe this foreman would remember her, and hire her before she was eighteen.

"It's off?" she asked, checking the power switch.

"Course it's off," said the foreman. "Think you were with the Brotherhood with the way you're carrying on."

Without delay, she hopped nimbly onto the belt, feeling the rollers dent her knees as she crawled into the entrance. She had to flatten a little, but it was still big enough for her to fit. They didn't need Chip after all.

Squeezing her body under the spray bar took a little work, and she coughed as the acid fumes burned her throat and nostrils. A glance to her left told her that the foreman and a couple other workers were watching. She needed to do this quick and right.

Carefully, she flipped over on her back, staring up at the metal stamper above her head. A sudden thrill shook through her. If that came down it would flatten her. It would crush her. If they turned on that switch, or if she shook a piece loose, she'd be a goner.

Breathing fast, she searched the area for something out of place, but she didn't know the machine well enough to know what she was looking for. Finally, a sliver of steel caught her eye. It was lodged inside one of the gears near her right shoulder. Hoisting herself up on her elbows, she grabbed it, and yanked twice before it fell loose.

The machine gave a creaking moan. Ty held her breath.

The stamper didn't fall, but she'd had enough. She didn't even bother flipping over. Still facing up, she clambered out like a crab, knees bent, arms holding her chest up. She moved as quickly as she could. So quickly, she banged her head on the spray bar.

A fizzling sound, and a clear liquid bubbled out from one of the nozzles. She saw it gather as if in slow motion. Then it fell, and landed with a hiss just above her left eyebrow.

It felt like liquid fire.

Ty screamed. The acid burned straight through her skin to her skull. She swiped at it, but accidently hit the bar again, and this time a wave of droplets sprinkled down over her.

"Pull her legs!" she heard a woman yelling. But she couldn't move. Ty covered her face and tried to wipe away the acid but it was tearing her skin away. And then it was in her eye, and everything went white on one side. Panic scored through her. She was going blind.

Hands on her legs, jerking her from the machine. A smack of her head against the plastic rollers on the belt. Then she was on the floor, and someone was trying to pull her hands away from her face, but she wouldn't let go.

It hurt.

It hurt.

It *hurt*.

"Ty, listen to me. Put your hands down. Do it!" Ty recognized the woman's voice, as if she were coming from far away. But one eye saw only white, and the other was pinched so tightly it saw only black. The left side of her face felt like it was being buffed with sandpaper.

A cool liquid was sprayed over her skin, but it brought only a little relief. Then she was being lifted by the shoulders, and dragged into the office, where she was laid out on a lumpy couch. She curled into a ball around her knees, rocking back and forth.

"She needs a doctor!" The woman's voice again. More cool water was sprayed over her face. It ran through her hair and made the cuts on her head burn, but it soothed a little of the edge off. Ty blinked open her good eye and recognized Ida, Colin's ma.

"She'll have to go to the Charity House," said the foreman with some uncertainty.

"What are you talking about? Call the Brotherhood's doctor!"

"Watch your mouth, Ida," said the foreman. "You know as well as me, Brotherhood docs are only for charter workers."

Ida swore sharply. "She's a kid."

A strange, unbidden desire rose within Ty. She wanted her parents. She wanted her father. Why, she didn't know. She couldn't even remember the shape of his face.

"No doctors," whispered Ty. She couldn't afford them. "I gotta go back to work."

"Absolutely not," said Ida. Ty felt her body clench up, tighter than the panic. She was going to be fired, and the only other work for minors was in food testing and whoring.

But she couldn't see.

"Shima," she whispered.

"What's that?" the foreman asked.

The pounding in her head had turned to a sharp throbbing in her skin. Each beat of her heart brought a new, choking pain.

"All right," said Ida with a frustrated sigh. "Shima's a friend. Give me an hour to take her, will you, Max? I'll work over to make up for it."

Ty felt herself pulled up, and tucked under Ida's arm with a tenderness she'd never experienced before. Even though her whole body hurt, she grew stiff. Her legs barely worked when Ida pulled her to a stand.

"Can you walk?" Ida whispered.

Ty nodded.

* * *

When Ty opened her eyes, she had no idea how much time had passed. The small room was lit by candles; the flickering flames threw bright waves across her vision. She kept blinking, but something blocked her left eye. She tried to push it aside but her hands were wrapped.

With a groan, she turned her face, and saw two wide blinking eyes staring back at her.

The memory hit like a sledgehammer to the temple. Minnick and Chip. The Stamping Mill. The poison machine.

She scrambled back, a blanket falling off her shoulders. She was only wearing an old T-shirt, one that wasn't even hers, and socks had been tied at the wrists over her hands. Her legs were bare. She tried to cover them with the blanket, but couldn't separate her fingers in order to do so.

"Up!" screeched the child who'd been staring at her. "Up! Up!"

"Hush!" Ty registered a shadowed figure that entered from her bad side, and she tried again to loosen the socks from her hands.

Shima grabbed her wrists and held them down. "Ty, be still." She purposefully adjusted to Ty's good side, showing the feathers of black hair and a sturdy, calm gaze. Her amber eyes were lined with crow's-feet, the only hint of her age.

"What'd you do to my hands?" Ty slurred. She felt dizzy.

"You were scratching." Shima untied the bindings. "You need to see a doctor. At least when McNulty ran these streets you could go to the damn doctor."

Ty couldn't remember a time before the Brotherhood. It was hard to imagine a Metaltown that Jed Schultz didn't rule.

···103···

A hazy memory slid into place. A white office. A *doctor's* office. Strange devices that let you hear a person's heartbeat. Someone must have told her about it; she'd never been to a clinic before.

"How do you feel?" Shima asked.

"Doped up," said Ty, shaking off the image. "You gave me something." She hated feeling woozy and tired. Out of control.

"Corn whiskey," said Shima. "Little Benny's dad pays me in the stuff. Knocked you right out." There were more children around her now, all blinking at her with their mouths open. None of them were older than five.

Ty inhaled sharply. "I've got to get back to work. Where are my clothes?"

"I'm washing them. Though maybe I should have just lit them on fire." Her voice took on a tone of reprimand. Ty suspected her clothes weren't the only things that had been washed. She smelled like lye soap. The panic rose within her. She was practically naked.

"My clothes, Shima. I need my clothes."

"You'll get them," assured the woman. "Your shift's over. Ida covered for you. She told Small Parts that you were staying at the Stamping Mill through the afternoon."

Ty felt a little relief, but was reluctant to believe Minnick would grant her a second pass after missing so much work.

"Here," said a little girl, placing something in one of her hands. "For your owee." It was a little rope doll—the kind Shima made from mops for the kids she watched. Ty had never been given a doll before, and didn't really see the point in one. Still, she took it with a curt "thanks."

A knock came at the door. "Shima, it's me."

Ty recognized Colin's voice and jolted up. Head still muddled, she grabbed for the blanket. Shima stood, but Ty stopped her. Having him see her like this—without her clothes, without her pride—it was too much.

"Ty, are you in there? Let me in, okay?"

"Sounds worried," commented Shima, quirking an eyebrow.

"Tell him I'm sleeping," Ty said. "Tell him I'm not here. Tell him whatever you want, just get him out of here, okay?"

After a moment, Shima nodded. Ty stumbled into the tiny bathroom, and pressed her ear gently against the door. She could hear Colin telling Shima that his ma had filled him in. Shima was right, he did sound worried, and that made her buzz even stronger.

A few minutes later, the room fell silent. He was gone, and she was glad, but part of her wished he had stayed, too. That was the crazy corn whiskey talking, she told herself.

There was a little aluminum mirror above the sink, and Ty startled when she caught her reflection in the low light. The bandages had been wrapped at a diagonal across her head, and her cropped hair stuck out through it like a patch of grass.

Gently, she unwound the dressing, shuddering when the vision on her left side stayed bright and unseeing. Through her good eye she saw herself in the mirror. Saw purple skin and hideous welts and yellow-tipped blisters. Her stomach turned, and she dry heaved into the sink. She looked like a monster. Like someone half-human, half-dead.

Good, she thought. *No one will ever want to look at me again.*

Then she melted into the floor, and covered her mouth with her hands, and wept.

12

LENA

For three days Lena locked herself in Otto's office at the Hamptons' estate. He made no attempt to stop her, but instead gave her free rein of his case files, stating that he could care less how she wasted her free time. So, while he was gallivanting around the River District with precious Ms. Dwyer, Lena read his reports.

Or rather, his lack of reports.

Otto paid shoddy attention to the details of the business. There were discrepancies, errors, missing income. And some months, there was more money reported than there should have been. A lot more.

"How is it possible to double your profit without doubling your workforce?" she asked herself, glowering out the window at the blue river.

The water gargled and hissed as Darcy poured another cup of hot peppermint tea. Lena knew the extract was meant to soothe her, but this was no time to relax. Otto had made an unintelligible mess of things.

"Why don't you take a break, Miss Hampton? You've been at it all day."

"We spend money on raw products, supplies, power, and staffing," Lena ticked off, ignoring her. "Our expenditures don't change month to month, so unless the employees are working in the dark . . ." Lena blew out a long breath, feeling as though she could sink into the floorboards.

Darcy's face went grave. "Some tea?"

"He's not paying the workers," Lena realized. "My brother's not paying the employees." It was the only way the figures made sense. The only way they could increase their income without making any other changes.

Darcy gave a shrill, forced laugh. "Now, Miss Hampton, that's your brother we're talking about. The Hamptons are fair, honest employers. The whole of Metaltown would starve to death otherwise."

"Have you seen them lately? They *are* starving." She remembered the people working in her brother's factory. The rashes from the cold, the prominent lines in their necks and their jaws, the way they barely filled their clothing.

The hungry way they looked at you through those piercing blue eyes.

The way they'd give you the clothes off their backs just to keep you warm.

She shook her head quickly, noticing how her hand had gripped the scarf she'd folded on her lap. She'd washed it, of course; who knew what kind of germs he carried. But regardless, she found herself stroking the soft fabric through her glove, reminding herself how it had lain against his neck. *Colin's* neck.

When she'd seen him working she'd been surprised. In hindsight she didn't know why; of course he was a laborer. He dressed like one, acted like one: hard and rude and arrogant. Even if he was handsome in a way that made her brother's *refined* friends seem as two-dimensional as bad art, he'd done nothing but ogle and annoy her in their short time together. But seeing him there, sweating, worn out, had put her on edge.

She didn't know why she felt sorry for him. Honest work was a point of pride.

Which was why she was here, digging through these files.

Brows drawn together, she looked again at the spreadsheet for last month. Six workers laid off and six new hires. And double the net income from the previous month. She was sure she was right; Otto wasn't paying them.

"Why would these workers continue to show up if they weren't getting a paycheck?" This wasn't the Eastern Federation, where workers' wages went to support the masses. If someone worked for a living, they should be compensated. Anger boiled inside of her. Her brother would ruin their family name.

Darcy fidgeted uncomfortably, her elbows pointed out like wings. "Miss Hampton . . ."

"If you're not going to say anything substantive, simply don't speak," snapped Lena. "I don't want any more of that damn tea, either."

Darcy frowned, and placed the cup and saucer on the table. As she retreated toward the exit, Lena felt the prickling of shame.

"Darcy, wait. I didn't mean to be rude. I just . . ."

Darcy paused at the study door.

I just want to show them there is more to me than songs and dresses. That I have a brain. That Otto isn't better, just because he's a man.

That I can do this.

"Be careful," Darcy whispered, refusing to look back. "No one crosses a Hampton, not even you."

"But . . ."

"Just be careful."

* * *

Lena was still considering Darcy's warning when her father walked in. She stood, slyly leaving the scarf on the chair behind her, and straightened her blouse.

"Where's Otto?" he asked, his face as telling as marble.

"Out, I suspect," she said.

Her father narrowed his eyes, and she swallowed. "I have some business I need to discuss with him," he said. "When will he return?"

He was already annoyed, which meant Otto was in trouble, which in turn meant she was in trouble.

"He said he had a meeting. With the foreman, I think," she lied, hurrying around the desk. "You can tell me." A slight grimace crossed his face, making her feel like a too-eager puppy. "I've been reviewing the books since I went to the factory earlier this week. I've noticed several things I wanted to discuss with you—"

"You can ask your tutor or your brother if you have any questions."

Lena frowned. "*You* could teach me. About the business, I mean."

Her father's brows lifted in genuine surprise. He took a step forward, placing a hand under her chin. "Had a good time in Metaltown, did you?"

She hated the way he played it off as if she'd gone there on some shopping trip. "It was very enlightening."

"Good. I find a little time there is all I need."

Lena stepped back. "For what?"

He opened his arms. "To remind me how grateful I should be for all I have."

"Oh." She hung her head, feeling worse than when she'd yelled at Darcy. She was grateful. Every day her meals were prepared for her, and sampled by an employee for her safety. She was driven where she needed to go, had her clothes tailored to fit her shape. And every night she fell asleep in a big, soft bed.

"Lesson learned?" The superiority in her father's tone made her cringe.

"Yes. Sir," she added.

"Good. Then tell Otto I need to speak to him. The winds are changing, it appears. The Advocates attacked another supply train heading for the front lines."

"One of ours?" The last rebel attack had been detrimental, wounding their efforts to keep back the Eastern Federation. She'd seen a report that nearly two thousand soldiers had died, which was substantial in a war that had already claimed nearly thirty thousand lives since the fighting had sparked, almost forty years ago.

"That's right," he said. "The war's crossed onto Northern soil again, and our men need more ammo to push those bastards back across Eastern Federation lines. We'll need to increase our shipments by a quarter. Business, dear daughter, is good." His eyes sparkled like ice.

"Business is good," she repeated. "Has anyone found the Advocates?"

"No." He gave a short, confused laugh, as if surprised she had taken interest. "Tell Otto the news, will you?"

She forced herself to smile, though her insides withered.

"I'll tell Otto."

"That's a good girl."

* * *

Otto was nowhere to be found. Lena even called on Ms. Dwyer, but was told she was out shopping with *Mr. Hampton*. The maid seemed pleased with the social match.

When it was clear Otto had no intentions of coming back soon, Lena made her decision. Maybe her brother didn't care about the family business, but she did. And if she just could take care of some of the problems he'd let slide, her father would see her competence. He'd know she was grateful. He'd be proud of her.

Darcy's words echoed in her mind. *No one crosses a Hampton, not even you.* The woman was out of line, making statements like that. Lena would talk to her about it first thing tomorrow. Maybe the men in her family didn't see her as an asset yet, but they would. They just needed proof.

She would give them proof.

While Aja drove the electric car across the beltway, Lena practiced what she would say to the foreman. They needed to increase their output, and if that meant dedicating more resources to overtime pay, then so be it. There was a war going on, and the Northern Federation's military depended on Hampton Industries.

He'd agree, of course. He was paid to take orders from a Hampton; it didn't matter which one.

Maybe she'd even see Colin.

The scarf he'd loaned her was in her bag—she'd return it if they had a moment alone. But that was foolish; of course they wouldn't be alone. Technically, he was her employee. They would never again talk to each other as freely as they had in the alley, when neither had known the other's station. The thought distressed her, and she plucked at the black pin-striped skirt and suit jacket she'd chosen to wear. She'd changed three times before picking the right outfit, a fact that made her feel ridiculous. This was a factory; no one was going to notice the way she looked.

Aja parked on the curb, activated the car's security device, and walked her through the front doors of the factory. The checkered tiles on the floor stopped abruptly as she passed through the staff entry and gave way to peeling yellow linoleum. She walked briskly to the foreman's office. Through the windows, she could see the floor below, and the bodies grouped around each station on the snaking belt.

The thought of those workers, most of them her age and younger, going without pay made her insides twist. She was glad they'd stayed loyal to the company. Hampton Industries wouldn't survive without them.

"Mr. Minnick?" She knocked twice on the door, fixing her black leather gloves while she waited. When no sound came from inside, she pushed through, frowning at the mess of papers on the man's desk and several half-empty mugs scattered around the room. The noise was louder here, but still muted by the glass walls overlooking the floor. She sidestepped through the office to the walkway, where the volume increased, and moved to the railing. There, she spotted the foreman near the center of the belt.

Talking to Colin.

He was wearing the same beige long-sleeved shirt he had been when she'd seen him the other day. The neck was ringed with sweat, and the sleeves were rolled up to the elbows. He was taller than the foreman, broader around the shoulders but leaner at the waist. So different from the men she'd seen in the River District. Less refined in every way, but somehow more real because of it.

And she was staring.

Why had she come down here? She could have just as easily called from home. She told herself she should wait in the office, but as she was turning away, she remembered that her family owned this company, and she could go where she liked. With her jaw set, she returned to the stairs, her heels clicking down every metal step.

If anyone noticed her, they did not acknowledge her presence. They kept their heads down, even the youngest of the children, who were sorting the pieces. She clutched her purse to her side, feeling distinctly invisible.

When she drew closer, she could hear the foreman yelling. Colin's eyes snapped to hers, held for a moment, and then lowered. The heat in the room seemed to increase by ten degrees. Beside him was a girl, the same who had been here the other day, only now she wore a knit cap. What showed of the left side of her face was covered by bandages.

"You're down in count, rat, and that's the bottom line," reprimanded the foreman, and Lena promptly forgot why she'd come here or what she'd planned on telling him—she was too shocked that he'd just referred to an employee as a *rat*. He looked as though he were about to carry on, too, when he noticed the way Colin and the girl had shifted their attention to her.

"Miss Hampton!" Mr. Minnick's face grew a bruised shade of red, and the rivulets of sweat rolling down his cheeks glistened. His eyes were bright with panic.

"What happened to you?" Lena asked, stepping toward the girl. She would deal with Minnick's behavior at another time. "Are you all right?"

"Yes, ma'am." The girl turned her face away, and to Lena's surprise, Colin positioned himself so that she was half-hidden behind him. Lena lifted her chin, surprised that he was attempting to shelter this girl when all she had expressed was concern.

"Some of these workers are unpredictable," said Minnick. "This one's down in count by thirty pieces over the past two days."

"Well, she's clearly injured!" said Lena.

"I'm fine, ma'am," said the girl. "Just a scratch."

Lena gave Colin wide berth as she approached the girl. She had thick eyebrows, horrible dental hygiene, and a mess of scars scattered over her flushed face. The heat in here had to be killing her with all those layers. Perhaps she'd just come in from the cold outside.

"Why is your eye covered? Did something happen?"

"She's fine," said Colin. Then, under his breath he added, "Back off, Lena."

The comment enraged her. She was his superior, and he was going to get his coworker hurt further making her stay on the job in this condition. Had he no compassion?

"You need to go home and rest," she told the girl.

"*No.*" The girl began working faster, churning out pieces that even Lena could tell weren't precisely right. "I can do the work. I'll meet goal today, I promise."

"She'll finish," assured Colin, glaring at Lena. "I'll make sure of it."

"Well, I'm hardly going to depend on you," Lena said.

They stared at each other in heated silence, and between them shot the glances of the other two. Colin looked away first, jaw flexing.

"You heard the lady," said Mr. Minnick. "Sorry, sweetheart, you're dismissed. Take care of yourself."

"Wait," said Colin, at the same time the girl sputtered, "You can't fire me."

"Who said anything about firing?" said Lena. Even if she'd wanted to, surely she didn't have the authority. Or maybe she did. Mr. Minnick looked eager enough to please.

"My apologies, Miss Hampton, I thought that's what you meant," said Mr. Minnick, motioning her off to the side. "We can hold her position if you like, but we can't hire someone to take her place while we do. Keeping her on the books will slow down production."

Lena thought of her father's news—that they needed to produce more weapons for the front lines. *Business is good.* For the Hamptons, maybe, but not for everyone.

"I see," said Lena, mouth going dry. She looked away from Colin's furious glare, and forced her gaze to the girl, trying to focus on what her father would do. "I'm sorry."

On her way out, the girl bumped hard into her shoulder, knocking the bag down to Lena's elbow. The scarf inside spilled out over the edge, and when Colin saw it, he shook his head, and turned away.

13

COLIN

"Snobby little greenback bitch!" Ty shouted into the night. The noise was enough to turn a few heads in front of them, but apart from some grumbled responses, no one stopped.

"What'd you expect?" muttered Colin. "She's a Hampton." They'd replayed variations on the same theme since he'd met her after work at Shima's. Not that she wasn't right—Lena had cost Ty her job, and in Metaltown if you didn't work, you ended up on the streets, and then you ended up dead.

Colin wasn't going to let that happen. Ty could come stay with him for a while if that's what it meant. He could float one more person—one more cup of water in the watered-down broth wouldn't exactly ruin the flavor. But telling himself this didn't cure the unexplainable rage he felt every time he pictured Lena's face.

What had *he* expected? Just because they'd talked didn't mean she wasn't a Hampton. Didn't mean she had any idea what kind of damage she could do with just a few words. She was probably home now, eating a big dinner with her dad and brother in her nice warm house. She'd probably forgotten all about what had happened at Small Parts.

A headache was brewing right behind his eyes. Another worker would take Ty's place tomorrow and Lena would never know the difference. But this would change everything for Ty.

"Well that *Hampton* is gonna be sorry when she's the one who's got to work the line because everyone else is either sick from the hot room or cut loose." Ty kicked an empty tin can across the street.

He pictured a nearly empty Small Parts factory, with only Josef Hampton and his two kids on the line. It helped his mood a little.

"My eye's just an excuse," she went on. "You know she came there to trim the fat. Probably was just about to pull names on who to sack when she saw me."

"She didn't come there just to fire you."

"Oh, is that right? And how would you know that?"

They rounded Whore's Corner to Market Alley, where the shops were bustling with the after-work crowd.

"You could see it on her face."

"On her stupid, flush face, you mean," bit Ty. "What are you talking about, *her face*? Who cares about her face? Her mouth is what fired me."

There was no winning with her when she was like this. "How's *your* face?"

She stiffened beside him. "Fine."

"Can you see yet?"

"Yeah," she said too quickly. "Almost."

Colin dragged a hand over his jaw. "You should have let them take the kid. If Lena hadn't fired you, Minnick would have, just for being a hero."

Ty had stopped walking, and when he noticed, he turned back. "What?"

"*Lena?*"

Colin felt his ears get hot. "The boss's sister."

"Oh, I know who Lena Hampton is," shot Ty. "Do *you*?"

Shifting irritably, Colin quickly explained the situation he'd walked into at the beginning of the week. When he was done, Ty was laughing. He might have taken this as a good sign of her recovery if she hadn't been so damn sarcastic about it.

"You're lucky she doesn't have you jailed for menacing," she said.

Normally he would have shrugged it off, told her, "We'll see," or something like that. But he knew she was right. In the two times he'd seen Lena Hampton since their first encounter, she'd treated him like the invisible man.

But she did still have his scarf.

It didn't make sense.

"It wasn't a big deal," he said. "I didn't even remember it until just now."

Ty made a noise of disbelief. "What did you need over here, anyway? I'm broke, in case you forgot."

"We're going to talk to Jed about your job."

"Schultz?" Her one visible eye widened.

"Do you know another Jed?"

"Uh-uh." She stopped and turned on her heels. "Brotherhood doesn't cover kids."

"The Brotherhood covers injuries on the job, though. And anyway, he likes me, and he knows you. He covered for you with Minnick when we went to Bakerstown." A chill ran through him at the memory of Gabe Wokowski and his father.

Ty shook her head. "I don't need his help. I don't need anyone's help."

"Shut up," he said. "You don't even have to say anything. I'll talk, you just stand there and look . . . desperate or something." Colin wasn't sure Ty even possessed such an emotion.

"I'm not desperate," she said between clenched teeth.

"You will be when you're working Whore's Corner."

She shoved him hard on the chest, and he bumped back into a cart of tableware. A set of metal bowls clanged together and then fell to the cement. He was pissed too; pissed that she was so damn stubborn she didn't get it. She was thicker than blood to him, and he wasn't about to let her freeze to death under the bridge.

"You want me to say it?" he asked, exasperated. "*Please*, okay? Please, Ty. Come with me. There, you happy?"

She melted back a step, rolling her shoulders to shake it off. "Fine."

He sighed, almost wishing she'd kept fighting so he could burn off some of his own pent-up anger. They pushed through the crowd, stopping at the Brotherhood's door. Colin stood a little taller, remembering how Jed had told him they were alike, and that he didn't need to lie.

Jed had been generous to his family. He hoped he wasn't stepping over the line to ask for one more favor.

He knocked on the door, throwing Ty a harsh look that told her to play nice. Imon opened the door, reminding Colin of just how big the man was. His flat face didn't show any recognition, but he did move aside, and led them down the narrow hall to Jed's office.

The People's Man was sitting behind his desk, wearing a new suit. A fancy one, like a greenback would wear. He almost looked like a different man in clothes like that, and Colin felt a cold feeling of dread come over him, like coming here had been a bad idea.

"Mr. Walter," said Jed with a yellow-teethed smile. "How are you, Colin?"

"Good," said Colin. "Real good. Got some new duds with the green you gave me."

"The green you earned," corrected Jed with a nod. "I see that. Not too shabby."

Colin felt his confidence build, even as Ty's jaw began grinding beside him.

"Is everything all right with Cherish?" Concern warped Jed's brow.

"Oh. Yeah," Colin answered. "I actually came by for a different reason." He swallowed. "Ty here was injured on the job. Well, not really on the job. The Stamping Mill pulled her out to fix a machine, and she got some burns on her face. And then Small Parts let her go because her eye's all messed up."

Jed's gaze shifted to Ty, and it struck Colin that he hadn't ever looked at her before just then. "What a shame. Take off your hat; let's see the damage."

Ty faltered. "It's just a few burns, sir."

"Take it off," Jed repeated.

"Do it," Colin hissed. What was wrong with her? You didn't say no when Jed asked you to do something.

Ty glanced over at Colin, her one eye pleading. A spike of guilt drove through him, but still he reached for her hat and pulled it back. Head hung, she unwound the bandages, and his breath caught when he saw the bright red welts on her skin. There was pus, too, leaking from the blisters, and her left eye was bloodshot and unfocused.

Ty had lied to him. She was blind. She was never going to see again.

He wanted to hit something. He chewed the inside of his cheek, biting down hard so that he'd think of anything else but how hurt she was. Shima should have told him it was this bad. *Ty* should have told him. And now he was making her show it off like some battle scar. Maybe someone needed to hit *him*.

Jed cringed. "Imon, come look at this." The big man stepped forward from the door, and bent down to see Ty's wounds. His expression didn't change. Colin's fists tightened.

"Well, that *is* bad," said Jed. "Does the doctor say it will heal?"

"Course it will," lied Ty, her voice so small it made Colin flinch.

"That's good news." He leaned back in his chair.

Colin noticed the cool tone, and realized that Jed wasn't going to offer anything unless he asked outright. He took a deep breath. "I was thinking you might be able to get her back in at Small Parts. Talk to Minnick or something."

"The Brotherhood doesn't extend to children's work."

Colin stiffened. He wasn't a child. "But since she was working at the Stamping Mill when it happened . . ."

"The fact that it happened at the Stamping Mill makes no difference," said Jed. He shook his head, disappointed. "You thought you could walk in here, after I put those clothes on your back, and ask me to break the rules?"

"No, sir," said Colin quickly, feeling the situation taking a turn downhill. "I just thought, since you'd talked to Minnick before about us being late—"

"You thought wrong." Jed leaned over the desk, dark eyes piercing. "Believe it or not, I don't owe you anything."

"I never thought—"

"In fact, if anyone owes anything, it's you, Colin. Your brother has a debt, did you know that? He borrows to fund that little fix he's got. Surely your mother would be distraught if we came to your home to collect."

Colin's mouth fell open. "You don't need to go to my house."

"Now that's just rude," said Jed, suddenly indignant. "After all I've done for your family, you wouldn't even invite me in?"

"That's not what I meant."

"An insult like that has me rethinking my generosity."

"I'm sorry, sir," stammered Colin. "I didn't mean anything by it." Beside him, Ty was quickly rewrapping her wounds. Panic blossomed, like the first draw of blood. Coming here had been a stupid idea. Jed was going to stop the payments that kept Cherish alive. He wasn't going to help Ty, either. Things had been fine one second, and the next had spiraled out of control.

Jed sighed. "I know you didn't. You were just trying to look out for your friend." He sat down again, and Colin became aware of his muscles humming, his organs vibrating. "Just a word to the wise, kid. This is a dog-eat-dog world. Sometimes the best thing you can do is cut your losses." He glanced over Ty again.

Colin went very still. Gone was the confusion. Gone was the anger. And in its place, remained a different kind of fury. A dangerous kind.

"Is that the Brotherhood's official opinion?" he asked.

"Colin," muttered Ty.

Jed smiled. "Of course not. If you paid your dues to the Brotherhood, I'd give you the Brotherhood's official opinion, but I'm afraid you don't. You just reap the rewards."

Colin stepped forward, but Ty grabbed his shoulder. He tried to shake free, but she wouldn't let go. Then Imon had his collar, and was dragging him down the hallway, out into the gray light of Market Alley.

* * *

Colin made for the river with Ty on his heels. He didn't speak to her; he couldn't even look at her. The shame was almost worse than the fury, and he was ready to rid himself of both.

He stalked down the crumbling sidewalk, past the pay-by-the-hour motels, to a bend in the road. The dive on the corner was alive with neon lights and already full of Metalheads—laborers mostly, avoiding going home. *Lacey's.* Where they served penny shots of corn whiskey, and never pretended the stuff was safe to drink.

The bouncer outside was meaty, and marked up the forearms by half-finished tattoos. Before Lacey's, Rico had worked at Small Parts. Exposure in the hot room had made him sick, and Minnick had turned him out to find the only work he could: food testing. A bad batch had messed up his lips, and as a consequence he wore a perpetual sneer. Lacey had hired him because he looked like a monster.

"Hayden in there?" Colin barked.

Rico rolled his head to the side. "You going to cause me trouble if he is?"

"No," Ty answered for him.

Rico's sneer deepened as he inspected her face.

"Keep staring," Ty challenged. "I'll make sure your eye matches mine."

Colin pushed past them inside, scanning the bar and the patrons huddled over their dirty glasses. Behind them was standing-room only. The laughter was already turning raucous.

"Colin!" Zeke called from over in the corner. Martin was there with him, and a few others from Small Parts. Colin didn't stop.

He wove through the bodies toward the back, to where Hayden was sitting on a fold-out metal chair, dealing cards onto a wooden crate. Four other guys watched his hands, waiting for him to slide a card and cheat.

Colin felt his control snap. The fury rolled through him, blocking out the lights, blocking out the other people. Blocking sound and reason. He lunged over the makeshift table, grabbed Hayden by the shirt and hoisted him to a stand. Cards and money scattered across the plank floor.

"What the—"

Colin hit him. Hard enough to crack his nose. His knuckles flared with the pain, but he didn't care. He wheeled back to hit him again, but Hayden had lowered, and he charged straight into Colin's gut, knocking the air from his lungs.

Colin crashed into a group behind them and hit the floor. Glass cracked somewhere near his head. He swung up, connecting with Hayden's side. A grunt filled his ear, brought on a dark satisfaction. He hit his brother again, and again.

Hayden's elbow swung back and knocked him hard enough in the temple to make his vision waver. And then the weight was suddenly absent. Colin sucked in a tight breath.

"No trouble, my ass," growled Rico, holding Hayden upright in a headlock.

Zeke's arms latched under Colin's and heaved him up. His brother's eyes were red-rimmed, his dark hair matted with sweat. The blood ran freely from his nose. He swiped at it with the back of his hand.

Fighting had erupted around them, a chain reaction of explosions. Glass shattered, voices raised. Colin saw Ty taking a swing at a guy in a chem plant uniform. Martin pulled her back.

"Get out," ordered Rico. "Work it out outside."

Hayden and Colin were shoved out the front door, into the empty street and the frigid night. Inside, the fighting raged on.

"I was on a streak," said Hayden. "You cost me half a day's wages in there."

Colin got right back in his face, sick when the sticky sweet smell of nitro wafted off of him.

"Why don't you ask Jed Schultz to spot you, then? I hear he's been loaning you all kinds of green."

Hayden fell back, brows hiking up his forehead.

"Where'd you hear that?"

"Where do you think? From Schultz himself. When he was telling me he could cut the money for Cherish if you didn't pay up." It was close enough to the truth, and Colin wanted nothing more than to make Hayden crumble.

"You don't want to mess around with Schultz, little brother." Hayden's voice was low.

"Oh, that's perfect," said Colin. "Go ahead, try to tell me what to do. You can't even take care of yourself. It's pathetic."

Hayden turned away, like he was going home, but stopped and came back to Colin, squinting, pointing. "Everything's so easy for you, isn't it? So goddamn easy."

Colin's head fell back. Easy? Nothing was easy. His mom was sick and his brother was a junkie and his best friend was half-blind. He was the idiot, yet again. Wanting everyone to be something they weren't.

"Yeah, everything's real easy, Hayden," he said bitterly. Glancing back through the bar window, he found Ty still standing, yelling something at Rico. She was all right—at least for now. But things were changing. She'd had her fair share of scrapes, but what had happened with her eye was different. It made her vulnerable, and he'd never thought of her that way before.

He forced a heavy breath, standing side by side with his brother, facing the black water that lapped against the concrete barrier beneath the bridge. A train was rolling down the tracks at the shipping yards, on the edge of Bakerstown, and the sound carried over the distance. He wondered if Lena could hear it all the way in the River District and then felt stupid for even thinking it.

"I'll get clean," said Hayden.

"Okay." He wondered if he sounded as skeptical as he felt.

The minutes passed. Colin knew he should go home. Check in. Take care of things. Try to get a few hours' sleep in before work tomorrow. He cringed when he remembered that Ty wouldn't be there with him. He hadn't worked a day without Ty by his side in four years.

"It's not so damn cold on the water," said Hayden, chin digging into his collar. "Sometimes, when the tide was out, we'd lay out on the dock in the sun. That kind of warm goes straight to your bones. Keeps you heated half the night."

Colin felt a pull deep inside of him. He wanted to feel that kind of warmth. The kind that burned off the chill, and the sickness, and the hunger. And the crushing defeat that he couldn't help anyone he wanted to help, including himself. But at the same time he wished Hayden would just shut up about it, because he was sick and tired of stories that never came true.

"You coming home?" Colin asked.

Hayden's eyes shot quickly to the door, then back to Colin. "Yeah. Now?"

"Now."

Hayden grumbled a curse as they turned up the street. "You messed up my back, little brother."

"Good."

14

TY

Ty wandered the streets, with no particular destination in mind. The shadows were thick this time of night, and she watched them like they were living, breathing monsters, rather than the shrouds of the sick who'd wandered aimlessly from Beggar's Square. No Bakerstown cops crossed the tracks to Metaltown. Not that they would have kept the streets safe anyway. Knife in hand, she walked faster, feeling the blisters begin to bite at her heels, and the cold claw under her collar.

She was tired of Lacey's. Sick of the noise and sick of people staring at her face. She could have gone to Shima's, but the sublevel apartment was cramped, and Ty didn't want to be a burden. She wasn't an invalid, after all.

She'd used up all her green from last payday; even if she had been able to forget what had happened last time, the Board and Care was out. If she'd stayed on at Small Parts until the end of the week she might have been all right, but kids who got fired didn't get to claim their wages. That was Minnick's rule.

So she walked, heated by her hatred for Lena Hampton. Hampton might not have been the one to dump the acid on Ty's face, or sic those mutts on her at the Board and Care, but her hands were still dirty. It was her people who owned stupid Small Parts, who allowed for knotheads like Minnick to take advantage. Her people who let Jed Schultz's Brotherhood protect the adults, but not the kids. Now there was nothing for her to do. No one hired a girl with one eye. And the Brotherhood would never cover her as an adult because she'd been injured before eighteen.

The despair clung to her back, sharp nails lodging in her muscles. She moved faster, trying to outrun it.

Lena Hampton had fired her. Ruined her. Ty remembered that pathetic puppy-dog look on Colin's face when he'd said her name. That had been its own special brand of betrayal. He just couldn't figure out where he belonged. Well, she was tired of reminding him.

It was long past midnight when she reached the familiar stone statue of St. Anthony. One thin stone arm stretched before him, the other broken off sometime over the years. He looked eerie in the dark, like a corpse in the streetlight. Ty quickly skirted by into the projects.

Twelve floors high, Keeneland Apartments was on the verge of ruin. The brick siding was crumbling, the windows almost completely boarded up. Graffiti marked everywhere within reach, and the fire that had scorched the west corner had become a hole for squatters since the owner—some pig-faced greenback from the River District—refused to fix it last year.

Ty hustled around the outside of the building, clambering through the weeds and empty bottles toward the fire escape. Just to the left of it was the Dumpster, and the smell coming from it was enough to make her gag. She froze when she heard several voices back near the statue. Someone broke a bottle against the stone, making her shudder. Laughter echoed off the brick siding as they moved on.

She climbed the fire escape to the second floor, and huddled in the shadows below the window. There wasn't much warmth coming from inside, but it was enough to take the edge off. She felt safer here, with her back against the wall. She felt safer knowing he was close.

Her eyelids grew heavy. Her arms pulled inside the sleeves of her shirts, wrapping around her bare stomach. Her knuckles grazed the two matching scars beneath her knife hilt, reminding her of a nun at St. Mary's, who'd told her when she'd gone to take a bath that she shouldn't let people use her body to put out their cigarettes. If that's what had happened, Ty couldn't remember. Probably better that way.

A hacking cough from within the apartment roused her, but when it quieted, she drifted again.

Get up, she told herself. *Don't fall asleep.*

* * *

The woman's hand was cold, and dry like bones. Not warm like her mother's. Not full like her father's. It grasped her fingers so tightly she recoiled, but couldn't shake it loose.

"Come on." The woman's voice shook, and that brought hot, fierce tears to the girl's eyes.

They were outside a stone building, the damp shadows clinging to their skin. The woman knelt down, scooped up icy mud water from a puddle, and sloshed it into the child's hair. It bit into her scalp and dribbled down her face. Her dress was ripped too—the collar shredded, leaving only her stained underskirt. The sounds were too much like growls in this strange place. The cold made her shiver so hard she could barely stand.

Finally, the woman knocked at a dingy wooden door, told the girl to stay put, and ran. She cried then, wailed, her tiny bare feet frozen to the step. She wanted her mother. After several moments the door was unbolted, and a lady appeared in the lamplight, a sour look on her face. She was dressed all in black, her hair and neck hidden by a scarf.

She only shook her head disapprovingly, and then picked the little girl up.

* * *

Ty surged to her feet, a rattling at the window above turning the remnants of that strange, familiar dream to dust as she sprung for the fire escape. She was too late; the plywood board was lifted off the frame and pulled inside, and the sharp curse from within had her freezing in her steps.

"Trying to kill me?" Colin whispered. He had a wastebasket tucked under one arm as he stepped over the ledge to the platform. Instantly, he replaced the board, coughing once as the cold air hit his throat.

Ty couldn't think of anything to say. Her tongue felt too thick. Dawn had come, and she'd stupidly fallen asleep outside Colin's door. For all the times she'd come here, she'd never been so lax.

He was wearing his work trousers already—the pants Jed had bought for him. They reminded her of what had happened the last time they'd gone to the Brotherhood's office, and she forced herself to look away.

"What are you doing?" he asked. "You crash out here again?"

Her teeth chattered. "No. Just walked over."

He went to the ledge and turned the wastebasket upside down, spilling half a dozen bloody rags into the dumpster below. Ty's heart clenched.

"If I was flush," she said, "I'd get her medicine."

When he rubbed his eyes, she noticed how tired he was. For an instant she let herself wonder what it would be like, living here with them. She could help him take care of the family.

"If I was flush," he said, a small, sad smile playing over his mouth, "I'd get your eye fixed."

Her throat tied in knots. She crossed her arms over her chest. "I was thinking I might talk to Hayden about a job at the chem plant." Maybe she'd talk to him about some other stuff too, like getting himself together.

One brow lifted. "They only hire over eighteen. You know that."

Of course she knew that. "People say I look older. Couldn't hurt to ask."

"You know . . ." He paused. Frowned. "You know you can stay here, right? Ma says it's fine."

She felt her spine zip up. "I can take care of myself, thanks."

He leaned against the rail, sighing. "Can you? I mean, you know I've got your back, but who else does?"

"What are you talking about?"

"I been thinking," he said. "About Jed."

She groaned. "Oh, here we go."

"Just listen." He chewed the nail of his little finger. "Jed started the Brotherhood because no one was protecting the workers. They were getting beat up and fired and not getting their pay."

"And . . ."

"And it sounds a whole lot like Small Parts, right? I mean, you've worked there since you were a kid. Never missed a day. And Minnick goes and sacks you the second you get hurt—on the job, no less."

"Minnick didn't fire me, Hampton—"

"Anyway, I started thinking. Why doesn't Small Parts have a Brotherhood?"

"Because Brotherhood is just for adults." She didn't know where he was going, but the scheming in his voice made her nervous.

"I mean our own Brotherhood. Why doesn't Small Parts have something like that?"

"A charter? The Hamptons would smash it."

"Why?"

"Because we're kids," said Ty. "Because we're nobodies."

Colin was pacing now, tapping the wastebasket under his arm like a drum. "Well this nobody makes eighty detonators a day, and I'm pretty sure a bomb's just a hunk of metal and nitro without that."

"So what are you saying? You want to stop making detonators to teach them a lesson? They'd fire you faster than they fired me."

"They can't fire all of us."

Ty laughed. "All of us? You mean all the workers at Small Parts? I'm pretty sure they can, Prep School."

"And do what? Hire a new set of workers? Who's going to train them, Minnick?"

Ty abruptly stopped laughing. He did kind of have a point. But this was crazy. "How are you going to convince over a hundred workers to stop their jobs?"

Colin grinned. "I'm not. You are."

* * *

They met at Lacey's after work, when dusk had lit the Metaltown sky a bruised yellow-gray. Ty had been sick with nerves since morning, but she'd come anyway, because as much as she thought their plan wouldn't work, a small part of her hoped it did.

Rico had boiled water for her in silence. When the parasites had all burned off, he poured it into a cracked mug and set it on the bar. Rico didn't like to talk much, on account of the pain in his mouth when he spoke, but it made her feel a little better being around him. His face was damaged too, and he'd still managed to find work.

Colin stood beside her while she slumped on the stool, gripping the mug so hard her hands shook. Chip settled in the front row, looking doubtful that this would be as entertaining as she had promised. Martin and Zeke had come, and Matchstick, who was forced to stand in the back because he was so tall. Others, too—a girl named Agnes Ty had known from St. Mary's who mostly kept to herself; Slim, who worked in Batteries; Noneck, whose ears rested right on his shoulders; and even some of the guys from the warehouse. All in all there were nineteen of them. Hardly enough to break Small Parts, but still more than she'd expected.

They quieted on their own, all watching Colin expectantly.

He cleared his throat. "So, like you've all probably heard by now, Ty got pretty worked over at the Stamping Mill a few days ago," he said loudly. Ty could feel their eyes boring through her and bristled at the attention. "Small Parts fired her, and you know nowhere else is going to take her with her eye all messed up like that."

"You blind, Ty?" called Martin.

"Maybe now you can finally kick her ass," joked Zeke, slapping him on the shoulder. Several people chuckled, but Ty felt too sick to join them.

"At the Stamping Mill there's rules the Brotherhood enforces when someone gets hurt on the job," continued Colin. "They get three days' leave, and a doctor's care. And most important, their job gets held while they're gone. The boss can't hire anyone to fill it. But at Small Parts, if you get hurt . . ."

"You get fired," said Chip.

Colin eyed him, annoyed, but the murmurs of agreement around the room returned his focus to the plan.

"At the chem plant they get protective eye masks and gloves. And they can't dock your pay whenever they feel like it. The foreman can't rough you up without the Brotherhood roughing *him* up."

Ty noted the distaste in his voice, but doubted the others knew what Jed Schultz had said to Colin when he'd asked for help. It was important that Colin point out the good parts of the Brotherhood, like they'd discussed, rather than the dangers of it. They needed people to want to join them, not to get scared off.

"That true, Hayden?" asked Zeke. Everyone looked back to where Colin's brother stood beside Matchstick. Hayden jerked up awkwardly, but his eyes were clear. It was strange seeing him sober.

Colin went rigid, obviously surprised he'd shown.

"Yeah," said Hayden. "Yeah, he's got it right."

"My sister works at the uniform factory," said Noneck. He'd just been transferred to the hot room after a year in Plastics, and his eyes were already bloodshot. "They get two breaks a day. Small Parts, we only get one, and only for five minutes. Barely get to the front of the line at the can in five minutes."

More nods of agreement.

"I don't see folks at the Stamping Mill pulling doubles and not getting paid for it," said Agnes.

"We get sacked if we don't work them, and then stiffed when we do," said Henry, a musclehead who worked in Plastics. "I say we torch the place and be done with it."

"That can be arranged!" called Matchstick from the back. One of the defective detonators was swinging around his pinky finger by its thin copper wiring, and he grinned as the others broke into laughter.

Ty couldn't believe how the mood in the room had changed. She lifted her chin for the first time, pushing her hat back off her forehead. Colin smirked down at her. Maybe he'd been right. Maybe people would make a stand.

Maybe she'd even get her job back.

"Pissing and moaning is one thing," said one of the boys from shipping. "But this is the kind of stuff that gets us all sacked. Nothing good comes out of it."

"What if it could?" said Colin, stepping forward. "Nobody over eighteen puts up with this crap, why should we?"

"Because we're grunts," argued the same boy. "Ty had a tough break, could've happened to any of us, but that's the way it is. She knew the risks when she took the job."

"She took the job because there wasn't another one," said Colin, and Ty swelled at the bite in his tone. "Look, alone we're just like Ty, sacked and homeless, and—"

"I get it already," inserted Ty.

"—Minnick is one man. There's over a hundred of us at Small Parts," Colin continued. "If we tell him we want changes . . ."

"He'll fire us," said Martin. "Plain and simple." Colin glared at him as the others began to protest.

"I was quitting anyway," called Matchstick, puffing his chest out. "Once I collect my inheritance, that is."

It was an old joke in Metaltown. Years ago, before Ty could remember, the owner of the food testing plant had died. His kid had gone missing—likely killed by the same illness he'd tried to destroy. Hampton himself had posted a reward for information, but no one had dared to collect. Only a fool went toe-to-toe with the big boss and demanded money.

Several people fought Matchstick for the title, all demanding that they were the rightful heir. That was how the joke always went.

"You know I got your back, Ty," interrupted Zeke, "but I got my sister to look out for. I can't be getting myself fired just 'cause you did. You understand."

"I understand," said Ty, hands gripping the mug again. "I understand you're full of it."

"Don't be like that," said Zeke, frowning.

"Be like what? Honest?"

"Stop," Colin hissed at her. "Of course you have to take care of your sister," he said evenly.

"But don't say you got my back if you've only got hers," Ty finished, skin hot. Chip burst to his feet and stood beside her. There was fire in his eyes as he glared back at the crowd.

Colin stood his ground. "How'd you like it, Zeke, if you were in Ty's place right now, and she was the one saying 'sorry 'bout your luck'?"

"Come on, man," groaned Zeke.

"If we stand together, we can look out for each other," said Colin. "They can't run a factory if all the workers refuse to work."

That got some laughs. Ty felt a familiar itch inside of her. Soon her hands were fisting and her eyes had narrowed to slits.

"All the workers," mocked Noneck. "None of us work, just to make a point."

"Why not?" asked Colin. "We can keep taking it, or we can crew up and do something about it."

Martin was shaking his head. "You're talking about organizing a press."

Ty had heard of a press—once upon a time the Stamping Mill had pressed for rights. They'd refused to go into their factory, and instead stood outside and blocked the doors, stopping production completely. They even got their own shirts made. The Stamping Mill press had been organized by the Stamping Mill Charter, a group of workers tired of their boss's crap who'd joined up to make things better. The Brotherhood, they called themselves. Led by slick Jed Schultz.

"That's right," said Colin. "We hold out, stop working, and press the boss for what we want."

"Since when did you get so goddamn noble?" chided the second shipping boy.

"Since I figured out no one gives a damn about us."

"What about Jed Schultz? What's he got to say?"

"Who cares?" shot Colin. He hunched suddenly, Adam's apple bobbing.

A hush came over the room; Colin had spoken blasphemy. Ty wanted to stuff the words back in his mouth. Even if Jed was slippery as the grease in his hair, you didn't bad-mouth him in public. That was dangerous.

"Jed Schultz must believe the same thing, otherwise he wouldn't have started the Brotherhood," she said, but it was too late.

"Sorry, guys," said Martin. "But some pay's better than no pay."

One by one, they fell into their old conversations. Their old jokes. Their old fights. And Ty and Colin melted onto their barstools, defeated.

"I got your back," said Chip to Ty. "I'll pledge right here."

"Pledge to what?" muttered Colin.

"Pledge to the code," he said, as if this were obvious. "Street code."

Ty smiled despite herself, and the movement hurt her face. Street code. That said you didn't beat up on kids smaller than you. That if you didn't call dibs, your stuff was up for grabs, and if you shared food with someone, they owed you later.

And that said if someone said they had your back, they had your back.

15

LENA

Lena's room sparkled. Her clothes were refolded, or straightened on their hangers. The floor had been scrubbed. Her sheet music on the stand was organized and filed away. Everything was in its proper place. There were staff members to do the housework, of course, but with her mind reeling, Lena had demanded to do it herself.

She scrutinized the mirror over the dresser, searching for streaks in the glass. Every time she thought it was perfect, she noticed another one and had to start over. It had been this way since Aja had driven her home from Metaltown the previous afternoon.

From the cage before the window came a high trill. Lena glanced up—her yellow bird stood out sharply against the black night outside.

"It's not my fault," she answered.

The bird cocked his head to the side, then jumped to another wooden dowel.

"It's *not*." She collapsed on the parlor chair, groaning at the tight muscles in her lower back. "Letting that girl go was the ethical thing to do. What if she'd hurt herself more? What if . . ." She balled her rubber cleaning gloves and tossed them across the room. She'd been so flustered by what had happened, she hadn't even told Minnick he couldn't call the employees *rats*. "Managers have to make tough decisions, that's the bottom line. The Small Parts factory cannot afford to fall behind right now."

The bird trilled again, and she could hear the accusation in his song. *Then why haven't you told Otto or your father what you did? Why haven't you been able to stop thinking about the look on Colin's face when you fired his friend?*

"I don't have anything to be ashamed of," she said, hating the defensiveness in her tone. "In fact, I'll go downstairs right now and tell Father." The idea lifted her spirits—maybe this would show him that she cared more about the company than Otto. She quickly changed into some casual slacks and a soft, blue blouse, and was padding down the stairs barefoot before she remembered that she wasn't wearing gloves.

She hesitated, but didn't stop. Riding high on momentum, she searched the second floor, not finding him in his bedroom or his office. Perplexed, she returned to the stairway, taking the steps down to the ground floor, and passed through the kitchen with its broad marble countertops and cherry cabinets. The sound of muffled voices in the parlor froze her in her tracks. It was late, but not unreasonable for her father to hold a meeting. Still, she was usually informed of such things so she would know to stay out of the way.

Curiosity had her tiptoeing to the swinging door. She pushed it gently, ears attuned to the conversation in the next room.

"For five hundred units, I'll expect a little more, my friend." There was ice in her father's tone.

"A little more," sputtered another man. "I get the feeling it's always a little more with you, isn't it, Hampton?" Lena recognized the voice but couldn't place it.

"War's expensive."

"That it is." A sigh, and the clink of ice in a glass. "The business of war," he mused. "Tell me, Hampton, are you as cunning with the Eastern Federation as you are with your own people?"

Lena's stomach tightened. Her father had no contact with the Eastern Fed. The two federations had been in hostile negotiations over food and water rights since before she'd been born. When he'd served on the Assembly, he'd supported legislation to increase the North's military, to keep their way of life protected. A defensiveness rose within her. To suggest her father was communicating with the enemy was to imply he was a traitor.

"My business with the Eastern Fed is my own," answered her father. "Tonight, let's focus on what we can do for each other."

The other man laughed, and placed himself in Lena's memory. The stranger who had watched her sing and asked why he should enter into business with her father.

"Very well," he said. "In order to keep our little rebellion in action, we'll need five hundred units of artillery, delivered by railway, in unmarked crates to Billington. It's quiet there; we'll run no risk of this going public. Oh, and *without* armed security this time, if you please. I'd hate to have our shipment steered toward your front lines. That hardly does us any good." Another clink of ice within a glass.

"General Akeelah was pleased with the last shipment, I take it."

Akeelah. Lena recognized the name. He was the leader of the Advocates.

A cold dread whispered across her nerves.

"I assume so. He did take the product, didn't he?" The man gave a short laugh.

The breath locked in Lena's throat.

The groaning of a leather chair—someone was getting up. "Half of the payment now, half upon receipt," the man continued. "That ought to fuel this damn war for another eight months, at least."

Lena's hand slipped, and the door whined softly on the hinges before she caught it. She eased it back on the jamb, wincing as a second passed in silence.

"And if it doesn't," said Lena's father, "then we'll be in touch." She could hear the smile in his voice.

The meeting was drawing to a close, and Lena had heard enough. Heart pounding, she darted silently to the stairs, and ran up to the top floor. Only in the safety of her room did she finally release the breath burning inside her lungs.

Billington was in the Northern Federation, near the border of the Yalan Mountains. Her father was arranging to ship weapons there, quietly, in order to support a rebellion. And not just any rebellion. He was supporting the Advocates, the very group responsible for destroying the Northern military's supply train. The radicals who would see the North—her father's *own federation*—fall, and turned over to a bunch of starving farmers who had no business running it.

Even as she processed this, she doubted it. Her father was a powerful man, maybe the most powerful in the Northern Federation. He employed thousands of workers, and supported their military with weapons and supplies. He was a patriot. It made no sense to betray his own people—no sense to fund the group who would see him taken from power in the name of fairness and equal rights.

Unless he then planned on sending more weapons the other way—shifting the tides back and forth at will.

War was a business, as the man had said. Her ears could not deny what they had heard. Her heart could not deny the dread squeezing it.

Hampton Industries was selling weapons to their enemies to keep itself in business.

Business is good.

Footsteps on the stairs stopped her from pacing, and automatically, she pulled back her hair and inhaled several deep, composing breaths. It was likely the maid, checking to see if she needed anything. She could not appear flustered. Nothing could appear out of order until she figured out what was going on.

Two successive knocks, and her father pushed into the room.

Lena's eyes shot to the floor, and she concentrated on slowing her heart.

"Up late, aren't we?" he asked. "Oh. Are your gloves in the laundry?"

She hurried to the dresser and slipped an extra pair on from the drawer. As she picked up her comb, her hands shook. She couldn't think of what to say.

Her father wandered to the window, unbuttoning his suit jacket and leaning down to face her bird. "Do you remember when I got you this?"

She unlatched her long braid and began combing through the strands, watching him in the mirror's reflection. "Yes, sir."

"You were so happy that day. As a child should be. A songbird for my songbird."

Her shoulders lowered an inch. "We built the cage together."

He laughed. "Yes, we did. I'm surprised you remember."

"Of course I remember," she said quietly. When he smiled, she felt the blush stain her cheeks. This was not the man she'd heard downstairs. In a surge of relief, she realized she'd misheard. Her father was a good man, a *grateful* man, like he'd told her. She was wrong not to trust him.

"Your mother used to sing to you as a baby," he said wistfully.

Lena felt her heart skip a beat. He never shared anything about her mother. "She did?"

"Yes," he said. "You were so little. You'd fit right here, in my arm." He crooked his arm to show her. "The first time I saw you, I couldn't believe how much you looked like her. How fragile you were."

Lena's hand had paused midstroke. Her father had never before spoken so tenderly.

"You're still so fragile," he said.

He undid the latch, and in a quick move, grabbed the bird, holding it firmly in his hand.

The brush fell from Lena's hand with a clatter, and she quickly righted it. Forcing herself to be calm, she crossed the room to where her father stood, a serene look on his face. Softly, he stroked the bird's belly while its head twitched side to side.

A sob rose in her throat.

"Do you have what it takes to be a Hampton, Lena?"

"Yes. Of course," she said, her voice cracking. Her eyes stayed glued to her little yellow bird. The friend who sang with her, who listened when she needed to talk. Who she never once had dared to touch. His chest was rising and falling too fast.

"Please," she said. "You're hurting him."

"You will hurt people, Lena."

"I can . . ." *I did. Just this week.*

"I thought you said you wanted to learn about the business," he said, squeezing tighter. "I thought you wanted me to teach you."

"Please, Daddy," she pleaded, the tears stinging her eyes.

"Then you must be willing to learn."

One clench of his fist, and the bird's neck was broken.

Lena's hands covered her mouth, the tears streaming down over her covered fingers. She stared at her bird's poor lifeless body as her father placed it back in the bottom of the cage, and latched the door, leaving it there for her to gaze upon.

16

COLIN

In Ty's absence, Minnick temporarily moved a kid named Henry up the assembly line until he could hire a replacement. Henry was big, Colin's height, but built like a tree trunk. Perfect for Plastics, which was where he'd come from, but crap for the intricate work that fuses required. He was all thumbs, which meant Colin ended up doing both their jobs.

He'd had it good with Ty. She was quiet, efficient, and dependable on the job. She knew when to talk and when to get busy, and best of all, he didn't have to explain every little thing to her.

Part of him thought he should just let it go. Meet half his quota, and blame the loss on Henry. Maybe they'd let Ty back then. But what did that prove? That he'd been all talk last night at Lacey's. That he didn't really give a damn about anyone but himself. Which made him just like all these other cowards who wouldn't stand up for one of their own.

Hell, if he was really Ty's friend, maybe he would have quit with her.

But two missing workers didn't make an impact like fifty. Or a hundred.

There had to be a way to get them to see.

He was still mulling over options when Martin's voice carried over from Batteries: "On the floor!"

A moment later the foreman appeared, red in the face and practically steaming. He stomped down the stairs and yelled across the belt to Colin and Henry.

"Think he wants you," said Henry morosely.

Colin tensed. Apparently this day *could* get worse. As much as he'd wanted to stand up for Ty, getting fired was about as much fun as a kick to the face. "Damn."

He grabbed his handkerchief from the table and stuffed it in his pocket, then wiped the white chalk on his hands off on his shirt. Minnick turned back up the stairs without an explanation, and as Colin followed, he tried to think of how he was going to explain to his ma why he couldn't help her with rent.

At the top of the stairs, he followed Minnick into the office, raising a brow at the big foreigner—Lena's bodyguard—standing with his arms crossed across his massive chest.

You're lucky she doesn't have you jailed for menacing, Ty had said. His muscles grew tight, his spine straight as a ramrod. Little greenback had sure taken her time telling Daddy. He never should've talked to her.

"Let's get this over with," Colin said. No point in sitting down or making himself comfortable. Getting cut loose was one thing, but if she wanted him jailed she had another thing coming. He studied his exits, ready to bolt.

"Someone wants to see you," said Minnick. Not quite as freakishly happy as when the boss was around, but not his normal, sneering self either.

"I can see that."

"Outside," said the bodyguard. He looked angry.

"Oh, right," said Colin. "I get it. I just step outside and then what?"

Minnick's jaw twitched. "You tell us, kid."

"Miss Hampton would like a word with you," said the man. "And you'll treat her with the utmost respect."

"Or else?" Colin taunted.

"Or else I'll break your legs," said the man.

"Like that wasn't the plan all along," he muttered. He wiped the sweat off his forehead with the back of his hand. Lena wanted to see him? Right. More like this guy and a few of his friends wanted to send a message. Where was Ty when he needed her? He was glad his boots were already laced up tight, because he doubted they were going to let him go back to the lockers to get his knife.

He might not have been a Bakerstown pansy, but he could still run.

"Let's go," he said, adrenaline pumping.

The man disappeared through the door that led to the front of the building, but before Colin could follow, Minnick snagged his forearm.

"What's your game, rat?"

"I'd tell you, Minnick," said Colin. "But I don't think you'd understand."

Minnick squeezed Colin's wrist until his fingers started to tingle. His other fist was ready to strike. If he was going down, he might as well go down in flames.

"I understand that you're stepping on toes, rat. Big toes. Jed Schultz kind of toes. Heard he's gunning for you. What'd you say, huh? What's got the white knight all riled up?"

Colin jerked out of his grasp, feeling the blood drain from his face. "Don't know what you're talking about."

Minnick smirked. "Sure you don't."

Someone had gone to Schultz after last night. They'd probably told him about the meeting, how Colin wanted to start his own Brotherhood. How he'd said he didn't care what Jed thought. As if he weren't on bad enough terms with the man already.

Colin turned away and pushed through the door. This wasn't the time to lose focus. He had more pressing issues.

It occurred to him that maybe the Brotherhood was who would be waiting outside.

Slowly, he entered the empty lobby of the building. There was nothing here for him to grab, nothing to use as a weapon. He looked outside, but the street was empty. Hiding, he thought. Someone's out here waiting. But all he saw was that sleek electric car parked on the street, and the Hamptons' man standing beside it.

Warily, he pushed through the doors outside, feeling the cold air punch all the sweat-soaked patches in his shirt. His heart was pounding.

He crossed the street.

The man opened the car door.

Inside was Lena Hampton.

Word traveled fast—even the boss had heard what he'd said last night at Lacey's. Doing one final survey of the area, he leaned down to face her.

"You wanted to see me?" She was wearing a soft-looking sweater and pants that showed the shape of her legs. Her eyes were bright with worry, the kind that had had him talking to her in the first place. Still not altogether sure he wasn't about to get jumped, he drew in a slow breath, and reminded himself to keep a safe distance.

"Please sit. Colin." The tentative way she tried his name on for size had him scowling. She patted the seat beside her with one satin glove, making him realize how little skin she showed. Just that thin, graceful neck and her pretty face.

"I'm fine right here," he said. Trouble followed this girl. She'd been the one to cut Ty loose, and was probably about to do the same to him.

"Oh. Of course." Her chin dropped. "I just wanted to return this to you." She reached into the purse at her feet and removed the scarf he'd given her.

Damn. He hadn't thought she'd kept it, but seeing that she meant to give it back stung a little. Realizing it was best to get this over with quickly, he scooted in beside her, and pulled the door closed, feeling immediately warmer inside the small compartment. Outside the window, her man glared at him, and he raised both hands to show he wasn't doing anything worthy of a leg breaking.

She offered the scarf again, nearly shoving it into his lap.

"It's yours." He wasn't so sure he wanted to keep the memory of this encounter wrapped around his neck.

"But you said you'd get it back when I saw you next."

"And I didn't."

Her mouth formed a small O. She unfolded the scarf, refolded it, and then tried to hand it to him again. "I'm sorry for the delay. I'm sure you've been missing it."

"It's a scarf," he said, and then gave a short laugh. "You think I can't afford another one. I'm sure I'll survive somehow." The color brightened her cheeks. He liked that more than he cared to admit.

"That's not what I meant," she said. "I'm not used to people giving me things."

"Somehow I doubt that."

"No. Gifts, that's what I mean. Unless . . . I could pay you?"

"What did you have in mind?"

Her eyes grew wide, and she glanced to her bodyguard, still outside.

"Take it easy," he said. "I was joking. You don't get out much, do you?"

"I've been here twice this week already."

"Yeah." He frowned. "I remember."

She straightened, turning more to face him, and when she did, her knee bumped against his. She apologized, then backed into her door to widen the space between them. "That's why I wanted to speak to you, actually. To talk about what happened."

"And here I thought you just wanted to get me in the backseat." He drummed his fingers on the driver's compartment, directly in front of them.

"Are you never serious?"

He snorted. "Are you really dragging this out?"

"Dragging what out?"

"Aren't you here to fire me?"

"What? No. *No.* I'm not here to fire you. I just wanted to talk to you. I wanted to see if that girl had found work, and if not, maybe I could help her find something."

"That'd be nice, since she got hurt on the job and all." He bit the inside of his cheek, not meaning to have been so free with his words.

Lena's mouth dropped open. "She did? I thought . . . Why didn't Mr. Minnick tell me?"

"Probably because he's the one that sent her to the Stamping Mill, where it happened."

Lena's face, drained of color, fell into her hands. He blinked down at her, surprised that she was genuinely upset. When she sat back up, several hairs had slipped from her braid. She looked better that way. Like she wasn't trying so hard to be perfect.

"It'll be all right," she said in a way that made him think she was talking to herself, not to him. "It won't be hard to find her something else. There are plenty of jobs that don't require a lot of experience."

"She had years of experience." He scoffed. "You think we're born knowing how to wire fuses?"

"That's not what I meant," she said. "I meant that the work she was doing . . . it's not exactly skilled labor." Her face turned red.

His probably did too.

"So anyone can do it."

"I'm not saying that." She cringed, likely because she *was* saying that. "I didn't mean to offend you."

"I know. That's what makes it worse."

She clasped her hands over her lap, squeezing to the point of shaking. "I'm sorry. I've really made a mess of things. That wasn't my intent."

He shrugged. "Don't take this the wrong way, Lena." He paused, checking her response to the use of her name. "But what do you care? You're a Hampton. She's nothing to you. None of us are."

She stared at him. "You don't know me."

"Yeah, I'm beginning to get that," he said quietly.

"I'm talking too much." She looked flustered again. "Please tell the girl that I'd like to make up for things."

A moment of awkward silence passed.

"Okay," he said. He could already imagine how well that would go over.

Lena's back straightened. Her chin lifted. "You don't believe I'm good for it."

"Does it matter if I do or not?"

"Yes," she answered. "You should trust your employers to keep their word."

Her tone was so genuine he almost pitied her. She really believed that this was the way it worked. The fence around her house must have been sky-high to keep her so sheltered from the real world.

"Trust is a hard promise to keep," he said slowly.

"Trust is earned," she said. "I understand that."

He scratched his jaw, suspecting this was an act, and curious what she had to gain if it was. He was a nobody at the factory; he hadn't been there half as long as some of the others and he sure wasn't Minnick's favorite. He was just a guy she'd met on the street, a tiny piece of the big Hampton machine. Winning his allegiance was useless.

But winning hers might not be.

If she really did intend to help Ty, maybe she could help all of them. Minnick didn't listen, Otto Hampton didn't care. But Lena had the positioning to make things happen. Goggles and suits in the hot room, maybe. Clean water for the workers. She'd bat her eyes at Daddy and they might even get overtime pay.

"I'll tell her you want to talk," he said.

"Good," she said. "And thank you. For your time."

And just like that, he'd been dismissed. He pulled the door open and stepped outside. Right into Otto Hampton.

Startled, he jerked back. Otto was wearing a collared shirt, neatly pressed, and his short, dark hair was greased to the side. He was standing beside Lena's driver, thumbs tucked into his trouser pockets.

"Hope I didn't interrupt," said Otto. Colin's shoulders rose.

"Otto!" Lena jumped from the passenger side. "What are you doing here?"

"Surprised, sister?" asked Otto. "Mr. Minnick works for me, as you seem to have forgotten. As do the rest of the *employees*." He sent an appraising glare Colin's way.

Lena's surprise iced over. She marched around the car until she was standing between them. "I reviewed your reports, Otto. It appears as though I'm not the only one forgetting things."

Colin was impressed. Maybe he knew even less about her than he thought.

Otto Hampton snorted, his expression slick with arrogance. "Does Father know about this?" He tilted his head toward Colin.

"About what?" *Say it,* Colin silently dared. *If you're man enough.*

"Oh, this is rich." Otto cracked a smile. "He's going to defend your honor."

Rage, hot and sudden, struck him. Otto's smart mouth was about to earn him a broken jaw.

Lena turned to Colin, her eyes pleading. "Go. You've been excused."

Excused? The fun never ended with this family.

"Yes, go back inside," said Otto. "Before I change my mind and have you arrested for assault." Colin looked to Lena once more, and only when she nodded did he start walking.

"And one more thing," said Otto, slapping his palm on Colin's chest. Colin looked down at it slowly, imagining how he could break each finger. "Next time you put your hands on my sister, at least have the decency to bathe first."

Colin mustered a cold smile. Without a word, he walked back inside.

17

TY

Days lasted forever when you had no green and no work.

Ty waited in the alley outside Small Parts at closing time, but no one came out. An hour passed and still the doors stayed locked. Just before dark, she walked to Beggar's Square and got a cup of broth and some corn mash from the line, but when she returned, there was still no movement.

"Come on, Minnick," she groaned. She'd hated overtime when she was working, but now that she wasn't, she sort of missed it. There was something calming about knowing where you were supposed to be and what you were supposed to be doing. She'd been good at her job, and everyone knew it. Now what did she have? Nothing.

She kicked a broken bottle against the door, and as if by magic, the chain inside rattled, and it swung outward.

She recognized the faces. Harker, T.J., and a quiet kid Colin called Loudmouth. None of them looked at her. They wanted to play the high-and-mighty game? Fine by her. She didn't like them anyway.

When Colin emerged the load on her shoulders lightened. He spotted her across the alley and walked over, yawning and stretching his arms.

"Take all night, why don't you," she said.

"Miss me, Ty?"

"Kiss my ass." She spat on the ground. "Thought maybe another supply train had been taken out and Minnick was making you work a double."

At the mention of the Advocates, he groaned—they were all still burned from the extra work they'd had to do last time the rebels had struck, only to have more overtime stuffed on—but something else was bothering him. A few days ago he wouldn't have had to tell her. She would have known, because they would have been together. But now she felt a space between them.

Zeke tore out of the exit, his face set and furious. He was running by the time he reached the street.

"Late to pick up his sister," said Colin.

Ty snorted, remembering the way he'd used her as an excuse not to make a stand against Minnick. "Too bad for him."

Martin came up behind them. "How's the vacation, Ty?"

She wove her fingers, stretched them before her. "Wouldn't know. Spent all day at the train station loading boxes." It was half true, anyway—she'd been to the train station looking for work, and when they'd turned her down she'd gone to the Uniform Division. She'd spent four hours in their lobby before the foreman finally came out and told her they didn't need a girl with one eye.

Ty looked away when Colin's brow lifted. "You hungry?"

"Starved," he answered.

"Hayak's still got his cart out," called Martin.

When they reached the street, it became obvious that most of the others had the same idea. Ty was hungry again—the broth and mash hadn't done much to quiet her grumbling stomach—and she began taking stock of everything hanging low enough that she might be able to grab without the old man catching on.

Colin was surveying the line before them, brooding.

"Spit it out already," said Ty, tired of him holding back secrets.

He pulled his hat down over his ears. "You hear anything today about last night?"

"No, why?"

"I think someone told Jed Schultz what happened at Lacey's."

"Someone did, in fact," said a man behind them.

Ty spun around, her knife already palmed before she realized Jed himself was standing three feet away. Beside him were Imon and three more men from the Brotherhood. They were big, dressed like greenbacks, and didn't look particularly friendly.

"Mr. Walter," said Jed, flashing a fake smile. His harsh gaze was pointed at Colin.

"Mr. Schultz." Colin's ears turned faintly pink. Ty placed herself on his left side, where he was weaker, even though it kept her blind on the outside. A mix of fury and fear scored through her. After their last meeting in Jed's office, she didn't know what to expect.

She became aware that the line had gone quiet. Everyone's eyes were upon them.

"Some concerning news has come my way," said Jed. "Unexpected news."

Colin didn't say anything. Jed leaned back, hands in his hip pockets.

"Do you know what an organized press is, Colin?"

Ty's shoulders jerked. Colin was right. Someone had ratted to Jed.

"I've heard of it," said Colin carefully.

"Do you know what happens to workers that press when they don't have a charter?" When Colin didn't answer, Jed took a step forward. "They get fired. They lose their jobs. And then they go hungry and lose their homes. Do you know what happens to the man that leads them?"

Colin stood his ground, silent.

"He gets blamed. For all those hungry stomachs and cold nights on the street."

"Some of us are hungry now," said Colin. Ty bit down on the inside of her cheek.

"I know what it's like to want to help," said Jed. "I know better than anyone. And so I've been thinking." He glanced behind them, making sure everyone was listening.

Here it comes, thought Ty.

Jed opened his arms. "Small Parts would be a welcome addition to the Brotherhood. We can look out for these people, take that heavy burden off your back."

Slick. So slick it made Ty feel slimy. He wouldn't be offering unless it helped him somehow. Behind her, people had begun to murmur.

Colin contemplated this. "We'd get the same rights as the other factories? A doctor, and pay when we work overtime?"

"Of course," said Jed, eyes gleaming. "I'd make sure you get everything you need."

"And what do you get out of it?" he asked.

Jed's smile faded. "The satisfaction of helping the children, of course."

"And our money," said Ty. Jed barely glanced over.

"There would be a small fee," he acknowledged. "Members pay dues."

"Of course," mumbled Ty.

"I got to *pay* you to watch my back?" shot Chip. Ty hadn't heard him approach. He stood on her bad side, where her head was still bandaged.

"Get out of here." She pushed Chip behind her, willing Jed to forget his face. The streetlamps flickered on.

"I'll bring the paperwork tomorrow," said Jed with finality. He turned.

"Wait," said Colin. "You didn't answer the kid's question. Why should we pay you, when we can do the same thing ourselves?"

Jed turned slowly. "Because I talk to Hampton, and you do not. You need me."

"No," said Ty, feeling all eyes turn her way. There was no going back now. She took a bold step forward. "You need *him.* You need all of us. You wouldn't get paid otherwise." It was all coming together, all making sense.

"If I recall, you were fired, weren't you? This doesn't affect you."

Ty's face went red. She could still feel his disgust when he'd looked at her eye. She could still see it on his face. "Why now? You were doing fine without Small Parts. Why do you care now?"

Jed ran his tongue over his top lip. "Keep your dog on a leash, Mr. Walter." He spoke in a low, threatening voice that only Colin and Ty could hear. "That's your second warning."

Colin's chin lifted. "You haven't seen her off the leash, believe me."

The smirk on Jed's face faded, and was replaced by the same darkness Ty remembered in his office. "Well, consider this. Her smart mouth just got your mother kicked out of the Brotherhood. Do you know what that means? No more protection. No more charity."

Ty felt a shimmer of fear work through her. "You can't do that!" Beside her, Colin shifted, teeth grinding.

"Oh, believe me," said Jed. "I can do anything I want." He backed up, and looked slowly around the crowd of workers. "All right, let me try this again. Tomorrow, Small Parts will join the Brotherhood. You'll pay your dues, and if you don't, I'm sure they'll find a place for you in food testing."

The anger was rolling through Ty, hot and heavy. Jed Schultz thought he could walk in here and flex his muscles after years of ignoring them. Thought that everyone would bend to his whim, just because he said so. Who did he think he was, a Hampton?

The other workers said nothing. How were they not furious? She couldn't tell if they were afraid of losing their jobs, or relieved by Jed's offer.

"What's wrong with you guys?" she said.

"Ty, shut up!" Martin hissed behind her. "We don't really want to press," he added, loud enough for Jed to hear. Ty flinched.

"That's good to hear, son," said Jed. "We're looking forward to tomorrow." He turned, the others on his tail, and made for the front of the line, where a somber Hayak gave him his choice of anything on the rotisserie.

"That arrogant prick!" Ty growled. Martin glared at them before walking away.

"Shut up, Ty," said Colin quietly.

"He just threatened your jobs!" He wouldn't look at her, and the sick feeling inside of her spilled over. Colin didn't have the money to buy the supplies Cherish needed. If he lost his job at Small Parts, she'd die even faster. Ty had done that to them. It was her fault.

"I'll get some green, don't worry. Cherish—she'll be okay." Ty took a step forward. "I swear I'll help out. You believe me, right?"

"Back off," he said. Her chest tightened, the muscles wrapping tighter and tighter around her ribs, making it difficult to breathe.

"Colin . . ."

But he had already turned, and was walking away.

LENA

Lena paced across the study, awaiting her father. She expected him home any minute, and she intended to intercept him before Otto did.

Her brother was the worst kind of bully. The way he'd treated Colin was intolerable. The sneer in his tone when he'd told him to bathe. The accusation that they'd been doing something inappropriate together. She'd covered for her brother enough. He'd gone too far, and it was time her father heard of it.

She smoothed down her sweater, hands pausing over her slim waist. As much as she hated Otto's methods, she found herself worried. Meeting with Colin alone had been a risk; she'd known that to begin with. She hadn't meant to confess the things she had, and she certainly hadn't expected him to speak so frankly now that he knew who she was. It should have been insulting—her family employed him. He was from Metaltown, and she was a Hampton.

Yet the only reason she'd gone to him in the first place was to prove to herself that she wasn't like the rest of her family.

She thought of his scarf, hidden in the adjacent bedroom beneath her mattress.

The front door opened. Lena's heels clacked against the hard wood as she jogged down the stairs toward the foyer. When she reached the bottom, her heart sank. There, beside her father, was her brother. Otto shrugged out of his jacket and placed it on the coat-rack.

"Come to greet us at the door, Lena? How very sweet."

She swallowed, ignoring him. "Father, I . . ."

"I'd like a drink," he told the maid. He didn't look at Lena as he swept into the parlor.

"What did you say?" she hissed at Otto.

Her brother's eyes twinkled. "Who says I said anything?"

She tailed after Josef, Otto gloating at her heels.

In the parlor, the maid delivered a tumbler of corn whiskey to her employer, and then quietly took her leave. Otto collapsed on one of the leather couches lining the room. The light was low, but did not hide the hard lines etched around their father's eyes.

Josef tossed back the first drink, then went behind the bar to serve himself another.

"What were you doing in Metaltown today?" he asked without looking up.

She slowly filled her lungs, summoning control. "I went to speak to an employee regarding a girl I fired earlier in the week."

"A girl you *what*?" Otto lurched up, shoes clapping against the tiled floor. "You fired someone without running it by me?"

"You didn't even notice," said Lena.

"I'm not interested in that," said her father. "I'm interested in why you were outside the factory, alone, with the help."

She didn't like the way he said *help,* as if Colin was no different from their maids, or any of the other workers. "I wasn't alone. Aja was there."

"And I've dealt with Aja."

A beat passed, and Lena's mouth fell open. "You let him go." Aja had been with the family for years.

"Could I have done any different?" Her father came around the bar, a hint of flush showing on his neck.

"Aja did nothing wrong. I told him to take me to Metaltown."

"He works for me, not for you, Lena. Though, apparently you can be quite persuasive."

Her chin pulled inward. "What is that supposed to mean?"

Her father came close, grabbing her chin harshly and lifting her face to his. Gone was the gentle reminiscence of the previous night when he'd talked about her as a baby. This was the man who'd held her bird—the only gift he'd given her—only to crush it in his fist.

"Father." Otto had risen and was standing several feet away. The concern in his voice frightened her. Otto should have been enjoying himself.

"Stay out of this," Josef said evenly. "If you had any self-respect you would have managed this yourself."

"I didn't do anything." The tears burned Lena's eyes, but she blinked them back. "I just went to speak to him."

"Don't lie to me." His level, emotionless tone made her insides tremble. "Do you know what it looks like? You, rolling around in the back of *my* car with one of them?"

She lifted her chin. Forced herself to be still. "It's not what you think. Otto, tell him."

Otto said nothing.

A sharp pain lit up her jaw as her father squeezed harder. His eyes were black and bottomless. She became unable to remain a statue. Scratching at his hands, she tried to pull him off, but her satin gloves slipped.

An image of her nanny flashed through her mind. The only person in this cold house from whom she'd ever felt love. But looking into her father's stare, that love felt wrong, undeserved.

"He's a worker, Lena. Do you want to spend your days hunched over a sewing machine or stamping metal? You wouldn't last five minutes." He breathed in slowly, then out, nostrils flaring.

"I think she understands," said Otto weakly.

"I didn't do anything wrong." Her voice cracked.

"You fraternized with an employee," said Josef. "You told me you wanted to learn the business. You wanted to take on responsibility.

But all you wanted to do was play in Metaltown. You *lied* to me, Lena. I trusted you, and you made a mockery of our family."

A great rage rose within her, like a tidal wave blocking out everything behind it.

She shook herself free from his hold, his thumb and forefinger leaving aching points on either side of her jaw as her narrowed gaze burned up at him.

"*I* lied? I'm not the one selling weapons to the other side just to prolong this stupid war. I wonder how long ago the fighting might have stopped if not for your clever interference. A year ago? Longer? Tell me, Father, do you leave the crates of artillery unattended on the supply trains, or do you have them delivered all the way to General Akeelah's doorstep?"

His hand came down hard against the side of her face. So hard, she felt her brain rattle, and her joints and muscles temporarily give out. She hit the ground on her hip, tumbling on her side, vision wavering, static in her ears.

He'd hit her. He'd never hit her before.

The shock gave way to fear, and rage, and disgust, creating a potent, suffocating mix in her lungs. Small gasps were all she could afford, but she closed her lips. Her hot, burning skin became a mask to hide the horror beneath. She willed steadiness, calm. Maybe it was stubborn, or maybe it was just her Hampton blood. Either way, she kneeled, smoothed down her skirt, and rose on shaking legs.

Josef's head had fallen forward. His hands rested on his hips. He looked exhausted.

"This life you love so much has a cost," he said, raising his chin. "This house. These things." He held his arms wide, but they collapsed again at his sides. "Without the war, we have nothing."

A weak laugh slipped from her throat. These fine things were theirs because they'd funded the enemy. This house was built on the backs of workers who weren't even paid half the time. If this was what this life cost, she wanted none of it.

"We already have nothing," she said.

Without looking back, she walked from the room—slowly, as her legs were still unsteady. She climbed the stairs, entered her bedroom. With numb hands and a numb heart, she reached beneath her mattress for Colin's scarf, and within it, a doll, given to her long ago by the only person who'd ever really cared about her.

Her eyes landed on the birdcage before the window. Empty now, since the maid had removed Lena's only friend. She went to gather some things and reached for a silver-backed hairbrush on her dresser. How much had that cost? A day's wages at one of her father's factories? A week's? Enough to send the girl she'd fired to the doctor, at least. And yet, it wasn't even one of her most prized possessions. If she lost it, she'd just get another. She left it where it was.

She needed to get out. Out of this cold house. She'd crossed a line downstairs, told the truth, and been punished accordingly. This family didn't honor honesty. Northern Federation soldiers were dying at the hands of well-armed Advocates, just so she could wear nice clothes, and eat clean food. Everything she touched felt tainted. She'd never been less hungry. She wanted to give everything she owned away.

Her feet carried her down the stairs, to the door where her coat hung. She grabbed it and calmly walked outside into the freezing, black night. No one chased her, no one called for her. She didn't expect them to. She found the carriage house, and the car in the garage. The keys were hanging on a rack on the wall, and with shaking hands she took them and pressed the button to open the door.

She'd never driven before, but it couldn't be that difficult. She'd seen Aja do it enough. Scan the key, start the ignition. When the car began to roll back she tested her foot on the brake, yelping when the vehicle jolted to a stop. Setting her grip on the wheel, she eased off the pedal this time, backing down into the circle, and pressing the button that said DRIVE. The steering was sensitive and the car jerked each time she shivered.

Away, she thought. *Anywhere but here.*

Some of the streets were familiar, others not. Squinting into the black, she drove on, never slowing, never stopping. There were no cars on the road this late anyway.

Soon she recognized the beltway that led to Metaltown. *The factory,* she thought. She could go to the factory. It might be open. Panic chipped through the numb shell encasing her heart. If it wasn't open, she didn't know where she would go. She didn't even have her nanny's address anymore, not that it was right anyway.

No, she would just keep going. Keep going until the Tri-City was so far behind her, she couldn't even remember what it looked like. She would be fine on her own. She was strong. She *would be* strong. Anywhere was better than her own house.

A figure in the road caught her attention and she slammed on the brakes, swerving across the empty lanes. She was thrown into the side window. Spun and spun until her stomach was in her throat and she was sick with dizziness. The rear of the car hit the median with a metallic crunch. The back window shattered, sending a blast of cold air into the compartment.

And then everything went still.

She was shaking. Every part of her. She couldn't breathe. She couldn't think.

Someone came running at the window. Through the thin glass she heard the footsteps. Terrified, she searched for something she might use to defend herself. She hadn't brought a defuser. She didn't have anything. *Glass,* she thought. She was just reaching over the seat to grab a shard of the broken window when the driver's door was yanked open.

A startled cry burst from her throat.

"Lena?"

She spun toward the familiar voice. In the moonlight she could see his face, the shadows on his jaw, the surprise in his eyes. The thin scar cutting through one eyebrow. For a fraction of a moment she wondered what he was doing there, and then realized she didn't care. Her hands covered her face and she screamed silently, rocking back and forth, yielding to the twisting inside of her.

"Are you hurt?" he asked. She felt his hand on her back, sliding down to her hip. Then another on her ankles, moving them from the floorboards. She couldn't catch her breath, couldn't find her Hampton mask to hide beneath. Every jagged, raw emotion spilled from her, uncontained, and trying to collect the pieces just made her feel more fractured.

"Okay," she heard him say, voice soft. "Come on." He slipped one arm under her knees, and the other behind her back. She felt her body shift beyond her control, and then her cheek was against his shoulder, and he was lifting her to the front of the car.

He sat her on the hood, where she curled into a ball, knees against her chest, hands gripping her shins. The cold air wedged itself between them, and when she looked up she saw he was standing a few paces back, arms crossed over his chest. Her whole body was quaking so hard he seemed to vibrate, but she couldn't stop it.

"What are you doing here?" She forced herself to breathe, the shuddered breath ice cold in her throat.

"Dodging cars," he said with a frown. "Makes it harder when they don't use their headlights."

She knew she'd missed something.

"I've never driven before," she said.

"You don't say."

She realized how insane she must have appeared. It disgusted her, how little pride she had. She fixed her gloves and slid down the front of the hood to stand.

As if he'd been waiting for this, he shot forward, gripping her elbows. "You should sit awhile. You're shaking."

The flush crept up her cheeks. Gradually, he released her arms, and she found he was right—she nearly tipped over. He didn't reach for her again; he stayed where he was, pulling his coat tighter across his chest.

"What are *you* doing here?" he asked.

"It's not been the best day." She glanced up at him.

He pulled off his hat and scratched his head, then replaced it. "No, it hasn't."

She wrapped her arms around her chest, shivering, though now from the cold. She probably looked ridiculous, blotchy cheeks and smeared makeup, but she didn't care. He didn't seem to either.

Reaching around her, he picked something up off the hood of the car where she'd just been sitting. His scarf. It must have slipped off her lap when he'd set her there. He gave a small smile as he held it out for her, and she hesitated before taking it, unsure if she should put it on, and she hesitated before taking it, unsure if she should put it on.

"Thanks. Again," she said, laughing once awkwardly, and then wincing because she sounded so stupid. The doll within fell to the pavement, but before she could reach it Colin had stooped beside her. Bent low, with the shards of glass reflecting the moon like diamonds, they found themselves face to face. His gaze caught hers, deep and steady, and though her breathing slowed her heart beat harder.

"Where'd you get this?" he asked.

"Oh." She remembered herself then, and grabbed the rope toy, tucking it into her coat pocket. "My . . . um . . . nanny made it for me. When I was little."

"Ah."

"No witty remark?" she huffed. "No comment about the poor little rich girl and her nanny?"

"I guess I'm fresh out." His lips straightened, as if he were trying not to smile. "Stick around, though, and I'm sure I can come up with something."

A laugh bubbled up, sealing the ache beneath her collarbone. Less than an hour ago, her father had struck her, and here was this Metaltown boy who didn't even know her, trying to make her feel better.

She looked back at the small, wrecked car. The tire that was pressed against the median had popped. The rim rested directly on the ground. She couldn't even run away without making a mess of things.

He cleared his throat.

"Your family's probably wondering where you are," he said. "I can take you somewhere to call them. Doesn't look like you're going anywhere in this." He kicked the deflated tire.

"I can't go back," she whispered.

The truth settled over both of them, cruel and cold as the Metaltown night.

He stepped closer, making her heart trip in her chest. "Come with me, then."

"I . . ." She frowned. Could she go with him? What would her father say about *that*? Realizing it didn't matter, that she didn't care, she made her decision. "Okay."

"It's a walk," he said. "Sure you can handle it in your poor little rich girl shoes?"

She smiled down at them. "I think I can manage."

19

COLIN

By the time they had reached the end of the beltway, Colin had herded Lena to the opposite side of the street. Every step he had taken closer to her, she'd moved subtly away, like the wrong end of a magnet. The game amused him, though he doubted she even knew they were playing.

Stealing a glance in her direction, he found her chin buried in his scarf, and her gloved hands deep in her coat pockets. She'd stopped trying to fix her hair, and it hung loosely over her shoulders and back. Not that anyone cared, but he thought it looked better that way.

He didn't ask what had made her run away, but the bruise still forming on her jaw gave him a good idea. Thinking about someone laying a hand on her burned him up. Surprised him a little, too. He wasn't sure when he'd started thinking that the Hamptons were all on the same side. It was possible he'd never considered they weren't.

The fog from the chem plant may have muddied the shape of the moon, but it brought up the temperature and took the edge off the chill. Fifty feet below them, a single train began to chug down the tracks. It was striped head to toe with green graffiti—the mark of McNulty's gang. The heavy sigh of the engine filled the night.

"It's late for a train, isn't it?" she asked quietly. She had paused by the edge of the sidewalk and leaned over the railing, gazing down on the parallel tracks below. He thought of all the times he and Ty had come here, wishing they were someplace else. Ty would kick his ass all the way across the bridge if she knew what he was doing now. She'd be right, too. Lena Hampton's business was not his business. He needed to stay out of it.

And first thing tomorrow, he would.

"Supply cars," he said, moving beside her. When she didn't scoot away, he inched closer. "Probably taking weapons to the front lines. The fighting's getting worse, I heard."

When she stiffened he stifled a groan. Stupid, bringing that up. She probably didn't want to talk about her family's business right now. She'd taken off in the middle of the night for a reason, after all.

"How did you hear that?" She side-eyed him from above his scrunched scarf.

"Longer hours means a big order's coming through. Big orders of weapons usually mean more fighting."

"Oh." Her gaze locked on the trains again, so intently that he wondered if she knew more about the war than what had come through the factory line.

"*Is* there more fighting? Last I heard, the North was winning." He snorted. "I mean, we have to, right? We've got the best weapons."

Word on the line was that the North was getting closer to pushing the Southern lines back, that soon the Eastern Fed would surrender and the Advocates would disband—but then they'd get more orders. It seemed the war would never end.

Lena gave a bitter laugh, and sort of crumpled in on herself.

"Do you even know why we're fighting?" Her words may have been snobby, but her voice was heavy, sad.

Colin thought back to the lessons he'd learned in school in Bakerstown. They'd watched movies about it—Eastern soldiers in their black and red uniforms raiding houses, taking anything they wanted. People in jails, crying for the Northern Fed's help. Hungry people, waiting in lines for corn bread, which was probably contaminated anyway. It had been shocking, until he'd moved to Metal-town and seen the same thing.

"Because they're the enemy," he said, chewing his chapped bottom lip. That's what people always said anyway.

"*They're* the enemy," she said. "How do we know *we're* not the enemy? What if we're the ones who are wrong?"

He supposed there were two sides to every story. Still, he couldn't figure her out. She should have wanted this war. Her family was getting rich on it.

"Maybe you should join the Advocates," he said, then held up his hands when she spun toward him. "Just a joke," he added.

Slowly, she turned back.

"No one wins," she said, and it made him think of Small Parts, and Ty, and even the Advocates, facing up against the whole Northern Federation. How none of them ever seemed to get ahead, no matter how hard they tried.

"I know," he said. "That's why I'm getting out of here."

She turned to face him. "You are?"

"Sure," he said. "There's this place on the coast, Rosie's Bay. You heard of it?"

She shook her head. "Our coastline is prohibited. The oil spills ruined it."

"Not all of it," he said. "Rosie's is way up north. There's sand there, and fishing boats. And these little houses. They're on stilts because the tide goes in and out underneath them."

"That sounds nice." There was a smile in her voice.

"Yeah. Soon as I finish up some stuff here I'm heading out."

"Oh." He thought she might've sounded a little disappointed, but he probably made it up.

She ran her hands up and down her arms, and he thought of how she'd trembled when he'd pulled her from the car. Part of him hadn't wanted to let her go, but the bigger part remembered what she was capable of. She was a roaming disaster. She'd almost run him over to prove it.

He pushed his hands deeper into his pockets.

"Is that what you were doing walking to Bakerstown in the middle of the night? Finishing up some *stuff*?" Her voice had taken on a sharp edge.

He couldn't bring himself to tell her that he'd tried to get the workers to make a stand against her company. Or that Jed Schultz was a common criminal, no better than McNulty over in Bakerstown. Or that he couldn't go home because he wasn't ready to face his ma and explain to her how he and Ty had gotten her kicked out of the Brotherhood. He never wanted to make things harder on her, but that was all he seemed to do.

He leaned back against the railing. Lena still refused to look at him.

"You caught me," he said. "I was on my way to rob the Cat's Tale." *The bar right beside Gabe Wokowski's house.* He picked at a loose thread on his coat sleeve.

Her eyes darted to his. "You're kidding."

"'Course I'm kidding," he said. "Cat's Tale has security guards. I was going to hit up the liquor store across the street."

She laughed, and then covered her lips with her hand.

Before he thought about what he was doing, he reached for her wrist, drawing her hand gently away from her face. He'd never met a person who tried so hard to stuff their own happiness back down their throat. She tracked the motion of his arm, caution pinching the corners of her eyes.

"It's all right." He didn't know why he said that, or why he'd touched her again. Whatever was happening here, it was definitely not *all right*. His hands returned to his pockets where they belonged.

She chewed her bottom lip. He stared at her mouth.

"I suppose it's easier to be a thief if you're charming." She stared at the ground between them.

"Am I charming?" He leaned closer.

Her lips quirked up, then down. Then suddenly she backed away, chin jutting toward him. "You're after money. That's why you helped me back there. I didn't bring any, okay?"

"I'm not after your money," he said, a little irritated that she'd brought it up. He knew if he pursued she'd bolt, so he stayed where he was. Did she think money was all he wanted? What *did* he want? It had already occurred to him how reckless it was to be alone with her. Ty was right, Lena could say anything she wanted about what had happened here. That he'd attacked her, robbed her, worse. If she did, he'd be dead before dark tomorrow.

"How could I be so blind?" She glanced back at the car, across the beltway.

"Lena, I don't want your money," he repeated. "You crashed your car. I didn't even know it was you."

"And once you found out it was, it didn't even cross your mind you might get a reward?"

It might have crossed his mind.

"I just wanted to make sure you were okay. Not everyone thinks in terms of payout."

Her hip cocked to the side. She crossed her arms over her chest. "They do where I'm from."

"Well, I guess you left for a reason, didn't you?"

He felt like an ass when her eyes glassed over with tears.

"Lena, I . . ." He took slow steps toward her. "Look over there." He pointed across the beltway toward Bakerstown. The lights in the center of the city still twinkled. "I used to live out there. My brother and I went to school, and came home, and did homework, and hung out with our friends. We ate dinner together at night like a family. And then Cherish got sick, and my brother and I had to work. We couldn't afford our place anymore, so we moved out to Metaltown. Sometimes I come out here, and look across the bridge, and just wish . . . I don't know, I just think about those times, okay? That's what I was doing tonight. Just walking and thinking." He swallowed a breath. He hadn't told anyone that, not even Ty.

She studied him for a long time. He would have cut off his own finger to read her mind.

"It's not always better over there," she said finally.

He glanced over. From this side he could see the bruise on her cheek more clearly. "I hope you hit him back."

Her posture went more rigid, if that was possible.

"Hit who back?"

Right. Pretend nothing had happened. She was just like Ty when she'd lost a fight.

"Here, face me." He turned her, feeling her tense beneath his hands. "Gloves off."

"*No.*" She clasped her hands behind her back.

His brows lifted. "Okay, gloves on. No problem. Lift your hands up, like this." He showed her how to guard her face, and slowly, she mimicked his stance. "Elbows in, stagger your feet. There you go." She was a quick study.

"Now swing."

"What?" She dropped her arms. "I'm not going to hit you."

"I know." He smirked. "You couldn't if you tried."

Her eyes narrowed. She lifted her hands back up and swung, nearly tipping over. He caught her around the waist and righted her. "Told you."

She swung again.

"Thumbs in," he cued, dodging to the side. "Follow through with your shoulder." She bounced a little, trying to copy him. Cute. "Come on," he said. "I know three-year-olds that can scrap better than you."

She swung again, dropping her guard hand, and he reached in and tapped her once on the nose. "Got you."

Her eyes narrowed and her nostrils flared. She locked her jaw, and the growl that came from her throat nearly made him laugh out loud. But she jumped at him with a burst of speed, and kneed him hard, right between the legs.

For thirty seconds there was nothing but pain. The worst kind.

The kind that made you wish you'd never been born. When he opened his eyes he was on his knees and elbows, trying not to puke.

"I got you," she said.

He winced. "You got me."

* * *

As they entered the heart of Metaltown, he made her walk close. He kept to the more heavily traveled streets, but hugged the shadows, not wanting anyone to see the way she was dressed. Mostly just junkies were out now, trying to scrounge up a way to stay warm. They weren't generally trouble.

"I'm going to put my arm around you," he said.

She missed a step. "Why?"

"So people know you're with me."

She stared at him, but before he could explain that she didn't exactly blend in, she nodded.

He liked the way her small body fit against his. She smelled like vanilla, sharp and sweet. He rubbed one hand up and down her bicep, feeling her withdraw just slightly from his touch, then settle into him. She did a good job keeping up, and didn't once complain about the heels on those shoes she wore. Maybe she was less fragile than he thought.

"It's rude to stare, you know," she said, without looking up at him.

"Not where I'm from," he said. "Take it as a compliment."

He was careful not to be so obvious after that.

They came to Market Alley, and Colin walked faster, refusing to look at Jed's office in the back. The Brotherhood would absorb Small Parts tomorrow. It should have made him happy, but it didn't. It stuck in his jaw like sour candy. Jed was a bastard and a liar. He wasn't one of them. He may have come from the streets, but he didn't honor the code of it.

He wondered again who had ratted them out.

They rounded the corner between the two brick buildings. The doors to the basement apartment were down a few steps, and metal fire escapes rose above on both sides.

"Look familiar?" he asked her.

She glanced around, relaxing a little when she saw the way was empty. "This is where we met. Is this where you live?"

He scratched his head. "Not exactly." Part of him wanted to bring her home, but it probably would have run her off. Shima's place was nicer than his. Less crowded. Cleaner. More what Lena was used to.

Who was he kidding? Nothing here was even close to what she was used to.

"I'm not staying with you? I mean . . . I didn't mean to assume . . ." She wriggled. "You can let go of me now."

She wanted him to stay.

"This is the safest place I know," he said. He didn't want to let her slide away. Soon, she'd realize he was trouble, that Jed was after him, and that he'd tried to get the others to stand against Small Parts. There'd be no more backseat chats then. No more talks on the beltway. No more forgetting, just for a little while, the heavy weight of Metaltown.

He knocked once on the door before he said something stupid.

"Wait. Before we go in, I need to tell you something," she said, fidgeting from side to side. "Something bad."

"And things were going so well." He took a deep breath, bracing for what was to come.

"My father was angry that I met with you this afternoon. Otto told him, and . . . he assumed things had happened that certainly had not happened."

Colin tilted his head. "What kind of things?"

"*Things*. You know." She circled her hands. "Anyway, I . . . I think Otto might try to take it out on you."

He'd like to see him try. Still, a knot tied in his gut. "I can handle myself."

"He might fire you," she said in small voice. "I tried to tell them the truth—that I called on you, and that you didn't do anything wrong—but they wouldn't listen. I'm so sorry."

He thought about Small Parts, about Jed Schultz and Minnick. About Ty and how no one else would stand up for her. "I'm probably going to get fired anyway," he said.

Her chin shot up. "You shouldn't go back. It's not safe."

"You're worried about me."

"I am not," she said, frowning. "Don't be silly."

Slowly, gently, he touched her face, pressing his cool skin against the heated patch below her eye. Was that why she'd been hurt? Because of him? No one but Ty had stuck their neck out for him before.

"I don't have much of a choice." If he didn't go to work, Otto and Lena's father would use it as proof that Colin was hiding something. Were they right? He'd broken the rules the second he'd offered to bring her here. Anyone in their right mind would have taken her straight home.

Her eyes were so bright when she was angry, and her cheek was even softer than he thought it would be. He moved closer, feeling the warmth of her, hearing her breath catch. Her lips parted.

The door behind him swung out, and Shima blinked at him. "For God's sake, Colin, it's the middle of the night." She pulled her shawl closer around her shoulders. "If it's Hayden again, I swear I'll beat that boy myself . . ."

Lena stepped out from behind Colin, her mouth open in surprise. "Shima?"

20

TY

Colin hadn't gone home. Ty waited outside his place for an hour before heading to Lacey's, but no one there had seem him either. She felt sick over what had happened. She'd known Jed was trouble from the beginning, but Colin hadn't believed her. Now he was on the warpath, stopping payments to Colin's mother, forcing the workers at Small Parts to join the Brotherhood. He was more dangerous than she'd ever imagined.

Her stomach clenched again. She'd known he was trouble, and she'd mouthed off to him anyway—in public, no less. Now Colin's family was going to pay for it.

Not if she could help it.

She was going back to Jed Schultz. She was going to do whatever it took to make things right. He wanted her to apologize? Fine. She'd eat crow. She didn't have to believe it.

She walked fast back toward Market Alley, pausing when she saw a man coming up from Factory Row. He was broad in the shoulders and looked to be sober from his even gait, which meant he'd be harder to beat in a fight. With her eye she couldn't chance the trouble. Ducking into the shadows, she held her breath and waited as he approached from across the street.

Something moved behind her. A scuffle on the sidewalk brought the knife from her belt to her hand. She stayed low, peering into the darkness. A bottle rolled across the hard ground. Maybe it was a cat on the prowl. It was hard to tell with half her vision.

Whatever it was moved closer.

One in front, one behind. A quick glance up the road revealed that the man was still far enough away not to have seen her. Run or hide—she had to choose fast. Making her decision, she charged the shadows behind her, heart in her throat, hoping to catch whatever tailed her by surprise.

She collided with a boy almost half her size and pinned him to the ground.

"Get off!" he squeaked, reeking of garbage.

"*Chip?*"

"Course it's Chip. What are you doin' out here?"

Ty rolled off to the side, pulling him into a sunken doorway. "Shh!"

"I looked for you at Beggar's Square, but you never came." He wiggled in her grasp.

"Shut. Up." He finally went still.

The man up the street slowed, and Ty could make out his white chem plant uniform pants below his coat. He passed the Stamping Mill, pausing to gaze in their direction. A moment later he continued on, disappearing around the corner of the building toward the Brotherhood office.

"Who is that?" Chip whispered.

"Hayden," whispered Ty. Why was Colin's brother coming to see Jed this late? She knew Hayden had gotten into business with him; that's why she and Colin had gone to Bakerstown in the first place. Despite the knowing, his presence here, now, didn't sit well with her.

"Go back to the Board and Care," she told Chip.

"No," he said stubbornly. "I got your back."

The reference to his pledge to street code pulled at something deep in her chest.

"Chip . . ."

"You're tracking that guy, huh? Why you following him? Is he going to the Brotherhood?"

She shook her head. "I don't have time for this. Stay back here."

She kept low and ran across the street, staying beyond the stretch of the yellow streetlights. She inched around the corner but the way was clear. The carts from the day were absent. The door to the Brotherhood was wide open, the lights within burning. Curiosity taking over, she tiptoed closer, catching laughter from within.

And footsteps from behind.

Go, she mouthed to the kid. He mocked her and continued on, holding an old rusty fork in one hand like a shank.

Half of her meant to turn back. If Chip had her back, she had his, and this put him in danger. She should have taken him to the Board and Care and dumped his skinny ass in the kids' room. But she remembered her last time there and wondered if he wasn't safer by her side.

Giving up, she crept forward, honing in on the voices. Holding her breath, she looked around the corner. Three jackets hung on a standing rack in the hallway. Cigarette smoke gathered at the ceiling. Against all good judgment, she snuck inside.

"What's wrong, boy? Run yourself dry already?" Jed asked. "What do you have for me tonight?"

"Nothing." Ty's hand closed around her knife at the sound of Hayden's voice.

"Oh, come on, you know that's not how it works. Is your brother planning to organize or not?"

"He's not doing anything."

"That's not what you said last night."

"I was wrong last night. Listen, Jed . . ."

"Mr. Schultz," corrected Jed. Hayden cleared his throat.

"Mr. Schultz, whatever you've got going on with Small Parts, Colin's got nothing to do with it. I was off last night. I wasn't thinking clear."

"And you are now, is that right?"

There was a pause, and then a crack as something hit the wall. "We can't have a charter organize at Small Parts, do you understand?" Jed's voice was low, menacing.

"I understand," choked Hayden. Ty was torn. Colin's brother was being roughed up, and he would have counted on her to step in. But if Hayden was the leak, she couldn't possibly help him. He'd ratted them out. He'd put Colin in danger.

Her loyalty was to Colin. Always.

"I'm not certain you do," said Jed. "Those kids build parts of bombs. The steel mill builds parts of the same bombs. The chem plant, where you work? Guess where that nitro goes?"

"Into a bomb, sir."

"The same bomb," Jed told him. "Every factory in Metaltown works together to make one product. So do you know what will happen if those kids refuse to work? Every other factory in town will have to stop production until we find replacements. This town will shut down. Hell, I might as well gift wrap it for McNulty."

Another crack, and she could hear Hayden's groan and labored breaths.

"So they all join the Brotherhood," he gasped. "They get what they want, you get their dues. Everyone's happy."

"This is what happens when you take too much nitro, boys," said Jed. A few other disembodied voices chuckled at the joke. "Nobody's happy unless Hampton's happy, and Hampton's not interested in giving kids *rights*. He's interested in profit."

"But he supports the Brotherhood everywhere else."

"Wrong," said Jed. "He supports me. You think a rich mug like Hampton couldn't shell out double for every one of those workers? But he doesn't have to, because I make sure his workers think they've got as good as it gets. He pays me good money to keep them quiet. Whatever it takes."

Ty's brows scrunched together. Jed Schultz was taking bribes from the Hamptons? That didn't make sense. He was supposed to be on the side of the workers—a representative of the people, not the other way around.

But he was a greasy liar; she'd known that from the moment she'd first laid eyes on him. He was taking money from both sides—dues from the workers, and payments from the boss to stay in his employees' good graces. He'd been keeping Colin's family quiet with green to buy new clothes and clean water. Gifts, so they never questioned his loyalty. She remembered the fear in that Bakerstown man's face when she and Colin had run Jed's errand. What had happened to them for refusing the money?

"And you're going to stay quiet too, aren't you, Hayden?" continued Jed after another crack against the wall.

"Yes, sir. Of course, sir."

"Because you know what happens to your little brother if you don't?"

Ty jerked, then froze when Chip pulled down hard on her arm. She glanced his way for the first time, seeing that he'd emptied the coat pockets from the rack, and held three wallets in his little hands.

Swearing under her breath, she grabbed one, ripped it open and lifted the bills. He followed her lead, replacing the wallets back in the pockets.

She'd heard enough. She had to find Colin fast.

Before Hayden was turned out, she'd stuffed the green in her coat, grabbed Chip's collar, and pulled him outside. They didn't stop running until they hit St. Mary's.

21

LENA

Lena sat on the edge of a sagging couch, tapping her heels. Her eyes fixed on the peeling wallpaper opposite her, and the brown water stain that ran from the ceiling to the floor. The room was small, much like the entryway at her estate, but with two couches crammed within, and a patchwork quilt tossed across the floor. Two children were sprawled out in the middle of it, one no more than a few months, the other a toddler. Both were fast asleep.

It made sense that Shima still watched children—she'd been Lena's nanny for as long as she could remember. But for some reason seeing these children made her insides prickle. It felt like she and Otto had been replaced somehow.

Shima came out of her bedroom with a steaming mug. She'd changed from her nightclothes into a shabby black dress, and combed her hair. Lena hadn't meant to intrude. She'd never felt that way with Shima before.

"It's just hot water," said Shima tentatively. "I know you like steamed milk before bed . . . at least, you used to . . . but I'm fresh out."

Lena doubted she was "fresh out." By the looks of this place, she didn't even have an icebox. Lena shifted, the borrowed clothes rough against her skin. Shima had made her change when she'd begun picking shards of glass out of her sweater.

"Thank you," whispered Lena, afraid of waking the children. Her old nanny sat beside her, a few feet away, and passed over the mug. Her gaze lingered on Lena's dirty black gloves.

"Are your hands still . . ."

"They're fine," said Lena quickly. "They're just cold, that's all."

Shima jumped up and returned with a knit quilt. She mimed wrapping it around Lena's shoulders, and Lena nodded, unable to sit back and relax. For the last hour they'd teetered on the edge of formality, neither sure how to begin. The last time they'd seen each other had been one of the worst days of Lena's life. That was, until today.

"A car wreck." Shima shook her head. "I can't believe your father let you drive alone. Thank goodness Colin was there."

"Yes." Thank goodness Colin had not disagreed when Lena had said she'd simply been out for a drive.

Shima slowly reached for her cheek, brushing her thumb along the bruise. Her look was not that of concern, but pity, and Lena suspected she knew the mark had not been caused by any accident.

"You're so lovely," Shima said. "More lovely than I remember, and I thought that was impossible."

That was all it took for Lena to unravel. She hiccuped a sob, the tears gathering in her tired eyes and spilling down her cheeks.

"Oh, Lena." Shima wrapped her arms around her, and for a moment, Lena was a child. Otto had just bullied her but it was all right. It was all okay now because Shima was here and she would fix it.

She didn't need to explain what had happened; with Shima she never would. She buried her face against the woman's neck and cried until all the tears were gone, and even then she didn't pull back. She stayed in her arms, and found comfort in her soft hum, and the gentle stroking of her hair.

"Why don't you rest," Shima said after a long while. "It's late, and you've had quite a day. First thing tomorrow we'll get you back home, safe and sound."

Lena pulled away, feeling the cold air brush her cheek.

"I'm not going back." She hadn't known it was true until that moment.

Shima's golden eyes, the eyes Lena had always trusted, grew wide. "Lena, you have to go back."

"I can't." Lena felt her throat closing. She sipped the hot water and it burned her tongue. "Maybe I could stay here with you? Just for a little while. If it's all right, I mean."

Shima scooted closer, the crow's feet around her eyes even more pronounced. She hadn't had those before, nor had she ever been so thin. "Your father must be so worried."

"He isn't, trust me."

Shima's thumb pressed against her temple, something she used to do when Otto had pushed her too far. "Your father can be *hard-headed*." She chose the word carefully. "But he's your father."

Which meant what, exactly? That it was okay that he was a traitor? That it was fine for him to strike her? Even if Shima didn't know the details of what had brought them back together, Lena didn't like what she implied. Just because he was her father didn't mean he could do whatever he liked without consequence. If he'd taught her anything, he'd taught her that.

She stood up, looking for somewhere to place the mug. She never should have come. Colin had been trying to get rid of her, and while Shima's care may have been comforting once, it was not anymore.

"I should go." Where, she had no idea. She'd run out of options. She hadn't had many to start with.

Shima stood, reaching out and taking her hands. "Stay. We'll talk about this in the morning, okay? Just rest now. We'll figure it all out."

Her grip was gentle, thumbs moving over Lena's wrists. Her smile was soft and sincere. Lena was exhausted, and despite her pride, Shima was right. She needed rest to form a plan.

Slowly, she sat, then curled into a ball on the thin cushion. She rested her head on the hard arm of the couch, and let Shima pull the blanket down beneath her feet.

"It'll be all right," Shima said. When Lena's eyes were closed, she went to her bedroom, leaving the door cracked. Lena could hear the whine of the mattress as she sat upon it, but though she listened, she never heard the blankets move, or the rustle of sheets as Shima lay down.

Tired as she was, it was a long time before she finally fell asleep.

* * *

In the morning Shima made porridge that was so bland Lena could barely swallow it. She wondered what her father and brother were eating. Omelets, made from eggs imported from their farmlands outside the city. Grapefruit and freshly squeezed juice. All tested by a servant to ensure their safety. The three of them would sit at the table, each consumed by their electronic readers, waiting for the cookstaff to clear their settings. She wondered what Darcy would think when she didn't show up for tutoring. She'd probably be relieved.

Instead, Lena was surrounded by children. Two more came in the early hours of morning, jumping and screaming as if they'd woken that way. One boy pulled another girl's hair, and Shima made him sit in the corner. A little girl played with a rope doll—the same doll Lena had in her coat pocket, folded neatly in the corner. The same doll she refused to take out.

Just after breakfast a knock came at the door. Shima made her way there, a child attached to one leg. She squeezed Lena's shoulder as she walked by, but it settled her stomach only a little. The long night was over, and the morning had brought even deeper uncertainty. She didn't know where she would sleep tonight, but it wouldn't be here. This house was too full. She was in the way.

Besides, if her father knew she'd come here—to a woman he'd dismissed from his service—Shima would be in trouble. Lena didn't know what he'd do, but after their fight yesterday, he seemed capable of anything. It was better if she didn't linger.

"Miss me, Shima?" Colin came in like he owned the place, and was immediately attacked by one of the children—a boy named Ben, if she remembered correctly. Colin kissed Shima on the cheek and hoisted a giggling Ben over one shoulder.

"Oh, because it's been *so* long." Shima rolled her eyes. "You want some breakfast?"

"Sure." Colin tossed Ben down on the couch and grinned at Lena. Her heart stuttered, remembering last night too clearly—everything from the way he'd taught her to throw a punch to how his fingertips had brushed her cheek outside Shima's door—before she reminded herself it was just a smile. It didn't mean anything. It shouldn't have meant anything anyway, because she had about a hundred bigger things to worry about today, including finding food and a place to sleep tonight.

He placed himself in her line of vision, refusing to let her avoid his gaze, and she remembered other things, too. Like how her father had accused her of rolling around in the back of his car. Though he'd been wrong, and though she didn't want to care what he thought, she still placed the folded blanket on her lap as a barrier.

"How you holding up?" he asked.

"Fine," she said. "And you?"

"Never better." Shima handed him a bowl, and Lena couldn't hide the cringe when he stuffed a big, heaping spoonful of gruel in his mouth.

She lowered her voice. "Have you thought more about what I said last night?"

He leaned down conspiratorially, eyes flicking from side to side. "The part where you called me charming?"

"The part where I told you to stay clear of the factory."

He took another bite. "Right, that part. I thought about it." She waited expectantly while he took another bite. Could he be serious about nothing?

"I'm still going," he said finally.

"You need to reconsider."

"You're cute when you're worked up, you know that?"

He was messing around again. Still, Lena fixed her hair, wishing she had a comb.

"Colin," warned Shima from across the room. She was eyeing him like any of the other children who'd broken the rules.

Colin tapped the spoon against his bowl. "There's some stuff going on today. Something I need to do." A shadow of doubt passed over his face.

"What's going on?" She hadn't heard Otto mention anything new happening at the factory, not that he would anyway.

He didn't meet her gaze.

"Nothing you need to worry about."

She planted her fists on her hips. "No? And why is that?"

"Because it involves the workers."

"I see," she said. "And you think I wouldn't understand because I'm not a worker."

"I think you got a different factory tour than the rest of us."

Her chin lifted. "Mr. Minnick showed me everything."

He laughed, bringing a flood of heat up her neck. "Aren't you always on your best behavior when the boss is around?"

She wouldn't know. She'd never had a job before—not before she began researching a role in Hampton Industries anyway. But she knew the way she acted when her father was in the room was vastly different than the way she was with Darcy, and if this was what Colin meant, she had a keen desire to see the differences for herself.

"What exactly goes on when I'm not there?" she asked.

"Believe me," he said. "You don't want to know."

Her curiosity deepened, along with the lines between her brows. "Is there trouble at the factory with the workers? Is that what you mean? Trouble with . . . your salaries, perhaps?" She visualized the forms she'd seen in her study, the discrepancies in pay. In her mind, she cursed Otto again.

He took another bite. Swallowed.

"Is the management doing something they shouldn't?"

His head tilted slightly. "Now why would you say that?"

It was her father's factory, one she'd wanted to run one day. She knew he was making terrible, dangerous decisions when it came to sales, but had thought that Otto's neglect was the extent of the problems on-site. But Colin was alluding to more issues, maybe even larger than what she'd already discovered, and though part of her knew it was unwise to probe after how she'd left things in the River District, she felt a burden of responsibility to know just how bad things were.

"I'm going with you," she said, placing her back to Shima.

Any amusement in Colin's face faded. "Now *that* is a really bad idea."

"Why? It's my factory."

"Exactly." He lowered his voice. "What do you think your father will do if he sees me bring you in?"

"He never goes there. And Otto won't even be awake for another two hours. Besides, I'll be going in with you. As a worker."

"As a worker," he repeated, dumbstruck. "You want to work at Small Parts."

I want to see what you see. She put her hands on her hips. "You don't think I can handle it?"

You wouldn't last five minutes, her father had said.

"Umm . . ." Colin tapped his spoon against the bowl again. "I don't think I said that."

"Well, lucky for me it doesn't matter. I don't need your permission." It irritated her that he thought she couldn't do what he did. She might not have lived in Metaltown, but the River District wasn't exactly the safest place either.

"You should stay here." His voice was harder without the sarcasm.

"Lena's going home today," said Shima, approaching them.

Her blood began to run hot. "I am not going home. And I'm not staying here. I am perfectly capable of making my own decisions."

Colin and Shima looked to each other for support.

"I'm going with you," Lena said. "That's final."

* * *

She followed him through the employee entrance and into a dingy locker room that smelled strongly of body odor. The place was crowded and people kept bumping into her without any awareness of personal space. A few of them said hello to Colin—a dark-skinned boy about her age that he called Zeke, and a little kid who said someone named Ty was looking for him. Colin kept chewing his pinky nail, something she realized he only did when he was nervous.

It made her realize how truly dangerous this could be for him. In all her life, she'd never considered that she might be more dangerous to a boy from Metaltown than he was to her.

He stripped down to the thermal he wore on the floor, and when he lifted his arms over his head the hem of his shirt rose, revealing a pale, smooth belt of skin. Even after it was gone, the image still lingered inside of her. Though it was warm, she refused to take off her borrowed sweater, as if she had been the one exposed.

"Stay close to me," he said between his teeth. "Follow me when I clock in."

She kept on his heels, heart pounding as she passed the check-in station. Her eyes stayed down as she made it through the metal detector. A thrill filled her; she'd never imagined in a million years that she'd be sneaking into her own factory. Now she could see exactly what it was like to work under Otto's rule, and he wouldn't be able to deny it later.

If she saw him later.

She still hadn't figured out where she would go next. When she'd left the house, she'd left all her belongings. She didn't have money to go to a hotel, or rent an apartment, or hire a car. She didn't even have money for food.

Surely she couldn't live and work in Metaltown. Her stomach

sunk at the thought. Unless she went home to face her father, she didn't have much of a choice.

The line moved forward, and soon they'd reached the foreman.

She'd braided her hair back, and wasn't wearing any makeup, but even so, her pulse spiked when the foreman snagged her wrist. She looked down at his hand, fighting the urge to shake him off.

"Who are you?" he asked.

She slipped free, hung her head. "Mary, sir," she said, coming up quickly with the name. "From . . . the uniform factory."

"Uniform factory?" the foreman mocked, making her wish she'd said another division. "You blind? This is Small Parts."

Colin stopped in his tracks and sent a wary glance over his shoulder.

"They sent me as an extra," she said quickly, keeping her eyes down. "They said you needed more hands on the line because there was more work coming through."

The story fell from her lips as if it were practiced, but she wasn't even sure she was using the terms correctly. Still, she knew how to play a role under pressure. She'd entertained her father's party guests, after all, and they were some of the most dangerous men in the whole country.

"A sub you mean?" Colin suggested, glaring over his shoulder. "They send you to sub in for someone?"

"Call it what you like," she tossed back. "I just do what I'm told."

Minnick's face had seemed stuck in a frown, but at this, the lines around his mouth and eyes relaxed. "You're damn right you do. Hear that, rats? Mary here's gonna do what she's told, just like the rest of you."

There were some mutters ahead, but no one looked back.

The foreman pulled up his pants, but his belt buckle disappeared below his paunch as soon as he released them. "Haven't hired a re-placement for fuses. You work hard today, I might consider keeping you on. *If* you make quota, understand? No messing around. I don't know how they do it at the uniform division, but here, you don't pull your weight, we say good-bye."

"Understood, sir. I won't mess around, sir. Thank you."

He grinned, revealing yellow, crooked teeth. He snapped his fingers at Colin. "You show her how it's done. She falls behind, it's on you, got it?"

"Come on," Colin grumbled, motioning for her to follow.

The main room opened up to the floor. The machines were already loud and cranking—she remembered the volume from her last time here—and it was already warm. As they went down the stairs, it occurred to her that she'd made a huge mistake. She didn't belong here. She wasn't trained. She'd never worked a day of labor in her life.

But when she thought of home, and the things her father and brother had done, she thought maybe she didn't belong there, either.

Colin motioned her to the station where she'd seen him before. Wincing at the memory of firing the girl, she ducked under the belt and took a place beside him, opposite a big boy Colin called Henry.

"Mary," Lena said, introducing herself. "I'm a sub from the uniform division."

Colin quirked a brow, impressed.

"They all look as good as you over there?" Henry asked.

Lena's mouth fell open. Colin chuckled.

"What?" Henry grinned. "Just asking."

"Shouldn't you be getting back to Plastics?" Colin asked him.

He smiled again at Lena. "I will soon as the boss tells me to, and not a moment sooner."

Colin just shook his head.

He showed her how to wire the detonators by sticking a small copper wire into a narrow metal rod. He asked her again to take off her gloves but she refused. Still, she wished she could—her hands were sweating fiercely within them, and they made the task cumbersome. For every piece she completed, Colin finished five. Frustrated, she tried to pick up the pace, but she kept screwing up.

"Lose the gloves or we won't make quota," he said.

She locked her jaw and ignored him.

The heat increased. She longed to take off her sweater, but Henry kept staring, and winking whenever she caught his gaze.

At the end of the second hour she stretched her back. Standing on the cement floor had made her heels begin to ache, and she longed for a glass of water.

"When's our break?" she asked Colin.

"You had one," he said. "All last night."

"What about lunch?"

"Sorry, Mary," he said. "No lunch today."

Her mouth grew dry. A water girl came through, ogling Colin unabashedly. Lena passed; there were clearly things floating in the jug the girl had strapped over one shoulder. She might have fished it straight from the river.

Lena's head was pounding.

"You all right?" Colin asked. One brow, the one divided by a scar, arched. She hated that he was waiting for her to give up.

She wiped the sweat from her forehead and pushed on. "That area behind the curtain, what is that?"

"The hot room," he said. "Don't go near it. It'll singe your hair off."

"Don't tell me what I can and can't do," she answered, temper on edge. But she worried what he meant.

She waited for noon, then drifted nonchalantly toward the hot room. Thick plastic strips blocked a clear view, and she blinked back the tangy burst of chemicals that assaulted her senses as she drew the strips back. Inside were a dozen workers near her age, dressed the same as Colin. They stood around a table where a line of metal cylinders waited for their unprotected hands. She opened her mouth in shock, tasting the sour air. No gloves. No masks. Her father would have to be informed immediately. This was unacceptable, inhuman treatment.

A thought sank its teeth into her: what if he already knew?

And then, as she watched, a boy darted to the corner, leaned over a trash can, and vomited. Less than a minute later, he was back at his station.

"Does this look like social hour, sweetbread?"

Lena spun, the hard plastic sheaths slapping together behind her. Mr. Minnick glared down at her, his face red. Immediately she lowered her gaze, skirting by him.

Don't recognize me. Please don't recognize me.

He didn't. And not just because of the way she was dressed, or her disheveled appearance. Something was off about him. As she passed by she caught a strong whiff of something like cigar smoke, but more potent.

She shot across the room to go to the bathroom, but two other girls had the same idea, and when Mr. Minnick caught her in line he locked them all out with a sneer and a reminder that every minute wasted belonged to him. She dragged herself back to their station.

The minutes drew together. Her vision became blurry. She would have killed for a cold glass of water and a sandwich. The heat became unbearable, and the stench of working bodies and chemicals that infused every part of Metaltown made it even worse. Her stomach turned.

"It's like this all the time?" she asked, but she already knew the answer.

"Welcome to Small Parts," said Henry. "You don't look so good."

"Go home, Lena," whispered Colin. He looked angry. "Tell Minnick who you are. He'll call your family."

I have nowhere else to go. "I'm not leaving."

He shook his head.

The wires poked holes in her thin gloves and the sensitive pads of her fingers bled through. She didn't stop. The ache between her temples turned to a throb. She didn't stop. Quitting time came and went. She didn't stop.

Nearly two hours after the plant should have closed, Mr. Minnick reappeared at the top of the stairs.

"On the floor!" shouted someone from her left. The blond boy she'd seen before, working in Batteries. He hadn't noticed her when they'd run into each other this morning.

"On the floor!" Colin called on. Lena's back objected when she straightened.

Two men appeared at the top of the stairs. Mr. Minnick, and a man with long hair that she recognized from her father's party. The one her brother had paid for what she'd assumed was a gambling debt.

"Listen up, rats!" called Mr. Minnick. "You all know Schultz is here to talk to you about the Brotherhood, so don't look so surprised. Wrap your crap up, and get your scrawny asses in line."

One by one the machines shut off. Lena blinked back the dizziness, and pushed away when Colin placed a steadying hand on her elbow.

"Are you done proving you're tough?" he asked.

"Not quite," she said, still wavering.

He pointed her toward the stairs. "Go home, Lena. Things are about to get ugly."

She mustered her best pithy look and shot it his way. What was she, a child? Exhausted, she followed him up the stairs, straining on every step. She was starving, and wanted nothing more than to fall into her bed at home and sleep. Anger scalded her insides. She couldn't do anything right, not even day labor.

The boy she'd recognized from the battery department approached. The sweat made his short blond hair look crunchy. He glanced back at her. "Who's she?"

"Just a sub," mumbled Colin.

She kept her eyes trained on the backs of his heels, relieved when the boy took Colin's word for it. If she could just get past them, to the bathroom, to the foreman's office, *anywhere,* she could hide. Wait until they were all gone. Then figure out what to do.

"I thought Minnick hated Schultz," said the battery boy to Zeke.

"He does," said Colin. "If we sign up for the Brotherhood, Minnick won't get to work us to the bone like he likes."

Lena wondered what the Brotherhood was. It sounded like a cult. She'd seen the man beside the foreman—Schultz—but never had heard his name associated with a Brotherhood before.

Zeke leaned in, lowering his voice. "I heard Minnick hates Schultz because Schultz beat the holy hell outta him when he was a shell."

"Minnick was a shell?" Colin asked.

Battery Boy's face scrunched. "What's a shell?"

"A fill-in worker," said Zeke. "No skills, no nothin'. Just some bum off the street who's so hard up he's willing to work for half our wages."

"Half of nothing . . . ," Battery Boy mused. "I think that's still nothing, Zeke."

She wondered what they did make—in all her research she hadn't found a pay scale. Since she was technically a substitute on the line today, that should have entitled her to wages at the end of the day, but something told her not to hold her breath.

"What happened with Schultz?" Colin asked as they crowded forward.

"Schultz led the Stamping Mill press way back when, and while they weren't working Hampton hired all these replacement shells to do their jobs for cheap. Minnick was one of them. Schultz and his crew worked them all over pretty good, and there's been bad blood ever since."

"So Schultz can press, but we can't?" asked Colin. Lena perked up. Colin wanted to stage a protest? She felt a bite of betrayal, but could only blame herself. She was the one who'd walked into this situation blind.

"We don't want to," said Battery Boy. "Come on, leave it alone already."

Colin grumbled something as they got in line. Lena knew she should leave; she didn't really work here, and besides, Mr. Schultz might recognize her. Still, interest had her standing close behind Colin.

"Doesn't look like they hate each other anymore," commented Battery Boy.

"Someone's got his fix, that's why," said Zeke under his breath.

As Lena drew closer she saw what he meant. Mr. Minnick's eyes were bloodshot and too open. His cheeks were too rosy. His right shoulder kept twitching. Was he using drugs? At *work*? Automatically, she recorded this in her mental files, wondering if a time would come that she could tell Otto or even her father.

"Mr. Walter," called Mr. Schultz, who had set up a table beside Minnick's office. "Why don't you come to the front of the line?"

She saw Colin's shoulders tense. She dodged through the noisy crowd after him, grabbing onto the back of his shirt. "You were going to organize a press?"

He breathed in slowly. "I told you not to come today."

Her hand dropped. He'd had plenty of opportunities to tell her this and had knowingly hid it. It wasn't even like he could play it off that it wouldn't matter to her, or that it wasn't her business either. Her father *owned* this factory, and he knew it.

"You lied to me," she said. "You told me what was going on involved the workers, not management." A press directly involved her family—it meant work would come to a *halt*, and that was a big problem for Hampton Industries.

It shouldn't have mattered. She didn't know him. He had no reason to show her loyalty. But still, she felt like he'd left her out in the cold.

"I didn't lie." He paused just before reaching the front desk and faced her fully. His gaze reached deep inside of her, until she felt exposed, like everyone here could see who she was. "I just didn't tell you everything. I liked it when you didn't hate me."

What was that supposed to mean?

A second later he reached the table. The line behind him went silent.

He cleared his throat. "Thanks, Mr. Schultz, but I can't join the Brotherhood. Not when I can get someone to watch my back for free."

Lena's throat was parched, her cheeks too hot. Everyone was still staring since Colin had spoken to her. Who was Colin talking about? *What* was he talking about?

A girl with small, mousy features appeared in front of her, and as Lena watched, her face fell out of focus.

"Are you okay?" the girl asked, her voice far away.

"I'm just hot," Lena said. But the room was already spinning, and before she could grab onto something solid, she fell backwards into Zeke.

22

COLIN

Jed's lips twisted into a strange, satisfied smirk. Colin returned his stare, unwilling to be the first to look away.

"Sign the form, Mr. Walter." With an ink pen, he tapped the clipboard, then laid both on the table.

"No thanks." The act of defying the most formidable man in Metaltown filled Colin with a dark, dreadful power. It hummed through his veins like the last moments before a fight.

Jed's smile faded. "There are consequences to every action."

Colin rested his knuckles on the table. "Not many people tell you no, do they?"

An image of Gabe Wokowski's father picking money up off the cluttered floor shot to the forefront of his mind. At the time he hadn't understood how anyone could turn down so much green. He did now. Everything had a price.

He caught movement behind him out of the corner of his eye. Several people had begun talking all at once. He hadn't been sure how the others would take his refusal to join, and turned quickly, ready for anything. Before he could make out what was going on, Jed had reached across the table and snagged his forearm. His eyes were beady with anger.

"I'm offering you the Brotherhood's protection, Colin. You'll keep your job, and get all the pay you earn. No more stealing pigeons from the corner cart. I'll make sure your family's taken care of. All of them."

Colin felt his confidence waver. "How do I know you're good for it?"

Jed relaxed his grip. "You'll just have to trust me."

Trust. He trusted Ty. He trusted his family. They'd never threaten him if he didn't do what they wanted. Trusting Jed felt about as solid as trusting Minnick.

But if there was even a chance Jed was telling the truth, he was crazy to turn it down.

"Colin!" Zeke called.

He glanced back, then did a double take. Zeke was hoisting someone up—a girl, limp as a rag doll. Lena, he realized a moment later. Her head hung forward, sweaty strands of hair clinging to her pallid skin. Cold filled Colin's lungs. He jerked out of Jed's grasp and lunged toward them, sliding under Lena's shoulder.

"She's asking for you," Zeke said, brows scrunched together. "Who is she?"

Martin and Agnes looked to him with wary curiosity.

Colin tilted Lena's face up to his. Her eyes were open but her gaze was blank. She blinked.

"Come on," he said, taking her from Zeke.

"Wait!" Chip succeeded in pushing through the line and ran straight for Colin.

"Get back in line, rat!" belted Minnick. The foreman grabbed the kid by the collar and shoved him into Zeke and Martin. Chip hit the floor with a small cry.

Biting his tongue, Colin readjusted Lena's arm over his shoulder, and led her to the door. He'd deal with the Brotherhood, and Minnick, later.

"I'll be by later to settle your family's debts," said Jed as Colin passed. He didn't even glance over. Colin paused, his insides turning to ice.

Zeke, who was next in line, stepped nervously to the front. He glanced up at Colin, apology in his eyes. Zeke had his sister to look out for; what did Colin expect him to do?

What had he expected any of them to do?

* * *

Ten minutes later he'd traded his gloves to Hayak for a mug of water from the rotisserie's steamer. Lena sat on the curb beside the cart, elbows on her knees. Her quaking hands spilled liquid all down her chin and the front of her sweat-drenched sweater, but she didn't move to mop it up. When she'd finished gulping it down, she wiped her mouth with Colin's scarf, and sheepishly passed it back to him.

"What were you thinking?" Colin snapped. "I told you not to come. And when you did, I told you to drink. And when you didn't, I told you to leave. And you didn't listen to a damn thing I said, and now look at you."

She shot up, hands balled into fists. "Thank you for pointing out how stupid I look. As if I couldn't figure that much out on my own."

"How stupid you *look*?" He leaned over her, blood burning. "You have no idea what's going on, do you? Of course you don't. This was all some game to you. Play poor for a day. See how bad it is. Then go home to your big house and your rich friends and pretend it never happened."

"You don't know me." Her voice hitched. "You don't know any-thing!"

"I know this is my life. I know this is all I've got." He spread his hands wide. "I know you don't belong here." He jabbed her hard in the shoulder, and she stumbled back into the wall.

"I don't belong anywhere." The tears leaked from her eyes, cutting through the thin layer of powder from the factory floor. They stabbed into him, like needle pricks across his chest, but he was rolling downhill, going too fast to stop.

"You don't belong on the line, that's for sure. You belong back in that office where you can actually *do something,* not just make double the work for everyone else."

She stared at him, lip trembling, then swiped at her eyes with the back of her hand. There were holes in the fingers of her gloves from the wiring. She turned fast, hurling herself down Factory Row toward the Stamping Mill.

"Lena, wait." He ran after her. When he reached for her arm, she jerked away. "Let me at least take you back to Shima's."

"I'm not going back to Shima's."

He groaned. He had to get home. He had to be there before Jed came by. What he would say to him then, he had no idea, but he wasn't about to leave his family undefended.

"Then we'll go in the Stamping Mill. The foreman can call your parents."

She walked faster.

"Lena." He took off his hat and twisted it until he heard threads pop. "Come home with me."

She didn't stop.

"Come home with me," he repeated.

"Why? So you don't have to feel guilty for walking away?" She slowed, but didn't stop. "Here. I'll let you off the hook. I'll be fine on my own, Colin. You're not responsible for me."

But he was. He'd brought her here, hadn't he? He grabbed her arm and yanked her to a stop, not letting go when she tried to pull away.

"Are you always this big a pain in the ass?"

She turned her nose up. "Yes."

He sighed. He knew he had to tell her something, but didn't know where to start.

"That man who came to Small Parts? His name is Jed Schultz. I pissed him off back there, and after he's done at Small Parts, he's going to come to my house and collect on some bad debts. I need to be there when he does."

A crease formed between her brows. "You owe him money?"

"Yes. He's . . . *helped* my family out in the past." He didn't even want to get started on Hayden.

"If it was help, why does he want the money back?"

"Because I won't join the Brotherhood—the charter."

"Why?"

He frowned. "Because I thought I could do better."

As she considered this, he took a step back. Maybe he'd said enough to scare her home. It was just a matter of time before she realized they were fighting on opposite sides of the same war.

"Could you?" she asked finally.

"Could I what?"

"Do better. Organize the factory workers. I heard you and your friends talking about it back there."

He slung a hand around the back of his neck, confused. "Um. Yeah. Not me, though, everyone. I thought if we could all get together, they'd be forced to make some changes."

" 'They' being my family."

"Right." Something was working through her head, but for the life of him he couldn't figure out what.

"How?" she asked after a moment. "What would you see done?"

He shrugged. "I have a few ideas."

She watched his shoulders roll back, his mouth harden into a straight line, and suspected that he knew the faults of this place— and what should be improved—better than anyone.

"I don't belong on the line," she said. "I belong in the office."

"Look." He scratched a hand over his jaw. "I was mad. I didn't mean—"

"I'm going home with you." She pulled the hair back from her face.

"Lena." He chuckled dryly, as if anything could possibly be funny. "I just told you I wanted to fight your family, and that a very dangerous man is going to come looking for me. Why aren't you running?"

She pursed her lips, and met his gaze at last. The sadness in her eyes humbled him.

"Because I think I can help."

* * *

By the time they'd passed the St. Anthony statue, he'd chewed his nails down to the quick. He'd lost his mind—why else would he have brought her here? Or walked away from the Brotherhood's offer? Or told her he'd wanted to organize a *press*?

He was insane. That was all there was to it.

He watched her take in her surroundings, wondering again how she'd tricked him into telling her so much. The little greenback was full of surprises. An hour ago, he'd figured he would never see her again, but instead of taking off, she'd stuck. Despite what he'd said, she hadn't done so bad on the line, either, aside from keeling over. Slow, but precise.

As they walked, an idea formed in his mind. If he had a Hampton in his corner, the others might actually listen. Josef Hampton himself might actually listen. He and Otto wouldn't give the workers time to say their piece, but they couldn't write off Lena. She could be the voice they needed to get the same rights as the Brotherhood.

If they hadn't already cut her out of the family, which, by the look of her cheek, they might have.

The sign for Keeneland Apartments was covered with graffiti. After reading the string of curse words, Lena had snorted, and then blushed, and coughed delicately. She wasn't used to the nitro fog from the chem plant. Colin hardly noticed it now, but from the way she kept pressing her thumb on her temple, he bet it was giving her a headache.

Outside the first building, a group of kids were playing kick-the-can while a couple guys chucked knives into a wooden sign. A few thin souls, sick with the flu, wandered around aimlessly. Beside the dirt path a man with a mangy dog smoked a hash pipe. The dog barked as they passed, and Lena jumped in the opposite direction.

Colin led her around the side of the building through the weeds. Jed and his men were nowhere to be seen—not yet, anyway. They needed to get inside. It would be dark soon.

"You live here?" She stared up at the boarded windows and the laundry hanging from the fire escape. A couple somewhere upstairs was fighting.

He hunched. "Just for a while." Not forever. There were no old men in Metaltown—no one lived long enough.

"I didn't mean . . ."

"It's fine." He knew what it looked like. When they'd first moved here he'd thought the same thing—how could anyone live like this? But expectations changed over time. You made the best of what you had, or you ended up like Hayden. Forgetting yourself one fix at a time.

He opened the door to the building, remembering what his mom had told him once about ladies, and how it was polite to let them go first. That had been when he was little, in Bakerstown, before she stopped expecting him to bring a girl home. The metal creaked on the hinges, and the hallway stunk of rotten things.

They crossed to the stairway, and each step up brought more tightness to his chest. He didn't know when Jed would come, or what he would tell his family. He didn't know what Lena would think once she saw where he lived.

She followed wordlessly to the second floor and down the hall to apartment 205. It wasn't locked—thieves had broken the lock years before they'd moved in. He rested his hand on the handle for a moment, glancing down, wishing he could apologize. Hating that he wanted to.

She gave him a small smile and he pushed inside.

With one bedroom, one bathroom, and a living area, the Walters' house was a tight squeeze. The carpet was pea-green and stained, a tightly woven mat that shredded at the base of the walls. A crate and a piece of plywood leaned against a futon couch, and a hot plate and assortment of dishes were stacked on a nightstand. Broth was heating in a large steel pot; the smell of synthetic beef stock made Colin's stomach rumble.

A hacking cough emanated from the bedroom. A moment later a rail-thin woman in a pink bathrobe stepped out, a wastebasket under one arm. Her thin yellow hair was missing in patches.

"Oh good, I thought the foreman was going to hold you over . . ." When she saw that Colin wasn't alone, the red blotches on her cheeks grew brighter. She dropped the basket and backed up quickly the way she'd come.

"Cherish . . ." Colin motioned for Lena to sit down and crossed into the bedroom. Cherish was coughing again, and searching frantically through a pile of laundry on the floor. He placed one sturdy hand on her shoulder, and with the other, gently pounded the corners of her back to break up the mucus in her lungs. Her breathing slowed to a rattling wheeze.

She stuffed a blue, handmade knit cap on her head to hide her hair.

"I didn't know you had company," she said, still breathing heavily. Her lips were redder than usual.

"Is it okay?"

"Yes! You just surprised me, that's all. Where's Ida?"

"Still at work, I guess." Probably pulling another double.

"Okay, how do I look?" Frail hands with paper-thin skin pulled the hat down over her ears. She straightened her back.

Like you're dying. "Fine. Pretty."

She slapped him lightly on the cheek and smiled. He held her elbow to steady her as they walked out the bedroom door, and found Lena was still standing, staring over the couch at a framed certificate.

"You won the spelling bee?" she asked, humor in her voice. Colin pinched his eyes closed.

"This is Cherish. My mom."

She wobbled forward, hands outstretched. Lena smiled warmly and took them, never faltering. Unafraid. "I'm Mary. It's lovely to meet you, Cherish. Thank you for having me."

"So polite!" Cherish grinned at Colin, just like she'd been doing since she'd married his mother fifteen years ago, and then wavered as the vertigo hit. He jumped forward, guiding her to the couch, then grabbed a clean rag off the shelf and passed it her way. The blood soaked through the cotton within seconds. She was getting worse.

"Mary, tell me all about yourself," she said through labored breaths, tucking the rag into her sleeve.

Lena's eyes flicked to Colin. "Well . . . I, um . . ."

"Mary's tired," cut in Colin.

Cherish smiled in a knowing way and patted Lena's hand. "How about you take a bath and we'll have some soup, and then I'll tell you all about how Colin used to bring home stray cats and dress them up in his old baby clothes."

Lena giggled. It distracted him until Cherish began to cough again.

A moment later a rattling came from the door's broken lock, and before Colin could reach it, his ma entered. There were bags under her eyes, and her nose was red from the chill. She pulled off her scarf, hanging it beside the knife they kept near the exit. Colin braced himself for her disappointment; she wasn't going to like what he had to say.

"Ma, this is Mary. Mary, this is Ida."

"Oh," said Ida, her brows lifting. She passed an unmistakable look of pleasure to Cherish. "Mary. Welcome. You're Colin's girl-friend then?"

"Ma." Colin groaned.

"*Ida*," whispered Cherish. "You're embarrassing him."

"What?" Ida crossed between them and pressed her hand against Cherish's forehead. "Colin's never brought a girlfriend home."

"Oh, I'm not . . ." Lena hesitated. "I think I'll clean up now, if it's all right."

"This is great," muttered Colin.

"Isn't she pretty?" said Cherish.

Both his moms were grinning like they were posing for a damn picture.

"Come on." Colin grabbed Lena's arm and directed her to the bathroom. There wasn't much to the shower besides a low spigot and a bucket, but there was lye soap, and at least it got her away from the women.

"Which side is hot?" she asked, staring at the knob.

"Keep turning, you'll find it." Did it look like they had hot water? He closed the door behind him, realizing suddenly that she was three feet away, taking off her clothes.

And that his ma and Cherish were also three feet away, staring at him.

"Try to hold yourselves together," he told them.

"Put the table out," said Cherish. "I'll get the bowls."

"You'll sit down." Ida kissed her knuckles and placed them in her lap.

Colin pushed the crate out in front of the futon, and laid the plywood on top. Ida set out four bowls and filled them with broth. He had to get this out fast, otherwise it would burn a hole through him.

"Ma, I have to tell you something."

"Oh God," said Cherish. "Mary's pregnant. I knew it."

"Cherish!"

The look on Ida's face could have pinned him to the wall. "*What*? How many times have I told you—"

"Nobody's pregnant," interrupted Colin before she could launch into his favorite, not-at-all-awkward responsible-relationships speech. Quickly, he told them what had happened at the factory, carefully leaving out his thoughts of pressing at Small Parts or Hayden's drug debts.

"Well, if you don't want to join the Brotherhood, that's up to you," said Ida slowly, her brows knitted together.

Ty already tried that. "Jed didn't like that answer. He . . . he says you're out too, Ma."

Ida's face went ashen. She didn't look over to Cherish, though Colin knew she wanted to. "I'm out. What's that mean? I've still got my job, haven't I?"

Colin wanted to disappear. "I don't know. He's not going to send by any more green. In fact . . ."

Cherish leaned forward. "What, honey?"

"He wants to collect."

Ida placed her face in her hands.

"Ma, I'm sorry."

She didn't say anything for a while, then looked up sharply. "You stay out of his way, all right? I'll take care of this. I don't want you trying to cover for me."

"Yes, ma'am," Colin lied.

"I mean it, Colin." He nodded, the shame hot and heavy.

"Never liked him anyway," said Cherish, placing one hand on her back. "All tail feathers and no bird, that one is."

The seconds ticked by. Colin could barely swallow. Life was hard enough on his Ma already without him screwing it up.

"I've been thinking more about Charity House," broached Cherish. "If I stayed there—"

"No." Ida's voice broke. "Don't even say it. Don't even *think* it."

"Ida," hushed Cherish. She reached for Ida's cheek, cupping it in her hand.

Colin spun when he heard footsteps behind him on the rug. Lena was standing beside the bathroom door, shivering in Shima's pants and one of Colin's clean long-sleeved shirts. Her dirty gloves peeked out at the hem. What was it about those damn gloves?

Her wet hair was down. Her face clean.

"I didn't mean to interrupt," she said. Colin couldn't immediately remember what they'd been talking about.

"Join us," said Cherish. She was sweating. Sitting up this long had been a strain.

"I hope it's all right I borrowed a shirt," whispered Lena.

He nodded.

While they ate they talked about other things, life in Bakerstown, stories of Colin and Hayden growing up. His ma and Cherish settled into their rhythm of finishing each other's sentences, making Lena laugh. He didn't even mind their jibes after a while. For the first time in a long while, he didn't wish he was somewhere else.

But when a knock came at the boarded window, it all came crashing back.

He rose quickly, reaching for the knife still in his boot. Ida joined him, grabbing a tire iron they kept at the door to tuck behind her back. She stood beside him, giving him one quick nod before he slid the board aside.

Ty was standing outside, hands on her hips.

"Where in the holy hell have you been?" she shouted. "I've been looking everywhere!"

"Hey, Ty," said Ida, rubbing the knot out of her chest. She retreated to the couch to help Cherish to bed.

"Hi, Ida," Ty said, motioning Colin through the window. "Come on already! Outside. By the statue. You have to come!"

"Ty, I can't," he said. He couldn't leave now, not when Jed still might be coming by. But she was already gone, sliding down the fire escape.

"Is that . . . Tell her to hold on!" Lena was standing, already reaching for her sweater to follow them. With everything that had happened, she still wanted to talk to Ty?

He dragged a hand over his face. "Ma, I'll be right back. Don't answer the door."

"Don't give me orders," she retorted, hoisting a quiet Cherish over one arm. "I'm the mom, I give the orders."

He shook his head. "Yes, ma'am."

"Be careful." Cherish wheezed, and Ida patted her back, no longer watching their son.

Colin helped Lena over the windowsill, wondering if it wouldn't be better to leave her inside. It was dark now, and who knew what kind of trouble Ty had stirred up.

From the bottom of the fire escape, he could hear it—a crowd, over near the statue.

"Lena," he said. "You should go back up."

"I need to talk to that girl," she insisted, pushing past him.

As they rounded the side of the building, he saw them. Ty and Martin and Agnes. Tall Matchstick and Zeke and his little sister with her poofy hair. Noneck and even some of the warehouse guys. Chip pushed to the front, ordering everyone to "shut up."

"What's all this about?" Colin asked.

"We didn't sign," said Zeke.

"Better make it worth our while," grumbled Martin.

"They're here to pledge to the code," Chip said excitedly. "Like I did."

Colin could hardly believe it. They weren't joining Jed Schultz; they wanted their own Brotherhood. A new Brotherhood.

"What the hell is *she* doing here?" asked Ty, pointing an accusing finger at Lena.

23

TY

Ty's glare tracked from Lena to Colin, every hair standing on end. What she saw didn't make sense. A Hampton, wearing scrap clothes? Out in the slums? With *Colin*?

The only conceivable answer was that it wasn't her. It was a look-alike. Just a girl, and it wasn't like Ty hadn't seen him with other girls before.

"Why didn't you sign?" Colin asked Zeke and Martin after his shock passed.

"I told them not to," said Chip, arms crossed over his chest. "That's why."

Ty grabbed Colin's arm, angling him away from the Hampton imposter. "Last night I snuck into the Brotherhood office and over-heard Jed having a little conversation." *With Hayden.* She bit the inside of her cheek. Better not to mention that yet. "The bastard's taking bribes from the Hamptons *and* dues from the workers. He's playing both sides."

"Why?" The yellow streetlight cast an ominous glow over his hard features.

"To pack his pockets with green. Because he's a worthless pig-face. You choose."

Colin swore. All the times Jed had given them money, he'd said he was looking out for them. He told everyone that. That he was protecting them from the boss.

Ty motioned toward the others. "Chip and me, we told the guys. I looked all over but couldn't find you."

Colin glanced over her shoulder to the girl he'd come with. She was talking to Zeke and his sister. "I've been busy."

A frustrated noise came from her throat. "Great, you found a Hampton replacement."

Colin didn't say anything, and in the silence Ty felt the smirk melt off her face.

"You're kidding me," she said.

Colin swiped his knuckles over his lips.

"What the hell is wrong with you?" In a surge of fury she shoved him, and he staggered back. He didn't attempt to defend himself.

"Excuse me," said the girl—*Lena Hampton.* "I've been meaning to speak with you."

Ty ignored her. "Why is she with you, Colin?"

He took a deep breath. "It's a long story."

"I wanted to help you." Lena's voice had grown strident. Others had turned their way and were watching now.

"I think I've had about enough of your help," snapped Ty, baring her teeth.

"Ty." Colin stepped between them. "Keep it down."

"What's a greenback—no, not just a greenback, a *Ham*—"

"Ty!" Colin grabbed her shoulder.

"It's not his fault," said Lena. She looked around, clenching her fists as the others began to whisper. "I know things are bad at the Small Parts factory. I worked there today, I saw everything. I've read the reports . . ."

"You haven't worked a day in your life," spat Ty. "Maybe all these Metalheads are scared of you, princess, but guess what? I'm not. You already fired me. Can't do much more."

"Ty, shut up!" hissed Colin, releasing her arm.

She turned to him, mouth open, vision shaking with fury. So much for loyalty.

"Think about it," he said, leaning close. "Think about what she could do to help us."

He stared at her as if willing her to understand, but she couldn't. Even if a Hampton were in a unique position to help, it didn't matter. She was on the wrong side of the fence. You couldn't fight the enemy by recruiting the enemy; it didn't make sense.

"You've lost your mind."

He reached behind him and pulled Lena to his side. "She wants to be a part of this. *Mary* wants to help."

Ty couldn't believe what she was hearing. A Hampton didn't belong in Metaltown. She had to be a spy, sent by her father to bring them all down. Colin could be reckless, but this was downright crazy. He was going to get them all thrown in jail.

"I'm calling safety on her, Ty."

His words raked under her skin. To call safety on someone meant to claim responsibility for them until they could stand on their own. They both knew how serious it was—Ty's safety on Colin when he'd first moved to Metaltown had been the only thing that had stopped the older guys at Small Parts from eating him alive.

"You're making a mistake," she said. Her heart twisted in her chest. Lena glanced up at Colin, confusion in her eyes, and Ty saw the bruise on her cheekbone that disappeared behind her hairline. It made her remember her own wounds, and she pulled her hat down to cover the bandage.

"It'll be fine," Colin whispered to Lena. Ty would rather have been punched in the gut. A Hampton was here in Metaltown, and somehow it was Ty who felt like the outsider.

"What's our move, Colin?" interrupted Zeke. "Schultz says we can't work for Small Parts anymore unless we join the Brotherhood."

"That's a lie," said Lena. All eyes turned to her and she dropped her head. *Good,* thought Ty, willing her to cry, or something equally as pathetic.

"Keep talking," prompted Colin.

To Ty's irritation, Lena lifted her chin. She tucked her hair behind her ears.

"No one is obligated to join a charter. In fact, the ... um ... *Hamptons* don't favor it. It slows production."

Ty settled back to watch the show. If Lena kept using words like "favor," people would see she wasn't a Metalhead. They'd turn on Colin, and she'd have his back like always, and then he'd see what a fool he'd been.

"What if we press for rights? That'll slow production!" called Noneck.

Lena squirmed a little. Ty cracked a smile.

"You don't have to press," Lena told Colin quietly. "There's a clause in the Hampton Industries contracts that says that a representative of the employees is permitted to meet with the owners. Mr. Schultz takes advantage of this frequently."

"And then he takes advantage of everyone else," said Colin.

"Choose a side, greenback," said Ty. Why was Colin listening to her? Obviously she was putting her company first.

"So we'll go all the way up the ladder," Colin considered aloud. "Just like Schultz does. We tell Hampton what we want, and we won't work till he gives it to us."

"Wait ..." Lena grabbed his shirtsleeve.

"What *do* we want?" asked Martin.

"Not to work in the hot room anymore," grumbled Noneck.

"Decent pay," said Zeke. "Overtime pay. Hell, any pay at all." Several people agreed.

"I want Minnick off my ass," called Matchstick.

"We need to get organized," said Martin. "Make a list."

An eager, hungry feeling was taking hold of them all, Ty could see it. It was contagious, and biting, like the night's chill.

"You're serious about this?" asked Colin, crossing his arms over his chest. "Because back at Lacey's I remember quite a few concerns. In fact, I remember half of you were flat-out yellow about the whole thing."

"That was different," said Martin.

"Oh yeah?" said Colin. "How? What's changed?"

Martin mumbled an answer, and Colin snorted.

"Oh," he said. "I get it. Now it's not just Ty who's in trouble, it's all of you."

Beside him, Ty puffed up.

Colin's gaze swept around the crowd. "If we do this, we've got to stick together. As a crew—a *charter*. It's that way or no way."

Some of the others nodded, that wild Metaltown edge in their eyes. Ty thought of the leak from Lacey's—Hayden, Colin's own brother—and cringed.

"All right," said Noneck. "We got to sign something or what?"

"No papers," said Colin, looking down at Chip and smirking. "I think Chip had it right. We got our own rules anyway. Our code goes deeper than anything the Brotherhood's got."

Zeke's white teeth gleamed.

"What *is* your code?" whispered Lena, wringing her hands together.

Colin grinned. His hand rested on Ty's shoulder. Squeezed. "What's our code, Ty?"

Ty wavered. Everyone knew what it was but the stupid greenback, and if anyone but Colin had asked, she would have told them to shove it.

"We got each other's backs," she said, stepping closer to Colin. "No stealing, no fighting, no holding back if you got something to share. And if you break the rules, you get busted up."

They cheered.

She wiped a smirk off on the back of her hand. Nobody had ever cheered for her before. She didn't like them looking at her, but it felt all right.

Colin picked up a stick off the ground, and dragged it through the dirt, stopping when he hit the statue. He stepped away from the group, to the opposite side.

"No one joins unless they want to join," he told them. "If you cross the line you're with us. You're loyal to the Small Parts Charter and you follow street rules. You break the code, you're out. Everybody clear on that?"

Martin nodded his agreement, expression grim.

"Why not?" mused Matchstick. "This doesn't work out, I've always got my inheritance."

Martin shoved him.

"*Colin.*" Lena's tone was filled with begging. He didn't hear her. Or he ignored her.

"Go home," Ty said under her breath. "Whatever brought you here is over."

But instead of cowering, Lena glared at her. Ty snorted, then tilted her head sharply to the side to crack her neck.

Ty made sure she was the first to cross the line. Matchstick came next. Then Agnes, and Martin, and Noneck. T.J. and Loudmouth. The warehouse boys. The kids from sorting. Henry and the guys from Plastics. Ty's chest swelled every time another person crossed over. Thirty-two workers. A third of Small Parts. Not enough to break the factory, but enough to slow things down.

At the end there were only three people across the line. Zeke and his sister, and Lena Hampton.

Zeke was on his knees in the dirt, fixing his sister's coat. He was speaking to her quietly, pointing across the line to the others, who waited in quiet anticipation. Finally, she turned to them, a huge grin plastered across her little face. She skipped over, big hair bouncing, and planted herself proudly next to Chip. Zeke followed, shaking Colin's hand.

"Come on, Mary," called Henry. "Tell your pals at the Uniform Division to join too!"

Lena dug her heel into the ground.

Stay. Good dog. Ty smirked.

Colin turned around to face the group, expression unreadable. "Tomorrow we meet at Small Parts like normal. But we don't go in. We stay outside the doors. Try to get as many people to join us . . ."

He hesitated when Lena Hampton crossed the line and stood beside him.

The group erupted. Henry picked her up and tossed her over one shoulder. She shrieked. When he put her down, her cheeks were rosy, and she was laughing. Ty kicked a rock as hard as she could across the field.

She was just about to kick another when Chip grabbed her arm and yanked down hard.

"The Brotherhood. They're here!"

24

LENA

Excitement stormed through Lena's veins. She'd never felt such exhilaration. At home she would have been in bed hours ago. She would have completed her assignments with Darcy, and taken her meal alone in the dining room before turning in. Her life at the Hampton estate was as predictable as her brother's arrogance.

Here nothing was safe. Nothing was certain. She'd committed treason against her family, and if her father ever found out, he'd do a lot worse than hit her. Still, the danger of her actions made them that much more potent. For the first time ever she was doing what she wanted, without knowing the outcome. For the first time she felt as though she belonged.

But just as the elation was swelling, it died. The girl who hated her—Ty—ran to speak to Colin, and Lena bristled watching them together. Lena liked being close to him. It was as if all the energy in the world came from him, and the farther away he was, the colder she felt.

The conversation heated quickly, and after a moment, Colin twisted away, searching urgently for something, or someone, in a way that made her body tense. She lifted on her tiptoes and tracked his gaze.

"Brotherhood!" he called suddenly, and she saw them—three, no, more than four men approaching through the entrance of the complex. Immediately Colin's call was passed around.

"Brotherhood!" someone beside her yelled. Then another voice raised the call.

Without thinking, she pushed to the front. Colin had said that Mr. Schultz would come collecting on bad debts. He'd been afraid for what the man would do to his family when he couldn't pay. If she was there, they wouldn't dare hurt him.

But they'd know who she was.

She faltered just behind him, unsure of what to do.

The man who approached wasn't Mr. Schultz, though, it was his assistant—the big bodyguard who'd kept his company at the Small Parts factory earlier that afternoon. Four other men were there, dressed in laborer clothing, and the sight of them sent a chill through her. They didn't look like they'd come to talk.

"Imon," acknowledged Colin. The others crowded behind him, bumping her closer to his back. "Mr. Schultz couldn't make it, I guess."

Imon glanced at the group. "Meetin' with Hampton," he grunted in a heavy Northern accent.

Lena's stomach clenched. Had Schultz recognized her earlier? He could be telling her father right now. Were these men here for her?

"Look at that—he speaks," said Ty under her breath.

"We'll be meeting with the boss soon too," said Colin boldly. "Small Parts has its own charter now."

Zeke hoisted his sister on one hip, and made for the back of the crowd with some of the younger kids. To protect them, Lena realized. There was going to be a fight. She'd never been in a fight before, apart from the confrontation with her father. She didn't know the first thing about what to do.

What she did know was that she should have followed Zeke. But she didn't.

Imon's lips curled up. He turned to glance at the others and they all began to laugh.

"You owe Mr. Schultz some green," he said. "Lots of green."

Before her, Colin's weight shifted. "I . . ."

"How much?" asked Ty.

Colin's gaze shot toward her. She tucked her thumbs in her belt and cocked her head to the side.

"Well?" she asked. "How much does he want?"

Imon chuckled. "Two-fifty."

Lena wasn't exactly sure how much the Small Parts workers made, but from the gasps and whispers of the charter, and the laughter of the Brotherhood, she imagined this was an unattainable amount.

At least, to them. She'd easily spent that much on weekend shopping trips without even thinking. She sunk into the shadows, regretting that now.

"Two-fifty." Ty whistled. "That's a lot of green."

"That's at least twice what he's given us," Colin said.

"Interest," said Imon.

"All right," said Ty. "All right. We settle with you, and there's no need to come back here, right?"

Imon's lips tilted up, but she could see in his eyes that his confidence wavered. The group before him held thirty people to his five. Even if they were bigger, the Small Parts Charter could easily overwhelm them. If they dared.

Ty reached into her back pocket and withdrew a stack of bills, folded neatly in half. She made a big show of counting them, then slapped them into Imon's open hand. Lena marveled at her fearlessness, and thought maybe she shouldn't have felt bad for firing Ty—the girl obviously had sufficient funds.

Though Colin's mouth gaped, he didn't say anything.

Imon counted the bills, brows furrowed. Finally, he tucked them into his breast pocket.

"More," he said. The crowd shifted restlessly behind her.

"What?" asked Colin. "That was a year's wages!"

Imon slowly, carefully, reached for Colin's arm, then flicked his sleeve. "Doesn't cover thievin'."

Colin took a step forward and met Imon nose to nose. "I didn't steal anything. Jed bought these clothes for me."

"Now he wants them back." The others behind Imon closed rank. The closest—not more than a couple years older than Lena—slid something metal over his knuckles.

"That's completely out of line!" she snapped, finding herself shoulder to shoulder with Colin. "There's no need—"

In a flash, Imon had grabbed the scarf Colin had given her and twisted it around her neck. Vaguely she was aware of the movement around her. Her gloved fingers slid off Imon's hold, and she kicked out, connecting with his shin. When they locked eyes, Lena felt the dread thicken like tar inside her organs and halted her struggle.

Something cold and sharp pressed into her belly.

Yelling. Words she couldn't make out. The fighting around them stilled.

"Fine, okay," said Colin, voice low. "Let go of her, and we'll talk."

Lena's gaze flicked over to him. A young man behind Imon was snickering. Both sides watched her intently.

"The clothes," said Imon.

"Don't do it," warned Ty. Lena felt the sob tumble from her throat.

"Think she'll bleed much?" Imon wondered aloud.

Lena inhaled sharply, feeling the metal cut through her clothing and knick her skin. He was going to cut her open. She sucked in her belly as far as it would go, trying so hard to hold absolutely still, but she couldn't stop shaking.

"Okay!" Colin tore off his coat, and then the wool sweater underneath. The boy with the brass knuckles held out his hand to take it.

"And the rest of it," prompted Imon. Colin swore under his breath.

He removed his boots, taking care to place his knives inside. Then he pulled down his wool trousers, wearing nothing beneath but long underwear. Lena knew she ought to avert her eyes, but she couldn't look away. His face was red, even in the streetlight. She felt the cold then, felt it snake through her. He must have been freezing, but he hardly moved.

With hardly an expression, Imon released her. Her trembling legs gave out and she sank to her knees. Imon turned, exposing his back as if daring Colin to stick a knife in it, and walked away. One by one the Brotherhood thugs followed.

Then Colin's hands were on her shoulders, lifting her to her tiptoes. "You okay?" The adrenaline screamed through her ears, distorting his voice. Her knees wobbled. It was all she could do to stay upright.

"Safety!" Ty said, pushing him aside. "You and your goddamn safety!"

"Should we go after them?" Noneck asked, looking anxious.

"Course we're going after them," said Ty, though she wouldn't look at Lena.

Colin scratched his hands through his short hair, then snatched his coat off the ground and shoved it over his shoulders.

"No."

"What? Why?" Ty's arms dropped to her sides. Lena caught the glint of a knife in one hand and shivered uncontrollably. In her pocket was the little rope doll Shima had made her when she was little, and she squeezed it as hard as she could.

Home, she thought. *My bed. My sheets. My pillows.*

But these thoughts didn't warm her.

"Schultz knows they were here. We go after them, we have the rest of the Brotherhood on our backs tomorrow."

"So what?" countered Ty, placing herself right in front of him. The others looked uncomfortable—more afraid of their own fear than of their enemies, yet angry at the same time. Henry had come to Lena's side and thrown a clumsy arm over her shoulders. She wanted nothing more than to shove him away, but she was so cold.

"How are we going to fix Small Parts if we declare war on the Brotherhood?" Colin asked them. Some of those closest tried to argue, but he stood his ground. "Schultz is baiting us. He thinks we're just a bunch of kids. The only way to get payback is to show him we're not. We've got to beat him at his own game." Colin jabbed the shoulder of a tall boy who was coiling some copper wire around his finger and looking mutinous. "Not get distracted."

"So says the guy in his underwear," said Zeke. A tense laughter broke over them. Lena laughed nervously, then clamped a hand over her mouth.

The humiliation cracked open inside of her. Colin was laughing, but he must have been mortified. He'd been stripped down in front of all his friends. Made to look like a fool.

"All right, all right," said Colin. "Get out of here. Don't be late tomorrow."

They filtered away, one by one. Back to their apartments, or back to the streets. As they cleared, Colin approached Ty, whose mouth was still set with fury.

"That was a lot of green back there," he said casually, as if he weren't half-clothed. Lena stared at the outline of his legs in the darkness, long and muscled. Men in the River District would never be so unashamed. Her gaze shot away.

"Eavesdropping wasn't the only thing we did last night at the Brotherhood office," she snapped. "Chip's got sticky fingers."

Lena closed her eyes. Who were the bigger crooks? The Brotherhood or the Small Parts Charter?

Colin tilted his head back toward his apartment. "You coming?" The invitation was directed at Ty, and made Lena feel small, like she didn't belong, even when Ty shook her head to decline.

"Why don't you take the little princess home?" Ty said. "Looks like she misses Mommy."

Lena's knees locked.

"My mother's dead." She wasn't sure why she said it, but the way Ty hunched at her words brought on a wave of victory. Still, the girl had a point. Where would she go? Back to Shima's? Even though she was tempted, she couldn't walk there now, not with Mr. Schultz's gang on the streets.

Colin didn't look at her right away, and she worried what that might mean. When Otto didn't look at her, he was angry, and his anger was far worse than his playfulness. She heard a small tear, and realized she'd been stretching her gloves too far up her wrists.

"There's a spot on the couch if you want it," Colin said to her.

Ty's spot. Lena wasn't in a position to decline.

A different kind of nerves tightened her insides. She nodded.

* * *

She clung to his shadow as they moved through the weeds. Her footsteps on the metal stairs of the fire escape were nearly silent—her goal to draw as little attention as possible. But her hands gripped the handrails, and her gaze darted to all sides.

When they reached the top, he slid aside the board blocking the window and offered his hand to help her over the ledge. She was still straddling the windowsill when a movement inside made her pulse skip.

A man—nearly as tall as Colin, but thinner—waited within, a tire iron slung loosely over his shoulders.

"Nice work, little brother," he said, gazing over her appreciatively. He barked out a laugh when Colin followed. "Looks like you forgot something."

Brothers. Her pulse settled. That explained the resemblance. They had the same long face, like Ida's, and the same cocky grin. But the spaces below this man's cheeks were hollowed and she thought his eyes looked a little jaundiced, though maybe that was the yellow light from the buzzing bulb overhead.

"Your friend Jed sent his dogs to collect," said Colin harshly. "Don't worry too much, all right? I took care of it. Me and the Small Parts Charter. Maybe you saw us outside."

His brother tensed, mouth set in a grim line.

"What are you doing?" he asked, though from his flat tone it didn't sound like he really expected an answer. The tire iron hit the floor with a flat clunk. "Schultz will roast you for this. No one else makes a run on Metaltown. Not even McNulty."

Lena didn't know who McNulty was, but he didn't sound good.

"I'm not scared of him, Hayden."

"Then you're a fool." He stepped up to meet his brother, nose to nose.

As they squared off, Lena braced herself for more violence. "Stop!" she whisper-shouted. "Is killing each other all you people want to do?"

They both turned to stare at her. Hayden tilted his head, cocking one brow in the same way his brother did.

"Kinda feisty, aren't you?"

Colin snorted. "You should have seen her kick Imon."

"Yeah?"

She crossed her arms over her chest, still jittery. "Well, he did a little more than kick me back."

Colin's shoulders dropped. Abandoning his argument with Hayden, he led her past the quiet bedroom, to the bathroom, where he shut the door behind him. It was a tight squeeze with two people. Too tight. Her head began to buzz like the overhead light.

"What are you doing?" she asked, voice thin. It wasn't appropriate for them to be in such tight quarters together. His brother was right outside, likely thinking the same thing.

He reached around her to the plastic shelving unit on the wall. When his chest grazed hers, she backed up even farther, locked between his body and the cracked porcelain sink. The sweat began to dew on her hairline.

"Back up," she said. "Please."

He withdrew a first aid kit and a ratty towel, and motioned toward her sweater. Now that she looked down she could see where Imon's knife had ripped it.

"Let's see the damage."

"Back up!" She tried to keep quiet but her voice broke. "You're not wearing pants."

His mouth turned up the tiniest bit. "Is that the problem?"

"I . . ." She placed her hands on his chest, shoving him back sharply. Her gaze lifted to the ceiling, focusing on the light. A wave of nausea crashed over her. "I don't like small spaces."

He hesitated, as if to ascertain that this was true. "Fair enough."

Without another word, he left. She locked the door before crumpling over the sink. A ragged breath scraped down her throat, and she forced herself to focus on the overused toothbrushes and powdered dental paste on the ledge. What was she doing here? She didn't know this boy. His friends were rough and crude, and associated with criminals—one who would have taken her life without a second thought.

So fragile. Her father's words echoed in her head.

She fanned her eyes, willing the stinging to stop, then rolled up her sweater. The wound was small, merely a puncture, but she'd bled enough for a thin, orange rose to blossom on the skin from her ribs to her pant line. It stung when she prodded it. A hiss escaped through her teeth.

Cleaning and dressing the wound steadied her hands and calmed her mind. This, she could do. This, she had practiced. Turning to the side, she inspected the yellow-brown bruise that remained from Otto's careful hand. A reminder that no matter who tore her down, she could always put herself back together.

* * *

When she left the bathroom, Colin was alone. The crate and plywood that had served as a table had been pushed back against the wall, and a line of light pink rags were hanging to dry on the windowsill.

He shrugged grumpily when she asked where his brother had gone.

She crossed her arms. Uncrossed them. She pulled her sleeves down over her hands, debating if she should sit beside him on the couch. Was that where he planned on sleeping? She hadn't seen another bed. Lena had never slept with another person in the room, not counting Shima, who was a girl, and her nanny besides. She was clearly imposing.

Colin rose, and she was relieved to see he'd put on some pants. They were too big, and hung low on his hips, drawing her eyes to the place where they connected with the bottom of his shirt. He laid out some blankets on the couch, scratching the back of his neck.

"Not exactly what you're used to, I guess."

She had the sudden urge to show him what it was like at her house. Big, spacious rooms, heated to comfort. Food available any time from the kitchen staff. Bathtubs and hot water and a plush, oversized bed.

"Not exactly," she said quietly.

He frowned, and then the lines below his eyes pinched in anger. There was a bedroll of some sort in the corner, and he tossed it out on the floor.

"Well, we can't all be greenbacks," he said.

She'd heard the word before, but no one had ever called her it to her face. A hot flush burned through her. She hadn't asked to grow up in a big house. No one had given her the choice. And even if they had, he couldn't blame her for wanting nice things. He would have taken them, too.

She lowered to the couch, settling delicately so the springs wouldn't groan, and pulled the scratchy blankets to her neck. When he switched the light off, her hand rose to her breastbone, to rub out the hard, hollow ball formed beneath it. Cherish's hacking cough came through the thin walls in the adjacent room.

The mat crinkled as he lay down, and she listened for several minutes to the sound of his breathing. It made her conscious of her own breathing, and she opened her mouth to make herself as silent as possible. If she were still enough, maybe he'd forget she was there, and maybe she would, too.

"If you want to go home tomorrow, I understand," he said.

She thought of the soup she'd eaten earlier with his parents, the pride in their eyes when they talked about how well he'd done in school, or what a hard worker he was. Despite the fact that their table was a board tilted up against the wall, and they had barely enough blankets to stave off the chill, he didn't seem so poor right then.

"I meant what I said," she whispered. "I want to help."

She remembered what he'd told her—that she couldn't help on the line, she probably couldn't even help in the charter. But she *could* help in the office of the Small Parts factory. That's where she could make changes that would matter.

But that meant going home, and speaking to her father. He probably wouldn't even consider giving her a role in the business after what had happened, especially not after he learned that she'd agreed to assist the charter.

What Ty said had been true. Colin had made a mistake trusting her.

"Your friend was right about Mr. Schultz collecting money from my family," she said. "I saw my brother pay him at a party at my house." Admitting this to Colin felt wrong, but what Otto had done was wrong, too. If the payment had been a legitimate business transaction, it would have been recorded. She would have seen some reflection of it in the documents she'd pored over preparing for her factory visit. She pushed aside her feelings of unfaithfulness. Outside, she'd joined Colin's cause. She would do what she could.

"Ty never liked Jed." He sighed. "I should've listened to her."

"She doesn't like me, either," she said.

Colin didn't answer right away. "You fired her."

"I know."

"Do you?" She could hear the mat rustle as he rolled toward her. "That job wasn't just a job to her. It was the only thing keeping these streets from eating her alive."

"But, her family . . ."

"I'm her family," Colin said, and the edge in his voice made her lie still in attention. "Half the time that stoop outside is her home. Work is all she had. These jobs, they're not just jobs, Lena. They're the only things keeping us going."

Which was why they were willing to fight armed men for their right to form a charter. Why they were going to press, and take on one of the most powerful men in the Northern Federation.

She felt sick. Disgusted with herself. How arrogant and limited she'd been to think patching things up for Ty was as easy as getting her more work. When she'd told Minnick to let her go, she'd displaced Ty from her family. She'd taken away food, and clean water, and all the things Lena had taken for granted.

"I didn't know," she said.

"I know." He rolled back.

"I'll make it right."

He said nothing. He probably didn't believe her. Why should he? Trust, as he said, was a hard promise to keep. But she *would* keep it. Even if that meant going home to face her father, just so she could set up a meeting for the Small Parts Charter.

"Thank you for letting me stay," she said. And she listened as his breaths grew longer, and heavier, and free of all worry.

* * *

Dawn found them outside the Small Parts factory. Thirty-five of them. Everyone who had promised they'd be there, even herself.

Zeke and his sister brought signs. "WE GOT RITeS," one said, "SP CHARTER" said another, and while they waited, some of the others painted more on trash can lids and soggy boxes. Lena thought she might be the only one dreading the day; everywhere she looked people were grinning, laughing, even boxing in their own teasing, Metaltown way. But for Lena, the gray sky seemed heavier than before, and the fear inside of her was thick.

She'd been gone two days, and her father had not come looking for her. He didn't know where she was, but that didn't matter. He had the resources to send out a search party. He could have found her if he wanted to.

He would never forgive her for this. He had a long memory, and prided himself on learning a lesson from every experience. She had taught him one in return. That she was a traitor. That she couldn't be trusted.

She'd learned from the best. After all, he'd betrayed his own federation.

In her heart she knew that the treatment of the Small Parts workers had been wrong. She'd known it since she'd reviewed Otto's books and seen the discrepancies—the missing pay, the absorption of the Medical Division from its missing heir. Then she'd been to the factory, and sweated beside them on the floor. No breaks, no set hours, dirty water, and abuse by the foreman. Not to mention the exposure in that dreaded "hot room." It was barbaric. Humiliating to the core. And she'd been there one day.

Worse than the danger they endured was the fact that her father would hire replacement workers as soon as they were gone. *Shells,* the people called them. The ones who covered, but weren't the meat beneath. Josef Hampton didn't care how the job was done as long as it was done—as long as he had weapons that he could ship to the Northern Fed to fight the East, and the Advocates to fight the North. If this kept up, there would be more weapons than people left to fight.

If she'd stayed at home, if she'd swallowed her pride and been patient, she might have been able to help the charter. Her father would never listen to her now, but maybe that was for the best. Stopping production at Small Parts meant stopping production at all the weapons factories—they couldn't build their bombs without the necessary pieces created by this division. Stopping weapons production as a whole meant stopping her father from fueling the Advocates, but it put a lot of people out of jobs.

There was no way to win.

She sat on the sidewalk, separate from the others who congregated outside the alley that led to the entrance. On the walk from his apartment, she'd told Colin all she could about how to list his suggestions for change, and the proper ways to address her father to elicit respect. He'd listened carefully, seeking her advice in a way her family never had. But when they'd arrived he'd joined his friends, leaving her on the outside. She couldn't say for sure, but maybe the safety he'd called on her was some sort of protection from the others. They seemed intent to keep their distance.

Not that she knew what to say to them.

Ty walked past, bumping into her so hard she spilled across the sidewalk.

"Oops." Ty kept walking. Lena saw her find Colin, and take a place beside him. Her skin burned. But when she looked down the street, at the homeless, at the scantily clad women, she couldn't help feeling like she deserved everything Ty threw her way. She'd banished her to this life, and until last night, hadn't realized exactly what that meant.

She'd thought she could wipe away what she'd done with an apology, but nothing could fix what she'd done. Nothing, except perhaps supporting the charter—Ty's family, as Colin had put it. And even then, forgiveness would be hard earned.

Mr. Minnick arrived first, scowling as he approached the building.

"We got rights!" she heard the little one—Chip—yell. The others cheered behind him. Lena got to her feet.

"What the hell is this?" Minnick demanded.

"We want to talk to Hampton," said Colin. "We're not working until we do."

The throbbing at the base of Lena's skull had begun again. Before she knew it, she'd backed away from the group, biting her lip so hard it had begun to bleed.

"You want to talk to Hampton, you go through me," sneered Minnick. "Then I go through Mr. Schultz. Then he goes to Hampton."

Colin took a bold step forward. "See, that's not going to work," he said. "We didn't sign with Schultz, and we don't want to talk to you."

"Listen here, you self-important little prick," he growled. "Get your ass inside, or you're all fired."

"Call Hampton," said Colin. "Tell him the Small Parts Charter wants a meeting."

Minnick's fist shot out, but Colin ducked out of the way. The momentum swung Minnick forward, and he crashed into Ty, who shoved him back. With a thump and a grunt, Minnick hit the ground. The crowd laughed. Lena's breath caught. They couldn't fight the foreman. What were they thinking?

The cheers erupted as Mr. Minnick retreated. He pushed his way back to the employee entrance, his face a furious shade of red. The door slammed shut behind him.

Lena kept her eyes trained on Colin, fearing the reckless smile that lit his face. Yesterday he'd called off the mob from attacking the Brotherhood, but this was no better.

"We're pressing, Minnick!" he yelled. The others joined in. "Press! Press! Press!"

No. She bounced on the balls of her feet.

Hampton Industries had its faults, but it had kept all these workers alive.

Hampton Industries couldn't care less if these workers lived or died, just as long as they produced.

When they produced, their products went to the enemy.

Hampton Industries was fueling a war.

Choose a side, Ty had told her.

The sun came, eerie and pink through the haze, lighting the hard, serious faces of the Small Parts Charter as they chanted. The day shift had begun to arrive. A few people joined Colin and the others. Most attempted to push through the gauntlet to the safety of the factory, but found the foreman had locked the doors behind him. Lena watched, terrified, unsure how long they would be able to withstand the pressure of the charter, who hurled insults and blocked their retreat. Finally, Minnick emerged, and her throat clamped shut when she recognized the black pistol in his hand.

"Back up, rats!" he said. "Let the *employees* through!"

People began to yell, curse, focusing their efforts down the alley at Minnick. Lena took another step back, into the street. To her horror, Ty took a swing at a boy trying to get inside the factory. He hit her hard in the jaw with his elbow. She saw Colin take him down and screamed his name.

Minnick raised the gun in the air and fired. The blast smacked against the walls and Lena slapped her hands to her ears to muffle the ringing. Everything was spiraling out of control. Someone was going to be killed. What had she done, joining them?

"New plan," Minnick shouted. "Those of you who want jobs, prove it. Get this scum out of my sight and I'll even bump your pay."

His words hung in the air like the reverberation of the shot he'd fired. Then, the employees turned from Minnick back toward the charter, faces grim. It was obvious some didn't want to fight—their reluctance showed in their shaking fists as they raised them in defense. Others took hungrily to the challenge, eager to please their new foreman.

The two opposing waves collided. The employees attacked the Small Parts Charter, and the charter countered every blow, taking Mr. Minnick to the ground. Lena lost Colin, lost the foreman, even lost Ty. A girl screamed—a young girl. Maybe Zeke's little sister, maybe another of the young children who worked at the factory. The fear swelled inside of Lena, planting her feet in the asphalt, making it impossible to move.

Someone grabbed her arm and spun her away from the alley. The boy from last night who had come with the Brotherhood. A mess of dirty dark curls were plastered to his broad forehead, and his eyes were too far apart. He bared his teeth, then reached back and yanked her braided hair.

She screamed.

In a flash she remembered Colin on the bridge outside Metaltown. *Hit me,* he'd said. *If you can.* Concentrating all her strength in her right arm, she balled her fist and struck out. *Crack.* The pain ricocheted up her arm.

He released her at once, stumbling back and grabbing his face. The blood that ran through his fingers filled her with a primal thrill. He'd deserved it. He was going to hurt her and she'd hurt him first.

Men were running at them from up the street. Fifteen. Twenty. Maybe more. She recognized the guy who'd threatened her the previous night—Imon, they had called him. He held a knife in one hand. She remembered the way it had felt pressed against her stomach.

Fire burst through her blood.

"Brotherhood!" she shouted as loudly as she could. "Brotherhood! They're here!"

She was pushed down and hit the ground hard, scraping her knees and her elbows raw. Half crawling, half stumbling, she pushed to the opposite side of the street, away from the fighting.

"Brotherhood!" she heard the others yell. As they carried back the message, she felt the twisted validation within her sour. The Small Parts Charter was outnumbered. It was hard to tell what was happening across the street, but it looked like they were pulling back, away from the big men of the Brotherhood, away from her, deeper into the alley. She couldn't see Minnick; he must have been on the ground somewhere.

Then the Small Parts Charter began to disappear. It took only a moment to realize they had broken the barrier and were pushing into the factory, behind the brick walls to safety. She knew she had to get to them. She couldn't stay out here alone.

Jolting to her feet, she attempted to run across the street, but one of the Brotherhood's men caught her and whipped her around. She kicked him hard in the knee and ran for the alley.

"Colin!" Frantically she searched, but she couldn't see him.

The Small Parts Charter was almost all inside. The Brotherhood didn't know who to attack, and had turned on the employees, striking any kid who was still standing. Just as she reached the alley, a man stepped into her path. She registered the yellow stains on his bared teeth and the greasy tail of chestnut hair.

Jed Schultz.

"You," he said, his eyes widening with recognition.

She glanced down at the short leather club in his hand, stained red with blood. Someone grabbed her from behind and she wriggled away, heart bursting in her chest. Behind Schultz, the Small Parts Charter slammed the employee door shut.

"No!" Her eyes shot right, to the main entrance of the building. No one guarded it. A fleeting hope passed through her that it was still open.

She made a run for it, dodging through the bodies toward the double doors where she'd first been introduced to her family's factory. Ten steps—the breath seared her lungs. Four steps—she dove for the handle.

It didn't budge.

"Come on!" She jiggled it as hard as she could. "Come on come on come on!"

She banged her fists against the door. She kicked it. Her gaze flicked up and relief punched into her. Someone was coming. She could see their shadow through the dirty windows. But the Brotherhood's men were coming for her too. They were closing in on the side of her vision. Stalking her.

"Hurry up!" she shouted. Her pulse hammered in her ears.

The person inside ran to the door and grabbed the opposite side of the handle. Their eyes locked through the glass.

Ty.

And then Colin's friend straightened, and with a self-righteous smirk, lifted both hands, and stepped back.

25

COLIN

"Zeke!" Colin yelled down to the floor. "Len— . . . *Mary*—she with you?"

The machines were silent, but the voices resounded off the walls. Yelling, cheers. A few of the younger kids crying. The floor was packed with workers, some of them waiting nervously at their posts as if for the machines to start, most of them gathered in groups. Martin, Henry, T.J., and a few others were still upstairs guarding the employee door. Those injured in the fight were up against the walls. He recognized Agnes, who gripped her side, panting. A long smear of red wrapped around her waist.

"She's not here!" Zeke called. He'd gathered his sister and some of the smaller kids in the center of the floor.

Noneck came up the stairs, two at a time, blood still trickling from his nose.

Colin steered him toward Agnes. "Have you seen Ty or Mary?"

Noneck shook his head. "Saw Ty outside. Not since." He kneeled down to Agnes and pulled her hands away to see the damage. Colin felt a cold chill tremble through him. She'd been stuck, right above her hip. The blood that leaked out was almost black.

I did this to her. Colin forced himself to back away.

"Mary!" he shouted. He'd claimed safety on Lena, then thrown her to the wolves. If she'd been hurt it was on his hands. Ty never would have done this to him. That's because Ty was smart. What kind of person brought a greenback to a street fight?

He'd forgotten who Lena was. Or he'd ignored it, and seen only what he wanted to see.

He entered Minnick's office, which had been overturned since they'd taken the factory. Papers were spread across the ground, furniture tossed, but he only considered this a moment before shoving through to the opposite door, which led to the main hallway.

"Is the front locked?" someone asked behind him. Colin turned, startled, and found Henry on his heels.

He didn't know.

They raced toward the main entrance of the building and burst into the waiting room. Someone was beating on the door; its hinges squeaked with each hit.

Colin siphoned in a breath. Ty was here. Her bandage had been torn off, revealing the ugly brown welts on her cheek and her light blue iris, but she was still standing. *Smiling,* of all things.

And then he looked behind her, to where Lena slapped her hands against the glass windowpane.

Before he could speak, he'd sprinted to the door, but Ty blocked his way. He pushed her aside, lunging for the door handle. He could see Lena's terrified expression; her eyes, round with panic, her lips pulled into a thin line. It was just like after he'd found her in the car, and the sight of her like that shredded his insides.

I'm coming. Hang on.

"You open that door, everyone will get in," warned Ty.

Lena's muffled scream came through the glass as someone grabbed her around the waist and jerked her back. She held on to the handle, but those stupid gloves she wore wouldn't hold their grip long.

"Ready when you are," said Henry. He pulled a handful of white powder from the factory floor out of his pocket.

Colin unbolted the lock, planted his feet, and jerked the door inward. Henry threw a handful of dust into the face of Lena's attacker. The man cried out, and dropped her so that he could cover his eyes. She stumbled into the building, landing in a heap on top of Colin. Henry slammed the door shut and threw his body against it.

"Lock it!" he shouted at Ty. She flipped the bolt. The man outside kicked the door, but then disappeared from sight, leaving a prickling silence in his wake. The second he was gone, Henry began to barricade the door with furniture from the lobby.

Colin held Lena tightly against him. If he could only pull her close enough, she'd stop shaking. She'd see he still had her back, that she was safe.

"I got you," he said into her messy hair. Her fists knotted in his sweater, her knees curled under her, beside his hip. For one breath, in and out, he forgot the others. Forgot what was happening outside. There was only the firm floor beneath his back and her small body on top of his.

Then she withdrew, and smoothed down his shirt.

"Thank you." The rawness in her voice tugged at him.

Then she stood, straightened her sweater, and charged Ty.

His friend was too shocked to defend herself. She crashed into the back wall and huffed out a breath as Lena's shoulder slammed into her ribs. Lena clawed at her clothes like she might rip them to pieces. Colin jolted to his feet.

"Whoa, hold up!" Henry grabbed Lena around the waist and trapped her arms down at her sides. "You Uniform Division girls like to play rough, don't you?"

"Let go of me!" Lena kicked through the air as Henry dragged her back.

Ty wiped her mouth with the back of her hand. "Careful. I'll put you back outside."

"Ty!" snapped Colin. She met his glare, then turned, knocking him hard in the shoulder before striding down the hallway toward the main floor.

Something dark spilled over inside of him. She could have helped

Lena. Could have opened the door, called for backup, something. But she hadn't. She'd stood inside, behind the safety of locked doors, and *smiled.* His memories tinged red around the edges until he was so furious he thought he might break something.

"Stay here," he told Henry harshly. "Yell if someone tries to get through."

Henry nodded.

"Colin," he heard Lena say, but he couldn't face her. He didn't remember moving, didn't remember getting back to Minnick's office, or the platform outside it, but somehow he was there, burning a hole in Ty's back as she marched down the stairs.

Noneck grabbed him on the way by. "We got to get Agnes out. They stuck her good, Colin. She's bleeding bad."

"What's our move?" Martin glanced down at the girl in question, face pale. "We can't stay here. They'll break down the doors before long."

Colin's composure broke. His fist slammed against the railing. This was his fault. Agnes. Lena. The whole Small Parts Charter. The weights grew heavier, crushing his chest, grinding him into the floor.

"Some of the warehouse guys have cleared the back exit by the shipping dock. There's no Brotherhood back there." Noneck stayed where he was, awaiting orders.

He couldn't make these decisions. He couldn't hold Agnes's life in his hands. It wasn't supposed to go this way. Minnick should have called Hampton, and then they would have had the meeting. There was never supposed to be a fight.

"Take her," he said finally. Down on the floor, every dirty, sweat-streaked face was now pointed his way.

"The back by the shipping docks is clear." His voice was weak.

"Louder," prompted Martin, standing beside him.

"The back door is clear!" *Please be true.* "We need to get the people who are hurt out now. Zeke, take the kids with you." He swallowed. "Ty, you're going too."

She paused, halfway down the stairs, shoulders bunched, then continued in her descent.

"Ty, I'm talking to you!"

There was venom in her eyes as she slowly turned to face him.

"You can't kick me out."

He stomped down the metal steps, feeling dangerous, feeling like he didn't know her at all. "You turn your back on one of us, you turn your back on all of us."

"*She* is not one of us!" Ty shoved Colin back a step. "And you're not like her, either! She's a greenback. A *Hampton*."

Colin followed her gaze behind him, to where Lena stood on the stairs, sun-touched skin taking on a yellow hue. The others were whispering, pointing at her. She straightened her back and lifted her chin, but he knew she had to be melting inside.

"Mary crossed the line. She pledged," said Zeke. "I saw her."

"She's with us," Colin told them.

Martin's jaw fell open. "She's a *spy*?"

"I'm not!" Lena said.

Zeke had lifted his sister up on his hip. "What's this about, Colin?"

Colin stared at Ty, remembering when he was thirteen and she'd stuck up for him. Remembering when she'd taught him to throw a punch. Remembering day after day of working beside her, and night after night of searching for food. The day she'd found out Cherish was sick, and spent all her pay to buy her clean water. The time they'd taken on four guys from the Board and Care for stealing her shoes while she'd been sleeping.

Then those parts within him grew cold, and hard as ice.

"She's Lena Hampton. And I've called safety on her. Anyone who doesn't believe she's with us can take it up with me or hit the road. But that doesn't change anything. I'm staying here until we get a meeting with the boss."

They whispered among themselves, and Colin held perfectly still, unwilling for even his feet to falter.

"They came after her, too," said Henry. "I saw it."

A few people voiced their agreement. It should have brought relief, but all Colin could feel was frozen.

"She's the one that warned us about the Brotherhood," said Noneck. Colin turned to see him carrying Agnes's crumpled body down the stairs. They didn't have time to fight over this; they had bigger problems.

"In ten minutes I'm sending a message to the Brotherhood. If they break down those doors, we'll break every machine in this building. They don't want us to work? Nobody's going to work. Not until we talk to Hampton."

It was bold. Too bold, maybe. But the wheels were already in motion. There was no turning back now.

He closed the space to Ty, wishing he could take back the last hour, when she'd made her decision to break the code and lock Lena out of the building.

"You need me," Ty said in a low voice. "Don't do this."

"You did it to yourself," he said, feeling something inside him break wide open.

She looked up at Lena, desperation filling her face. She rubbed her hands on her pants. "All right, I broke the rules. Bust me up me if you have to. First hit's free. I won't even fight back."

Her words disgusted him. He didn't want to fight her. He wanted her here, by his side, the way it was supposed to be. But she'd ruined it, and as much as he wanted to, he couldn't let that slide. If it had been him locked outside that door, Ty would have torn apart whoever had done it. He owed Lena the same.

"Get out."

He was vaguely aware of the boy pushing at his side, yelling his name. Someone grabbed Chip, and pulled him back.

"Get. Out."

Ty went still, cheeks burning. "I guess Hayden isn't the only one in the family selling out for a fistful of green."

Colin pressed his teeth together so hard he thought they might crumble. She glared over his shoulder to Lena and he wondered how many others thought the same thing—that his loyalty had been compromised by her status. What that had to do with Hayden, he didn't know.

Ty turned and walked away, ignoring Chip, who clung to her side. Ignoring Noneck, who struggled with Agnes, and Zeke with the kids, and a line of those who hadn't bargained for this. Those who wanted no part in the Small Parts press, or the brutality of the charter.

He sagged back into the stairway railing and wondered what the hell he had done.

26

TY

Sunrise found Ty at Shima's apartment. She hadn't planned on coming here. She hadn't planned on a lot of things happening.

After she'd been kicked out of the factory, she and Chip had gone with Noneck to Charity House. They'd left Agnes on the front steps, knocked, and then hidden by the Board and Care across the street. It had taken three weak corn-flu victims to lift her, but they'd brought her inside. It wasn't great, but it was the best they could do for her.

Then they'd snuck back through the cluttered, sticky alleys to the factory. Even across the street Ty could feel the thick veil of tension surrounding Small Parts. Though no one had broken in, the front of the building was still teeming with Brotherhood thugs. Minnick and a few yellow-bellied workers were there too, but no Schultz. The stray pack of dogs snapped and snarled, waiting for their alpha to return.

Ty didn't know where the white knight of Metaltown had disappeared to, but if she had to bet, she'd say he'd run to squeal to Hampton. If Colin hadn't stabbed her in the back she might have warned him. As it was, Noneck delivered the message when he snuck back in through the shipping docks.

She could see the longing in Chip's face as they watched him disappear.

"If you want to go, just go," she'd said. "I don't give a rat's ass."

It had hurt his feelings, but he'd stood his ground. And that pissed her off. She didn't need a mama, especially not one half her age.

"I don't know how else to say it, kid. I'm sick and tired of you hanging around all the time. Go back to St. Mary's, or get in there with the others, but either way get gone. I've got enough to worry about without you hanging on my back."

Tear tracks made stripes down his dirty cheeks. "You don't mean it."

She forced herself to stare him straight in the eye so he would know she wasn't messing around.

"I wouldn't have said it if I didn't."

He'd kicked her, hard, right in the thigh. So hard it had knocked him over. Any other time she would have beat the snot out of him, but instead she was grateful. It stole some of the pain from her chest, just for a minute.

He'd snuck back inside, leaving her alone. Just like she was supposed to be.

And then, for the first time since she was a kid at the orphanage, she prayed.

Keep him safe, all right? Just do that one thing for me.

* * *

Shima opened the door on the third knock, just before Ty was about to turn around and leave. She didn't know where she'd go. She was so tired she thought she might just lie down in the alley and let the cold take her.

"Goodness, girl, you've seen better days."

Shima didn't look much better, though. The woman's hair was disheveled, her eyes red and swollen. She looked like she'd been crying. Ty immediately regretted knocking. If there was one thing she couldn't stand, it was someone else's tears.

When Ty didn't move, Shima grabbed her arm and pulled her in, checking the alley behind for any followers. Two children were on the floor. One was playing with a little rope doll Shima had made. The other was passed out on his stomach.

"Sit down," ordered Shima. Ty collapsed on the couch, only to have a bowl of corn mash shoved into her lap. The warmth made her numb fingers feel like they might crack. She wasn't very hungry.

"Did you run out of bandages?" Shima reached for Ty's wounded eye—the stupid marks that had made Colin unable to even look at her, that had sent him straight to that greenback spy Lena Hampton. Ty jerked away.

Shima set her teeth, scowling. "You need to keep it covered until it's healed."

Ty shrugged.

"Why aren't you eating?"

Ty looked at the pale mash, feeling her stomach turn. She handed it back to Shima.

"Small Parts Charter took over the factory," she said.

The woman ran a thumb over her own eyebrow. "I heard that. Should I ask why you're not there?"

Ty dug her heel into the carpet, staring at the wall. "Too much to do. I don't have time to mess around with that lot. I've got to find myself a job, remember?"

Neither of them said anything for a while, and Ty was glad. She didn't want to talk about it. It felt like more of that acid that had dripped on her face was being dumped in the empty cavity in her chest every time she thought about it.

"I'm sorry," Shima said finally.

"Didn't ask for your pity."

"Tough luck," said Shima. "You've got it."

Ty turned away, unable even to get up off the couch and escape her. "You know what the worst of it is?" she heard herself say. "All this? The charter, and the fighting back, it's all because of me. It all started 'cause *I* got hurt." She could feel the resentment spreading through her, sour and sticky as tar.

"And now you're not a part of it."

She curled her fists into her pant legs. She didn't need Shima making her feel bad. She didn't need anyone.

"We're not so different, you and me." Shima pulled her hair back, patting down the flyaways. "Before I came here, I worked as a nanny in a big house in the River District. Did I ever tell you that?"

Ty slouched, fitting her body around the couch's springs. Great. Story time. The babysitter was confusing her for one of the kiddies.

"My employer was young, handsome. He had a baby girl, barely standing on her own when I got there, and a little boy who was in constant need of a time-out. They were broken people. The poor mother had died of the corn flu, and left a hole in their lives a mile deep."

Ty knew what it was like to feel that hole. It existed inside of her, right now.

"The man ran a business, and worked too hard. Too many long nights. Too little time with his little boy, who pulled ten kinds of trouble trying to get his father's attention. Still, though, when he was home, my employer was kind to me. He talked to me like I was a lady, brought me back little gifts from his business trips. I'd never had things like that growing up. We became *close*." She glanced at Ty, as if checking to see that she understood what was meant by "close."

Of course Ty understood. She wasn't an idiot.

Shima hunched over her knees, resting her chin in one hand. "He sometimes said he'd move me into his big house, and we'd live there as a family. I didn't tell any of the other staff. It was a secret he and I shared. It was the best secret I'd ever had."

Her voice was quiet now, reminding Ty that there was only one person she'd ever shared her secrets with, and now a wall of stone and a Hampton stood between them. No one knew her like Colin, and when he was gone, no one knew her at all.

The haziness on her left side grew suddenly annoying, and she turned to face the woman more fully.

"So what happened?"

"Our arrangement was not as exclusive as I thought." She tapped her mouth with her fingers, sighed. Her face disappeared behind her hands. "He held frequent business meetings at the house. That man will stop at nothing to make a deal."

Ty didn't need to ask what that meant either. She remembered her nights at the Board and Care, the feel of another's weight on top of her, their breath in her face. Things weren't so different in the River District after all. She felt for the knife in her waistband, running her fingers over the steel to calm her nerves.

"So you quit," Ty guessed.

"I stayed on. For the children. The little girl. The boy . . . he'd already learned too much from his father, I suppose."

"But . . ."

"It's complicated." She stood suddenly, taking Ty's bowl back to the pot and dumping the contents inside. When she spoke again, her voice had softened. "It's complicated, loving someone so much you'd swallow hot coals every day just to see them done right."

Ty understood. She could have hopped a train, gone to Rosie's Bay like Hayden had all those years back. She'd thought about it more than once. It wasn't like she had anything worth staying for.

Especially not now.

"Now who's pitying who?" Shima asked, gauging Ty's response. "Don't bother. He sacked me soon enough. His son—that rotten little bastard—did something awful to his sister, and when I got in the middle of it my employer sided with the boy, and turned me out."

"What happened to the girl?" asked Ty. She remembered only glimpses of her own mother, flashes from her time before St. Mary's. A silver hairbrush. Her chiming laughter. An exotic perfume—something dark and spicy—that Ty had spilled across the floor. But those memories were only the dreams of a lonely kid. No Metalhead could afford perfume.

"She grew up, I guess."

"Do you think she misses you?"

Shima returned to the couch and collapsed again. "I know I miss her."

They sat in the silence, facing the wall, both missing their old lives so much it made the air between them heavy, palpable.

"What am I supposed to do now?" Ty whispered.

Shima grabbed her hand, and Ty didn't even flinch.

"Fight, because it hurts too much if you stop."

27

LENA

Lena spent half the night alone, cold and hungry, curled up in Mr. Minnick's office on a lumpy tweed couch. The foreman's chair beside her sat empty. Now that people knew who she was, they couldn't trust her. Even Colin was keeping his distance. Being *someone* felt a lot worse than when he'd told his friends she was just a sub.

In the middle of the night, a bone-rattling buzzer rocketed her back into high alert. But as suddenly as it started it was over, leaving a strange, screaming silence in its place. She held absolutely still, as if waiting for the floor to drop out from beneath her. A moment later the building plunged into darkness.

The power to the building had been shut off.

A chorus of protests sang out from the floor. Though she knew where she was, the familiarity of the dark, enclosed space was too strong. The muffled jeers from outside too reminiscent of another time.

Bile boiled in the pit of her stomach.

She stumbled to the door, clumsy fingers fumbling with the handle. Finally she jerked it open and swallowed the tepid, metallic air from the floor. It filled her mouth and lungs and pushed down the panic attempting to break free.

The emergency lights flickered on—one set of overheads in the far corner of the room. Their dull glow was just enough to create an obscure canvas in shades of gray. A winding, snakelike belt. Monstrous silver machines and black barrels. Not many people were left. Twenty, give or take a few. Counting them did nothing but increase her anxiety, and make her question, as she had a thousand times, what she was doing in a place she didn't belong.

Neither the Brotherhood nor the police had attempted to take the factory by force. But there were other ways to smoke them out.

Eyes adjusting to the poor light, she returned to the office and pulled open the top drawer of the foreman's desk. Inside, a bottle of liquid and a narrow glass figurine of some sort had been set atop a cluster of papers. She palmed the figure and riffled through the documents, lifting them close to her eyes to read. Incomplete pay ledgers, blank end-of-shift production reports. There was a thin piece of paper at the bottom, and on it was scratched a name: *Astor Tyson*. Beside it read: "*Call McNulty IMEEDEATLY*." Clearly it was important, even if the person who'd written the note had had the spelling capabilities of an eight-year-old.

She removed the small piece of paper from the drawer, frowning down at it. McNulty's name was familiar—Hayden had had mentioned it when they'd met at Colin's apartment. *No one else makes a run on Metaltown. Not even McNulty.* Perhaps he was another charter leader. If so, he might have been just as corrupt as Mr. Schultz. Maybe this Astor person was in on it, too. Lena shoved the paper into her pocket on the slim chance that she would be able to look into the issue when this was over.

After neatly stacking the remaining papers, she continued to another drawer, searching for a flashlight or something to quell her grumbling stomach. The figure remained in her hand, her thumb rubbing small circles over the smooth glass. She hummed softly to herself, lost in the task of sorting.

But when something shifted by the door, the song was swallowed.

"Don't stop because of me," said Colin, leaning against the frame. Heat flooded her cheeks.

"How long have you been standing there?"

Even in the dim light she could see his smirk. "Just twenty, thirty minutes tops." He made his way to the couch and collapsed, draping one long arm over the back cushion. "I see you've found Minnick's dope pipe." He pointed at the figurine in her hand.

"Dope . . . oh, yuck." It slid from her fingers and shattered violently against the floor. She grimaced and wiped her gloves on her pants, then fought the sudden urge to sweep it up.

Colin's chuckle rolled through the room, a breath of warmth in a cold, dark space. How could he laugh with everything going on?

"I thought you were avoiding me." She wished she hadn't said it the moment the words left her mouth.

The couch settled under his weight as he adjusted his position.

"I'm here, aren't I?" He tapped the seat next to him, and gradually she made her way over, sitting carefully, so as not to encroach on his space. "You're good. You know that, right?"

"What?" Her gaze found his, even in the low light.

"Your voice." He looked away. His fingers were tapping on the back of the couch behind her shoulders. "You could make a lot of green singing like that. Not that you'd need it."

Good God. She really had been absorbed in the task. She hadn't realized she'd been actually *singing*. Still. It felt different from when her father or his associates complimented her. Genuine.

"Oh," she said.

He scratched his neck. "You didn't say much earlier about our list of demands."

In the afternoon, Colin had gathered those who'd chosen to stay and compiled a list of requests they would take to her father when the time came. Lena hadn't said much; in all honesty she doubted the great Josef Hampton would ever see them. Their only audience would be their cellmates at the county jail. Of course, her father would never allow her arrest. Unless he wanted to teach her another lesson.

"It's a good list," she said, remembering the items. Pay twice a month and extra for overtime, two breaks a day, protection from the hot room chemicals and from firing in the event of sickness, and a new, fair foreman that wasn't "pervy," as they put it. Someone had asked for clean water to drink, but they'd all laughed like this wasn't even a possibility.

She'd been so embarrassed, she hadn't been able to look anyone in the face after that.

"Don't call them demands," she said. "My father doesn't respond well to people telling him what to do."

"I guess you two do have something in common."

She supposed he had her there.

"So what *do* I tell him?"

When she leaned back, his fingers skimmed over her hair, and she tensed.

"T-tell him you have some concerns about the Small Parts factory you'd like to discuss."

He snorted. "I'd say that's pretty obvious by now, isn't it?"

Perhaps so. "Tell him you'd like to invoke collective bargaining."

"Fancy words."

"It means you want to sit down with him and negotiate for more rights." She was struck by the sudden memory of the story she'd read at home about the rebel leader Akeelah wanting a seat in the Northern Assembly. *Perhaps he just wants their voice heard,* Darcy had told her. She couldn't help thinking Colin's plight wasn't so different.

"But what if I don't want to negotiate?" Colin's fingers slid over her hair again, though from his faraway gaze she doubted he'd done it on purpose. "What if I know what I want?"

She swallowed.

"Then you say it as honestly as you can," she said. "And hope he listens."

His shoulders rose as he breathed in, lowered as he exhaled.

"Thank you." The way he said it made her sit taller. Made her lungs expand. She felt like she could take on her father herself just then.

"You should know," he added. "We're not going to stop until we get what we came for."

"I know." She couldn't help but admire his commitment, but she wished there was another way. The sooner the charter went back to work, the sooner her father would ship weapons off to the Advocates. He might agree to Colin's demands just to get employees back on the floor. This victory would only mean a greater loss, more soldiers dying for a war they couldn't win, and the burden of that knowledge pressed her down into the lumpy seat.

Still, it wasn't as if the press could go on forever. They couldn't live here, locked inside a factory with no lights and no heat and no food. They would have to face Josef Hampton eventually.

She wanted to tell Colin—tell *anybody*—what her father was doing, if only so she wouldn't be the only one carrying this enormous secret. But she didn't know how to start. The words stayed locked in her throat, a family issue to be handled by family. Even after he'd admitted to treason, it still felt wrong to expose him. Wrong, and dangerous. He'd struck her for mouthing off. What would he do if he knew she'd really betrayed him?

She didn't know what to do. Even with the entire charter downstairs and Colin right beside her, she felt alone.

Glancing over, she found him lost in his own thoughts, chin buried in the collar of his shirt. She longed to read his mind.

"What's a safety?" she asked. "I heard you say it before."

He brought his arm back down to his side. It seemed to put more distance between them and she wished she hadn't brought it up.

"It's just this stupid Metaltown thing," he said, heel beating a rhythm into the linoleum. "It keeps you protected from anyone who tries to mess with you. It means that if they do, they mess with me."

Her mouth formed a small O. It didn't sound stupid. It sounded like more than her own family would have done for her. Still, she found herself thinking of Ty, the only other girl she'd known here, and she doubted he'd had to do the same for her.

"You don't think I can take care of myself."

"It's not that," he said, mulling over his words. "It just helps sometimes to have a friend here."

A friend. Was that what they were? She didn't have any friends, not real ones anyway. No one she would invite to have lunch or tell about her day. The thought that Colin had a whole charter of friends who would raise their fists in his defense made her warm behind the neck.

"I'm not sure the others agree with your choice."

He breathed out through his nostrils. "They're scared of you is all."

"Scared of *me*?" She laughed. "That's the oddest thing I've ever heard."

"Is it?" He shifted to face her. "Your family makes more money in a day than we'll make in a year. If one of us looked at you wrong, you could have us jailed, or fired, or . . ."

Guilt curved her spine. Regardless of what Ty had done, Lena knew that forcing her to leave had been harder on him than watching thirty other people march out the back door, and for that, she felt responsible.

She shoved the feeling aside. Firing the girl didn't equate to being shut out with the wolves.

"You wish she hadn't left." It tightened Lena's throat to say.

"She messed up," he said, shoulders flinching. "Even after what happened with her job. It just doesn't make sense. Street rules are the code she lives by. She's never done anything like that before."

Lena frowned. She knew why Ty had done it. Because Lena had hurt Ty, and now Ty wanted to hurt her. Because she thought Lena was a *greenback* spy. Because Lena had gotten her fired from Small Parts.

Because she cared enough for Colin to protect him.

"Do you ever wish you were someone else?" She glanced over,

worried that she had offended him. A girl who had been given everything didn't wish for such things.

"Most of the time," he said, words hanging in the air as if to say *but not right now.* His gaze deepened, seeing too much, and because she feared that what he saw would only let him down, she looked away.

"Your mother and Cherish are probably worried." She thought again of the frail woman, and wondered how long she'd had the corn flu. The prognosis for victims was grim. It had taken Lena's own mother before she'd been a year old.

He nodded. Then cleared his throat. "Your father's probably blown a gasket."

She wasn't so sure; he'd not even acknowledged her taking a car in the middle of the night. Again she wondered if he was looking for her now. If he knew she was here. If he was disappointed. The prospect gave her a twisted kind of hope. If he didn't care about her, she couldn't disappoint him.

"Is he why you wear the gloves all the time?"

She scooted to the edge of her seat. "No. What makes you say that?" Her hair was messy, and she tried in vain to keep it smoothed behind her ears.

He took her hand, weaving her fingers between his before resting them on the couch between them. He did this without any obvious thought, even while her heart pounded madly. "I thought maybe they were special or something. When I was a kid, Hayden gave me this coat he outgrew, and I wore it until the sleeves hit my elbows and I split the back down the middle."

His thumb trailed lightly over hers. She bit her lip, feeling her pulse quicken.

"You don't have to tell me," he said after a moment.

"I've worn them since I was ten," she said. "Not this pair, any pair." Only a few people knew what had happened, and she'd never dared to speak of it since.

"My brother liked to play this game," she continued, voice shallow. "Whenever I did something good, anything that got Father's attention really, Otto would lock me in the bureau in my bedroom. He was a lot bigger than me then."

Colin stilled. He said nothing.

Stop talking, she told herself, but the words kept tumbling out.

"One day my father left for a business trip and Otto locked me up and turned out all the lights in my bedroom, and then told Shima I'd gone to play by the river with the neighbors." *If Father really loves you, he'll find you.* "Shima was my nanny then. I think she panicked, guessing I'd fallen in or something. She didn't find me upstairs until the next day." That tightening in her chest was back, constricting her lungs. "I broke off some of my fingernails trying to get out." Sticky, splintered stumps. Wet blood running down her hands, her wrists, dripping from her elbows. "It's not that bad, but they didn't grow back. The gloves just cover up the mess."

She felt young again. Alone. Shima had left that day. Left her to Otto and her father. If Shima had really loved her, she never would have gone away. Lena didn't care if her father *had* fired her.

Colin had begun to squeeze her hand. "Damn."

His pity made her wish she hadn't said so much.

"I know it may not seem like it, but Otto's normal most of the time." They'd played together as children. Until he'd taken over the factory, they'd been tutored together as well. Most days they were perfectly respectful of each other.

"When he's sleeping?" asked Colin. "When he's eating? I hate to tell you, but even murderers are normal sometimes."

She pulled her hand out of his grasp. He didn't understand, and she couldn't explain it so that it made sense. Otto had not been born this way, he'd been made this way, a product of her father's worst qualities. Even if he applied himself, he'd never reach Josef's high standards. The bar would be raised just as it came in reach, and Otto would find himself lacking over and over again.

She was not the only Hampton with bruises. The difference was most of Otto's were on the inside.

"You shouldn't have to make excuses for him," said Colin.

He was right, of course. Regardless of what Otto had gone through, it didn't excuse what he'd done, or what he'd become. A younger, not quite as cunning version of their father.

Lena was glad her hair was down now; it hid most of her face.

"Can I see your hands?"

"What?" She jerked back, alarmed. "No. That's very rude of you to ask."

"Trust me," he said.

She wanted to believe him. She wanted to trust him. But the back side of trust was disappointment. In her world, one did not exist without the other.

Slowly, his hands slipped under her right sleeve. His touch seared a circle around her bare elbow and tucked just underneath the edge of the tattered satin. Every part of her braced, awaiting his next move.

His fingers grazed over the inside of her wrist, going no further. She nodded.

He eased the fabric down, holding her small forearm between his calloused hands. She gasped; her skin was sensitive, burning. Lightning shot up her arm, branching across her body. Her other hand, still covered, twined in her sweater, working the fabric between her thumb and forefinger.

He bared the delicate skin of her wrist, then the pale flesh of her thumb. He stripped each finger, one at a time, until she felt completely and utterly exposed.

Fear. Shame. But something more, something deeper, swirled inside of her. Her pulse beat frantically beneath his grasp. Her breath came in one hard shudder. It was easy for him, she realized. So easy to touch her this way. So easy to touch *anybody*. She'd seen him with the others—patting their shoulders, shaking their hands, grasping the backs of their necks. They all did it like it was nothing, but to her, it was complicated, and intrusive, and wonderful.

He turned her hand gently, his fingertips never ceasing their caress. She knew she should look away. She couldn't take his reaction when he saw the bruised nubs that would never fully heal, unprotected by fingernails that would never grow back. Seven nails were missing. Four on this hand alone.

It was unsightly.

But she couldn't take her eyes off his face.

He didn't cringe, or even pause. The skin became more sensitive the longer he continued, and a great dark whip curled inside of her, waiting to crack. Rough and smooth and raw, all blending together. He was so gentle. How could he be so gentle? She was shaking to pieces.

He pressed one finger against her empty nail bed. "Does it hurt?"

She shook her head.

"This right here," he said. "I think it's the part of you that's most like me."

She couldn't process what he was saying. It was all too much, too much exposure, too many feelings she didn't understand.

"I . . . all right." She snatched the glove. He gave her room as she thrust her hand within, but when she was sufficiently covered, he reached for her again. A sigh of relief escaped her lips at that small barrier between them.

Then he lifted her knuckles to his mouth and kissed them.

"Thanks," he said.

Her heart throbbed so sharply, it stole her breath.

"Colin!" called someone from downstairs. A tall, redheaded boy they called T.J.

They both jumped up, and she couldn't help but feel that she'd been caught doing something wrong. That concern was replaced by another as they raced out of the office: it had been too quiet through the afternoon. The Brotherhood was finally attacking the building. Or maybe her father had sent the police.

What would he say when he found her?

There was chaos, directed toward the side of the building. Henry had let someone in. A big man with white hair and a thick, grungy beard pushed a metal cart to an open area in front of the dormant machines. The emergency lights flickered above his head.

Colin skipped down the stairs two at a time, and Lena followed quickly. She recognized the visitor up close as the man who owned the corner rotisserie cart. The one Colin had traded his gloves to for a mug of oily water.

"Hayak?" Colin crossed his arms over his chest.

Martin shoved past him. "Uncle H.?"

He smacked into his uncle hard, and as they embraced the tears began to flow from the old man's eyes.

"This is your uncle?" asked Colin meekly. When Hayak's head lifted, he didn't look particularly pleased.

"What are you doing here?" asked Martin. Lena wondered the same thing.

"You are my sister's son," said Hayak, mussing Martin's short blond hair. "That is what I am doing here."

"How'd you get in?" asked Colin.

"Mr. Schultz's men have pulled back across the street. They are standing down, I think. Your foreman allowed me entry."

Lena's heart lifted as those around her cheered. "What about a meeting with the owner?" she asked. "Has anyone said anything about that?"

A fleeting moment of mortification as all eyes turned to her, and then it passed as they awaited Hayak's answer.

"You must be Miss Hampton," he said stoically. Lena's stomach plummeted to her feet. So Mr. Schultz had informed her father that she'd been sighted. What Josef's next move would be, she had no idea, but she dreaded it all the same.

Martin detached himself from his uncle's side and slapped a hand companionably on Lena's shoulder, jolting her back to the present.

"She's with us, Uncle H."

Hayak blew out a slow breath. "That is not what they are saying outside."

Colin took a step closer to her. She was glad, because her blood had begun to buzz, and she was getting that terrified gnawing again at the base of her spine.

"They are saying she was kidnapped by the Small Parts Charter," finished Hayak.

"*Kidnapped?*" Lena's head fell back. The second the word left her mouth she could see how her father might have believed it. Or worse, how he had fabricated this rumor to save face. An abducted daughter was far less shameful than a runaway.

Those around her resumed their quiet whispers, and began to distance themselves again.

"I wasn't kidnapped," she said. "I pledged. To the street rules. And anyway, if he really thought I'd been kidnapped, wouldn't he have tried a little harder to get me out?"

She thought of all the times he'd been gone, all the times he'd let Otto hurt her. How he'd turned Shima away for protecting her. How he'd struck her, and killed her favorite bird, and taught her lesson after lesson with the intention of making her strong.

He'd succeeded. She was strong.

The emotion was back, clogging her throat. She pushed it down. She would not give up any more tears to him. He was her father, but he would never have her back.

Colin was scowling. She reached for his hand, and he didn't pull away. He hadn't upstairs, either, when he'd seen her scars. He hadn't even when the others thought she was a spy. She squeezed his fingers.

"Will you pass on a message to Mr. Minnick?" she asked Hayak. "Tell him I refuse to leave the Small Parts factory until we have a meeting scheduled with Mr. Hampton. Tell him those are the terms of my release from this ridiculous *kidnapping*."

Someone whistled from upstairs. She glanced back to see Henry leaning over the railing, clapping for her. She smirked back at him.

"Lena," said Colin quietly. "You sure about this?"

"I'm sure." She nodded, moved by the concern in his face. "Don't worry. When we go to my house, I'll call a safety on you."

A smile broadened over his face. Martin shoved him, laughing.

Lena turned back to Hayak. "Tell Mr. Minnick that if anyone else is hurt, I won't be coming home. And tell him if my father denies this meeting, I will tell everyone exactly why this holdout helps the people of the Northern Federation more than a working factory."

There was a silence around her, and with it came an awe, an acceptance. For the first time she could remember, she was not afraid.

Hayak agreed to her message, and shook her hand. Before he left, he fired up his cart and fed them all fry bits and salty corn mash and pigeon stew.

It was the best thing she had ever tasted.

28

COLIN

A car came for them in the afternoon. The driver, a thick man with deeply set eyes and bushy brows, knocked heavily on the front door. Colin peered over his shoulder to inspect the street and see just what kind of tricks the Brotherhood might try to pull.

The terms had been laid out by Minnick two hours prior. Colin and Lena would be taken to a location of their choosing—Lacey's Bar, down by the river—to meet with Hampton, and in exchange the Small Parts Charter would vacate the building. There was to be no fighting among the Brotherhood, the holdouts, or the shells until the issues were resolved. Mr. Hampton had sent an army of police from Bakerstown to ensure his conditions were met.

Colin's palms were damp. A cold bead of sweat dripped down his spine. He'd assured the others that this would go well, but he knew the moment he left the building that there'd be a target painted on his forehead. As if the press weren't enough, Mr. Hampton was not going to be happy that his daughter had taken up with a working-class stiff.

Which was why all eighteen of them were going together.

Lena was close on his right, Martin on his left. Henry and Noneck and Matchstick clumped around him. Chip, invincible because he was too young to know any better, took the lead. Part of Colin wanted them to stay back—carrying their loyalty was a heavy burden and too many had already been hurt. The other part of him was proud, and hungry for justice. He was ready to end this.

The street was silent. A crowd had gathered on the south side, blocked by a line of police in black uniforms with Hampton Industries defusers and handguns latched to their hips. On the opposite side waited the Brotherhood—thirty thugs, Imon and that knothead with the brass knuckles standing before them. A sneering Minnick and a dozen Small Parts shells waited by the alley to be admitted into the building.

"Sellouts," muttered Noneck. "Yellow bastards."

Colin's mouth was dry. He set his jaw, told himself to toughen up.

"Think we can all fit in that thing?" Henry pointed at the little electric car as they huddled out in the open. Some of the others laughed nervously.

"It's ten blocks," Colin told the driver. "We got legs. We'll walk."

The driver shrugged, then backed away. Colin squeezed the knife in his palm and wondered what would have waited for him should he and Lena have gone alone. Hampton's man could have pulled off into any alley and fixed the game before it had even begun.

Now he didn't have the chance.

There was a commotion to his left. Someone crossed the police line, ducking between two officers. Zeke. His dark skin was already slick with sweat. As he sprinted toward them, one of the cops reached for his defuser. Colin siphoned in a breath, ready for a fight.

"Let him be!" shouted a voice Colin would know anywhere. "He's just a boy!"

A knot wedged in his throat. His ma stood right behind the line looking proud, and hard, and, well, more than a little pissed off. He remembered every time she'd told him to *do the right thing*. He wanted to tell her he was, but he didn't, because after Agnes and Ty and those who'd scrammed, he wasn't entirely sure.

As they moved closer, he could see that she wasn't in her Stamping Mill uniform, but in ragged trousers and one of Cherish's hand-knit sweaters. His fists clenched. The foreman must have fired her. Jed probably talked him into it—he may not have run the mill, but no one there was crazy enough to tell him he was wrong. The questions tore through Colin's mind: Was Cherish okay? Where was Hayden? What were they all going to do now?

He scanned behind her, looking for someone else. Someone he knew wouldn't show. Who he didn't *want* to show, but hoped would all the same.

But Ty wasn't there.

"Hi, Ma," he said as they shuffled by, so tightly packed they could barely take full steps. The blank-faced policeman between them made him feel like he was already in jail.

"I love you," she said, dark half-moons beneath her eyes. "But you're in big trouble when you get home, you understand?"

His ears got hot. Lena looked away. They moved on, past the crowd.

Each step they took seemed to bring them no closer to Lacey's. It was as if they were moving backwards, farther and farther away. The seconds turned to minutes. The chill sunk down to his bones.

He glanced down at Lena. Her chin was lifted regally, like it had been the first time he'd seen her and she'd stared down her nose at the rest of the world. Something was different about her, though. Something deeper than the clothes or her messy hair.

"Stop biting your nails," she said, pulling his arm down. "You don't want to show him you're nervous."

"Who says I'm nervous?" he asked, holding his arms so still they didn't move naturally when he walked. She rolled her eyes at him.

The broken curb ended at River Road. They'd reached Lacey's.

* * *

Hampton wasn't messing around. Lacey's had been cleaned out—no sloppy Metalheads hanging over the bar, no bums outside begging. Even Rico, his deformed mouth grimacing more than ever, had been replaced by ten Bakerstown rent-a-cops. But the light was still low, and the place still smelled like corn whiskey and dirty feet, and that was enough to remind Colin that they were still on his side of the tracks.

Jed Schultz met them at the door. His smug face had been wiped clean of all emotion. *Slick,* Ty would have said. The fact that she wasn't here weighed him down like a brick in his gut.

"Miss Hampton," said Schultz. He reached for her hand, and Colin smirked when she didn't return the gesture. "I wanted to apologize for our misunderstanding yesterday."

"What misunderstanding is that, Mr. Schultz?" asked Lena sweetly. "If you're referring to the fact that you ordered your men to have me beaten in the street, I can assure you, there was no misunderstanding. I was crystal clear on your intentions."

Colin settled back on his heels, hooking his thumbs in his pockets. Jed's expression went grim, then flashed back to shameful. *Slick.*

The white knight tilted forward, lowering his voice. "If I had known you were there . . ."

"Then you still would have attacked dozens of *children* and *teenagers,* thirty workers employed by my family, Mr. Schultz. Now, are we finished here? Mr. Walter and I need to speak to my father."

She breezed by him, pretty hair streaming behind her. Colin couldn't help but chuckle into his fist as he followed. Jed remained at the door, seething.

The back room was open to the bar, but typically reserved for card games. Only one table had been left out, and at it sat two men in black suits. One stretched back arrogantly, jacket unbuttoned, as if he owned the entire Northern Federation. The other's posture was rigid, but his head hung low like a child afraid of his teacher.

Colin had never seen Josef Hampton in person. He looked like Otto, only older, sharper, and more distinguished. His eyes were hard and glassy, like a snake's. Lena didn't share that feature, but did have his narrow build, and his light brown skin, and his raven black hair.

It took everything Colin had not to toss Otto out of his fold-out chair and beat in his skull with it.

"Colin Walter, I presume," said the elder Hampton. Neither he nor Otto rose.

"That's me," said Colin, glancing at the policemen stationed at every corner. *Show no fear.* "Thanks for seeing us, Mr. Hampton."

"I don't see that I had much of a choice," he replied.

Otto folded his arms over his chest and burned Colin with a glare that went deeper than annoyance, deeper than hatred. Colin had clearly taken something important from him.

"Let's get this over with." Otto nodded to the single chair across from them.

Colin's eyes flicked to Lena. An angry blush crept up her neck. He understood why. Her father and brother had yet to acknowledge her presence, and from the looks of it, they had no intention of doing so.

The chairs had been stacked against the wall behind Otto, and Colin walked around the table to grab one. He placed it beside the other and motioned for Lena to take a seat. Her brother's condescending laughter did not escape him.

"Awfully polite for a man charged with kidnapping my daughter," said Josef evenly. Colin pulled his shoulders back. Maybe if he had a flush suit and a shiny tie he would have told Hampton where to stick his accusations, but he didn't. All he had were his ripped slacks, his sweat-stained shirt, and his oversized jacket, all streaked with white powder from the factory and grime from the streets.

But he had Lena Hampton sitting beside him. And he had the Small Parts Charter right outside the door.

"We all know I wasn't kidnapped." Lena's words were tough, but her tone wasn't as sharp as when she'd talked to Jed at the door. She pulled at the ends of her gloves.

Josef ignored her.

"You've lived in Metaltown some time now, is that right, Colin?"

"That's right."

"Since your mother's *friend* became ill, if I'm not mistaken." Colin didn't like the way he said "friend"—like Cherish wasn't real. Like she was imaginary or something. Hampton ran his thumb down his jaw. "That's when you and your brother Hayden were moved to Keeneland Apartments, when you began to work for me at the Small Parts factory."

Colin shifted. "Looks like you've done your homework."

Lena placed her hands on the table. "Father, what does this have to do . . ."

"What will happen to your family if you don't have an income, Colin?" His eyes were black as ice over asphalt, his tone just as cold.

The muscles in Colin's thigh had begun to twitch. His heel tapped against the floor. Intimidation. He knew what Hampton was trying to do, and had to figure out a way to stop it.

"I didn't come here to talk about them."

"Victims of the corn flu don't last long without the proper care," continued Hampton. "Medicine. Clean water. Doctor's visits. Even then, there's no cure. Maybe Lena has told you about her mother. I'm just thankful that we were able to make her comfortable in her passing. That she didn't have to die somewhere cold and filthy, like the Charity House."

A veil of red dropped over Colin's vision. He could see his fist connecting to Josef's jaw, pounding it again and again until it cracked and shattered. He gripped the seat of the chair so hard his knuckles turned white.

"Father," said Lena. "Please."

"Just making conversation." Josef flicked a speck of dirt off his suit jacket.

"I know what I stand to lose," growled Colin. "Do you?"

Josef smiled slowly. "I have a feeling you're about to enlighten me." He crossed one leg over the other, shoes polished and gleaming.

"A third of your workers. More, if things continue the way they're going. Maybe all of them."

"Half of the Northern Fed is starving," said Otto. "What makes you think we can't replace those workers by the end of the day? We could pay them half of what we pay you and they'd still do it. Or didn't you stay in school long enough to learn the state of the economy?"

Colin smiled savagely. "I stayed in school long enough to learn that the guy with the biggest mouth better be the fastest runner."

Otto flew to his feet. "You pretentious—"

"Otto, sit down." Josef's harsh gaze never wavered, and bound by it, Colin fought the urge to slouch or look away. He'd crossed the line. Hampton had gotten under his skin and he'd lost his temper. He'd meant to play it cool, polite, but all he'd done was provoke a lion.

He was aware of Lena's shallow breaths beside him.

"You're catching me at a very precarious time, Colin." Josef sighed. "It so happens I lost a lot of money today with your little demonstration, and I don't have the time to lose any more." He leaned back in his chair, his cold stare falling for an instant on his daughter before shifting back to Colin. "I'm a businessman. What will it take to get these workers back on the job?"

Colin moved to the front of his seat. Hampton would hear his demands after all. He could feel his friends just outside the door, counting on him to do this right.

"We work twelve-, sometimes sixteen-hour days and never get overtime. Every couple months we don't even get paid. We get sick, we get fired. We miss call, we get fired—"

Hampton raised a hand to cut him off.

"You're not hearing me, Colin. What would it take *you* to get these workers back on the job?"

The momentum building inside of him slammed to a halt. A bribe. Hampton was going to bribe Colin to convince the Small Parts Charter to end the protest. Just like he'd done with Jed Schultz and the Brotherhood.

"Father, I've been to the factory, on the floor with the workers. You must listen," said Lena.

Josef pulled an envelope out of his breast pocket and opened it. He laid out a stack of green an inch tall. Otto looked away, as if annoyed.

"That ought to cover your rent for a while, I'd say."

Colin choked.

"And," said the elder Hampton, "I'll arrange for Cherish to have a bed at the hospital in the River District by nightfall. She'll have a nurse as well, on call, to get whatever she needs."

Colin couldn't take his eyes off of the cash. It was more than Jed had given him to take to the Wokowskis. More than he'd seen all in one place in his life. The empty paper envelope made a crinkling sound as Josef folded it.

"Consider it an act of patriotism," the man said. "Your work supports the war effort, builds the tools our front lines need to defeat the enemy. To rebuild the Northern Federation."

Lena made a sound between a cough and a choke, and was silenced by her father's appraising stare.

Colin could see the white sandy beaches and the cool, blue water of Rosie's Bay. The houses on stilts, the docks where you lay in the sun. It was just beyond his fingertips. Screw the hospital. With that much green he'd be able to get his Ma and Cherish, even Hayden, to the coast. They could leave everything and start fresh.

Josef lowered his voice. "Think about your future. Is this really all you wanted for yourself? To be trapped in Metaltown?"

"Colin," Lena whispered.

"Stay out of this," Otto hissed at her.

Colin's head snapped up. Otto Hampton. The rich boy who locked his sister in a closet. The rich family who thought they could buy themselves out of anything.

"No," he said. "It may work with Schultz, but it won't work with me. Small Parts Charter wants change, and we won't work until we get it." Inside of him, the image of Rosie's Bay grew darker and darker, until it disappeared completely.

Josef's eye twitched. Slowly, he gathered up the bills, and replaced them in his coat.

"Very well," he said. "Otto, see that we have a third of the staff replaced by the end of the week."

Colin gaped. "You're firing me for *not* taking a bribe?"

"*Firing* you?" mocked Hampton. "Did you really think that was the biggest consequence you'd face today? You halted production on what should have been a very profitable work week. You mercilessly attacked a foreman. You *held my daughter hostage.*"

"I was not held hostage!" shouted Lena. "I left because of you!"

Josef joined them standing. "Lena, the driver is waiting outside. Go and get in the car."

"No." She grabbed Colin's hand. He could feel her shaking. He felt sick thinking of what horrors might await her if she went with them.

And what would happen to him? What did Hampton mean, *consequence*? A man as powerful as Hampton could bypass jail. He could make Colin disappear and no one would ever know what had happened to him.

Josef breathed in slowly, then exhaled with a flare of his nostrils. "This meeting is over. I'm genuinely sorry we couldn't come to an agreement. I'm sure there'll be others who will jump at the opportunity I've offered today."

He'd never intended to listen. And Colin, blindly optimistic, had cleared the building so the shells could go right back to work. The thought crossed his mind that Ty never would have been so trusting.

One of the policemen approached behind Lena. Colin jerked her out of his reach. Three more officers closed in behind them, and those at the door approached slowly, defusers in hand.

He looked at her one last time, hoping she knew he was sorry. He knew they wouldn't hurt her; they were here for him, and though his arms felt like lead, he detached her hand from his. He'd been in enough fights to know when you had a chance and when you were going to get beat, and today his odds didn't look good.

But that didn't mean he was going to lie down and take it.

With a burst of speed, he charged the nearest cop, who grunted in surprise and toppled backward onto the floor. A boot landed hard in Colin's gut, making the edges of his vision turn black. The air in his lungs expelled in one hard cough.

Then there was a searing pain in his shoulder. A million lightning bolts charged through him, sending him into convulsions. Somewhere far away he heard Lena scream his name. And then he heard nothing.

29

TY

Bakerstown was quiet at night. The kind of quiet that snuck into the back of Ty's head and planted ideas about people following her, watching with their alley-cat eyes. She didn't like the place anyway, especially after the last time she'd been here with Colin. The streets were unfamiliar. The overhead streetlamps too bright and accusing.

At least the last time she was here she hadn't been alone.

She kept her head down and hustled past the park and the closed deli to Fifth Street, then turned left. The bottoms of her boots scraped over the sidewalk, an unavoidable giveaway of her location.

Her knife hand was sweating.

Shima had been right. If she stopped fighting, she'd start hurting, and that scared her more than dying out here alone.

For the hundredth time that day, Colin came to mind. His blue eyes, hot with fury. His words: *get out.* Her heart, if she had one, felt like it was being mashed over a grater.

A figure stepped out from the dark parking garage. He was lanky, with a mess of black dreads and a green pullover that clung to the lean muscles of his shoulders. She recognized him immediately from their last encounter.

He stayed quiet as she approached, but it was clear from the way he glanced to the side that more of his friends were hidden just out of sight.

"I want to see McNulty," she said as confidently as she could. She showed him her knife. "I'm not going to ask twice."

He started to laugh. "She-man the Metalhead. I thought I smelled you crossing the tracks. Looks like someone got a workout fixing up your face."

His friends filtered out of the garage's entrance, making a circle around her. She tracked them with her good eye. Brainless muscle. McNulty's crew. Her lips peeled back, the knife out before her. Her bad eye put her at a disadvantage. Screwed up her balance and hid half the playing field. She'd latched her belt so tightly it made it difficult to breathe, but she wasn't taking any chances that someone might try to rip it off.

"Tell me where he is or I'm going to stick one of you," she said.

They all laughed, bringing the heat to her skin. She hated having her back exposed. If Colin were here . . .

Stop. If Colin hadn't kicked her out, she wouldn't be here.

"Why should we take you to McNulty?" asked the boy with tight curls—the one who was bent about being taken out of school. "You trying out to be a working girl?"

"She's too ugly to put on the books," replied Dreads. "She'd have to pay them to take their pants off!"

More laughter.

She lunged at Dreads, catching the collar of his shirt and twisting it around his neck. Her knife point pressed into his jugular, and when he swallowed, the metal tip broke through his skin.

Five other blades were pointed into her back.

"No one's laughing now," she observed. Rings of white surrounded the boy's irises. The shallow breaths made his damp chest shudder.

"Let him go, Metalhead," said Schoolboy. "Or we'll cut you open."

"Not before your friend chokes on my knife," she answered. "Anyone want to see if I'm lying?"

Try me, she thought. She had nothing left to lose.

Silence.

Dreads motioned for the others to stand down. "What do you want with McNulty?"

"I have a proposition for him. And information he wants to hear." Her grip relaxed on his shirt.

The boy hesitated, looking for a weakness, but her gaze didn't falter.

"Fine," he said. "Let's go. Hands off the Metalhead, got that?" he told the others.

Dreads led the way, while the others walked behind her. Ty kept her knife ready, just in case one of them decided to try to take her down, but her hands were shaking now.

They reached the apartments where she and Colin had met the Wokowskis. Below them was a dingy bar with an old-fashioned carved wooden sign hanging from a wrought-iron hanger. The Cat's Tale.

Dreads trudged down the concrete steps, peering suspiciously back over his shoulder at her before banging on the door with a heavy fist. A moment later a thin line of light sliced through the peephole and a pair of beady eyes assessed them from within. The door pulled inward, and Ty was bathed in a muted yellow light.

The smell hit her first. Cigar smoke and too much perfume. She followed Dreads tentatively, gauging her surroundings, learning quickly that the only accessible exit was the door just behind her. Raucous laughter, both male and female, bounced off the walls. Most of it came from a felt-topped poker table in the center of the room, where half a dozen men played cards and tilted back shots of corn whiskey.

The bouncer stopped Ty with a heavy hand on her bicep. Automatically she jerked out of his grasp, only to find a pistol pointed at her chest. The breath choked off in her throat. The man's mouth was set in a firm line. A scar hooked around his cheek from his right eye, like a falling teardrop.

"I'll take the shank, and any other piece you might have on you," he said gruffly.

McNulty was here. If she wanted to see him, it would have to be on his terms.

She handed over her knife, and pulled another from her boot. When he patted her down, her forehead broke out in a cold sweat. The moment his hands were gone, she backed away, then made for the table.

Dreads shoved in front of her. "Either you want to die, or your head really is filled with metal."

She ground her teeth and let him take the lead. The card players lapsed into silence as they approached. The yellow lamplight cast a circular glow, and she stayed just beyond its reach in the shadows.

Across the table through the thick smoke, a man settled back in his chair. His hair may have been red once, but now it was a dull orange, tinged with white around his ears. A smattering of black freckles covered his cheeks, and his eyes were green, like the color of his clan. There was a hooker on his lap, a girl not much older than Ty, skimpily clad in a lacework bodice. McNulty lowered his hand of cards and tapped her on the lower back with one monstrous hand. She stumbled away, a sloppy smile on her face.

Dreads cleared his throat.

"One of Schultz's Metalheads is here to see you, sir," he said. "She says she's got information."

"I'm not working for Schultz," Ty said quickly, fingers flexing over her trousers.

McNulty cocked one brow, chewing on the end of his cigar. He was perhaps the only man in the Cat's Tale not wearing green. His gray button-up spread across his ample midsection.

"She was here just last week on Jed's pass," Dreads pointed out.

"Well, that was last week," snapped Ty. "I got nothing to do with slick Jed Schultz *this* week."

"Why are you here then?" asked McNulty. He had a strange

lilting accent, one she'd never heard before. His eyes drifted over her bandaged face.

Ty glanced behind her to the others, who were crowding too close for comfort. "Jed Schultz is taking bribes from Hampton. They're thick as thieves, those two."

McNulty smirked, one gold front tooth winking at her. "And?"

Ty shifted. "And the workers who pay their dues to the Brotherhood aren't going to like that when they find out."

"A heart-wrenching story to say the least," McNulty said, tapping his cigar on the edge of a brass ashtray. "What does this have to do with me?" His gaze returned to the hand of cards, and he riffled through them, pulling the last two to the front.

Keep fighting. "Everybody knows you used to rule Metaltown. Word is that Jed Schultz kicked you across the beltway, and that you were too yellow to ever come back."

McNulty's jaw twitched. He placed his cards back down.

"Watch your mouth, kid," said the old man to his right. He was bald on top, with a thin hedging of gray at his temples. Dreads took a deliberate step away from her.

"I'm just saying what I heard," said Ty. She'd gotten to him, she could tell. The air between them thinned, like a ratchet had pulled it tighter.

"The story's changed some in the telling," said McNulty.

Ty shrugged, trying to look like she didn't care. "All I know is the Small Parts factory refused to join the Brotherhood this week, and won't go back to work until Hampton makes some changes. Once the other factory workers see we can do it, they'll do it too, and that puts slick Schultz in quite a bind, if you know what I'm saying."

Schultz's words, as he'd said them to Hayden at the Brotherhood office, replayed in her mind: *Every other factory in town will have to stop production until we find replacements. This town will shut down.* Metaltown depended on the factories. The factories all depended on each other—they all built parts of the same weapon. The charter needed to show the other workers they weren't afraid of the Brotherhood, and to do that the Small Parts press wasn't enough. They needed muscle.

McNulty tapped his cards on the table. "Schultz is just Hampton's lapdog without his Brotherhood."

"That's right," said Ty. And none of them were anything without the workers.

"Hmm . . ." McNulty scratched his thumb over his chin. "If he loses his workers, the McNulty clan can take back Metaltown."

Ty nodded.

"If you don't work for Schultz, what could you possibly be getting out of this?" He leaned down to stare at her square in the face.

"My life back," she said simply.

Work. Enough green to buy some food. *Colin.*

He laughed then, a deep, throaty sound that grated against Ty's nerves.

"If only you were trustworthy."

Someone grabbed her from behind. She jerked against him, swinging back with her elbow and cracking against something solid. A flash of short curls, and the red smear of blood. The schoolboy latched her arms down to her sides while she struggled.

"Bring her into the light," ordered McNulty.

"Let me go!"

"Schultz has outdone himself this time," said the crime lord, rising. He flattened his hands on the table, leaning forward so that the table lamp illuminated his face and made his rough skin glow. "It's clever, actually. Well played. Taunt the McNulty clan to cross the beltway and violate the truce, then when he retaliates we'll be on his turf." He shook his head. Some of the other men at the table laughed.

"I don't know anything about a truce!" Ty's heart slammed against her ribs. Schoolboy swore and gripped her harder when she swung back her heel and connected with his shin.

"Of course you wouldn't," said McNulty. "Schultz is too smart to tell his spy the whole story. Tell me, kid, what'd he offer you?"

"Nothing, because I'm not working for stupid Schultz!"

McNulty smiled, rounding the table slowly. He was big. Bigger than she'd thought. Two heads taller than her. A few of the girls pulled away, toward the back of the room.

It was in that moment she realized just how much she didn't want to die.

Her limbs went cold. She locked her jaw and told herself to be brave. Not to cry. If he was going to kill her, she'd go out like a Metalhead, kicking and screaming to the end. Not like some Bakerstown pansy.

She shoved her weight back, trying to throw Schoolboy off balance. She kicked at him, swung her body from side to side.

"*Stop,*" said McNulty, the word so firm she actually did. Everyone did. No one moved as he reached overhead for the chandelier and tilted it her direction. Her shirt had come up over her belt in the struggle, and he focused on the uncovered skin at her waist.

"What's a roughed-up roach like you doing with vaccine scars?" he asked.

Another man from the table rose and came to take a look for himself. She didn't like that one bit, but held still, because even if she didn't know what McNulty was talking about, anything that held off a knife to her gut felt like a good idea.

"You're too healthy for food testing," the giant mused, releasing the chandelier. It swung, throwing light across the room in waves. "'Less your insides are all melted."

"My insides are my own business, thank you very much." Sweat ran down the side of her face.

"They're old scars," said the other man, poking at her stomach with his finger. "Probably got them as a kid." She kicked at him, and he backed away.

McNulty nodded, never looking away from Ty.

"Where are you from?" he asked. Wrinkles formed around his eyes, his mouth, his nose—the marks of a hard-lived life.

"Across the beltway," she said between her teeth.

"Try again," he said. "Metalheads don't have enough money for food, much less vaccines."

He thought she was lying? There was no reason to pretend you were from the slums.

"I grew up at St. Mary's."

"An orphan," he said, eyes growing wide. "Your parents had the flu?"

Lots of orphans were orphans because of the flu. She didn't know where this was going.

"I guess."

"You don't remember."

"I was just a kid."

"How old are you now?"

"Why do you ca—" She hissed as Schoolboy twisted her arm behind her back. "Fifteen." She thought, anyway. She didn't know her birthday. The woman must have forgotten to mention it when she'd been dumped at the orphanage.

A quick hand snagged her chin and dragged her into the light. She blinked, trying to grab her hat as McNulty ripped it off her head. Her bandage came off next, and he tossed it onto the floor.

"Who are you?"

"What's all this about?" she asked.

He shook her so hard Schoolboy had to release his grasp. The room bounced in her vision. The muscles of her neck tensed against the whiplash.

"Who. Are. You."

"Ty," she said. "My name's Ty."

"*Ty*," he repeated, laughing. The other man laughed a moment later. Soon those at the table were laughing, too. "Ty, who just wants her life back."

"That funny?" She mustered a sneer.

"Oh, it is," he said, wiping his eyes. "Astor Tyson. Here, in my bar."

"No . . . I . . ." *Astor*. Why was that name so familiar?

"Impossible," snorted someone from the table.

There was a cloudiness in her head. Images, carried in the fog. A wooden train set on the floor. A thin woman in a black dress, dragging her through the streets. A pinch to her belly, from a long silver needle. Things she'd only dreamed about. Things that didn't always make sense.

Ty was a child when she'd been brought to St. Mary's orphanage. The nuns had called her Ty; she'd told them that was her name. She didn't know an Astor Tyson. She didn't understand why he thought she was this person, just from a stupid cigarette burn on her stomach.

She didn't remember being burned, though; the nuns had only told her that. It could have been a vaccination scar, like they'd said. But she didn't know anyone else with one. As far as she knew, only the rich kids got their shots. She didn't know why she would have been vaccinated, or against what. The corn flu? There wasn't a cure.

She flinched, realizing she'd gone still in McNulty's grasp. Her response was answer enough. A slow grin split his face, his gold tooth drawing her fearful gaze.

"I'm not Astor Tyson," she said. "I don't even know who that is."

Some of the older men were talking among themselves. The bald one approached behind McNulty, lifting a pair of spectacles to ogle her properly.

"Ten years late," McNulty said. "But Hampton'll be pleased nonetheless." He laughed. "We might get Metaltown back after all, boys!"

"What are you talking about?" she gasped as he tightened his grasp on her throat and pulled a knife from his belt.

"I'm talking about green," said McNulty. "My favorite color. Hampton's going to pay out by the bucket for your cold corpse."

He pulled his knife back, and in the lamplight she saw that one side was jagged, the other smooth as silk. She tried to loosen. A punch hurt less if you didn't flex; maybe the same was true for a stick.

Good-bye, Colin.

"I'll pay you double!" she shouted. One last ditch effort to save her own life. If green was what he wanted, she'd get it.

He froze. "What's that?"

"Whatever Hampton's paying you to kill me, I'll pay you double."

He laughed, but his knife lowered. Then he stopped laughing. The room went silent, but her ears were ringing.

"Help us in Metaltown, and I'll get you the money." She didn't understand why he believed her but knew better than to question it. If he thought she could get the money, she'd make sure he thought her blood ran green.

He released her shirt. She grabbed the back of a chair, drawing in a ragged breath.

"Might work, McNulty," said the old man.

"Or she might take the cash and scram," said another.

"I'm good on it," Ty said. "Help me and I'll help you."

McNulty turned slowly and paced across the room. He came back, bushy red brows scrunched together. Ty thought he couldn't possibly be more confused than she was.

"I need to think on it," he said.

Her chin jutted forward. "There's no time to think on it!"

"A general always thinks twice before marching his troops into war," said McNulty. "When I've made my decision, I'll find you. And know this: a girl with one eye can't hide in Metaltown. If you try to run, bet that we'll go with my first plan, and I'll deliver your head to Hampton on a stake."

Ty shivered.

Dreads motioned toward the door. She should have been grateful to be alive, but all she could think was how she'd failed on her mission. Swearing under her breath, she turned, and made for the beltway.

LENA

Lena stared, still seething, at the pile of kindling on her floor that had once been a birdcage. She'd thrown it there when her father's new driver had carried her over his shoulder up the stairs to her room. The defeat in his eyes as he'd slammed the door behind him had brought a wave of satisfaction, but then the lock clicked. She was a prisoner.

She tore off her tattered gloves and flung them into the pile, pressing her bare fingertips to her hot, swollen eyelids.

She kept seeing the same image. Colin convulsing on the floor, his jaw open wide in a silent scream, his eyes pinched shut in pain. Every muscle jerking against his will.

Her father had done that. It sickened her that the same blood flowed through her veins. He had never intended to listen to the workers, only to taunt Colin with money, to offer him a bribe to keep quiet and silence his friends. Nothing mattered to Josef Hampton but wealth. He'd even sold out the Northern Federation to the enemy to get more.

And Otto was just like him.

They'd taken Colin to jail. She knew that inmates were the first line in food contamination testing. If Colin was lucky, he'd end up like Cherish. More likely he'd be forced to test some new strain of manufactured corn product. His insides would melt. Burns would cover his skin. He'd go blind or deaf. Sores would line the inside of his mouth until he was unable to eat at all, and then he would slowly, painfully die.

She'd read about this in her lessons. Before her father had become angry with Darcy, and the content had turned to language arts.

This was her fault. If she hadn't encouraged Colin to bargain with her father, he might never have continued with his charter. If she had warned him about how dangerous Josef Hampton could be, he would have known to run.

But likely wouldn't have.

A groan started deep inside of her, making her insides tremble. He already felt dead. And despite all rationality, she felt responsible.

She returned to the door, slamming her fists against the wood. When the bruises bit down to her bones, she threw her shoulder into it, until finally she slid to the floor, wrapped her arms around her knees, and gave in to the exhaustion.

* * *

Movement in the hallway had her springing to her feet. She searched frantically for something with which to defend herself. A shard of wood from the birdcage stuck out from the pile and she snatched it, and braced it before her like she'd seen Ty do after Imon and the Brotherhood had come to the statue outside Colin's apartment.

Then she glanced down at the weapon, bewildered, wondering just who she thought might be coming for her. This was the River District, she reminded herself, not Metaltown.

The door pulled outward, and a narrow woman in a black dress backed in, carrying a silver tray of tea and crackers.

Lena shoved her aside, trying to get out the door, but it was too late. The heavy oak was already locked. The tray clattered to the floor. The teapot shattered.

"Well," said Darcy after a moment, wiping crumbs from her bodice. "I suppose this room needs a good scrubbing anyway."

"Where is my father?" demanded Lena, throwing down the scrap of wood. Darcy's consequent evaluation of Lena's clothing and naked, deformed hands had her brows arching high into her forehead.

"I don't know," she said. "The Hampton men have yet to return home."

Lena sighed heavily, realizing how disheveled she must look after seeing Darcy's neat appearance. Unconsciously she went to straighten the sweater she'd borrowed from Shima. Though it was probably better that they keep their distance, Lena missed her. Anything she touched, her father had a way of breaking.

"You have to let me go, Darcy," said Lena.

Darcy rolled her sleeves up to her elbows and knelt to the floor. She began to gather the larger pieces of glass to take to the wastebasket.

"You've had quite an exciting last few days," said Darcy. "You must be tired. A hot bath and a warm dinner, I think, and then straight to bed."

"Darcy!" Lena grabbed the woman's bony arm and hauled her up. "My father has sent an innocent boy to his death and I'm the only one who can stop it, do you understand? You have to help me get out of here."

Darcy's eyes lowered. "You know I can't do that, Miss Hampton."

"Oh, have some backbone, for God's sake!" cried Lena. "Someone's life is on the line!"

She turned sharply, and stalked to her window, staring out at the tall oak tree. The nearest branch thickened a few feet away. There, it would support her weight, but she'd have to make a jump for it.

"Where did you get this?" Darcy's voice was low. When Lena turned, her tutor was pale, her brow damp with sweat. In her trembling hand was a scrap of paper, which she extended Lena's direction. "This name. Where did you get this?"

Lena approached, glancing down at the slip she'd taken from Mr. Minnick's office when they'd been under siege at the factory. *Astor Tyson—Call McNulty IMEEDEATLY.* She'd forgotten she'd put it in her pocket. It must have fallen out when she'd thrown the birdcage.

"It was in the bottom of the foreman's desk. I think McNulty might be another charter leader or something. Not that it even matters anymore," said Lena, waving her hand.

"I told you to be careful," said Darcy. Her voice was firmer than Lena had ever heard it. "I warned you to leave this alone."

Lena's arms lowered to her sides. "What are you talking about, Darcy?"

Darcy's hand flew to her mouth, as if willing her to stop speaking. Lena closed in, grabbing the frail woman by the shoulders.

"Tell me what's wrong."

Darcy's nostrils flared as she inhaled.

Lena, at her wit's end, shook her. "Tell me!" The fear brightened her tutor's eyes, making Lena inch back. "Please, Darcy."

Darcy glanced at the door, then back to the window. Paranoid fear made her features more pointed and harsh.

"I used to work for another family in the River District," she said hurriedly. "A doctor who was researching a cure to the corn flu, who hired me to tutor his wife in society living because she'd been raised among the middle class in Bakerstown. They had a child, a little girl. A good girl."

Darcy crossed her arms over her chest, slouching.

"It was rumored the man came close to an answer—close enough to catch the attention of wealthy men—investors, who began funding his research. He built hospitals with that money. Clinics, throughout the Federation. They were worth more than the entire weapons division. Small Parts, the Stamping Mill, the Chemical Plant, *all of it.*" She hesitated, glancing again at the door. "When the war began, his work became more important than ever. The strongest federation would be victorious, and they'd be strong because they would have the *cure*."

She was referring to the Medical Division; Lena remembered it from their earlier discussions. *Once upon a time, saving lives was more important than ending them.*

"He didn't find it," Lena guessed. If someone had found a cure to the corn flu, she would have heard of it. Everyone would have heard of it. There would be no fighting over clean food. The war would be over.

"No." There was regret in Darcy's voice. "He thought he had it—he was so confident he tested it on himself, even gave his wife and daughter a vaccine he'd concocted. Horrible stuff, injected right into the belly. Left an awful welt."

Lena cringed. She'd had her vaccines against the pox and measles in her youth, but had been fortunate not to scar.

"None of it worked," Darcy went on. "Both the doctor and his wife contracted the very illness he was trying to treat. They held on for longer than most, but near the end, his investors began to prowl. The research in those labs was worth a lot of money, and the family's death provided enormous opportunity. Do you understand?"

Lena nodded. "The first to find the cure would be the most powerful person in the Northern Federation."

"Yes," said Darcy, lowering her voice to a whisper. "But the first to prevent someone from finding the cure would also be very powerful."

Lena couldn't wrap her mind around that. "Why would someone stop research that could end the war?"

Darcy breathed in slowly through her teeth. "Not everyone is so eager to end this war, Miss Hampton."

Lena closed her eyes, hearing the low voice of her father's associate return to her: *In order to keep our little rebellion in action, we'll need five hundred units of artillery, delivered by railway, in unmarked crates to Billington. That ought to fuel this damn war for another eight months, at least.*

The business of war.

She felt the sudden urge to touch the rope doll her nanny had made her all those years ago, but realized she didn't have it. She'd left it at Shima's. Before she'd gone with Colin to Small Parts. Before the press.

"What about the doctor's child?" Lena asked. His daughter would have inherited her father's work and income. In her absence, Hampton Industries had been absorbing the profit.

Darcy gripped her elbows tightly. "When she didn't get sick, one of the investors hired a gangster from Bakerstown—a man by the name of McNulty—to find her, and kill her."

Call McNulty. This note hadn't been about an unresolved work issue, it had been about a bounty, about a killer looking for his victim.

"My father was the investor." Lena's blood ran cold.

Darcy nodded. "The woman begged me to take her child away, to hide her, but your father's men were already watching." She reached for the tray, began stacking the larger pieces of glass on top of it. "I took the girl to an orphanage. St. Mary's, I think it was called. And then I caught a train. I thought maybe if I left, it would draw them away from Metaltown. I didn't know what else to do." A wedge of glass sliced open the tip of her finger, but she continued stacking, faster now than before. "Your father's men caught me near the southern border. They wanted the girl, of course, but how could I give her up? She was just a child."

"What did you tell them?" Lena asked weakly.

"That she was sick—that the vaccination in her belly that had killed her parents was killing her, too—and that I'd left her near the river. She'd go easy that way. Numb from the cold." Her eyes closed tightly. "They didn't believe me." She'd stopped stacking now, and one hand lifted absently to the back of her head. Lena wondered if she'd been injured. All the times she'd shied away from Josef Hampton stood out sharply in Lena's memory.

"You didn't go to the police?" But even as she said it, she knew this wasn't an option. She'd seen the chief of the Bakerstown police in her own house, sharing drinks with her father, who donated huge amounts of money to support the force.

Darcy gave a wan smile. "And tell them what? That I'd taken a child and left her at an orphanage? You know as well as I do where their loyalties lie."

"Why?" Lena pressed. "All these years you've been trapped here. Why not run?"

Darcy gave a watery laugh. "Do you think I haven't tried? I think they would have just killed me and been done with it if they'd found the child's body. The fact that she was missing turned out to be the only thing keeping me alive."

Lena felt ill. She'd been so preoccupied with her own problems she'd never considered that Darcy was her father's prisoner. She felt terrible for all the cruel things she'd said, all the times she'd taken out her frustrations with her family on her. Darcy hadn't chosen to be here, and Lena couldn't even begin to imagine the fear and abuse she must have received, or the bravery it took to get up each morning and guard her secret.

Her father had hired someone to kill a *child*. Another fragile yellow bird in the palm of his hand. And now he would go after Colin, and the Small Parts Charter. He would sell weapons to the Advocates, who would in turn kill Northern soldiers. He was a monster—one who owned gangsters, politicians, and police alike. There was no way to stop him.

"This girl—Astor Tyson—is she alive?" asked Lena. The dreadful meaning of the note she'd taken from Minnick's desk took full hold of her then. McNulty may have already found Astor Tyson, may have already been paid by her father to make her disappear.

Darcy had backed into the door, and was resting against it, worn down by the past.

"I don't know," she said. "But if she is, she'll be worth a lot of money. Astor Tyson is heir to Division IV—the entire Medical Division. She'd be worth more than you, Miss Hampton."

31

COLIN

It was the coughing Colin heard first. The sticky hacking that turned to a gasp, and then a desperate groan.

He pushed himself up to his hands and knees. His cheek was frozen from where it had pressed against the floor and when he blinked, his vision stayed blurry.

Rags. He needed rags. And a wastebasket. A cup of the clean water they saved for Cherish.

"Shut up and die already!" A man's voice echoed off the walls, its origin indistinguishable. Colin jolted up, reaching automatically for the knife at his waist. A sharp hiss of pain tore through him. The knife was missing, and in its place was a bruise.

Panic clawed up his spine.

He wasn't at home. His last memory was of the meeting with Hampton. And then Lena, shouting his name. The police, they'd attacked him. They'd brought him here. Wherever here was. Jail, if he had to guess.

He massaged the base of his neck, an attempt to clear the throbbing in his skull enough to think. His fingertips probed the darkness, inching over the cold, damp cement floor until it connected to a smooth stone wall. He followed it up, rising to his feet. Both arms extended, the heels of his hands flattening against each side. When he stood on his toes, he could reach the ceiling. The room had no windows. No light.

He tried to control his breathing, but it echoed in his eardrums like waves. Great ocean waves, like the ones he'd imagined at Rosie's Bay. He pinched his eyes closed and tried to conjure the warmth of the sun, but something bumped up against his shoe, and squeaked when he jumped back. He hated rats.

He found the edges of the door, blunt nails scraping down the seal. There were bars in the center, spaced widely enough that he could reach his wrist through. The hallway beyond was just as dark.

"Hello?" he called in a hoarse whisper. His muscles felt weak. Questions he couldn't answer slammed through his head, threatening his resolve to keep it together: how long he'd been here, and where Lena was, and if his ma and Cherish knew what had happened.

"Keep it down!" came a male voice from somewhere to his right. A laugh, or a sob, gripped his throat. He'd never been so happy to hear another's voice.

"Where are we?" Colin asked. "The jail?"

"No." The voice was closer now, and sounded vaguely familiar. Probably wishful thinking. "A facility. For food testing."

His stomach dropped. Hampton had bypassed jail and taken him right to the executioner. He tried to focus. He knew where the food testing plant was. On the outskirts of Metaltown, beyond the beltway.

"How long have you been here?" he asked, desperate to keep the conversation going.

The boy hesitated. "I . . . I don't remember. Four days? Five maybe? It's hard to tell in the dark." He paused when a groan came from a few cells down. "Hey, why'd they throw you in here?"

Colin succeeded in pushing his forearm through the bars, but he couldn't go beyond the elbow. He swore as the pain shot up into his shoulder. He swept blindly for the handle.

"Pissed off the wrong guy," said Colin. The boy laughed a little crazily. "What about you?"

"Same thing," he said. "Guy wouldn't happen to be named Schultz, would he?"

Colin hesitated, then continued his search, straightening out his arm to get through. "He was one of them."

"I think he killed my dad."

A grave pity mingled with his growing sense of urgency. Schultz might go after his ma and Cherish for what Colin had done. Hayden might not be there to defend them.

The thought of his brother drew Ty's words from his memory. *At least Hayden isn't the only one in the family selling out for a fistful of green.* Whether she'd meant Hayden's drug debt or something more, he didn't know. He just wished things had gone differently back at the plant. If Ty had been outside Lacey's, there'd be no way he would have gotten locked up, not as long as she was still standing. She had his back no matter what.

At least she used to, before the charter, and the press, and Lena.

"What happened?" asked Colin, trying to push Ty to the back of his mind by pressing the heels of his hands against his forehead.

The boy coughed once to clear his throat. "He went to work. He's a consultant at the chem plant. Anyway, he didn't come home. I crossed the beltway to find out what happened and woke up here."

"Schultz is a bastard," said Colin. He couldn't reach the handle, so he withdrew his hand, the sweat pooling in the divots of his collarbone. "I say we get out of here and return the favor."

The boy scoffed and the familiarity in his tone struck Colin again. "If I could get out of here, don't you think I would have done it?"

"If there's a way in, there's a way out."

There was a long stretch of silence, and then the boy spoke again.

"In school we read this book about a man who stole a loaf of bread to feed his family."

Colin closed his eyes, despising the darkness and the welling fear within him. He needed to get out, not chat about literature.

"They threw him in prison," the voice continued. "And they brought him out of his room only to torture him. Crazy stuff. Water up his nose and everything. But every time they took him, he learned a little more of the layout of the building. And then one day, when they came to take him out for torture, he made a run for it."

Colin was pacing the four steps to and from the door, wishing the guy would just shut up about torture. He hoped they hadn't brought Lena here—the tight space would make her crazy.

Just thinking about her made him crazy. He had to get out of here.

"That's a great story," said Colin, half listening as his hands felt their way over the cold stone walls.

"They bring us out twice a day for food testing," whispered his hall mate. "I think I know where the exit is."

Colin froze. He returned to the door, wrapping his fingers around the freezing metal bars. "Tell me."

"It's in the white room, behind the glass. Where the testers sit. The door behind it opens to the outside but you have to get into the testing room in order to see it. I think . . . I think two of us could get through. You sound like you're still healthy."

Colin didn't ask what happened in the testing room. He didn't want to know.

"I'm healthy enough," said Colin, a wild, desperate kind of hope thrumming through his blood. "What's this book called, anyway?"

"*Flight of the Fox,*" answered the boy.

Flight of the Fox. Colin searched his memory for where he'd seen that name before, and then pictured it. Sitting in a pile of papers on the table in an apartment in Bakerstown.

His insides bottomed out.

"Gabe?"

Silence. Then: "Who are you? Who's there?"

Colin swallowed. Schultz had killed Gabe's father, Mr. Wokowski, possibly because of him. Because he'd told Schultz Wokowski didn't want his money. He grasped the bars so hard his hands began to shake, but his body melted down, until all his weight was hanging onto them.

"It's Colin," he said weakly.

Gabe didn't say another word for a long time.

* * *

Hours, maybe days later, the lights in the hallway buzzed, then flickered on. Colin, curled in the back corner of his cell to keep warm, shoved himself up, blinking back the brightness. His squinting eyes shot around his cell—no more than a cement closet, the floor damp, the corners marked by black mold. It may not have been a jail, but it sure looked like one.

He was so hungry his stomach hurt.

A guard in a beige suit came to the front of his cell and told him to put his hands between two bars. They were cuffed; the cold steel bit into his wrists.

"You got a visitor," the guard said. The cell next to Colin's was silent. Whether that meant Gabe was sleeping or listening, he didn't know.

Colin had a hard time keeping his steps even and measured as he followed the guard through a maze of halls. There were no windows, no signs posted. He looked for something to track his progress—to learn the layout of the building as Gabe had suggested—but he was surrounded by white-painted bricks.

His pulse had doubled by the time they reached a small room, large enough only for a single metal table and two chairs. His Ma had come. Or Ty. Maybe even Lena. Someone was going to get him out of this place.

The guard told him to sit, then fastened his cuff to a circular ring at the edge of the table and left the room.

A frantic kind of hope exploded in his chest. The terror of what lay behind him seemed so much worse with even this little separation.

He couldn't go back into that cell. The cold floor, and the thick darkness, and the fear that no one was coming, had all been seared into his memory. So what if he *was* yellow about the whole thing. This was a place of nightmares, worse than he could have imagined. If leaving was a matter of telling Hampton he was sorry, he would do it. He would kiss his damn shoes if that's what the man wanted. He didn't care, as long as he didn't go back.

His hope was crushed by thoughts of Gabe, and Mr. Wokowski. He couldn't leave Gabe behind. No one deserved to rot here.

Colin waited. And waited. His nerves wrenching tighter with each passing minute. After a while, he began to think this was some kind of trick. They were going to tease him with the prospect of getting out, then crush his relief by throwing him back in a cell.

He stood, but couldn't extend to his full height with his cuffs locked to the table. Just when he was about to call out, the door opened, framing a thin man in a suit with a tail of slicked-back hair. A thick wool coat draped over his arm, and Colin shivered just looking at it.

"Colin," said Jed with a smile—the same smile Colin had once been warmed to see. He turned to the guard. "I'll knock when we're finished."

The guard nodded and closed the door. Jed laid his coat over the back of the chair opposite Colin, then took a seat. Overhead, the harsh yellow lights buzzed.

Jed kept smiling. Colin's hope dried, and turned sour, and burned in his chest. Slowly, he sunk into his metal chair.

"How do you like your new place?" Jed held his arms out.

Colin didn't answer.

"It's a little drafty," Jed said. "But I hear the food is wonderful."

Colin's eyes narrowed.

"Have you sampled any of it yet?"

"What are you doing here?" Colin asked.

"I thought that was obvious," said Jed. "I came to visit an old friend. We are friends, aren't we, Colin?"

He wanted, more than anything, to wring Jed's neck. To tell him what a liar and a crook he was. To call him out for being Hampton's pet, and maybe even *killing* Mr. Wokowski. But Colin was cuffed to a table, and Jed was not. He could go back outside, with Colin's ma, and Cherish, and the charter, and leave Colin inside this festering pit, wondering what was happening to them.

"You made a good run of it out there." The sudden drop of Jed's voice took Colin off guard. If it had been anyone else, he might've thought the sentiment was real. The People's Man looked down at his hands, folded on the table. The sleeves of his suit jacket covered his wrists.

"In this world, you have to fight to get to the top, or get crushed by the heap, am I right?"

Colin's fists bunched, and the chain between his cuffs clattered against the table. Much as he didn't want to go back to that cell, he'd rather be there, alone, than out here with slick Jed Schultz. He hadn't come here just to reminisce about the press, or philosophize on life. He had a purpose. He needed to get to it.

"You nearly did it," Jed continued. "You just forgot one crucial step."

"Yeah?" said Colin. "What's that?"

Jed spread his hands over the table. "You have to take out the competition."

Colin snorted. Of course it was too much to press for his own charter's rights while the Brotherhood was around. Two separate charters couldn't possibly exist in the same place at once. Not when Jed wasn't getting paid for both of them, anyway.

He forced his shoulders back, and his jaw to stop grinding.

"Is that what I am, Jed? Your competition?"

Schultz met his stare evenly, and despite himself, Colin was humbled. The man was conniving, but he'd survived Metaltown a lot longer than Colin had. Even if he'd gone about it the wrong way, he'd built himself a small empire, and that was nothing to sneer at.

"Not mine," said Jed. "Hampton's."

Colin gave a wry laugh. "Yeah, how's that?"

"You threatened him," said Jed. "Not with your little blade, or your little army. You yelled loud enough that he could hear."

Colin flinched. "We didn't ask for anything the Brotherhood doesn't get."

"Yeah," said Jed. "Difference is, I tell the Brotherhood what they want."

His meaning filtered slowly through Colin's irritation. "Hampton pays you to make it seem like it's their idea."

"It's called strategy," said Jed. "You listen to your people. I listen to Hampton."

"You do whatever he wants, you mean."

"I'm not stuck in here, am I?"

A thin, tenuous silence stretched between them.

"Why *are* you here?" Colin asked again.

"Guess I just wanted to tell you I was impressed you tried."

"You say that like it's over." Colin's voice broke a little as he said it. He hadn't truly considered that it was, even alone in his cell. Believing there was still something left to fight for was what had kept him from losing his mind. But hearing Jed say he was impressed tore the last shreds of confidence from his fists. You knew you were in trouble when the devil himself said he was proud.

Jed rose and pushed in his chair. "It *is* over, kid. We don't beat men like Hampton. We just find a way to live in their shadow."

He knocked on the door, and Colin was alone again.

* * *

Back in his dark cell, Colin's thoughts consumed him. Much as he hated to admit it, Jed was right. The press was only ever a dream. They were just kids in Hampton's eyes. Poor kids, who should have been happy to have jobs at all. He'd thought if they all came together things could be different, but this was Metaltown. Things didn't change in Metaltown. *You* changed, and if you didn't, you paid. You ended up here, in a place so bad even men like Schultz pitied you.

Jed had been wrong when he said you had to climb to the top or get crushed by the heap. Their places had been set when they were born. Jed was no higher than he was; sometimes Hampton just threw him a scrap from the table.

The anger sparked in him, warming his cold body. He didn't want Hampton's scraps. He didn't want Jed's pat on the back. He didn't want to take what was given, when what was given wasn't enough. He wasn't going to lie down and die—Ty had taught him better than that, and soon as he was back outside he was going to set things straight with her. Maybe the press was over, but he still had people counting on him. His family. Gabe, in the cell next door. Lena, wherever she was.

The only thing keeping him sane was believing that Josef Hampton, however ugly he could be, would not send his own daughter to this place.

Colin closed his eyes, and saved his strength. The next time the guards opened that door, he was getting out.

* * *

Hours passed before the lights were turned back on. A different guard appeared outside Colin's cell and told him to clear the door. He could hear other guards, including the one outside Gabe's cell, telling the other prisoners to do the same. Colin checked the weapon at the guard's belt and found a defuser. Just a defuser. Not a gun like the Bakerstown cops had carried.

His heart was pounding as the guard cuffed his wrists behind him and shoved him into the hallway. Gabe was pulled out a moment later, wearing the same old denim pants and loose shirt he'd seen him in before, only now his face was gaunt and pale as the moon, and his eyes tinged with red. A scab on the side of his forehead descended into a purple welt at the top of his jaw.

There was a fury in his glare that stabbed into Colin and painted him with shame. *You killed my father,* that glare said. And Colin wondered if he wasn't right.

Colin glanced back to the four other men behind him. All were in various stages of the corn flu. The closest had almost no lips, the scarring and burns on his mouth were so severe. The man behind him also had a red mouth, and red cheeks, too, but his gaze was so unfocused that Colin suspected he was blind. The others weren't much better.

Food testing.

He'd heard about it. He knew Rico had once worked for the food testing plant, and that was what had turned his grin into a perpetual sneer. The reason for the defusers was clear now—the guards didn't need guns; no one was strong enough to fight.

Colin forced himself to stand tall because he wasn't yellow. He wasn't a coward. He was the man of his house and people were counting on him. He hated that he had to lock his knees to keep them from giving out.

I will not die here. I will not die here.

They were led out of the cell block and into a brightly lit hallway, and Colin's eyes watered at the sudden white light. Here it looked more like the facility he'd pictured in his nightmares. Sterile. Cold. His wrists worked against the harsh plastic bindings, and his gaze locked on the backs of Gabe's sneakers.

They were brought into what he figured was the white room Gabe had talked about. It was segmented in the back by a separate observation space, the length of the far wall. A flat-faced, redheaded woman in a white lab coat ordered the guard to put Colin on a scale while she took notes on his height and weight. She made him open his mouth and looked inside for any previous scars, and then shined an even brighter white light in his eyes.

"Baseline readings: unremarkable," she said.

He felt a tug of resentment. *Unremarkable.* But gauging by the other poor saps in the room, he felt very remarkable, if only just because he could still make a fist. Which he did. That earned a clinical "relax" from the woman, and a sharp jab between his shoulder blades from the guard.

He broke down and asked, "What are you doing?"

She didn't look up at him. "Developing a safe balance of natural and synthetic materials to feed a hungry world."

Ever since Cherish had gotten sick, he'd never eaten anything that hadn't been tested. His ma had made sure to grind that lesson into his brain. He'd rather die of starvation than start now.

A man entered the room from behind the glass observation partition. His bald head was too shiny, and his eyes bugged out from their sockets. He carried a metal tray and set it on the counter near Gabe. Atop it was a clear glass bottle, filled with liquid.

Colin felt his palms go clammy.

"What is that?" he asked, bracing for another warning from his guard.

The woman continued to add to her notations.

"That's the cure to the corn flu," she said. He felt the acid churn in his stomach. There was no cure to the corn flu. They were still running tests. Experimenting on otherwise healthy people.

On him.

She motioned to the guard. "Motor skills."

The guard cut Colin's bindings, one hand on his weapon. Colin rubbed his wrists and followed the woman's directions, which involved tracing a pattern of circles on a piece of paper with his finger. She took more notes.

Colin took notes of his own. Six guards. Four testers. And only two subjects strong enough to fight. At least the security seemed relatively low here—it would have been a different story if they'd been at the jail.

His attendant departed to the front of the room and unlocked a door with a scan of her ID badge hanging around her neck. He watched her emerge behind the glass observation window and sit with three other scientists, all with no-nonsense expressions. Behind them was a metal door with a push bar handle. That must have been the exit Gabe had talked about.

He focused on that door through the glass. That was his way out.

They were brought to a long white table where Colin was forced to sit on the end. Gabe was seated next to him, then the blind man, and so on down the line, until the sickest man, an invalid who could barely register his guard's commands, was placed at the opposite side.

A woman with short hair, wearing a shabby gray uniform, pushed a metal cart into the room from the hallway where he'd entered. Corn mash. The sweet smell of it had Colin's mouth watering and his stomach clenching.

He couldn't eat it. It was tainted food. Poisoned. *Testing* food. He steeled himself against his own demanding hunger.

Then the bug-eyed man came down the line with the glass bottle and a little glass dropper.

"No," moaned a man three spaces down. "No, please. No more."

The guards had all been dismissed but one, and he stood by the closed door. Just Bug-Eyes and the woman with the cart remained before them. Colin frantically searched the room for a weapon, but the countertops were mostly empty.

The sickest man on the end had to be told three times to stick out his tongue, which was crusty and almost black. The scientist squeezed the top of the dropper, and a clear liquid squirted out onto his tongue. He was given a bowl of corn mash. The blind man beside Gabe began to whimper.

"We can take that guard," Colin whispered to Gabe, biting his pinky nail.

Gabe turned away.

Colin swore under his breath. He wished Ty were here. There wouldn't be a moment's hesitation. When it was time to fight, she had his back, no questions asked.

He leaned around Gabe to whisper to the blind man. "There's a door directly behind you, think you can find it?"

The man choked on a sob, but nodded.

"Hold it closed, okay? I'm going to get us out of here."

The man hiccupped, then straightened his back.

"Are you crazy?" muttered Gabe.

Colin ignored him. "We're going to rush the guard on three."

"I'm not helping you do anything."

"I didn't know," said Colin, watching the scientist move to the next prisoner. "I didn't know Jed was bad until after I came to your house. If I'd known . . . I wouldn't have done a lot of things, okay?"

Gabe didn't say anything.

"I'm sorry," Colin said. And he was.

The tester was two men down.

"Gabe. I can't do this alone."

Finally, almost imperceptibly, his old friend nodded.

When the tester reached the blind man, Colin burst from his seat and lunged across the table. The tester yelped, and as he stumbled back into the cart, Colin caught the glass jar, sloshing, slippery in his hands, and threw it with all his might at the guard, who was already drawing his defuser.

A loud clang, and a crash, then a scream as the tester knocked over the cart and the woman. The glass hit the guard in the face, spilling clear liquid and blood down his chin. Then Colin charged him, and the guard yelled out in pain as the back of his head bounced off the white wall.

They fell in a heap to the floor. He threw his weight on top of the struggling man, nearly tossed over the top of him. Desperately Colin tried to contain the guard's flailing arms. Fury and terror blended inside of him. *I will not die here.*

"Get his weapon!" Colin shouted.

Gabe jumped on the guard's arm, a sickening crunch coming from beneath his knees. He snatched the shockgun just beyond the man's reach and lifted it, wide-eyed, unsure of what to do next. A pained groan ripped from the guard's mouth, and his eyes rolled back in his head.

"They're coming! Help me!" pleaded the blind man. He'd found the door, but it was already being shoved open. One of the other prisoners staggered toward him.

Colin ran back to the table, lifted one of the metal chairs, and with all his might threw it into the glass observation window at the back of the room. It cracked. An alarm sounded in the building—a high-pitched *whir, whir*—spiking his pulse.

He picked up the chair and threw it again. The woman who'd taken his baseline readings, along with the other scientists, were all running out the exit door. Gabe was right—beyond the partition he could see natural light, the gray haze of Metaltown. Freedom.

Behind him, the other inmates were struggling to hold back the guards on the opposite side of the door. The siren screamed through his temples.

"Hurry up!" shouted Gabe, voice cracking.

A roar started deep inside of him, flexing through every muscle in his legs, his back, his arms. He whipped the chair through the air, and when it slammed against the observation window, the glass finally, *finally,* broke.

"Come on!" Colin yelled. The shattered pane sliced into his fists as he punched the hole larger. Gabe was up, defuser in hand, while Colin looked back at the other inmates.

If just one abandoned the door, the whole thing would cave in.

Leave them, screamed a voice inside of him.

He couldn't.

He bent down, running at the table, using his momentum to shove it forward. "Move!" he ordered, and the inmates scattered as he rammed the heavy wood against the door. It inched open, the silver barrel of a defuser sneaking through. The table would not block their way for long.

The guard with the broken arm had revived, and he took down the slowest, the worst of them, who could barely walk anyway. A low cry erupted from the poor man's throat, like the sound of a dying dog.

"Come on!" Colin grabbed the blind man's arm and propelled him forward.

The door slammed against the table. A second later it was wide enough to squeeze a body through, and a small guard scrambled over the table. An electric crackle snapped by Colin's ear. Gabe had gone around the testing room and opened the door, and the inmates dragged each other through it, ducking low behind a desk covered with papers and blinking screens.

The man behind Colin screamed, and with a clatter his body fell to the floor. Colin didn't look back. He put his hands on Gabe's back and shoved him through the exit door, into the light.

They were out.

Colin blinked to readjust his eyes. And saw the half circle of facility guards surrounding the door, all with their weapons drawn.

32

TY

It was nearing dusk when the alarm within the testing plant began to scream, the sound pumping electricity into Ty's body. She crouched low behind the crumbling wall on the opposite side of the street, knuckles scraping the bricks in her hurry to hide.

Colin.

The questions raced through her brain, as they had since she'd run into Martin and Zeke outside Lacey's. Was he alive? Had they started the testing yet?

Was she too late?

What had happened between them seemed so stupid now. They wouldn't survive Metaltown without each other. Lena Hampton wasn't big enough to get between them, and pigheaded McNulty was nothing more than a distraction. She kicked herself for not staying closer to Small Parts, watching for movement. She should have been with Colin when Hampton had unleashed his Bakerstown dogs. If she had, she could guarantee he wouldn't be stuck in food testing right now.

"They're moving, you see that?"

Keeping low, Ty sprinted to where Henry crouched beside Matchstick. There were six of them now—five who'd answered the call when she'd demanded they go after Colin. Matchstick, Martin,

Zeke, Henry, and Chip—and only because the kid had refused to be left behind. Everybody else was either home, or too scared of Hampton's bullies.

Henry pointed at the front entrance of the old stone compound, where a line of guards in beige uniforms raced out and around the side of the building. They filtered through a gate in a high chain-link fence topped with a coil of barbed wire, and disappeared out of view.

"Let's take a look," Ty said. "Matchstick?"

"Say no more." A wicked grin lit his face. Gently, he laid his over-the-shoulder pack on the gravelly ground, and withdrew half a dozen faulty detonators from Small Parts. A few glass capsules followed, filled with a clear, thick liquid. He shoved a ball of twine at Henry, and lifted a match.

"I'm not sure this is such a good idea," said Martin, easing back a step.

"It's just a little bump," answered Matchstick. "Don't be such a baby."

"Yeah," said Chip, squatting beside them with wide eyes. "Don't be such a baby."

Martin pushed him, and he fell into the dirt with a whining, "Hey!"

Before he could fight back, Ty had grabbed the kid around the ribs, and they were creeping away from the others in the direction they'd seen the guards go. Henry and Zeke were keeping watch intently, and both pointed silently toward the building.

She lifted her head, just above the wall. And her world stopped.

Before she knew what she was doing, she'd stood to her full height. Zeke tackled her, covering her mouth before she could yell for him to get off. The rocks on the ground jabbed into her back.

Colin was there. Colin, and that boy from Bakerstown, and a few other men. Their backs were against the wall of the building, and they were surrounded by armed guards. *Execution.* The word horrified her, but that's what it looked like. It looked like they were about to be murdered. From the distance she couldn't tell if their guns held bullets or shocking prongs, but she wasn't about to wait to find out.

She screamed against Zeke's hand, bucking her hips when his knees pinned her shoulders down. She fought him as hard as she could, eventually heaving him off to the side. When she was up, she grabbed a rock and hurled it back toward Matchstick. It fell close to Henry, who looked back. He was too far away to hear her call to hurry.

"Go!" she told Chip. "Tell them we can't wait!" He sprinted away.

The fear was thick inside of her. Thick and alive and venomous.

"We've got to distract them!" She grabbed another handful of rocks, gathering them in a pouch she created from the front of her sweater. The others followed her lead.

"Be quick, then get down," said Martin.

She didn't wait for his approval. She stood and launched a stone at the nearest guard. It fell short by five feet, but it was enough to distract him. He lowered his gun and stared back at the wall, but she'd already ducked behind it again, breathing hard.

Zeke fired next. Then Martin. Ty found a hole in the wall and watched their confusion. Three more guards spun toward them, and a few others nearby turned to see what they were looking at. *Over here!* Her shoulder burned as she flung the next rock.

One of the guards saw her. He pointed their way and shouted something she couldn't make out. She followed his gaze up, to a guard tower that reached above the fence. The last sight she saw before ducking down was the man within raising his arm.

A *zing,* then a *crack,* as a bullet embedded into the wall. A tight cry escaped her throat.

"They're shooting at us?" Zeke asked breathlessly. "No. Uh-uh."

Chip came running toward them, head low.

"What'd he say?" she asked quickly.

"He says get down." Chip covered his ears as another shot smacked into the wall. Zeke and Martin glanced at each other, jaws slack. They didn't ask questions, they just flattened down against the ground.

A moment later the entrance of the food testing plant exploded in a deafening crash of rocks and grinding metal. Ty grabbed Chip and pulled his little body beside hers, one hand covering the ear on her good side, the other cupped around his head. Small bits of debris rained down from the sky. Thick white smoke filled the air, heavy with concrete dust, tangy with the scent of nitroglycerine.

She blinked and saw Martin, his face covered with a thin sheet of white powder. He was trying to tell her something, but only mouthing the words. She opened her jaw wide, forcing her ears to pop. Again, and she could hear the shouts from the facility.

Another explosion, this time closer. She held Chip so tightly she was sure his ribs would break. The ground quaked. Part of the wall collapsed over them, a brick falling right between her shoulder blades.

When the ground settled, she glanced over Chip, then Martin and Zeke, finding them all powdered white like ghosts.

Then she was up. With a heave she lifted herself onto the wall, swung her legs over, and jumped down. There were guards scattered across the street, their beige uniforms gray with concrete dust. Some were standing and coughing. Others were on their hands and knees. One was out cold or dead, face down on the ground to her right. No one moved in the tower above her.

"Colin!" she shouted. "Colin!"

She ran through the smoke to where she'd last seen him, hoping that Matchstick wouldn't set off another explosion until she was clear. She pushed forward blindly, hand on her knife, knowing it would do little good against the force of a bullet but feeling more competent with the hard steel in her hand.

Then her hands found a wall and she pushed herself along it, beyond fear, beyond doubt. Her good eye was burning, her bad, too blurry to make anything out. Her lashes were matted with salt and muck, but through them she could see just enough to make out a shadowed figure in her path.

"Colin!"

He was leaning against the wall, hacking, his clothes and skin covered with powder. A thin line of blood trickled down the back of his neck.

At a sprint, she threw herself into him. His arms wrapped around her shoulders, then lowered to her waist, and when he squeezed back, all the cold, broken parts inside of her mended, and she felt more whole than she ever had in her life.

"You stupid bastard." She choked out the words. "You stupid idiot. I hate you." She realized suddenly what a fool she was being, and shoved him back.

A small grin quirked at the corner of his mouth as he bounced off the wall.

"About time you showed up," he said. She snorted, her throat tied in knots.

"What was *that*?" coughed the boy from Bakerstown. He'd linked arms with another man, an older man who looked to have withstood the blast all right. Another emerged from the smoke behind them, and began hobbling quickly away from the building.

"*That* was Matchstick," answered Ty.

She led them out of the dust, one hand covering her mouth and nose. When the way cleared some, they ran, helping the blind man over the lowest part of the wall, and then following, creeping against it back to where Henry and the others waited.

"Look at that," said Colin when Matchstick appeared, one eyebrow completely singed off, the rest of his face covered with black soot. "You're useful after all."

"More than useful," retorted Matchstick, grinning like a loon. "That's art, right there."

"Next thing you know, the Advocates'll be recruiting him," said Henry. Matchstick blowing up railway cars on their way to the front lines? Ty figured that might be the truest thing she'd heard all day.

"Move," she said. "Shut up and go already."

"Are you talking?" asked Martin. "I can't hear worth crap." He stretched his jaw wide in a forced yawn.

Zeke boxed his ears. "How's that?"

He was running before Martin could catch up.

By the time they reached the beltway, Ty's lungs were burning from the pace. They crouched behind an old tollbooth, frame bent and glass shattered by time and well-aimed rocks. No one had followed, no one seemed to have recognized them. But they were coming. They needed to hide, Colin especially, and Bakerstown, even with its cops, was safer than Metaltown right now.

The whirring of sirens on the bridge made them freeze, hold their breath. Ty's heart pounded in her chest. *Please don't stop, please don't stop.*

Three electric cop cars, sleek and black, whipped by, their red overhead lights flashing. They made a right at the first intersection, speeding toward the food testing plant.

Matchstick laughed nervously.

"Get out of here," Ty told Colin. "Lay low for a while. I'll tell Cherish and your ma you're all right."

He shook his head. He was a little too close; his shoulder rose and fell against hers with each gulp of air. His hand brushed her leg. She thought maybe he was looking at her, and for some reason that made her train her gaze straight ahead, and pull the brim of her hat down over her bad eye.

"Ty." The way Colin spoke her name forced her to glance over, just to make sure he was all right. His mouth opened, just a little, and she focused on his cracked lips, unable to look elsewhere. They needed to hide, she thought absently. They needed to go somewhere. Do something.

"I've got to find Lena," he said.

It took a moment for the words to sink in, but when they did, she felt them. Like they carried a physical weight.

"No."

"She's in trouble," Colin said, holding her gaze. His eyes showed pain, but not his own, and not for her. For the greenback. For the *Hampton.*

"You've got to hide," she tried to reason. "Look, she went back home. She's not here anymore. You don't still have safety on her if she's not in Metaltown."

He eyed her strangely. "When you called safety on me it didn't matter where we went."

Because it was us, she wanted to shout. *You and me. Not you and her, you and me.*

"At least flush old Hampton didn't get everything he wanted," said Martin, picking at a broken bootlace. Ty shifted back, as far away from Colin as she could get without moving her feet.

He wiped the sweat off his brow, smearing black grime across his forehead. "What do you mean?"

His friends glanced at each other warily.

"After you left . . ."

"Got the shocks, you mean," inserted Chip.

Zeke frowned. "Right. After they pulled you out of Lacey's, Old Hampton told us we could get our jobs back if we . . . you know."

"No," said Colin. "I don't know."

"Stopped the press," said Matchstick, rubbing the bald patch where his eyebrow used to be.

Ty tensed. "And you told him what he could do with his offer, right?" But the answer was clear on all their faces.

"While I was locked up you all took your jobs back?" Colin asked, disbelievingly.

Henry's face hardened. "What were we supposed to do? He said he'd blacklist us off every payroll in the Northern Fed. He was gonna replace us with *shells.*"

"That's nothing new!" Colin raked his hands over his skull. "You knew the risks when you crossed the line."

"Agnes didn't make it." Zeke's somber words tripped their heated momentum.

Ty remembered her from St. Mary's—a quiet girl, small, but

gritty—and then from the factory where she'd worked day in and day out without complaint. She'd deserved a better death. She'd deserved a better *life*.

"Hampton was going to sic the Brotherhood on us right there," added Martin. "I was good to go, but some of the other guys . . . they thought maybe it wasn't such a good idea." No one looked at Colin.

Colin said nothing

"So it's over," finished Ty, as Colin paced a short stretch away, hands latched behind his neck. The way they were treated at Small Parts would continue. The defeat was thick as the smoke after Matchstick's bomb. She'd never realized just how much she'd wanted them to win.

And now they'd just blown the side off a building. They weren't just hopeless, they were dead.

Chip pulled at her shirtsleeve, looking young. Too young. "We're not going back, right, Ty?" His hat was lopsided, his eyes tinged red from the dust.

As mad as she was at them, she couldn't help but wish Chip had sold out, too. Orphan kids had even fewer options for work than half-blind girls in Metaltown. The responsibility she felt for him was suddenly overwhelming.

"No," she said quietly. "We'll be all right."

Matchstick rose, and went to stand beside Colin. A moment later Colin nodded, then hunched, then punched Matchstick in the arm. They returned to the group still solemn, but less burdened.

"We're taking Jessop here to Charity House," said Henry.

The blind man's expression had softened since they'd escaped the jail. Colin grasped his hand and shook it. After quiet words of thanks were exchanged, Henry and Zeke were off.

"The Hampton girl—Lena. She went out like a Metalhead," Martin said, by way of an apology. The way Colin stiffened made Ty want to give him a good shake. Martin and Matchstick disappeared into the failing light.

"We've got to go." The worry was clear in Gabe's voice.

Colin turned back to Ty. She looked away. He moved closer, and her stupid eyes burned with tears. It wasn't supposed to be like this. He was supposed to come back to her. She had seen him first.

"Ty?"

She looked down. "Stupid dust," she said. "It's messing with me."

He put his hands on her shoulders, and aligned his gaze with hers.

"Thanks. I mean it, Ty. Without you . . ." He shook his head. "You're still my best man, you know that?"

His words were like a velvet-covered sledgehammer.

She forced herself to smile. "I better be."

As he and Gabe ran for the beltway in the fading light, she thought she might just be the biggest fool in all of Metaltown.

LENA

Lena toed the towel that she'd shoved under her door to her bedroom. It was a snug fit—enough to make the barrier nearly soundproof. She stepped back and shoved her dresser up against it to ensure no one else could enter.

After Darcy had left, she'd bathed; one last chance to use the cinnamon soaps and hot water. She'd asked for more food—enough bread, corn cakes, and syrupy fruit to last a day—and packed it all in one of her smaller handbags, alongside a modest amount of money she'd saved for shopping trips to the river pavilion. Then she'd changed into a sturdy pair of flat boots, leggings, and the heaviest sweater she could find.

She was going to escape through the window.

The sheets from her bed made a strong rope when tied together. Not long enough to take her to the bottom, but long enough that she could hook the nearest weight-bearing branch and swing to the base of the tree.

She'd never climbed a tree before, but there was a first time for everything. Darcy's story had been the final straw; she couldn't stay here any longer. She would renounce her Hampton name. There were things far worse than being poor.

Her heart was pounding. A thick pair of gloves waited in her pocket, but if she wore them now her hands would slip. Hooking the straps of her bag around both shoulders, she opened the window, letting in the cold black night.

And registered the blinking eyes staring back at her.

The only thing that stopped her from waking the whole district with her scream was her sudden loss of breath.

"Move back," whispered a disembodied voice.

She blinked, and slowly, a human figure in the tree came into focus. Her arms fell slack.

"*Colin?*"

"Move back," he said again. Confused, she scooted aside, just as he catapulted himself through the opening to the space where a pretty birdcage had once sat.

He rolled, tucked in a ball, then stopped himself with a hand slapping against the hardwood floor. The noise made him cringe, but a second later he'd leapt to his feet, searching the room with his steely blue eyes. He inspected the door closely, testing the heavy dresser.

When he was satisfied, he approached her, his face gleaming with sweat, his hands and clothing filthy.

"You okay?" he asked.

Lena couldn't find any words. Confusion and fear and elation all burst inside of her, making it hard to breathe, let alone think. He reached for her hands, touching the bare, exposed skin again as though there was nothing wrong with it at all.

"What are you doing here?" she finally managed.

His scarred brow rose in curiosity as he found the rope she'd fashioned from her bedsheets and the full leather handbag strapped to her shoulders. "What are *you* doing?"

"Why do you always insist on answering a question with another question?" she demanded, then groaned when she realized she'd only perpetuated the cycle. He hadn't released her hands, and even if his face seemed calm, his grip trembled slightly.

"I was leaving," she said. "I was going to climb down the tree and go to Metaltown and find you." The heat blossomed beneath her skin. It sounded foolish when she said it out loud.

"I hope you didn't plan on driving."

She snorted in a very unbecoming way, but when she tried to push away he drew her closer. The smirk on his face faded.

"You would have come back for me?"

She nodded. He inched closer, placing her hands on his chest and holding them there, where she could feel the rise and fall of his breath.

Surprise had softened the corners around his mouth—surprise she didn't understand, because he was loved in Metaltown. Surely he'd had a dozen or more people who would've done the same thing for him, but the fact that he seemed to care that she had planned on tracking him down made her stand taller, and prouder. Made her feel worthy.

There were so many things she wanted to tell him. *I'm sorry for my father. I'm sorry about the factory. I thought I'd never see you again.* All locked deep behind the fear of what would happen if they were caught together. In her bedroom.

"You shouldn't be here," she said. "My father . . ."

"I needed to see you."

She couldn't look away. Were they closer? She hadn't remembered moving, but now her forearms were pressed flat against his chest, and her toes touched the ends of his boots. He had thick eyelashes. She'd never noticed just how long they were before.

A thin layer of blood was smeared from his temple back through his short, dark hair.

She stepped away, feeling the room sway without his body anchoring her. "You're bleeding." She raced to the bathroom, unsure of what had just happened. Everything about him pulled her closer, pulled her off balance. She felt like she was still falling, even with her hands firmly gripping the marble counter.

When he appeared in the doorway, she busied herself with the first aid kit from under the sink. She'd kept it there since she was a child, for every time Otto came to assert himself as their father's favorite.

Colin placed his hands in his pockets, as if unsure of what to do with them. "We should go."

"I know," she said. She wanted a moment, just a moment, to put him back together. But when she raised a damp towel to his forehead she found she couldn't even do that, and instead passed it to him. He placed it on the sink and then, to her shock, reached for the hem of his shirt and pulled it off over his head.

"Oh, right." She laughed, then choked a little. She'd never seen a man shirtless other than Otto and her father, and even then not in a long time. The way Colin's hard, corded muscles moved beneath his smooth skin made her forget it was rude to stare. She couldn't look away from the straight line of his collarbone, and the swell of his shoulder, and the way the fine, dark hairs made a thin line that started at his belly button and dipped below his belt.

He leaned over the sink, turned it on, and let the silver spigot shoot water straight onto the back of his skull. The muddy runoff that poured from his forehead was tinged with crimson, and before she was completely mesmerized by the arc of his back, she turned, and ran straight into the wall. With a squeak, she hurried back into the main room, first checking the door for any sound in the hallway, then running to her bag, where she'd packed the shirt she'd borrowed from his home.

Her father could be back anytime, and he could not find them together. They needed to leave immediately.

When she returned to the bathroom, Colin had dried his face and head, and was toweling off the countertop. Though urgency raced through her, she couldn't bring herself to raise her eyes.

"Don't bother." She wasn't coming back here anyway. "Here." She shoved the shirt in his direction, then backed away against the wall, giving them an arm's length of separation. Enough space to think clearly.

"I thought my father had sent you to jail," she said, wincing a little over the memory.

He washed his forearms, up past the elbows. "Not jail. The testing plant. It didn't stick, though." He didn't explain further.

"Did you walk all the way from Metaltown?"

He shook his head, and she could smell the cinnamon soap on him. "I borrowed a friend's bicycle." He stumbled a little over the word *friend*. His eyes met hers in the mirror. "It was easier to find this place than I thought. You can see it all the way from Bakerstown. Biggest place in the district. I've never seen a place so nice in my life."

She picked at the sleeves of her sweater. "It's just a house." A big, beautiful, quiet house. A pit of silence after the racket of Metaltown. "I guess you got past the security gate."

He hid a smile behind his hand, but his eyes flickered with amusement.

"Rode in on the back of a delivery truck. We used to do the same at a grocery depot near the apartment until the owner got wise."

She was impressed, but that truck he'd snuck in on was probably filled with food for the next few days, already clean and tested, and the thought made her shrink a little.

His expression had sobered.

"Did they mess you up any?"

She shook her head quickly, but his asking brought a sharp pain behind her sternum. "No. They didn't even come home. I don't know where my lovely brother and father have been."

"Trying to get the Small Parts Charter back on shift," he said bluntly. "Your dad offered their jobs back in exchange for stopping the press."

"And they agreed?" She pushed off the wall, fury clenching her fists. "After everything that's happened?"

Colin stared down the drain, the despair so heavy on his shoulders that she was ready to march back into Metaltown and start another riot, just to ease his suffering.

"Maybe they're right," he said after what seemed like forever. "We were never going to win. We already had it as good as it gets."

"Don't say that," she said, moving behind him. "You can't quit. You can't give up."

"Why not?" The exhaustion was clear in his voice now. "What difference does it make?"

"It makes all the difference!" She made herself stop, take a breath. "The workers listen to you. They care about you. They know you care about them. That skill . . ." She looked away, ashamed of a time she'd thought his job had required no skills at all. "I thought it was just a matter of fitting pieces together, but it's so much more than that. It's about fitting people together. That's something not everyone can do."

He turned slowly, leaning back against the counter.

"Do you know why my father needs those workers?" she continued. "Because he's sending weapons to the war—to the *Advocates*. To keep the fighting going because as long as there's a war, the military will need more weapons, and as long as demand is high, Hampton Industries profits. Don't you see? This is so much bigger than all of us. The Small Parts demonstration could have changed the course of the war."

He straightened, taller than he had been seconds before. A line had furrowed between his brows. "We did it so we could keep working, not so we could stop working."

"I know," she said. "I know. And I want that too, I just . . ." She turned away in frustration. "It's all so wrong. And there's nothing I can do to stop it."

Though he moved in silence, she could feel him approaching. Feel it in the way her skin tingled and her pulse began to race. Maybe she shouldn't have said what she had, but she trusted Colin. More than she had ever trusted anyone.

She faced him, trying to be brave. "I want what you want," she said. "But one day the war won't need Hampton Industries, and we won't need the war, and then we'll all have to find something better to do."

His fingertip trailed down her cheek. She could feel his touch, even after his hand lowered.

"You're not what I expected," he said.

Before she could tell him that he wasn't what she had expected either, he lowered his head, and closed his eyes, and pressed his lips to hers.

She blinked rapidly, unable to breathe, unable to think. Her body went completely rigid, the only movement beneath her ribs, where her heart punched through the bones.

His hands slid slowly over her shoulders, down her straight arms to her bunched fists, and he lifted them and placed them behind his neck. She could feel him smile against her mouth, and then kiss her again, slowly, pulling lightly on her lower lip.

It was like colors she'd never seen, light, brighter than she'd ever known. It was new, and soft, and terrifying, and perfect.

When her back bumped against the wall, she froze. A small dose of panic shot through her as Colin's arms surrounded her, caged her in. He must have felt the change in her because he slowed, and shifted, so that it was his back against the wall. So that it was her leaning in, testing, taking.

Her hands gripped his shoulders of their own accord, and her eyelids drifted closed. She followed his lead, parting her lips the way he did, gasping when his hands tangled in her hair. Her legs grew weak, and her body melted, and soon his skin, hard and warm, was pressed against hers and his hands were inching down her spine.

Every part of her came alive all at once—parts of her she hadn't known had been sleeping, parts of her she hadn't known were empty. It all became so clear. Her life before this moment was a hollow shell. She'd been lost, and alone, and aching for this. For Colin. For the acceptance he showed her now.

Her fingers spread over his chest, exploring, asking questions of their own, and his body answered in goose bumps and tensing muscles and the pounding of his heart.

"Lena," he whispered, kissing her jaw. "There's something I've got to tell you."

She hesitantly touched his cheek, rough with stubble and still damp from washing, and traced the thin line of his ear. The pads of her fingers were sensitive, and maybe they made him sensitive too, because he was breathing hard.

"Tell me," she said.

And then he froze. Because outside the bathroom, in her room, someone had placed a key in the lock, and was unbolting the door.

34

COLIN

They'd stayed too long.

Colin shoved his shirt over his head, sliding on the slippery wood floor as he followed Lena around the corner. His brain tried frantically to catch up: the screaming alarm between his temples battled the smell of her, still on his skin, and the feel of her softening against him.

The door shoved inward and banged against the dresser, leaving only enough space for a man's delicate hand to grope through. Colin reached for the knife in his waistband, but he didn't have it. They'd taken it from him in jail. He clamped down on Lena's shoulder and jerked her back.

Her eyes snapped to his, filled with horror.

"Hide!" Had the word come out with any volume at all, it would have been a scream. As it was, it was barely louder than a breath.

Hide? She wanted *him* to hide?

"Lena," taunted a voice from the hallway. "Are you barricading the door? We haven't played this game in some time, have we?"

Colin felt time slow as he processed Otto's words. Lena tried to drag him back, clutching at his clothes, but he wouldn't budge.

"The bathroom!" she whispered. "Quickly! He can't find you here!"

His eyes flickered to hers, and despite the roaring hatred within him, he stalled. Her fear was evident. If he was seen, they would both be punished for it.

Otto's fist slapped against the door, tearing a short cry from Lena. He shoved it again, and this time the dresser squealed and slid back a few more inches. His menacing laughter filtered into the room.

"Lena . . . oh, Lena," Otto sang.

Colin faltered back a step. Then another. He ducked into the bathroom, and Lena shoved the door closed behind him.

"Don't come out," she said. "Whatever you hear."

He clenched his teeth.

A skidding sound, like the stuttering growl of a machine gun, and Colin knew Otto had pushed past the dresser.

He pressed his ear against the doorjamb, sick that he was hiding like some sort of coward.

"Look at those hands," Otto mused, his voice muffled through the wood. "I'd forgotten what a number you did on yourself. Why don't you do us all a favor and put your gloves back on?"

"Where's my guard?" Lena asked in a low voice. "There's been a man outside my room all night."

"I excused him," answered Otto, and Colin could hear the smile in his voice.

Lena paused. "Is Father home?"

"No," he answered. "Just you and me."

The floor creaked. *Don't come out. Whatever you hear.* Colin flexed his hands.

"And the house staff," she reminded him.

Otto laughed. "What? Think your precious nanny is going to come save you again?"

There was a skittering across the floor, and then the bathroom door vibrated as a body slammed against it. Colin turned the handle carefully, but there was too much weight against it to push outward without ramming it. A cold sweat broke out over his skin.

When Otto's voice came again it was much closer, just beyond the barrier.

"You were wretched today, Lena. Father is very upset. He means to punish you, I think."

"Then he'll be disappointed if you beat him to it."

Don't provoke him, Lena.

"Or he'll be glad I've taken care of business."

"For once," bit back Lena. "Because we all know you're doing nothing at the factory."

Then she gasped, and Colin's fury spiked.

He lowered his center of balance, shoulder against the frame. The adrenaline surging through him would make him strong enough to push through Otto and Lena both.

But then the weight was gone. He hesitated, focusing on Lena's plea. Maybe Otto was just trying to scare her. Maybe he was leaving. Colin pressed his ear back to the door.

"I hate the factory," Otto said absently. They were moving, but Lena didn't sound hurt. "He's starting to catch on, I think. He paid the bartender at the club to call him when I'm there. Can you imagine the humiliation? Checking up on me like I'm a child." Colin realized Otto was referring to his father.

"Probably another lesson," Lena mumbled.

"I hate the foreman. I hate the bottom-feeders that work there. I hate the factory district." He laughed cynically. "I hate being a goddamn Hampton."

"Give the factory to me," Lena said quickly. "Let me manage it. I could help you."

Otto groaned. "If only it were that easy. You know what he'd say, though. *Hamptons don't fail, Otto. He gave it to me. I'm* the one who has the responsibility."

"Let me take the responsibility," she said. "We don't have to tell him until we've found you something else. Something you like."

A quiet followed, and for a moment, Colin felt a surge of hope in her proposition.

And then Otto said: "Were you really with that worker?"

"Otto, the factory . . ."

"You know he wasn't really interested, don't you? They're color-blind. All they see when they look at us is green."

Colin wanted to close his fists around Otto's throat.

Don't come out. Whatever you hear.

"It's not like that," said Lena weakly. Colin hated that the fire in her voice had simmered.

"He wants the same thing everyone else does. A Hampton on their side. They're willing to do anything to get that."

The resonating sound of a slap against skin. For one shocked moment, Colin thought Otto had hit her, but it was a male voice that yelped in pain. A moment later, Lena cried out.

Colin had had enough. He shoved through the door, taking in the sight before him. The tall bureau beside the bathroom was open, Lena's clothing flung across the floor before it. Otto was behind her, and had his arms latched around her waist. His face was red, with shock, with anger. With the imprint of Lena's hand.

On the inside of the cabinet door were scratches, some deep enough to indent the wood. *I broke off some of my fingernails trying to get out.*

Colin went blind to everything but Otto. Voices came to him from far away, commands he couldn't process. And then he was somehow straddling Otto's chest, and he was hitting the sorry, pathetic bastard in the face again, and again.

"Stop!" screamed Lena. She tackled Colin from the side and they fell backwards in a heap. Otto Hampton's legs were limp, his arms outstretched to his sides. He did not move.

"What did you do?" Lena crawled to where her brother lay. She touched his face with trembling hands, the tears streaking down her cheeks.

Colin pushed himself up, confused. His knuckles stung now, and when he looked down they were red with Otto's blood and already beginning to swell.

"He came after you." Colin's chest was tightening, sucking in on itself. He'd hit a greenback. He'd hit a *Hampton*. He'd broken into the richest house in the River District, after breaking out of the worst place in Metaltown.

"You have to go," she said, voice hitching. "You have to leave, right now."

"What?" He stepped back. Her words were sharp as knives. "No. You have to come with me."

Her fearful look turned to exasperation. "I can't. I told you not to come out. *I told you.*"

"Lena . . ." His head was pounding. He searched for words, came up empty.

She stood, and when she looked at him again, her face was as calm as her father's had been when he'd handed over the stack of bills at Lacey's.

"You should never have come."

He reached for her, but she jerked away.

What did I do?

He glanced down at her brother, who didn't stir. The sickening thought occurred to him that Otto Hampton might be dead.

"You don't belong here," Lena said, voice low. "Leave. Leave Metaltown. And unless you want to end up back in food testing, you'd better never come back."

He stumbled back as though she'd hit him with a hammer. *You don't belong here.*

She had made her choice, and she'd chosen her brother. Even now he couldn't blame her. Hadn't he done the same thing, over and over, for Hayden?

He looked around her room at her nice things. At the furniture that would never fill his home. At the life he would never have.

At the girl who would never be his.

"Go over the south wall behind the fountain," she said without looking up. "I'll tell them you ran the opposite way."

It was the only good-bye she would give him. A cover, to get him out. A little time before she told her father what he'd done.

He made it to the window, leapt the distance onto the nearest branch, and swung his way down. The fountain was around the corner of the house—he'd passed it when he'd snuck by earlier. The security gate was an easy climb, no higher than the fences around the condemned buildings in Metaltown. It was easier than hitching a ride on the back of a delivery truck like he'd done on the way in the front gates, but less successful. By the time he reached the top he'd tripped the alarm. With the siren blaring, he stumbled through the dark to where he'd left Gabe's bicycle, down the street beneath a curtain of vines over a privacy wall. His coat was still upstairs with Lena, but it hardly mattered, because he could barely feel anything, much less the cold.

* * *

He didn't know what time it was. He didn't really care. It was still dark when he abandoned the bicycle outside the chain-link fence and found the panel that had come loose from the post. It was a tight squeeze through to the train yards; the chains that caught in his clothes conjured memories of how he and Ty used to sneak out here after dark to watch the trains and dream of places far better than Metaltown.

At some point those stories had lost their luster. Had turned to work, and real life. He and Ty had spent more time scrounging for food than dreaming. And then they'd stopped coming altogether. Their spot, on an embankment high above the loading station, was now covered with long grass and trash. Now they just watched from the beltway up above.

The way down to the tracks was rocky, and he slid once or twice on account of the darkness. It struck him when his stomach grumbled that he was hungry—he'd had only a quick bite at Gabe's before racing to the River District—and this annoyed him. Nearly as much as his chattering teeth, and the shivers that seized his body every few seconds.

Keeping low, he approached the train, careful to keep out of the reach of the security lights. The cars that had once been red were now the color of dry dirt. Rust had popped holes in the metal siding. He scanned for an open box and found one, four cars down. Quickly, quietly, he crept toward it.

And then he stopped, because there was movement to his left, up the rocky slope, in the grass above. He dove behind a stack of shipping crates, listening. Waiting. Though his eyes strained, all he could see through the dark night was the distant shadow of the beltway.

After a minute he reminded himself to breathe, and when he did, the air felt too thick, or maybe his lungs were just too small, and that annoyed him, too.

More lights flickered to life down at the main loading dock. A man yelled something he couldn't make out. Another responded. An engine roared to life. Colin pulled his knees closer to his body to ensure he wouldn't be seen.

You don't belong here, Lena had said. She was absolutely right. He could go anywhere; he didn't need Metaltown. He sure as hell didn't need Josef Hampton, or food testing, or the damn Small Parts factory. Even Ty was better off without him now.

But he would have stayed for Lena.

He rubbed his frozen jaw with his frozen hands. The smart thing to do was to get on that train. Disappear. Go anonymous, join the Advocates. *Something.* Once Otto Hampton woke up—*if* he woke up—Colin would be in a world of trouble. Trouble that would stack upon the trouble he was already in from taking over the factory and escaping the testing facility. Trouble that would carry over to his family.

With the racket down near the loading dock, Colin didn't hear the man coming up behind him until he was only an arm's reach away. He spun so fast he tipped sideways into the crates, gripping the splintering wood to right himself.

Hayden slid down the last few feet of gravel and stooped beside him.

"Where's your coat, little brother?" His eyes were clear, and his voice wasn't sloppy.

"Lost it." Colin shivered. The acknowledgment of the cold made his mind register the prickling in his hands and feet.

Hayden shrugged out of his jacket and passed it over. He rubbed his hands together, his breath clouding in front of his face. Colin pulled the coat over his shoulders, keeping his arms close to his body. The sun was coming up, lighting the haze a too-bright shade of pink. He could see his brother more clearly now, and was surprised to recognize the anger on his face. How many times had he looked that same way after spending all night searching through Hayden's haunts?

"Where you going?" Hayden stared straight ahead at the open compartment.

"Doesn't matter."

"Matters to me."

Colin felt a flash of guilt. "Thought I might try Rosie's Bay." Alone, he could be a stowaway. It wouldn't matter that he was broke. He'd catch however many trains he needed to until he reached the coast.

Hayden sat back, rubbing his shins to keep his legs warm. Down the way, another train engine roared to life. Colin felt the pressure kick alive inside of him. He needed to get into that empty car.

"I never pegged you as a runner," said Hayden.

Colin turned on him, teeth bared. "You never pegged me as anything because you were never around."

Hayden tucked his chin into his shoulder. Colin stood up, not caring now that he might be seen. He needed to get on that train. His feet needed to move. But instead he rounded back on his brother.

"What are you talking about, anyway? You left. Why can't I leave? It's my turn."

Hayden was silent for a full minute. "I never left."

Colin blinked. "What?"

"I never went to Rosie's Bay. I made it up."

"You made it up," Colin repeated. He tried to picture the white sand, the sunny dock. The sound of the waves. If he could hear them, they had to be real. "You're lying."

Hayden looked away. "I made it up. You liked the story so much, I don't know, it just went on from there."

"You were gone for *two years!*" Colin bellowed, forgetting momentarily about the train. Rosie's Bay couldn't be made up. It had to be real. But the Metaltown smog was now crushing him. Suffocating him. Filling him with doubt.

Hayden looked pale, but his cheeks were blotched red, like Cherish's.

"I was in Bakerstown. I went back to where we grew up, you remember? I thought I'd make a go of it, and then once I did, I'd come get you guys." He sighed, defeated. "I never meant to get hooked on the stuff. It was just to take the edge off."

Colin wanted nothing more than to strangle him, but his limbs wouldn't move. "You were just across the beltway the whole time?" The insanity of Hayden's claim was sinking in. He'd been close enough to visit, to send money, to help with Cherish, and he'd done *nothing*. For *two years*.

A dark fury swelled within him. He wondered if it was possible to hate his own brother.

"Ty said you were a sellout," Colin said. "What'd you do?"

Hayden closed his eyes.

"Same thing I always do," he said weakly. "Got my fix." He rubbed his hand over the back of his neck, standing finally, but looking small. "I told Schultz about your charter. I . . . I wasn't thinking straight."

Schultz had known about the charter the night after the Small Parts workers had met at Lacey's. There had been a leak.

The leak had been his own brother.

Colin took a step toward the train. He didn't know where it was going. It didn't matter anymore, just as long as it wasn't here.

Hayden was pathetic. A junkie. A sellout. Colin remembered all the times he'd lain out here with Ty and told stories about his brother's adventures. How many nights had he watched these trains waiting for Hayden to come home?

He never should have come home.

"I don't suppose it matters," said Hayden. "But I'm clean now. Three days. I won't mess up again."

Colin shook his head. *Right.* He contemplated whether lying down on the tracks was a yellow way to die. It was one thing to lose Lena. It was another to lose Rosie's Bay. It felt like someone had died.

The engine down by the station sighed. The car before them crawled forward.

"I'm leaving," said Colin, raising his voice over the grind of the machines.

"Okay." Hayden shifted. "I hope you find what you're looking for, little brother. I hope there is a Rosie's Bay."

But there never had been a Rosie's Bay. There had only been the false hope that there was someplace better than this place. A break from the daily grind. A shiny wish he could chase after, something bright enough to light the dark places. For a little while, Colin had thought that was Lena.

He thought of Ty then. Who never got a break. Who never quit. Of Matchstick, risking his life to blow up the jail. Of Martin, who'd turned into a believer, and Zeke, who looked out for his sister, and Noneck and Henry, who'd followed him straight into chaos. Of his ma, who never stopped to complain. Of Cherish, who didn't have much longer. And suddenly it all seemed like a lot to lose.

The train squealed, the sound of metal scraping metal, and when it pulled out of the shipping yards, Colin was not aboard.

35

TY

Ty hunkered down in the shadows of the warehouse on the opposite side of the street from the Small Parts factory. After busting Colin out from food testing, and her run-in with McNulty, going back to Beggar's Square was out of the question. Instead she'd come here. To think. To watch.

Three hours before the day shift and already there were Brotherhood goons milling around. Every lit cigarette cast an orange glow, a beacon in the early gray light.

She'd slept just a little, with Chip under her arm. She told herself it was only to keep him warm—the alley floor was cold and unyielding—but in truth she didn't mind. His heavy dreaming breaths soothed some of the questions in her head.

But they didn't take them away.

For years she'd tried to tell Colin he belonged in Metaltown. That to want anything more was wasted effort. Hope was a killer, worse even than the corn flu, because hope in Metaltown went by another name: disappointment. And to live with disappointment was to die of thirst holding a cup of clean water.

But Colin wasn't like the rest of them, not really. He'd taken on Schultz when the other Metalheads bent. He'd taken on Hampton because it was the right thing to do. He was meant for bigger things.

Every time she'd tried to tell him otherwise, she'd only been trying to convince herself.

It was just a matter of time before he moved on.

Maybe if she were flush like Lena Hampton, maybe if she were dignified, and had fancy things and smart duds, Colin would have taken her side. But even as she thought it, she knew that wasn't right. Colin wasn't shallow. It wasn't just Lena's pretty face drawing him across the beltway. He'd been with plenty of pretty girls and none of them had stuck. No, he was looking for a way out, and Lena was his ticket.

Ty could never offer what she did, and that made all the anger and panic and despair inside of her spark into a full-blown fire. Her thoughts turned to McNulty. He'd called her Astor Tyson. He'd made it sound like she was worth something. The truth was, she *could* have been worth something—she didn't know where she was born, who she was before she'd been dropped off at St. Mary's. There was no saying she *wasn't* this Astor Tyson.

Her dreams emerged from the tired parts of her mind, slipping past the barriers of her consciousness. The toy train, the smell of perfume. A woman, leaving her on the steps and running into the dark. Old questions she'd shoved into the boxes in the back of her mind had been seeping out—things she'd tried to forget about because knowing the answers didn't change anything. Who were her parents? Was the woman who'd taken her to St. Mary's her mother? Why had she left her?

Who was Astor Tyson?

Before she could wake Chip properly, she was scrambling to her feet. Maybe Shima knew what McNulty had been talking about.

"What're you doing?" Chip slurred, rubbing his eyes. "You got some food?"

"Come on." Ty grinned, feeling like she was standing on the edge of something big. If McNulty was right, and she was entitled to money, she could pay him to send muscle, get the press up and running again, and show Colin that he didn't have to go all the way to the River District to find a greenback. He'd had one in front of him the whole time.

But she didn't get far, because a moment after they'd started toward Shima's, a voice hailed them from around the corner.

"Hey!" he said. "Hey, get over here!"

"Keep walking," she told Chip, reaching for her knife. Her muscles tensed. Probably a junkie or a perv out trolling.

"Hey!" the voice called again, and through the gray, predawn haze she saw what looked like a man wearing a hat of snakes.

She squinted. Not snakes. *Dreads.*

She gripped the knife low at her waist. "Watch my bad side," she told Chip, who obediently jumped to her left.

They glanced around the corner and spotted two figures. It took her a moment to recognize them.

"About time somebody showed up," Dreads said. Beside him, Schoolboy folded his arms over his chest.

A dark understanding settled on her bones. McNulty hadn't sent anyone else, which meant that he didn't intend to take back Metaltown. He wanted her dead so he could collect his bounty from Hampton.

She crouched low, revealing her knife. If she ran into the street the Brotherhood would see her, and they certainly wouldn't help. But if she stayed here, she'd have to take them both. After their last interaction, she doubted they'd let her off easy.

"Why'd you cross the line, schoolboys?" she said, putting a hard edge in her tone.

Dreads gave a snort. "McNulty sent us."

She loosened her shoulders. Beside her, Chip flashed a new shank—a metal butter knife he'd lifted from St. Mary's. "What's McNulty want with us?"

"What's McNulty want with anyone?" said the boy with curly hair, clearly annoyed. "He wants to collect."

"Collect what?" asked Chip. "Ty doesn't got any green."

The two Bakerstown boys tossed their heads back and laughed, revealing a flash of their lime-colored belts.

"Your friend's worth more than your life, kid," said Dreads. "Her daddy used to own half of this hellhole."

Curiosity got the better of her. "He owned a factory?" Nothing else made sense—there wasn't anything else in Metaltown that carried any weight.

Schoolboy turned to Dreads. "Just one or two," he said, with a bite of sarcasm.

"Small Parts?" asked Chip hopefully. Ty was glad he asked.

"Try the entire scientific world," said Dreads. "Every clinic, hospital, and food testing plant. The Medical Division, ever heard of it?"

When he reached into his pocket, Ty hissed and nearly stuck him, but he only revealed what looked to be a crumpled wrapper. Slowly, he smoothed it out against his chest, then turned it to show them. The black and white image had been divided by fold creases where the paper had thinned, but a man's face was still visible in a small, boxed segment.

He had short, slicked hair, and a mustache. Round glasses. Serious eyes.

Ty felt her stomach drop. Her knife nearly slid out of her hands. The man was familiar. She'd seen him before. *Known* him before. Not just from a picture like this—news images were only on screens and tablets, and no one in Metaltown had one of those. The closest she'd gotten to one had been when Otto Hampton had once carried his through the factory.

No, she'd seen him before in person, she was sure of it.

She snatched it from the boy's hands, trying to sound out the words above the picture, frustrated that she couldn't read faster.

"Doctor and his wife succumb to flu, it says," Dreads told her. "Survived by their only child." She barely heard him snickering.

"Where'd you get this?" she said, unable to tear her eyes away.

"McNulty had it. Said you might want it. Says to tell you he plans on seeing you real soon."

She should have been looking for her nearest exit, but she couldn't take her eyes off the picture. She knew what this man looked like without his glasses. When he lay on the floor, and played trains with her. He helped people—he was a doctor. A *doctor.*

See you later, Astorgator, he used to say. Every morning before work. One hand went absently to her stomach, to the round scars there. He'd had to give her a shot. Something so she wouldn't get sick.

Astor, that was her name.

Her head throbbed painfully. Was she making it up? Forcing the pieces to fit in the outline of a puzzle they'd provided? It seemed too good to be true.

But it was true. She could feel it in her bones, the same way she knew that Jed Schultz was bad and Colin was, well, Colin.

Her family had owned the Medical Division.

She had heard the stories. That the heir had gone missing—a suspected victim of the corn flu. By the time she was old enough to work at Small Parts, that speculation was all gossip. A joke they would tell—Matchstick especially. *When I collect my inheritance . . .*

Hampton Industries had absorbed the division, and no one fought Hampton.

Until Colin.

"I told McNulty the deal," she choked out. "He helps me, and I help him."

"What did you think we were doing here, She-male?" asked Dreads. He held out his hand, and Ty jumped back, thinking he held a weapon. But it was empty.

"Skaggs," he said, then pointed to his schoolboy friend. "This is Liam."

"Ty," she said slowly. Then, "Astor." But the name sounded wrong on her tongue. "Ty's fine."

They shook hands. Then Liam led them back to a thin, dark street, and her mouth dropped open.

"Ty, what's going on?" Chip asked.

She couldn't answer. Fifty men filled the alley. Rough, ugly brutes. Muscle. All wearing some flash of green. They crowded together, keeping quiet, like a bomb ready to explode.

"What's the call?" asked Skaggs, grinning. "We gonna bust some heads or what?"

* * *

Dawn was breaking by the time they'd gathered the others. Word spread like wildfire in Metaltown. Ty found Matchstick and No-neck burning trash under the bridge, both of them wide-eyed with shock when they caught sight of the train of men lurking in the shadows behind her. They agreed to split up—one would take Keeneland Apartments, the other Beggar's Square. Chip had already torn off toward Lacey's to catch any stragglers.

Nerves rattling her clean through, Ty led the Bakerstown lot through the backstreets, toward the Small Parts shipping dock. Two Brotherhood thugs were waiting, but when they caught sight of the army behind her, they ran, just like the yellow cowards they were.

Ty knew they'd tell their friends. It would only be a matter of time before Jed gathered his troops and attacked—if the cops didn't come after them first for the damage at the food testing facility.

She glanced back at the Bakerstown boys and chuckled to herself. It would take a whole lot of cops to take them down now.

"So how is it a bunch of inbred Metalheads start thinking they can take on the big boys?" Liam fit a pair of fingerless leather gloves over his knuckles. When he made a fist, the hard material creaked.

Though the claim made her balk, she supposed he was right. They may not have started with the intention of going to war, but they were ready for one now. The poor workers of Metaltown were about to take on the richest man in the Northern Fed, and if they won, they would prove that a swarm of rats was a lot scarier than one big snake.

While they waited, Ty explained why they were pressing.

"If this works," said Liam, looking less burdened than he had when she'd seen him on his own turf, "if the workers get their rights, a lot's going to change. For everyone. Maybe us, even."

"You got something in mind?" she asked.

He scratched his ear. "Maybe after we give Schultz a workout, we can head over the beltway."

He wanted to take on McNulty. It occurred to her McNulty might be the Schultz of Bakerstown. She looked around, but if anyone had heard, they didn't seem too bothered. Could be they all felt that way.

Could be she'd need more friends in her corner when this ended and she had to come up with the green she owed McNulty. If they weren't firmly on his side, maybe they'd help watch her back while she figured out how to collect her inheritance.

Her *inheritance.*

It didn't seem possible. It certainly wasn't fair. She could have had everything, and instead, she'd lived thin, stomach aching with hunger, never certain when a knife might end up in her back. It was the only way she knew how to be, and imagining another life just felt wrong.

One battle at a time.

"I don't know," Liam added. "Things change over there, I might try to finish school."

Bakerstown pansies, thought Ty, but she smirked anyway. "Thought you had to be bright to go to school."

He grinned. "Least I can read, Metalhead."

She socked him in the shoulder.

The start of the shift drew closer. Chip reported that more of the Brotherhood had gathered at the front of the building, and soon Minnick and his shells would start showing up. They needed to make themselves visible, make their intentions known. To bring the bite to Hampton's door.

She was just about to give the order to creep around the building and block the entrances when Zeke showed up, two tall men in tow.

"Thought we might need some help," he said, white teeth flashing.

From behind him stepped the Walter brothers.

Colin was tired—she could see it in his eyes. Tired in the body, tired in the soul. Whatever had happened with Lena Hampton hadn't turned out the way he'd hoped, which didn't make Ty as happy as she'd hoped. Still, he'd come back to her, because they both knew she could fix him. She would do what she'd always done: give him something to fight.

As he looked over McNulty's crew, his jaw fell slack. "Ty, how . . ."

She beamed. "If I was flush, I'd build us an army."

He slung one arm over her shoulder, shaking Henry's hand with the other.

"Looks like you might be flush," he said.

She swelled with pride, feeling like she could take on the Brotherhood, the Hamptons, the whole Northern Fed. She wondered if this was how Colin had felt all these years. Bigger than life. Important. Meant for something more.

With a nod from Colin, she told Skaggs and Liam to get ready. They were about to go into battle.

36

LENA

Lena paced around the brightly lit hospital room. The monitor attached to the wall beeped the steady rhythm of Otto's heart, slowed by the drugs he'd demanded they give him to dull the pain. Now he was passed out again, as still as he'd been on the floor in her bedroom after Colin had beaten him to a bloody pulp.

She stared at him in a state of detachment, unsure what to feel. Otto's face was blackened, swollen. His cheekbone had been broken. He'd lost two teeth. Part of her accepted responsibility, and with it, guilt, because Colin had only attacked in her defense. But there was something else within her too. A wild streak of jealousy, as if it should have been her hands clawing Otto to pieces, her fists pummeling him raw. He'd hurt her, not once but many times, and right then she didn't care if he'd learned how from their father, or that he had suffered at Josef's hands too. She felt vindicated by his pain, and that made her wonder if she had suddenly become psychotic.

So she said nothing, and kept her lips closed in a thin, firm line while the nurses and doctors all fussed over Mr. Josef Hampton's son.

"You didn't recognize the assailant, Miss Hampton?" A police officer in a stiff black suit shot a glance at Josef Hampton, who'd arrived two hours after she and Otto had been shuttled to the hospital.

Lena turned and stared out the window at the river, wishing she could see the tainted sludge that ran beneath that dyed blue façade. Something real. Anything to distract her from the betrayal she'd seen flash in Colin's eyes.

She'd sent him away to save his life. She'd been cruel, and righteous, and so much like a Hampton that it had nearly torn her apart. But it had worked. He'd gone. He'd left her in the house he'd come to rescue her from. Watching him leave had been harder than kicking him out.

When she had called for help, she'd told the staff that Otto had come to her room when he'd heard a noise outside. She'd hidden in the bathroom, but after hearing a skirmish, cracked the door. Her presence must have scared the intruder away. He'd gone through her window, and run for the north wall. None of the staff had dared to question her, and it gave Colin more precious time when the alarm on the opposite side of the property had been tripped. Once her brother woke, the truth—at least what he knew of it—would be revealed. Hopefully by then Colin would be halfway across the Northern Federation, somewhere her father couldn't touch him.

"I only saw him from the back as he ran away," she said. "It all happened so fast."

"The color of his hair perhaps?" the officer pressed, looking again to Lena's father as if afraid he would be punished for her amnesia. "Was he about my size?"

"Now that you mention it," Lena said, spinning on him. "Yes, he was your size exactly. And with dark hair, cut just like yours. And green eyes. How strange that you have green eyes as well, Officer."

"*Lena*," said her father firmly. "I don't know what's come over you."

The policeman tucked his recorder into his breast pocket and wiped his sweating palms on his thighs. "It's all right, Mr. Hampton. Shock, I think. Understandable, given the situation."

Deliberately, her father reached for her hand, his expression warped with concern.

"I'm just glad she's all right," he said. "That my son was there to protect her."

She jerked her hand away, aware of each scar beneath the fine fabric of her gloves. *And where were you when I needed protection?*

"Indeed." Sensing the tension, but smart enough not to acknowledge it, the officer turned quickly to the door. "If you think of anything else, Miss Hampton, you know how to reach me."

Lena wished she could leave too, but her father's guards were keeping watch right outside the door. She was trapped on the ninth floor of an unfamiliar building, while Colin was running as far and as fast as he could.

She should have gone with him.

The monitor over Otto's bed beeped. Her boots groaned as she transferred her weight. She read her father's movements, trying to sense his mood behind that social mask.

"It seems the testing facilities across the river need to review their security protocols," said Josef, looking down at his son with clinical detachment.

So he did know, after all.

"Perhaps their ethical protocols as well," she said. "I know Hampton Industries does."

When he turned to face her, the lines beside his mouth and eyes had drawn tight. He tapped his middle finger against his thigh in warning.

She stared up at him defiantly.

"Hit me," she said. "And this time I *will* hit you back."

A strange light dawned in his dark eyes. Almost like respect.

"Metaltown has changed you, my dear."

"I find a little time there is all I need," she answered, throwing back the lesson he'd once taught her. "It reminds me how grateful I am for all that I have."

He bared his teeth in a grim smile. "Then it's a pity it's about to become a war zone."

Her blood ran cold. "What do you mean?"

"Your friend has been spotted back at the factory. It seems he's staging another protest. I warned him and his colleagues what would happen if they tried something like this." He sighed. "Their loss, I suppose. Mr. Schultz and his Brotherhood have kindly agreed to impart a lesson on my behalf."

This couldn't be. Colin was gone. She'd thrown him out. He was smart enough to run. But she knew from the way her stomach sank that her father was right. Colin took direction from his heart, not his brain, and he would fight to the end to see his friends protected.

"It's *your* loss," she snapped. "You're worried about slowing labor for the press, what do you think is going to happen if all of your workers are injured or worse?"

"Then I don't suppose they'll be much use to anyone, will they?"

She stared at him, fury scalding her. She wasn't shocked; he was beyond shocking her. But the fact that he was willing to lose his precious money just to keep his pride intact surpassed even his usual arrogance.

He turned and reached for Otto's leg, resting his hand on his ankle in a rare gesture of affection. "There will be something special for the boy, of course. I hope his mother and her sick playmate won't be too devastated."

"What have you done?" she asked weakly.

"Made a business decision. You do still want to learn what I do, don't you?"

Like she had in the house after he'd struck her, she felt the overwhelming urge to get out. Get away from him. Sick with fear, and with nothing in her mind but finding Colin, she strode from the room, only to be caught in the hallway by her father's new driver.

"Miss Hampton," he said, fixing his suit from where she'd rumpled it. His bushy eyebrows were drawn together. "May I escort you home?"

It was not a question.

She slipped by him and sprinted for the stairs. Ten steps away, his wiry arms clamped around her shoulders and lifted her off the shiny white floor. Swinging back, she booted him hard in the shin, and he let out a hiss of pain.

"Let me go!"

"Why don't we go back to your estate?" he asked between his teeth, tightening his grip. Around them, a dozen faces had turned their way. Hospital staff, policemen. Watching blankly. Refusing to help.

She struggled all the way down the stairs, but the big man was immune to her flailing elbows and snapping jaw. Warnings screamed in her head as he shoved her into the car. She couldn't go home. She had to get back to Metaltown. She had to warn them.

She tried to scoot across the seat, but he'd already locked her in from the outside. Frustrated, she beat her hands against the glass, screaming, hoping to attract anyone, but though two women watched with interest, they did little more than whisper and point.

"Nothing to see," he called, and they moved along, glancing back over their shoulders. They disappeared into the building, leaving the private parking lot empty.

Lena wasn't watching him as he opened the door; she was concentrating all her efforts on tearing the inner handle off the passenger door. But when she heard a short male yell, she spun back around. Her mouth opened in horror. The guard had fallen to the pavement, revealing a slight figure behind him, dressed all in black.

A moment later Darcy slid into the front seat, the defuser still in her hand. She shoved the key into the ignition, and brought the electric engine to life.

Lena's body was flung against the siding as the small car tore out of the parking lot. Without looking back, Darcy lowered the partition between them.

"What are you doing?" Lena screeched. They pulled onto the main highway, zipping in and out of traffic in the direction of Bakerstown.

"Something I've been trying to do for some time," Darcy said, more determined than Lena had ever seen her. "I'm getting out of

Tri-City, and if you have any sense, Miss Hampton, you'll come with me."

Lena stared at her in shock. This was Darcy, who frowned and fretted and worried, who Lena had once thought didn't have the spine to fight back. She knew better now. Darcy had survived her father, waiting for just such a moment to make her escape.

"How did you get out?" she asked.

"Your father's security is distracted with Otto's attack," she said. "I told the driver I needed to check in on you at the hospital. I was in the waiting room when you were removed. It is my place as your tutor, after all, to make sure you're safe."

She swerved across a lane, gripping the wheel with both hands.

"Take me to the Small Parts factory," said Lena.

Darcy's knuckles turned white as she gripped the wheel. "And what happens then?"

The sharpness in her tone made Lena scoot back an inch. *I find Colin,* she thought. *I help the Small Parts Charter.*

"I don't know," she answered honestly.

Darcy shook her head. "No disrespect, dear, but sometimes you can be such a Hampton."

Lena's back slouched against the seat.

"You can't fix this," Darcy said, veering into an open lane. "You can't sweep in on title alone and expect the world to change. The Small Parts factory is just a cog in your father's machine. One piece of the problem. There are still the other factories, the other workers, the poor who'd kill to fill those workers' spots. The *war.*"

Lena closed her eyes. "There are people in danger. If I can help . . ."

"Then today everyone will raise their glass in your honor," Darcy finished. "But what about tomorrow? What about a year from now? What about when the war ends?"

"I don't know!" Lena shouted. When the war ended, Colin would be jobless, along with all the workers she wanted so badly to protect. But if the Small Parts factory closed, the war could not sustain. She could hardly imagine a world without war.

"Come with me, while your father and his security are preoccupied. Leave this place. Let it destroy itself. I've heard the Advocates will take people over the border to the Eastern Federation."

The Advocates, whom her father was providing with ammunition to attack their own people just so that the war continued.

"Darcy, that's insane. The Eastern Federation? We're fighting against them!"

"We're fighting against ourselves," Darcy retorted, and Lena wondered just how much she knew of her father's weapons dealings. "The time has come to choose, Miss Hampton. The war in Metaltown, or the war outside it."

Lena considered it only a moment, and then she placed her hand on her tutor's tense shoulder.

"Take me to Metaltown."

"They're rioting there, last I heard." There was no surprise in Darcy's tone. Bakerstown rose on their left, a mass of red brick, with the shops clustered on the right side of the road and the residential towers and schools on the left. Lena thought of what Colin had told her one night, standing on the bridge. That he would come out here, and think of his past, and wish things were different.

"Then take me as close as you can," she said. "Thank you, Darcy."

A tight smile pulled at the corners of Darcy's mouth. "It's been a pleasure, Miss Hampton."

* * *

Darcy let her off near the bridge, across from Lacey's Bar, where Lena and Colin had met her family during the protest. She slammed the door behind her, and an instant later was running up the hill toward the Small Parts factory, Darcy's defuser tight in her grip. The sweat ran in her eyes and chilled her skin, and her blood pounded through her veins, but she didn't stop. She had to find Colin. She had to warn him of what her father had promised.

The noise could be heard three blocks down. A quiet roar, like all of the grinding machines had been left on, punctuated by higher-pitched screams. The sounds made her muscles seize, threatening to slow her down, but she pushed on, and made it as far as the Stamping Mill before the chaos blocked her path.

The fights had broken out all down Factory Row. It was like the press, but overwhelmingly larger. Brotherhood, and the Small Parts Charter, and others, too. Men and women in navy or white uniforms, employees of the Stamping Mill and the Chem Plant. There were people wearing green as well, and where they had come from, she didn't know.

They fought tooth and nail, throwing punches, attacking with their fists and their bodies, and weapons fashioned from whatever they could find. She saw a trash can flung through the air, and screamed when something exploded a hundred feet before her, on the opposite side of the street.

Too late. The fear echoed between her temples. *Too late to save him.*

Through the clatter of raining debris, she thought she heard a woman cry her name. But though Lena spun toward the sound, she saw nothing but violence.

Ducking low, she searched for Colin, but she could barely see ten feet before her for all the clashing bodies. If she could get to the front of the building, she could climb up the metal trash bin and get a better view from higher ground. She raced toward it, taking a hard hit to her ribs on the way.

Before her, a man hovered over a small figure on the ground, a child, curled up into a ball. She recognized the Brotherhood mobster by the flash of his brass knuckles, and stared in horror as he wheeled back and kicked. The boy went sprawling.

"Chip!" The familiar female voice broke Lena's sudden freeze. "Chip! *Get out of my way!*".

Lena's gaze shot up and locked on Ty, trying in vain to shove through the crowd to get to the boy. Lena recognized him now. He was one of the workers. Part of the charter.

The man attacking him wiped his sweaty brow on his bare forearm, and swung his leg back to kick Chip again. Ty was still too far away; even if she broke through from the fighting, she wasn't going to make it in time to help him.

Lena rushed forward.

"You bastard!" She stuck the point of the defuser into the man's back and pulled the trigger. He hit the ground in a fit of seizures, mouth gaping, eyes wide. She jumped over him to Chip and dragged the boy to his feet.

"Are you all right?"

Chip shook free. "I had him!"

Behind him, Ty's stare locked on Lena's. The hate she'd come to expect in the girl's eyes gave way to wariness. She gave Lena a brief nod, and then called for Chip, and disappeared back into the fight.

Before Lena could follow, iron hands clenched around her ribs, dragging her backward through the crowd. She dropped the defuser and lost sight of Chip as the others closed in around him. Terrified, she fought, twisting, kicking, sinking her teeth into the dirty, sweat-drenched sweater covering the man's shoulder. He growled and squeezed her harder, so hard that she could barely breathe.

She was pulled through a line of men, into the alley, where the sounds of the street echoed against the high factory walls.

"Let go!" she screamed. "Colin! *Colin!*"

And then they were in the Small Parts factory. Her heels couldn't gain traction as she was dragged through the employee locker room, past the metal detector to the foreman's office, where she was sat roughly in a chair. Immediately she attempted to leap out, but the man had grabbed her wrists, and fastened them behind her with a thin wire, which he wrapped tightly enough to make her fingertips prickle with numbness.

He spun the chair around, nearly tipping it over, and as he leaned down to meet her gaze she saw his face for the first time.

Lena's eyes widened. Before her stood Jed Schultz, the leader of the Brotherhood.

37

COLIN

Colin's pulse pounded in his eardrums. Before him, Imon swung a silver knife, nearly catching his gut. He bowed back at the last second, belly sucked against his spine, and stumbled backwards onto the crumbling sidewalk. He'd already landed a couple clean shots on the big man's jaw, but Imon was a machine—nothing seemed to slow him down. He loomed over Colin, knife low, face red, lips snarling over crooked, blackened teeth. Colin's heart kicked up his windpipe as he scrambled backward in an attempt to regain his footing.

And then Imon staggered, as if a pallet of scrap metal had been dumped onto his back. Hayden's face appeared over his shoulder, his forearm locked around the foreigner's throat. The look on his face was crazed, and as angry as Colin had ever seen it.

Hayden released Imon only for a second, and with his other hand wheeled back and knocked him hard in the back of the head with a broken brick. Imon collapsed with a grunt and a spray of dust.

The Walter brothers stared down at Imon for a full second, waiting for him to rise. When it was clear he was out, Hayden swiped the knife off the ground where it had fallen.

"Always hated the guy," he said.

Colin nodded, trying to say something, *anything*, but unable to because of the lump in his throat. He'd been sucked back to another time, another place, when they were both kids. Colin was wearing Hayden's coat, following on his heels, so sure that no one, not one single person out there, could beat his big brother.

"Me too," he finally said.

Around them, the war waged on. Another of Matchstick's explosions rocked the sidewalk beneath their feet, this one near the entrance of the building. Colin wiped the sweat from his eyes, torn. The Brotherhood had started the fight, and the Small Parts Charter, McNulty's boys, and the other workers who stood by them had answered. But blowing up the factory took things to another level. If there had ever been a shot Hampton would listen, it was gone now.

Or maybe this would be what it took for him to finally take them seriously.

Hayden squeezed Colin's shoulder and gave him one parting look before slipping into the crowd to join another fight.

"Get away from the building!" Colin shouted. Thoughts of Agnes burned through him. How many other kids would die out here today? He had to get everyone he could away from Matchstick's mayhem.

"Back up! Back up! Into the street!"

Henry appeared before him, nose bleeding like an open faucet.

"Form a line," Colin told him.

"Line up!" barked Ty, taking up the call. "Block the building! Don't let anyone through!"

"Form a line!" gargled Henry, standing to Colin's left. "Pass it on! Go!"

Gabe, who'd come just before the fight, took a space next to Henry, a tire iron braced before him. "Form a line!" he yelled. One of McNulty's boys stood beside him. Gradually, they pushed the fights away from the building.

A body shoved between Henry and Colin. It was a woman, nearly Colin's height, and he stared in shock at her profile—at her firm, set mouth and hardened stare.

"Ma? What are you . . ."

Her arms linked with his to make a chain. "Well? You're my boy, aren't you?" She turned to face him, the look on her face the same one she gave when he stepped out of line. "Is there a problem?"

Henry laughed at Colin's stunned expression, then took her other arm.

No, there wasn't a problem. Ty may have taught him how to fight, but his ma had taught him to be tough long before that. With her at his side, he felt every time she'd told him to pick his chin up, and pull his shoulders back, and do the right thing. He felt like the man she'd raised him to be.

"Keep together!" Ida Walter ordered, distracted by Zeke zipping past them.

"They took down Hayak!" he shouted. "Martin's holding 'em back by himself!" Colin followed his trajectory toward the street corner, where Hayak set up his food cart every morning. The lamppost marking the spot was now bent at an angle, and he could see nothing below it.

Hayden ran after Zeke, and Colin swore and closed the gap with his outstretched arms. He was just about to tell Henry to tighten the line when Chip yelled his name.

"The greenback, they got her!"

Colin froze. Ty, who'd taken his right side, turned her face to see him clearly with her good eye. She grabbed Chip's shoulder.

"What greenback?"

"The Hampton girl!" His face was covered with grime and tracks of sweat that ran down from his hairline. "They took her back to the factory—I tried to save her—you believe me, right?"

"'Course I believe you." She looked to Colin, mouth pulled into a tight line.

He took a step back, spinning to face the gray stone building, scorched black near the main entrance from Matchstick's bomb. There was a fire somewhere; he could smell it through the sweat and blood and nitro air. Horrified, he realized it was coming from inside the building. White smoke billowed out from the front doors.

Lena was inside the building. With the Brotherhood. With the fire.

"Stay." Ty's grip latched around on his biceps. "You have to stay. They listen to you."

"They'll listen to you now!" He jerked back. Another explosion, and pellets of concrete hailed down over them. From somewhere behind him came a man's fatal scream, and Colin's whole body cringed at the sound.

"Stop Matchstick!" he shouted to anyone who would pass on the call. Ty grabbed his face in her hands and forced him to look at her.

"You stay here," Ty said. "I'll get her. I'm your best man, right?"

The look on her face was absolute confidence. She was his best man. He trusted her, even when everything inside of him demanded he find Lena.

He nodded. "Yeah."

"Good," she said. "I'll bring her back to you. Don't worry."

Ty's gaze lingered a moment longer, flashing with something close to regret. And then she grinned savagely, and ducked out of the line. His last sight of her was her small form running toward the front door and disappearing into the smoke.

38

TY

The Brotherhood had blocked the alley leading to the employee entrance in order to secure the building, but thanks to Matchstick's bomb the front doors were clear. White smoke plumed out of the right side from where the glass had been shattered, but no flames were visible from the outside.

As Ty neared the entry, fear caught up with her—hot and thick and suffocating, like the smoke that had swallowed the whole Metaltown sky. She covered her mouth and nose with her sleeve, and shoved her feelings aside. The greenback needed her help. She'd taken on the Brotherhood to pick Chip up off the pavement. She'd taken on her father to stand beside the charter. She was one of them, as much as Ty had wanted otherwise. She was one of them, and that meant she wasn't going to get left behind.

Ty would not let Colin down. Not this time.

She squinted, and kicked out the ragged shards of glass to clear her path. She was just about to step through the door frame when a hand closed on her arm.

Turning, she saw Liam, his face smeared with soot, his face lifted with confusion. A trickle of blood ran from one ear; Ty suspected he'd been too close to the last blast. She glanced back at Colin, who was still holding the line, pushing the fights away from the factory. It worried her that Matchstick was nowhere in sight.

"They've got one of us in there," Ty shouted to him.

Liam's brows scrunched. "Better hurry. Cops are on their way. Word is, there's a suit on the beltway giving the order to shut this thing down."

A shiver passed through her. "Hampton."

The Bakerstown cops were dirty, owned by the man that owned everything. If Hampton ordered it, they would end the riots by any means necessary.

Without another thought, she ducked through the hole in the glass, her sleeve covering her nose and mouth. The fire seemed to be contained to the debris in the foyer; the door to her left was clear. She hopped over a burning board and shoved through into the hallway that would lead to Minnick's office.

It was quiet inside. An eerie, sticky kind of quiet that muffled the rebellion outside to only a faint roar. Keeping low, Ty raced down the hallway, but before she was halfway she heard a clacking of footsteps behind her and wrenched the knife from her boot.

Liam skidded on his heels, grasping the wall for support as she spun back to face him. In that moment, she thought she'd never been so happy to see a friendly face.

She nodded. He nodded back.

With silent, deliberate strides they approached the door. Ty pressed her ear against the wood and heard a crash, and then a stifled cry of pain.

Lena.

Ty shoved Liam aside and rammed her shoulder into the door. It cracked and gave way, and she burst into the room with a fierce roar. Bracing low, she prepared to defend herself, but found the office empty. It wasn't until she jogged around Minnick's desk that she found Lena, laid out sideways on the floor, still seated in the metal chair. Her wrists had been bound behind her and a gag filled her mouth. A closer look showed that the back of the chair was lying on her forearm, which was bent at an awkward angle, like Lena had another joint between her wrist and elbow. Her eyes had rolled back, revealing a thin line of white.

"Watch the doors!" Ty told Liam, then knelt beside Lena to release her bindings. The girl's fingertips were purple, and the wire had cut through the thin skin of her wrists in her struggle to get free. She'd probably tipped over the chair in her efforts.

Not bad for a greenback.

Once Ty had released Lena's arm, she kicked the chair across the floor, and slapped her across the face. "Hey!" When Lena blinked sleepily, Ty slapped her again. "Does this look like naptime to you, princess?"

"What . . ." Lena gulped down a deep breath, her cheeks and neck red. Her long black hair was plastered to her skin with sweat. "It's Schultz," she rasped as her eyes came into focus. "He . . . he left. He's looking for Colin. He was going to bring him here. He was going to use me to make him stop the fighting . . ." Her words turned to a groan.

Ty's lips curled back over her teeth. "Get up, come on." She jerked Lena roughly to a stand. The greenback nursed her arm against her chest, wavering once before leaning into Ty's shoulder.

"I have to find Colin," she said weakly.

"You have to find your father," Ty told her. "You have to stop him. You're the only one who can stop him."

Lena found her footing. "He won't listen to me."

"Make him listen! He's sending men here to end this. Not just Brotherhood knotheads—*cops*. Dirty cops. You know what that means?" *Guns*, thought Ty, her gut heavy and cold as lead. *The demolition of Metaltown.*

Lena swallowed. Nodded once. "What about Colin?"

"Let me take care of Colin."

Again, she nodded. Then her gaze met Ty's. "I'm sorry I fired you."

Her uninjured hand closed around Ty's wrist, and Ty glanced down at it, then back at Lena.

"Did you want a hug? Because now's not a good time."

Lena's lips quirked. "Later then."

Ty gave a snort.

"Astor, come on!" Liam shouted, just as one of Jed's men came bowling into the room from the main floor. Liam had the chair in his grip and swung it hard into the intruder's head. The man blinked, and fell like a stone.

"Astor?" repeated Lena, going still.

Ty glanced outside the door, knife ready. Footsteps were coming, though not at a hurried pace. *Click. Clack. Click. Clack.* As if there was no urgency to reach the office at all. Her fingers turned cold. She rolled her shoulders back.

"Astor Tyson?"

When Ty's gaze flickered over she found Lena's mouth open, with something between realization and horror playing over her reddened face. If Lena knew something about her past, if she could fill in the missing pieces of Ty's fragmented memory, it would have been great, but there wasn't time to ask.

"Go!" Ty shouted. "Liam, take her to the beltway! Make sure she gets there!"

He grabbed Lena's good arm and dragged her toward the door, but she shook him free.

"It's you?" she asked weakly.

Despite the urgency, curiosity was getting the better of her.

"Surprised?" Ty still was. She could almost feel the small, folded piece of paper in her hip pocket. The picture of her father.

"I know what happened," said Lena quickly. "I know about the Medical Division."

At her words, Ty's world quieted. Her knife arm lowered. Liam hesitated by the door. *It's true,* she thought. She wasn't sure she'd really believed it until just then.

"We'll get your division back," Lena said. "I'll help you."

Ty's breath released in a great shudder. *I'll be flush,* she thought. The reality of it rushed over her, hot water on an ice-cold day. All those times she and Colin had run their mouths about what they'd do with a little green came flooding back. All those nights alone in the Board and Care, gripping her knife. All the scraps she'd pulled from trash for just a little bit of food. The things she'd come to expect, that she prepared for *every single day,* could actually be over. The weight of their chains slid off her shoulders. She felt light then, young. It was the feeling of hope, just before the crash, but maybe this time there wouldn't be a crash.

"You mean that?"

"I mean that," Lena said. "I promise."

Ty felt herself pull taller. She hadn't fully trusted anyone besides Colin since she was a child. The feeling felt strange to her. Risky. And suddenly she got why her friend had given this girl a chance.

The slow click of footsteps drew closer.

"Go," Ty whispered. "I'm giving you a head start. Don't make me regret it."

Lena gave her a small smile. And then she and Liam bolted through the door and down the hallway.

* * *

Ty was blocking the factory entrance to Minnick's office with the chair when she saw him. Jed Schultz, greasy as the first day they'd crossed paths. He was alone, sweaty, and half-beaten already, and that centered her, gave her an edge.

"Where's your ugly friend?" she asked, bracing the knife before her. In her mind she tracked Lena and Liam's flight. They should have made it to the door by now. If they pushed, they could hit the beltway in ten minutes.

"Funny," said Jed, without a hint of amusement. "I was just about to ask you the same thing."

"Colin?" she asked innocently. "He's outside. Working your Brotherhood over."

Jed laughed dryly. He didn't have a weapon on him, not that Ty could see. That didn't mean he wasn't hiding one, though. She crouched, ready, as he continued to advance upon her.

"You set my little prize free," he said. "Typically, this kind of thing would rub me the wrong way, but as it turns out, I might still have won after all."

Ty flinched.

He stopped at the door three feet away, placing his arms on each side of the frame, exposing his chest. Daring her. Ty could smell him. Rank sweat and cinnamon cigarettes. She burned with hatred, for everything he'd ever done to Colin, and everything he'd ever done to her. She could stick him if she wanted, but her hand was unsteady. She'd never stabbed anyone before. She bared her teeth and gripped the knife harder.

"So it's true," said Jed with interest. "I can see it in your eyes— well, *eye*. Astor Tyson. The missing heir of Division IV."

An icy trickle of fear dripped down her spine.

"You know there's a reward out for information on you," he said.

"I heard that," said Ty.

"So that's why you hid," he realized.

No, she thought. *I hid because I didn't know.* But now there was no stopping the memories. An electric train set her father had brought home. It stammered over the carpet. It whistled when you pressed a red button. She'd dreamed of it. Thought of it every time she'd gone to the train yards with Colin.

"You think I didn't know you were the one behind the press? The engine driving the machine?" Jed glanced toward the main floor and its silent machines. "You got hurt, and Metaltown got behind you. They wouldn't have done it for Colin—not for a Bakerstown boy. But for you . . . That's some kind of power you got."

Sometimes the best thing you can do is cut your losses, he had once told Colin. He'd wanted her out of the picture because he thought she was strong, not because he thought she was weak.

Slick, thought Ty. She twitched when he lowered one hand.

"We could strike up an arrangement," he said. "It looks like McNulty means to take back Metaltown. With a little green, you and I could make sure that doesn't happen."

Ty narrowed her eyes. He didn't scare her, not anymore. Not now that she was worth something, and he was the one trying to make a deal. The tables had turned.

She forced a laugh. "Sound pretty desperate there, Schultz."

"Think of how it could be," he continued. "You can't work anyway. You could own a stake in the Brotherhood. You could have the respect of Metaltown. Protection. Enough food to fatten you up. Think of how good it could be."

How good it could be.

Her grip on the knife grew slippery with sweat. She didn't want to hear him, but couldn't help it. Once Lena Hampton helped her get her money, what would she do? Move to the River District? Live a flush, fat life with a defuser on her hip? No, she knew better. She didn't belong there. She was a Metalhead, but she was a greenback, too, and a single girl with her pockets full of money was a recipe for disaster without enough protection. She had Colin, of course, but he already had a home and a family of his own.

It was just her, and she needed to look out for herself. The Brotherhood could help her survive.

In that moment, she considered how different things could be. When someone came to her and needed help, she could help them. Chip wouldn't have to eat out of Dumpsters. She could take care of Cherish. She could make Metaltown safe.

It struck her that Schultz had probably thought the same thing once.

"No thanks," said Ty. "I'd rather gouge my other eye out than help you."

Jed's face tightened.

"Well," he said. "It's a good thing Hampton wants you dead then."

He moved fast—faster than she thought he could. He lunged, struck out with his fist like a snake. She raised her knife, but it was too late. He'd knocked it from her hand, and hit her hard on the side of her head. The vision in her good eye went bright white then exploded with color as she scrambled across the floor, searching blindly for the knife, surprise shocking every muscle into action.

He tackled her. Her cheek felt like glass when it slammed against the tile. The knee he planted in her back crushed the air from her lungs. Her vision refocused in a compressed point, and she screamed, a feral battle cry, and pushed up, every ounce of strength dedicated to getting free.

I've beaten better than you, she thought. Her fist sliced back and connected with his throat and he fell to the side. When he rose, his yellow teeth were bared, like a rabid dog's.

And then something sharp pricked her left side, just under her ribs. She gasped. It didn't hurt, but it stole her breath. Like her body was a balloon being deflated.

Jed used that moment to flip her on her back, and as he did she kicked out hard. His knee made a cracking sound, and he fell. With short, shallow breaths she prodded her side, and felt the handle of her knife, lodged up to the hilt.

No.

Her eyes welled with tears. She couldn't feel it, even as her trembling hand pulled it out.

Colin, help me.

Her vision began to grow dark around the edges.

Colin.

Then Jed was on top of her. She forced one hard breath, and when she did, her throat filled with liquid and she choked. Bright red spattered across Jed's shirt, and he looked down, not with disgust, but with victory in his black eyes.

Then his hands reached for her neck, exposing his chest. With all her strength she swung her knife arm up in an arc. The bloody tip implanted just below Jed's armpit. The metal hit something hard, and then gave way and slid all the way to the handle.

Jed's eyes opened wide with surprise. He leaned back, dazed, and looked down to where she'd stuck him. Then he fell backward onto the floor, dead.

39

LENA

The moment Lena emerged from the building, she was searching for Colin. She knew she had to find her father, to convince him to end the riots, but she couldn't help herself. Colin was out here, and while Jed Schultz was around he was still in danger.

There was too much smoke in the street to see clearly. More explosions had ravaged the side of the Small Parts factory; great hunks were missing from the gray stone, and what was left behind was streaked with black soot. The street below the explosion sites had been reduced to rubble.

Through the smoke and dust she could see a chain of people blocking the factory. They'd stretched beyond the alley leading to the employee entrance that the Brotherhood had previously been protecting, and blocked her path, reaching almost all the way to the opposite end of the building. Even as she watched, men and women thickened the line, pushing Schultz's thugs back.

Pride filled her, even above the urgency.

"This way!" Liam called, leading her left, away from the entrance, up the street. "We'll have to go around the riot!"

She followed him, running behind the line, searching for Colin's clipped hair, his broad shoulders, his stained thermal in everyone she passed. He could be anywhere. A quick glance behind her revealed that Ty had not yet left the building, and as the smoke grew black, her chest began to quake.

Ahead, a boy had a trash can lid braced in front of him like a shield. He was thick through the torso, with such overdeveloped shoulder muscles that it seemed he had no neck at all. She recognized him immediately from the Small Parts Charter, and slammed to a halt.

"Colin!" She lifted on her tiptoes to shout in his ear. "Have you seen him?" The searing pain in her arm, still tucked against her chest, was enough to bring a new wave of tears.

Noneck nodded. "Down the line!"

It was the only relief she was given, because Liam had doubled back, grabbed her shoulder, and was jerking her away. "Come *on*!"

They raced to the end of the crumbling sidewalk, where the street sloped up on its path to the Stamping Mill. Bystanders were watching the riots with interest.

"Look at that!" a man with a long scar down his cheek yelled. She and Liam both turned in the direction he was pointing.

The police approached from the direction of the beltway, marching down the open street with their plastic shields and helmets. They held a solid formation, a block of soldiers all in black, with guns already drawn and lifted.

"We're too late," said Liam.

But she didn't hear if he said anything else, because she was sprinting to the far side of the street, around the line, aiming toward them. Each labored breath scorched her lungs. Her muscles burned with fatigue.

She ran toward the closest officer, lifting her good arm in surrender. *Don't shoot me. Please don't shoot me.*

"Help!" she cried. "Help me! I'm Lena Hampton! I need to find my father!"

She couldn't see the police officer's face through his helmet's mask, but he faltered when she stepped in front of him, ten feet away.

"Please help! I'm Lena Hampton! My father is Josef Hampton!"
He lowered his weapon.

Jaw tight, tears streaming, she let him approach and escort her to the side of the road.

"My father," she whimpered. "Please get me away from here."

"I'll take you to him," he said finally.

He escorted her through the block of policemen.

* * *

Josef Hampton was stationed behind a full battery of his private security detail, buffered by another layer of police. He stood beside a long, tapered electric carriage—one of the many vehicles he stored in the estate's garage. His driver—the man Darcy had used her defuser on—was nowhere to be found.

Though the pain in Lena's arm had dulled to a pulsing throb, she still kept it locked in the center of her chest. Now that she had slowed, she felt how it affected her gait, making one step longer than the other.

As she was ushered through the sea of black, she thought of Jed Schultz, and how her father had contracted the leader of the Brotherhood to hurt Colin. She focused on the people of the Small Parts Charter, and all the wrongs her father had done to them.

As she approached, she saw that Josef Hampton wasn't alone. He appeared to be arguing with a woman with a long, dark braid that hung down the center of her back. Her oversized gray slacks and shapeless, hand-knit sweater told Lena she was from Metaltown.

An officer, who had been standing a few feet away, stepped forward and grabbed the woman's arm. She shook out of his grip. "Please," she begged. "She's down there. I swear, I saw her."

"You don't know what you're saying," said her father. "You forget yourself."

Lena felt the cold then, a stiff breeze, blowing straight to her bones.

"Father?"

At the sound of Lena's voice, the woman turned. The emotions flashed on her face. Surprise. Anger. Relief.

Shima.

Her old nanny half walked, half ran toward her, and shuddered as she wrapped her arms around Lena's shoulders. Lena squeezed her back, feeling stronger, less afraid. She wasn't alone. Not when Shima stood beside her.

She thought of Colin, of the workers who surrounded him. Of Astor Tyson, and the child, Chip, getting kicked in the street. Of Cherish and Ida. Of street codes and safeties and watching each other's backs, and it became as clear as the shouts ringing out from Metaltown: blood didn't make family, love did, and sweat did, and loyalty.

A wave of dizziness took her, and she rested her head on Shima's shoulder. Her nanny pulled back slightly, leaving a small slice of space between their bodies, and revealed the small rope doll in her fist.

"You left this at my house." A sob wracked through Shima, and she lowered her head. "I saw you by the factory. I feared the worst." Lena remembered the woman's voice, calling her name, just after she'd arrived on Factory Row.

The officer grasped Shima's sweater behind her neck, hoisting her up like a cat carrying its young.

"No!" shouted Lena. Her father had already sent Shima away once; he would not do so again.

The officer paused. Shima placed one tentative arm around Lena's shoulder.

"She stays with me," Lena told both of them.

Her father crossed his arms over his chest, looking out of place in his sharp black suit on this weathered, empty beltway. "You look a little worse for wear."

Lena stepped forward out of Shima's hold. She lifted out her broken arm, and fought the nausea when it bowed just below the elbow.

"Jed Schultz couldn't find Colin," she said. "Apparently I was his second choice."

His face flashed with surprise, then hardened into a grimace.

"What?" she asked. "Didn't you think someone could come after *your* daughter? At least I'm not a child, like Astor Tyson was."

He lowered his chin, challenge exuding from every feature. "In case you haven't noticed, I'm a little busy right now."

"Did her parents really die of the corn flu, Father?" *Or did you just get rid of them, like everyone else who stands in your way?*

The corners of his mouth twitched.

"Careful," he warned. "My patience runs only so deep."

She felt her body grow hard as the steel in their factories. She felt nothing. Not pain. Not fear.

"End this," she said. "Call off your dogs."

"I'm afraid it's too late." They squared off, him, tall and slender, ever perfect. Her, so like him in appearance, so different within. How long had she wanted to be like him? To gain his approval? Now the thought revolted her.

"It's not too late," she said. "People will die. People are already dying."

"That's the wonderful, terrible thing about Metaltown," he answered. "There are always more people to fill the void." He stared at her nanny.

Frustration stoked Lena's anger. He was blinded by his own arrogance. She would have to appeal to him in the only way he understood.

She straightened, and put on her calm, cool exterior. Her Hampton mask.

"You're going to lose everything. Your factory. Your workers. Your *family*." She closed her eyes, fighting the pain radiating through her shoulder. "You've lost hours of labor. Halted production. And worse, shown your employees that they're expendable. Why wouldn't they fight you?" She pointed behind her, to the smoke rising from Factory Row.

"I don't need my own daughter telling me how to run my business." For the first time, Lena's father raised his voice.

"You're right," she said dryly. "You have your son. Otto. Who is nothing if not dedicated to Hampton Industries."

He shook his head, his perfectly groomed hair falling loose around his eyes. His hands came to rest on his hips, and suddenly he looked old, older than she'd ever seen.

"You want weapons?" she continued. "You need Division II. Without the Small Parts factory, you're missing the necessary pieces to complete an explosive device. You have an empty shell of metal, with no mechanism to blow it up."

"I know what they do," he said.

"Then you know how important they are," she said, stepping closer. "You have deadlines. Shipments that will soon be overdue. There are soldiers waiting for weapons." *On this side and the other.* "Wasting time and money to stop a press is less lucrative than giving the charter what they want. They will still work for you, just as hard as before, if you bend just a little. If you don't, they won't be the only ones out of jobs; you will be too."

He looked past her, toward Metaltown, where more smoke filled the sky with every second that passed. Shima gripped her hand. She held on to it like a lifeline.

"Choose your war, Father. The one inside this Federation, or the one outside of it."

He faced her slowly, a curious, heavy expression weighing down his features.

"It was never supposed to go this far," he said, and whether he meant with the press or the Advocates, she didn't know.

He waved his hand to summon the chief of police.

COLIN

Colin pushed on. The Small Parts Charter and those who had chosen to fight beside them had thickened the chain before the factory until they were a giant, pulsing mass, unstoppable in strength. They pushed the Brotherhood into the street, across the street, straight to the sidewalk on the opposite side.

His pulse hammered in his ears. They were going to win this. The Brotherhood couldn't take the pressure.

A great cheer erupted near the front of the lines as Jed's men scrambled away. Colin jumped to see if others had followed, and when he found they had, he was filled with such a sense of triumph that he pumped his fist overhead and whooped right along with them.

We did it, he thought. *We beat the Brotherhood. We beat Jed Schultz.*

He was light as a cloud. Everything they'd wanted, everything they'd fought for, it all was worth it now. They'd shown a bunch of sellouts that they could not be pushed down or ignored.

He searched for Ty, wanting to see her face now. Wanting her to know that this, right now, was for her. With a sinking sensation he remembered that she'd gone after Lena.

He grabbed the nearest shoulder, which turned out to be Henry's. "You seen Ty?"

He shook his head.

Colin found Noneck, but he hadn't seen Ty either. Not since she'd gone into the factory.

He was just about to go in after her when he heard shouts to his right, fearful cries, in the direction of the beltway. The line collapsed near the employee entrance; the charter scrambled to escape whatever approached from the bottom of Factory Row. It couldn't be another explosion; there was no smoke, no quake. But all the same, he hadn't seen Matchstick in some time.

Colin stood as tall as he could and squinted, and then saw what had jarred the others.

A battalion of black uniforms, moving together as a unit, the way he'd always imagined the soldiers did on the front lines. They had gray shields and black guns, and were close, less than fifty yards away.

His ma kept by his side, unwilling to lose sight of him since they'd linked arms. She studied his face, searching for the answer.

"Cops," he told her. But it didn't matter, because the message was already being carried back. Some were running. Others were looking to him.

The guilt poured through him like hot, liquid metal. It was one thing to take on Schultz's men, but another entirely to face the police. The Brotherhood fought with muscle and blades—they had to get close enough to scrap. But cops . . . It didn't matter how hard you hit or how fast you split, they could pick you off from a distance and you'd be done.

"Run," his ma told him, iron in her tone. "They'll come for you, Colin. You have to run."

She placed her body in front of his, even as the fighters before her began to bolt. Standing solid, she looked ready to take on the whole lot of them, and in that moment he loved her more than ever.

But he wouldn't abandon his post. That wouldn't be right. He'd started this. The right thing was to finish it.

For the hundredth time he glanced back at the main entrance to the building. The smoke had slowed; the building wasn't going to burn after all. Lena was safe. Maybe she and Ty had gotten out when he wasn't looking. Telling himself this didn't make him feel any better.

He took a deep breath, and pictured Ty, and her face, and every nightmare she'd had to endure because of the Small Parts factory.

"Hold the line!" he roared.

His ma didn't turn around, but her body grew stiff, and she lowered, ready for a fight from any angle.

"Hold the line!" shouted Gabe. Colin nodded to him gratefully.

The word spread, and soon the running had stopped. The Brotherhood had disappeared, slunk away. All that remained were the good men and women of Metaltown who had faced them, who now waited in silence to see if the police would fight, or gun them down.

A tense anticipation blanketed them. Factory Row grew silent as a graveyard. Colin attempted to swallow, but his heart was lodged high in his throat, and he couldn't push it down.

Please don't be here, Lena.

He glanced around for Ty, wishing above all else that she was beside him. There was no one he'd rather have his back in a fight.

The army stopped. Colin and the others braced for them to discharge their weapons, but the shots never came.

A metallic hiss, then static, like the sound of Minnick's speakerbox in the factory. And then a booming male voice filled the taut space between them.

"The owner of Hampton Industries is ordering all factory workers to cease and desist their protesting until he can meet with charter leaders."

Colin heard the words, but they took a long moment to sink in. Cease and desist. Another meeting would occur, and this time Hampton was requesting it.

Their front line—men with helmets and long plastic shields—held their position, but those behind them turned and marched away. Those fighting watched in awe as the entire group retreated up Factory Row.

We're alive, Colin thought. But he almost couldn't believe it. He didn't understand what had happened, why the police had stopped. Did Hampton really want to end the press?

He couldn't help wondering if this was just a stunt to get him alone—to throw him back in food testing for what he'd done to Otto.

For a moment, no one knew what to say. It was Chip who spoke first, his high voice calling above the silence: "That's what I thought!"

And then there was cheering. Colin found himself at a loss for words, and gaped at the others, who slapped him on the back and offered their congratulations. His ma kissed him on the cheek, then disappeared to find Hayden. Henry embraced him so hard he thought his ribs would crack. Any confusion he felt, any doubt, was forced into the ground beneath his feet. The joy took him over like a tidal wave, and soon he was grinning and laughing and dancing, just like the others.

"Colin!" It was Martin who grabbed his shoulders and turned him away from the party that had erupted in the street. His face was pale as death, and for a moment Colin didn't understand why. Then he remembered that Zeke had said the Brotherhood had gone after his uncle.

"Hayak. Is he all right?"

"He's fine," said Martin, pulling Colin toward the building.

"Then what is it?"

There was a small crowd near the doors, and through their feet, he could see a body, lying out on the walk.

His ears began to ring; the sounds behind him disappeared. He didn't remember running over, or pushing the others aside. He didn't remember falling hard to his knees, and scraping his hands on the rubble as he crawled closer. All he knew was that he was suddenly crawling up beside his best friend, and she was bleeding from a great sopping wound in her chest, and her ribs were rising and falling, rising and falling, too fast. Her skin was white, and around her busted eye the blue twisted mass of skin was pulled taut.

"Ty?" His voice didn't sound right. Sounded like someone far away. He couldn't touch her. He was going to break her. No, that wasn't right. She was unbreakable. She was the strongest person he knew.

"Ty, stop!" he shouted, and then he did put a hand on her wound, and felt the warm, sticky liquid pool against his palm. "Stop, okay? Quit messing around!"

Doctor, he thought absently. And then: *the Brotherhood doctor won't see her.* It was stupid. They'd find a doctor, and he'd help her, and if he refused Colin would kill him, plain and simple.

"Colin?" Her voice was a weak groan. She held absolutely still, her hands clenched at her sides. The only things moving were her heaving chest and her fluttering eyelids.

"Where's the doctor?" Every muscle in him twisted. "Find someone!"

Footsteps as someone tore off toward the Stamping Mill. He followed the sound, eyes locking on the red path from the Small Parts main entrance that Ty had left on her struggle to this spot.

She was hurting. She'd been hurting a long time.

He pressed down harder, trying to slow her bleeding, but she cried out in pain, and he ripped his hand away. It hurt him, too. The pain was in his chest, in his muscles, but though he would have gladly done so, he couldn't bleed in her place.

"I'm sorry," he choked. *I'm sorry I wasn't there. I'm sorry I didn't have your back. I'm sorry I sent you for Lena. I'm sorry I'm sorry I'm sorry.*

Her lips were moving, and he leaned down over her face.

"Took you long enough, Prep School," she gasped.

The sob tore through him, like thunder from a black cloud. He gathered her close then, pulled her onto his lap and held her as tightly as he could. He could keep her here with him if he just held tight enough.

"Don't die," he whispered. "Don't die."

She choked, and he heard the gargle of fluids in her lungs. It was the same sound he heard at home, every night—the sound Cherish made when she coughed. But Ty wasn't sick. Not like that.

Fight harder, he willed, angry with her. Furious at how easily she was giving in after all they'd been through.

"Keep talking," she rasped.

"I . . . I don't know what to do." He didn't know what she wanted. He felt like an idiot. He was her best friend; he should know what to say.

"Rosie's."

His chest ripped wide open. He didn't want to tell her. He didn't want to say a word, because that made what was happening even more real. Real, in a way Rosie's could never be.

But this was Ty, and she never asked for anything. He couldn't deny her now.

He pulled in a shattered breath. "It's on the sea. Where the water's still blue." Her hands knotted in his shirt. "There's a dock in the sun, and it's warm, hot even, and when we get too hot, we'll just jump in the water."

She smiled against his cheek. Her breathing slowed.

He wanted to die.

"And we'll fish, you and me. We'll go out on one of those big boats like they used to have. And we'll catch all sorts of stuff, and then we'll cook it up and get fat. You and me, we're going to be old and fat one day, okay?"

Her hand slipped from his chest. It landed on the cement and lay unmoving, and Colin rocked back and forth and stared at the hazy sky and tried to imagine Ty as an old lady.

He tried and he tried. But he could never see her older than she was right then.

41

TY

Blue water. Blue like steel. Blue like Colin's eyes.

She could feel it. Filling her. Seeping between her fingers and her toes. In the spaces between her bones. In the gaps between her teeth.

"Ty?" His voice was far away. She clung to it, even through the water. Even after the sky went dark, and his face faded into memory.

"*Ty!*"

* * *

He was thirteen. All arms and legs. Fresh meat. The older boys at the factory, they knew it. They'd backed him into the corner, intending to give him a proper Metaltown welcome, and he snapped back at them like a wild dog that didn't know he was already beat. *Back off*, she snarled. *I've got safety on him. He's mine.*

* * *

They lay on their stomachs in the high grass, watching the trains. The bugs bit at her neck and her wrists but she didn't care. He told her stories about his brother. He told her about his family. And soon, they were her stories, too.

* * *

She taught him how to fight. To keep his elbows close to his body. To protect his throat. *Hit me,* she said. *If you can.* He would see how it felt then. He'd be ready next time.

He wouldn't hit her.

* * *

He was laughing with the others. He laughed so hard his eyes pinched shut, and he gripped her thigh and rocked back. Three layers of clothing to his touch. She could feel the heat from his palm. *Don't stare. Don't move.*

He laughed, and she wasn't hungry anymore. He laughed, and she wasn't cold.

* * *

They were walking to Beggar's Square and he was talking about Rosie's Bay. Blue water. White sand. Every time he talked about leaving her insides crunched up.

Once I get the money, we'll go, he said.

We, he said. *We'll go.*

He'd never said *we* before.

* * *

More water. She didn't know drowning could feel so soft. So quiet. Like relief.

Mine. He's mine.

"Mine," she whispered. From somewhere far away she heard his voice, strained thin, begging her not to go. She knew then that this was not a journey they could make together, that this was their good-bye. The one that lasted beyond sunrise. The one that lasted forever.

I am not afraid.

And then pain grew bright and sharp and white, and then was gone.

LENA

They met three days later in the foreman's office at Small Parts. Lena's father did not tell Otto of the meeting as he was still recovering in the hospital, nor did he request a police detail. Instead he arrived accompanied by only a few of his personal guards, and left Lena to reach the facility on her own.

His distance was fine with her. After he'd conceded to call off the Bakerstown police, he'd returned to his office in the River District. It wasn't until late that night that she heard him come home. His footsteps were heavy as he trudged up the stairs, and his tie was a slack noose around his neck when he appeared in her bedroom doorway.

"Are you leaving?" he'd asked, looking around her room as if for a suitcase.

Thinking that was an invitation to clear the premises, she'd reached into the bureau for her coat, exhausted by the long day. She looked at the long scratches her fingernails had carved with a vague, detached interest.

"If you stay, I'll let you manage the factory," he'd added. "A trial run, under my supervision."

She'd frozen in her tracks, and turned back to assess him. His hair was disheveled, the stubble on his face casting a shadow over his hard jaw. With the gleam and the ego stripped away, he really was just a man.

"What about Otto?"

"He's incapacitated, in case you forgot." Her father sighed. "Regardless. It appears Otto does not have what it takes."

She'd closed her eyes then, remembering the heat of the factory and those who had fought against it. Remembering the sound of Colin's mother coughing in the slums of Metaltown. Remembering Colin's tortured face, and his hands stained with blood, as they'd assessed the damage on Factory Row after the riots.

And then her father, crushing her perfect yellow bird in his fist.

Did she have what it took to do the right thing? Or was the Hampton blood running through her veins stronger than the will of her heart?

"What about the Advocates?"

He lifted his chin.

"I won't do it if you're only going to ship weapons off to the enemy."

It was a risk, and she knew it. He could retract his offer, and then she would be of no help to anyone. Even if she exposed her father's transgressions, which was dangerous, no one would take her word over his. The weapons he'd sold to the enemy, the things he'd done to Ty, and Darcy, and Colin, would never come to light. He would never go to jail, not while he still had connections in the police department. Would never be tried by the military after donating so much to the cause. And the other politicians, his friends, would never turn their backs on him. They were probably guilty of the same things.

Her father being cornered into doing what was right was the only punishment he would ever receive.

"They won't work for you," she added. "But they'll work for me."

A long, heavy silence stretched between them.

"When I was young, I was like you," he said finally. "I've forgotten what it was like to be so . . . idealistic. Pure in purpose." His head hung forward, and he rubbed the back of his neck.

It was neither an apology nor a compliment, but regardless, it meant something.

"Agreed," he said. "We'll supply the Northern Federation. No one else."

It was a victory, but maybe not the brightest of them. Even if she rebuilt the factory and put the charter back to work, they still built weapons. The war would continue, which meant more death, more hunger, more loss.

For now.

Two days later Lena had approached him with a stack of old reports and a proposal—an appeal to his arrogant Hampton greed. To her surprise, he'd considered it. Now she just hoped Colin would as well.

* * *

Lena paced in Mr. Minnick's office—or at least the office that had been Mr. Minnick's prior to her firing him. Her father had allowed her the honor of his dismissal as her first act of management. She frowned at all the things she would have to run by him, but it was better than nothing.

Josef Hampton sat in the chair across from her, his legs neatly crossed, hands folded across his vest. Whatever thoughts worked through his mind were locked behind his marble features. He'd been silent since their earlier report to the police, in which he'd explained that the explosion at the testing facility was a result of improper chemical treatment rather than an attack, as previously suspected.

In order for him to save his company—Division IV included—he needed the support of Metaltown, and Metaltown, for the moment, had rallied behind Colin. Making a martyr of him would only prolong the workers' holdout.

"Perhaps he's not coming," offered her father, a tinge of relief in his tone.

She shook her head. "He's coming." But she worried about how it would be between them when he did. They hadn't spoken since he'd hit Otto in her room at the estate. That felt like a lifetime ago now.

The floor had been cleaned, and the chairs replaced. Even the desk had been moved aside to the corner to make room for their meeting. It looked so unlike the place where Jed Schultz had imprisoned her just three days prior.

She shivered, remembering how the police had removed his body on a stretcher.

Her arm had been set in a sleek cast to her elbow. It barely impeded her movement, though it made her gloves bunch at the wrist. She pressed her opposite hand against the hard plaster, wishing her heart were so protected.

When the door opened and Colin pushed through, Lena's resolve weakened. Their eyes met for just an instant, just long enough for her to see the sorrow behind them. To feel it punch into her, real and unyielding. He wore a suit—one that was a little big, but clean. He'd shaved his face and trimmed his hair.

He looked invincible, even in his grief.

"I'm sorry I'm late." His eyes landed on the scarf—*his* scarf—that she wore proudly around her neck. "There was something I had to do."

She nodded, and noticed then that he hadn't come alone—Martin and Henry flanked him on either side. It was smart, considering their last meeting, but that didn't mean it didn't sting. She had assured his protection, threatened her father that she would tell everyone of his role in the war, and in Astor Tyson's death, if Colin was harmed.

The great Josef Hampton nodded. And to Lena's surprise, he waited for her to speak.

Her mouth immediately went dry.

"The Small Parts factory plays a crucial role in Hampton Industries," she began nervously, feeling their gazes upon her. Feeling like she had so many times at her father's parties. As the entertainment. As a piece of art on display. Unconsciously, she reached to smooth down her hair, but caught herself.

She was not meek.

"This war will not last forever, and when it ends, the weapons divisions will be forced to reduce staff."

Colin inhaled through his nostrils. Behind him, Martin balked.

"We all work, or we all don't," Colin said.

"Understood," said Lena.

"Hampton Industries is investigating the expansion of one of our divisions." Josef met Colin's gaze straight on. "The Medical Division."

There was a bristling in her nerves. It wasn't theirs, it belonged to a dead girl—but regardless, if there was opportunity in Division IV, there was work there, too. Despite their dual purposes, Lena felt a whisper of pride. Her father had read the reports she'd dredged up, those that contained figures Darcy had only alluded to. Once, the Medical Division had made more than the weapons divisions. Once, it had been believed that the federation that held the cure would be the strongest, and that they would win the war.

If Hampton Industries found the cure, they wouldn't need to sell weapons to anyone, their side or the other, to be rich.

"If we do expand, the Small Parts factory would transition its focus from weapons to medical supplies," said Lena. "Not immediately, but over time. Once a plan can be established."

The business of life from the business of war.

"And what happens to us then?" Colin frowned.

She cleared her throat. Then removed her black gloves, one at a time. Her fingertips lay exposed, black and distorted. Permanently bruised. Like so many here in Metaltown.

Martin and Henry barely noticed. But her father's gaze lingered.

"Membership in the Small Parts Charter would ensure that all workers would remain employed by Hampton Industries," she said. "You would keep your jobs. There would be training involved, of course, but no reduction in workforce as we transfer the factory's purpose."

Colin never took his eyes off her face. And when he smirked, the strength pulled through her, and turned to sheer determination. She owed it to him to change things. She owed it to all of them, and to herself as well.

"In the meantime, we're going to fix this. The right way," she said. "Tell me what you need."

A whisper of understanding, of silent, mutual respect drew Lena, Colin, and Josef Hampton into a central point. It turned their blunt words to dialogue and their rigid posture into the dance of negotiations. They discussed the demands of the Small Parts Charter one by one. They proposed solutions. They argued. They agreed. And when it was done, Colin shook Lena's hand and left.

Their final touch felt professional and stiff, and she wondered sadly if it was, in a way, his good-bye.

* * *

Lena exited the building through the employee entrance. There was much to do; she had to hire a new foreman, to start. Someone dependable that the employees trusted; perhaps Colin's mother, or the man who ran the corner cart. And then do something about that torturous hot room before Matchstick set the place on fire.

She mused about how ignorant she'd once been to all that went on inside the factory, and how fearful she'd been of all that existed outside. She knew better now. The workers needed her voice, just as they needed Colin's. And she had family here. Shima lived just down the street. Lena was bound to Metaltown in ways she never thought possible.

She pulled the door closed behind her, locking it with a key from around her neck.

"How's your stay so far in Metaltown?"

At the sound of Colin's low voice, she jumped and clutched her chest. Her gloves fell to the ground. He pushed off the wall where he'd been leaning and dipped down to pick up her things. It warmed her, knowing that he'd waited.

"I'm just here for work," she said finally, with a short laugh.

"What a coincidence, so am I." He smirked. The long shadows of the evening made him look taller when he stood.

He didn't offer the gloves right away, and when she reached for them, his fingers twined in hers. Gradually, they walked toward the street, where she knew her driver would be waiting to take her back to the River District. The thought weighed down her steps; she wanted to stretch out each moment before he came looking for her. To steal what time they had before life caught up with them.

Colin's thumb grazed the inside of her wrist and made her pulse flutter.

"I know what you did," he said, voice thick. "It was a good thing."

She watched their boots come to a standstill. Hers, polished and small; his, borrowed and scuffed. When she'd heard what had happened to Astor—to Ty—Lena had arranged for her body to be taken to Bakerstown for a proper cremation. It was the least she could do for the girl who'd saved her life. Though she had intended to oversee the arrangements herself, she'd silently removed herself to the back room when Colin had arrived. That time was his alone, and she could not take it from him.

He'd stayed with Ty until the very end.

"Chip and I took her ashes to the train yard," he said, squeezing Lena's hand a little harder. "She always liked it there. I think she would have gone away if she could."

Lena's throat tightened, for Colin's pain. For her own, as well.

"Will you go away now, too?" she asked. "To the Whitewater Sea?"

His chin rose, gaze drifting down the alley into the street where the lights were just beginning to flicker to life. Metaltown was changing, and not just because of her. The Brotherhood had disbanded in the loss of their leader, and even in the past day she'd seen more flashes of green on the patrons on the street. Evidence of an old gangster come back to port. McNulty, Darcy had called him.

"I thought about it," he answered, and in his pause her heart clenched. "Then I heard that the new boss is giving a portion of Ty's inheritance to the charter."

She blushed. Her father saw it as a bribe to go back to work. She saw it as reparations.

"I think we should take the green and get out of here. There's this place on the coast, I think you'd like it." When her mouth fell open, he laughed. "And if you say no, I was thinking about using it to open a clinic in Metaltown. But just so we're clear, that's my second choice."

She pulled her hand from his and threw her arms around his neck, not caring who might see. Joy speared through her. Joy and relief.

"You're staying." He held her against his body, and when she lifted her face from his neck his mouth found hers, and they both tasted the salty tears as they flowed from her eyes.

"I'm staying," he said with a smile. "Someone's got to keep the boss honest."

In the street she could hear Hayak shouting out his final call for dinner. She could hear the bells from Beggar's Square warning its patrons that the Board and Care would soon close its doors. She could hear the hiss and crank of a train pulling out of the station.

And somewhere in the distance, she could hear laughter.

ACKNOWLEDGMENTS

There are books that are easy to write (*Article 5*), and books that are hard (*Three*—but honestly, I was pregnant, so keeping my eyes open was hard, too), books that are emotionally wringing (*The Glass Arrow*), and books where you question every little decision you make (*Breaking Point*). And then there are books like *Metaltown*, which are just fun.

When I think of this story, the first thing I feel is lucky, because it was an absolute joy to work on from the first page to the last. Sure, I cried some (okay, that one part? I cried A LOT), and I smacked my palm against my forehead more than a few times, but overall, it was the best experience. I fell in love with Colin, Lena, and Ty from the very beginning. I thought of little else while writing their story. The words flew from my fingertips every time I sat down to work. It's not always like that, but it was for *Metaltown,* and I thank you, reader, so very much for giving it a chance. I hope you love this story as much as I do.

As always, it takes a village to raise a baby book. This never would have been possible without one of my favorite people in the world, Melissa Frain, sassiest editor in New York (I'm convinced), or her assistant, Amy Stapp, who just makes everything work (including the pranks I pull on The Frain). My agent, Joanna MacKenzie, is one of the coolest chicks ever, and I'm so fortunate to have Danielle and Abby from Browne and Miller on my side as well. Huge hugs, as always, to the team at Tor Teen (say that ten times fast!): my wonderful publicist, Alexis Saarela; Seth Lerner, who nailed it again with this cover; Christopher Gibbs, whose artwork has blown my mind again; and of course, Kathleen Doherty, the publisher who continues to make my dreams come true. I am grateful for you all.

A special thank-you to Adelynne, who was one of the first people to preorder *The Glass Arrow*, for generally just being made of awesome. If we ever meet, Adelynne, expect hugs. There's just no way around it.

Thank you to my friends, who make it possible for me to be me. Deanna, who keeps me sane (HAHA. YEAH RIGHT. Who allows for my crazy, is more like it!); Katie McGarry, who can always laugh us out of our worst moments; Jenny Z, I adore you, you know that; Kendare Blake, for your support of Ty and of me; the ladies at Jazzercise (UPTOWN FUNK GONNA GIVE IT TO YOU); and obviously Sara Raasch, for basically just being my everything.

Thank you so much to the people who were kind enough to write early reviews for the book: Cori Smith, Caitlin Fletcher, and Rachel Strolle, the best booksellers out there, I'm convinced; Jaime Arkin from Fiction Fare and Meg Caristi from Swoony Boys, I am forever glad that Chase (and Sean) brought us together; and Kristie Hofelich Ennis and Gwen Wethington, who fight on the front lines for literacy every day by placing books in the hands of their students. All of you make such a difference in the world. I hope you know you've made a huge difference in mine.

And as always, thank you to my family. My mom, who will never forgive me for how things went down with Brax, and my dad, who thinks every book is my best. I hope I can be the kind of parents you are. Thank you also to Lisa, Lindsay, Steve, and Elizabeth for your constant warmth and love.

Finally, thank you to Jason and Ren, who make me want to be better, and stronger, and more, every single day. There are times I swear I feel my heart stretching with the love I have for you both.

Tor Teen Reading & Activity Guide to
METALTOWN
by Kristen Simmons
Ages 13–17; Grades 8–12

About This Guide
The Common Core State Standards–aligned questions and activities that follow are intended to enhance your reading of *Metaltown*. Please feel free to
adapt this content to suit the needs and interests of your students or reading
group participants.
Supports Common Core State Standards: W.8.3, W.9-10.3, W.11-12.3; and SL.8.1,
SL.9-10.1, SL.11-12.1

Developing Reading & Discussion Skills
1. *Metaltown* is told from three characters' viewpoints. Have you read other
   novels told from multiple points of view? What might be some reasons an
   author would choose to structure a novel in this way?
2. As the novel begins, what are your impressions of Colin and Ty? What is
   their relationship to each other? What does it mean for a person to "have
   your back" in *Metaltown*?
3. How does Ty feel when Jed Schultz asks Colin to run an errand on behalf
   of the Brotherhood? How do the intended recipients react when Colin
   tries to deliver Jed's gift?
4. In Chapter 3, readers meet the third narrator. How do Lena's lifestyle, education, and understanding of her country's political and economic situation different from Colin's and Ty's? Whom do you think sees the situation
   most clearly?
5. Compare and contrast the power dynamics between Jed Schultz, the
   Brotherhood, and Metaltown; McNulty and Bakerstown; and Hampton
   Industries and the River District.
6. On page 59, Colin is tempted to hit a kid before thinking, "What did picking on a kid prove? That he was Minnick, that's what." How does this speak
   to a larger sense of the morality on the streets of Metaltown? Cite other
   examples from the story in your answer.
7. Describe Lena's relationships with her tutor, Darcy; her brother, Otto; and
   her father. Compare the ways in which Lena is vulnerable or trapped in her
   circumstances to the ways in which this is the case for Ty and for Colin.
8. Who is Hayden? How might Hayden's choices and actions be seen as a
   representation of many who feel powerless in Metaltown? What pressure
   does Hayden's situation put on Colin?
9. What is corn flu? How did it become the scourge of the nation? What other
   risks are part of daily life in Metaltown and even over the Beltway in the
   richer areas?

10. How does Lena first meet Colin? What problems with Hampton Industries does she begin to uncover as she reviews Otto's management reports?
11. What new tragedy befalls Ty when she is sent to help at the Stamping Mill, and how does Lena subsequently make Ty's situation worse? Compare this to the way Lena's father treats Aja and Darcy. Do these comparisons affect your views on where to assign blame in the novel, or where to place the responsibility for trying to bring about change?
12. How is Lena's Chapter 21 reunion with her old nanny a pivotal moment for her character and for the direction of the story? Cite quotes from the novel in your answer.
13. What is a "press"? As you consider the history of "presses" in Metaltown, do you feel that Colin is right or wrong to want to attempt a press by the Small Parts workers? Why or why not?
14. What action does Jed Schultz take when Colin refuses to join the Brotherhood? What threat does this cause to Cherish and the rest of Colin's family? How does it change Lena's understanding of what Colin wants to do in Small Parts?
15. What secret of Ty's identity is revealed in Chapter 29? What truth about Darcy's past is shared in Chapter 30? How do these revelations change the power dynamic between Metaltown and Bakerstown? How do they change Lena's view of her father's empire?
16. Where is Colin imprisoned? How does he escape? What secondary characters rise to the occasion during Colin's escape?
17. On page 308, just before chasing after Lena, Colin tells Ty, "You're still my best man, you know that?" How does Ty react to these words and why?
18. What is the truth about Lena's hands? Does learning it change your understanding of Lena? Does telling him this truth change Lena's view of Colin? If so, in what ways?
19. How does the author use objects of clothing as physical representations of Lena's, Ty's, and other characters' emotional states throughout the story?
20. How does Ty bring muscle to Colin's side as the press morphs into a battle? What alliances and loathings are revealed in Chapters 36 through 38? How does Lena bring the fighting to an end?
21. What is Rosie's? Why is it important? Who invented it? Why can't it be real?
22. War is a distant threat in the lives of the citizens in the book, while disease is a daily menace. Can you think of analogous menaces (near and far) in today's world? How do these threats affect your thoughts and behaviors?
23. On page 23, Lena notes that her father viewed the war as a conflict between "need" and "entitlement." Do other characters see the situation in the same way? How might this notion be viewed as a critical theme of the novel?
24. As the story concludes, Lena ". . . mused about how ignorant she'd once been to all that went on inside the factory, and how fearful she'd been of all that existed outside. She knew better now. . . ." (p. 376) How might *Metal-*

town be read as a warning about the dangers of ignorance—or of closing one's eyes to others' suffering and corruption?

Supports Common Core State Standards: RL.8.1-4, 8.6; RL.9-10.1-5; RL.11-12.1-6; and SL.8.1, 3, 4; SL.9-10.1, 3; SL.11-12.1, 3.

Developing Research & Writing Skills

Building a Story: Setting, Language, Plot, Character

*WORLD-BUILT HISTORY. The action of *Metaltown* takes place in the context of dramatic past events—famine, war, disease, strikes. In dystopian and science fiction literature, incorporating such background is part of the writing process of world-building. Use information from the text to write a short history of the world of *Metaltown* to present to friends or classmates. Discuss what questions you imagine the author may have asked herself to develop the world of the story.

*A METAL LEXICON. From slang like "green," "nitro," and "Metalheads," to phrases like "the truth settled over both of them, cruel and cold as the Metaltown night" (p. 163), the author uses powerful, specific language to script her story's world. Make a *Metaltown* dictionary, listing and defining at least twelve words or phrases to share with readers of the novel.

*CREATED CRISES. Over the course of the novel, Lena pieces together the terrible truth about Hampton Industries. Imagine you are a newspaper reporter who has the opportunity to interview Lena (and other characters, if desired) at the end of the story. Write an exposé article on Josef Hampton and the transgressions committed by his company.

*MOTHERS AND FATHERS. From the cruel Josef Hampton to the dying Cherish, the novel explores the positive and negative roles played by fathers and mothers and the ways their children embrace or reject the identities given to them by their parents. In the character of a parent from the novel, write a letter to your child which includes an element of praise, an apology, and a piece of advice.

*FINDING FAMILY. Is family made of people you can trust, those you must protect, and/or those who will love you? Create a chart comparing the way Colin, Ty, and Lena each define family in the early chapters of the book and toward its end. Note how each character's family circle evolves over the course of the story, and how this affects their actions and views of the world. If desired, write a poem, song, or essay entitled, "Family is . . ."

*WHAT HAVE WE CREATED? On page 252, Lena reflects that, "Otto had not been born this way, he'd been made this way, a product of her father's worst qualities. Even if he applied himself . . . the bar would be raised just as it came in reach, and Otto would find himself lacking over and over again. She was not the only Hampton with bruises." Is Otto a human manifestation of the state of the *Metaltown* nation, politically, economically, industrially, and even medically? Might Lena's reflection be applied to dangerous people in our real world—is she explaining how they reach the point of committing acts of terrorism or violence? Write a 2–3 page response to one of these questions.

Beyond the Covers: Themes, Concepts, and World Narrative

*UNITED. Former AFL-CIO Secretary-Treasurer Thomas R. Donahue once said, "The only effective answer to organized greed is organized labor." Do you agree or disagree? Divide into groups to research the history the American labor union movement. Then, debate Donahue's statement, referencing quotes from *Metaltown* and information from your research.

*REALITY BITES. From the risks of corn flu to the job of "taster," food is a dangerous thing in the *Metaltown* world. Assign each student a character from the story. From these viewpoints, have character pairs such as Darcy and Lena OR Josef and Otto Hampton OR Jed Schultz and McNulty OR Hayak and Colin role-play a dialogue in which they unravel and discuss how finding nourishment has become such a perilous activity. Compare and contrast the outcomes of the dialogues.

*REALITY RELATES. Could a toxic food scenario happen in America? Are we putting the food supply at risk through industrial farming and genetic modification? Go to the library or online to research your answer. (Hint: Resources could include *Food, Inc.* by Peter Pringle, *Foodopoly* by Wenonah Hauter, and websites maintained by the Food and Drug Administration at www.fda.gov/food/ and the Center for Food Safety at www.centerforfoodsafety.org). Organize your research on at least fifteen fact cards (index cards). Then use your research to write a newspaper editorial or a letter to a state representatives sharing your thoughts about the potential for a toxic food scenario.

*SOUND OFF ONSCREEN. Imagine *Metaltown* is being made into a movie. You have been hired as the sound designer. Select a theme song for each protagonist and a song to play during the title credits as the film begins. Write a short report to the production team explaining the reasons for your choices.

*KEEP WRITING. *Metaltown* ends as Lena hears laughter. Who is laughing? Why? What will happen next? Imagine you are tasked with writing a proposal for a sequel to *Metaltown*. List five questions you would like answered in the next book. Select six characters from the first book whom you would like to bring along into the second novel, and propose at least one new character. Based on your question and character lists, write a 2–3 page synopsis or an outline for the first 10 chapters of the story. What title would you suggest for this second story?

Supports Common Core State Standards: RL.8.1-4, RL.9-10.1-5, RL.11-12.1-6; RI.8.1-2, RI.8.8-9, RI.9-10.1-2, RI.9-10.7-8, RI.11-12.1-2, RI.11-12.7; SL.8.1-4; SL.9-10.1-4; SL.11-12.1-4; and W.8.1-4, W.8.7-8, W.9-10.1-4, W.9-10.7-8, W.11-12.1-4, W.11-12.7-8.